Snapped

Also by Tracy Brown

Dime Piece

Black

Criminal Minded

White Lines

Twisted

Snapped

Tracy Brown

St. Martin's Griffin
New York

This book is dedicated to the memory of my father, my best friend, my rock—William Brown, Jr. Whenever I see a little girl with her daddy—the way he plays with her and makes her eyes light up, how he acts silly with her but still makes her feel protected and special—I think of my own father and how he loved me, never wavering. He was always on my side, always in my corner and forever proud of me. They say a father is his daughter's first love. I'm a living testament to that fact. Seems like only yesterday I watched him strolling up Broad Street—slacks perfectly creased, shirt well pressed, pea-coat draping his frame, cologne lightly scenting the air around him as he breezed down the block with his signature Kangol cocked to the side. I never stopped being his little girl and I am so proud that he was my daddy. Long before my career as an author, he was my number-one fan. Shortly after I began writing *Snapped*, we talked about it one Saturday night as the summer faded into fall. His eyes lit up and he nodded his head and said, "Now *that's* the one!" He never got the chance to read it. But his approval will always be more special to me than any other review or critique that my work could ever warrant. He was one of a kind and I will miss him always.

SNAPPED. Copyright © 2009 by Tracy Brown. All rights reserved. Printed in the United States of America. For information, address St. Martin's Press, 175 Fifth Avenue, New York, N.Y. 10010.

www.stmartins.com

ISBN 978-0-312-55521-4

D 10 9 8 7 6 5 4 3

Acknowledgments

Monique Patterson, Holly Blanck, Talia Ross, and the entire SMP staff, thank you so much for your patience as I took longer than usual to complete this novel. Thank you for helping me through the grieving process with your wonderful cards, flowers, and prayers. Your kindness has touched me deeply and I am forever grateful for your compassion and your understanding.

Monique, you are the absolute best there is. Over the years we've worked together, we've formed more than a business relationship. I don't toss this word around loosely, but I truly consider you a *friend* who "gets" me and encourages me, and cheers me on as I face each project. Sometimes people are not aware of the effect they have on others. Perhaps without realizing it, during those days when I was holding vigil at the hospital, you were a breath of fresh air to me and gave me comfort by helping me to remember that I was not alone. Thank you, sincerely, from the bottom of my heart. Love ya!

And to the readers across the world who reached out to me to express sympathy or to share your own experiences,

I am so indebted to all of you. I'm just as much a fan of yours as you are of me, and I thank you for holding me up when I felt like falling down. You are wonderful and I appreciate you all greatly.

No More Mrs. Nice Bitch

The large house was still and dark, except for the flickering glimmer of a lone candle at the center of the dining room table. The linen tablecloth was spotless, decked out with Waterford crystal stemware and fresh flowers. The ornate table seemed only to highlight the enormity of the room and the scale of the silence within it.

Moonlight spilled through the venetian blinds, spotlighting her perfectly manicured nails and her diamond ring and bracelets. She was in a daze, staring at the wall, trying to make sense of what had happened. She had been sitting there for hours this way, replaying the events of the past twenty-four hours over and over in her mind. And it still didn't make any sense. Not even a little bit.

Everything had fallen apart. It had all come crumbling down. One day she was on top of the world. The next thing she knew, it was over. She stared blankly at the wall, oblivious of all the blood spattered across it. She was looking through that wall—looking into the recesses of her mind to see where it all started. How had she let this happen? she wondered. And what the hell was she supposed to do now?

The phone rang and snapped her out of her trance. She wondered who was calling, but didn't dare answer it. The house was empty except for her and the body lying still on the floor. The phone seemed to ring forever, each ring sounding louder than the last. Soon all she could hear was the shrill volume of the ringing in her ears. She knew she couldn't hide forever, but she wasn't ready to face what she had done. Not until she made sense of it herself. All she could think about was what she had done. And the only thing she felt was numbness.

The ringing finally stopped. It was over, she reassured herself. All the bullshit was over.

But actually, it was just the beginning.

The Early Days

Special Occasion

"*Surprise!*" the crowd shouted in unison.

Camille covered her mouth with her hands as she stood in the doorway in shock. Before her was a room full of everyone she loved. Her mother was there, her sister, her cousins and all of her friends. Balloons were everywhere, and there was a huge cake in the shape of the number 30 sitting on top of a long table. Camille felt like crying from sheer happiness, and she looked at her husband in wide-eyed amazement. "You did this for me?"

Frankie smiled at her and nodded, proud that he'd been able to pull this off without Camille getting wind of it. His wife was a hard woman to surprise, and he had gone to great lengths to make this happen. Camille beamed with joy and threw her arms around her handsome husband's neck in an ecstatic embrace. "Happy birthday," he said, hugging her tightly. Cameras flashed all around as if the couple were being swarmed by paparazzi.

Camille swirled around and faced the crowd of party-goers, a permanent smile plastered on her face. They began to rush her, planting kisses on her cheeks, hugging her and wishing her a happy birthday. Soon, Frankie got lost in the crowd, but Camille spotted him standing across the room with his cohort Gillian. Camille smiled. God, she loved him!

When they had gotten married seven years prior, Camille had been a twenty-three-year-old aspiring model/actress and Frankie had been a low-level hustler. He wasn't making any real money in those days, just enough to be hood rich and finance a ghetto-fabulous lifestyle. Today, the name Frankie Bingham (Frankie B, as he was known in the hood) was synonymous with respect, extreme wealth, and clout. He made major moves and major money, diversifying his criminal enterprise by investing in other ventures. Frankie made money not just from drug distribution, but from a myriad of businesses that ranged from a barber shop to a bar and grill. He always used the various connections he'd made over the years to keep himself plugged in to the newest get-money capers. It had been a rough road to the top. Through all the ups and downs, Camille had loved him.

Even in the early days, she could tell that Frankie was destined for greatness. He was a very handsome man, tall, brown, and sexy as hell. He was rough around the edges, yet more charming than anyone she'd ever known. He had broad shoulders and his toned physique made everything he wore look amazing. But most of all, he was focused. He was a risk taker, and he chased paper like few others. Frankie lived big. When he came around, heads turned. Camille herself was a five-foot-ten beauty with smooth chocolate brown skin, full lips, and flawless style. She complemented Frankie, and the two became fixtures in the circles of the ghetto-fabulous elite. They met at a nightclub in Manhattan and fell in love almost instantly. They got married after dating for less than a year and had lived together in a cramped studio apartment in the early days—Camille working hard to break into modeling and Frankie working his way up the ladder of one of New York City's most notorious criminal organizations. That seemed like a lifetime ago. A lot had changed since then.

Frankie had worked for Doug Nobles, one of the city's original drug kingpins. Nobles (as he was known in the streets) and his crew controlled the dope trade in Brooklyn in the eighties and nineties, and Frankie had been a bold young hustler who made a lot of money for them. Frankie had been hungrier than ever back then, eager for the lifestyle of the movers and shakers that he saw doing big business before his eyes. He wanted to impress Nobles and even the low-level street hustlers he dealt with day to day. So he had put in work, flying below the radar and never getting bagged, but bringing back double their investment at times. He gained the trust and respect of the men at the top—the ones who really had the power. Nobles took a particular interest in the young man and took him under his wing. And then Nobles got sent away for twelve years on a murder charge.

That was 1992. While Nobles did his time, his children corresponded with him via weekly letters. So did Frankie. And Frankie went along with Baron and Gillian when they visited Nobles up north. In some ways, Frankie became like a son to him. Nobles admired his work ethic and valued his loyalty. He schooled the young man on the ins and outs of the game, and he spoke from experience. Frankie grew to love Doug like a father. Though Doug loved and was proud of his own son, Baron, Doug felt especially close to Frankie.

In the years since his release, Nobles had wisely continued to play the background. He let his son take the lead
while he pulled the strings from behind the scenes. Nobles
had been quietly grooming his daughter for the business
as well. He didn't want her settling for a role as the wife of
some hustler. If she was going to be affiliated with the game
at all (which was likely, considering the fact that she had
been surrounded by gangsters, killers, and hustlers from
the moment she was born), Nobles wanted his baby girl to
be the one calling the shots.

By the time Nobles came home from prison, Frankie had
used his close relationship with Nobles to gain leverage in
the game for himself. Frankie eventually became the main
distributor for all of the Nobles family operations, and over
the years he had become a real part of the family. It wasn't
unusual to find him seated at the family Thanksgiving feast
or standing as a pallbearer at a family funeral. These days,
he ran a distribution empire that dealt in everything from
cocaine and heroin to prescription drugs. And he also owned
several legitimate businesses where he only made cameo ap-
pearances on occasion. He and Camille enjoyed a life of
luxury, and to her the only thing missing was the pitter-
patter of little feet.

Frankie had never really yearned for children, feeling that
parenthood would dampen their lifestyle. They wouldn't be
able to travel as often or move around as freely, he always
said. Frankie told Camille that he wasn't ready to change his
lifestyle to accommodate fatherhood. Plus, he felt that in
his line of work, having children could be a liability. He'd
seen his share of ruthless practices in his business, and families weren't always off-limits when there was beef. But the
truth was that the idea of having children scared him. It

reminded him of the misery he'd endured in his own childhood. He reasoned that someday he'd be ready for fatherhood—just not now.

Camille, on the other hand, loved kids and had always envisioned that she would be a mother soon after marriage. But she acquiesced, figuring that her life with Frankie would be enough to fill the void. And it was. Despite the lack of children, Camille was happy in her relationship with her husband. She had the man she wanted and an enviable lifestyle. She wouldn't have traded her life with any woman in the world.

As she greeted one person after another, a familiar face made its way through the crowd and Camille's eyes lit up with excitement. "Toya!" she exclaimed, throwing her arms around her old friend. Toya and Camille had gone to school together, and once upon a time they'd been inseparable. After high school, Toya had gone off to college in Atlanta while Camille began to pursue acting and modeling in New York City. The two friends had kept in touch at first, calling and sending letters and postcards. Camille landed ad campaigns for retail catalogs as well as print work for a number of high-fashion publications. As she hopscotched from one photo shoot to the next, Toya got acquainted with Atlanta nightlife and began to collect stamps on her passport by traveling from one exotic location to the next. They eventually lost touch with each other. It wasn't until a Kanye concert six months ago that the two friends had run into each other again. During an intermission at the famed Radio City Music Hall, Toya had spotted Camille, and the rest was history. Toya had just moved back to New York City a year earlier and was living her black *Sex and the City* dream. Now here she was, looking as lovely as ever in a short black dress. She also had another young lady in tow.

"Camille, this is my friend Dominique Storms," Toya introduced. "She's the one I was telling you about." As they had caught up on each other's lives during their recent phone conversations, Toya had told Camille all about her new friend.

Camille's smile broadened. "Hi!" she exclaimed. Dominique looked even more fabulous than she'd expected. She wore a white linen belted safari jacket and matching skirt. Her weave and her makeup were flawless. "I've heard so much about you."

Dominique frowned, wondering what they'd discussed. "What did she tell you about me?" Dominique asked Camille while looking suspiciously at Toya.

Camille laughed. "All she told me was that you were an A&R at Def Jam and that you two do a lot of partying together. It was all good things."

Dominique's lips twisted into a look of disbelief. She knew Toya well enough to know that that wasn't all she'd told Camille. Toya was a very matter-of-fact, no-holds-barred type of person. What she'd probably told Camille was that Dominique was a dumb young girl with potential whom Toya had taken under her wing. That sounded more like something Toya would say. Dominique didn't really mind, though. She loved Toya for her brash and cynical personality. Toya saw the world in black and white with no gray areas, a stark contrast to Dominique's sunny and optimistic outlook. It was an interesting friendship.

"Yeah, right. I'm sure she said something crazy, but it's all good. It's nice to meet you. I've heard a lot about you, too." She winked at Camille and they all laughed.

The party was in full swing. The deejay played one hit after another until the dance floor vibrated from all the people celebrating. Camille mingled and introduced Toya and Dominique to her friends and family. They danced, ate, drank, and let their hair down. It was a great party.

Soon the deejay announced that everyone should gather around the cake table. Camille and her girls made their way over and found Frankie standing with a microphone in his hand, Gillian by his side. Dominique's face lit up at the sight of Frankie, and she pulled Toya closer to her. "Is that her husband?" Toya nodded. "Damn!" Dominique said. "He's *fine!*"

"Can I have your attention, please?" Frankie's baritone voice boomed through the speakers. "I want to pay tribute to my wife."

"Awwww!" Dominique gave Frankie her full attention.

Toya elbowed her discreetly. "Stop cumming on yourself. He's already married!"

Dominique shot a wicked glance at her friend and rolled her eyes. She turned her attention back to sexy Frankie.

He held the mic in one hand, the other hand tucked. "I love you, baby," he said. "I really do. No man could ask for a better wife." He pulled a large square-shaped box from behind his back, and the crowd got excited, knowing that whatever was inside was bound to make their chins hit the floor. "Happy birthday!" He handed her the box, and Camille opened it to reveal a platinum and diamond spiral necklace. The brilliant carats sparkled in the light, and every woman in the room gasped. Camille jumped up and down and hugged Frankie tightly, kissing him over and over.

"Damn!" Toya said, admiring the stunning piece of jewelry. "That shit must've cost a grip!"

Dominique was in awe.

Everyone clapped and crowded around the couple to admire the necklace up close. Frankie helped her slice up her
beautiful cake, and the deejay got the party started once
again. While Camille attended to her guests, Toya and Dominique found an empty banquette and sat down. They ordered drinks from a passing waitress and watched the party
in full swing. It wasn't long before Camille joined them,
feasting on a huge slice of her birthday cake.

"Girl, that necklace is exquisite!" Toya said. "Frankie
did a good job picking that out."

"Thanks!" Camille touched the necklace delicately as it
graced her neck. She was so happy to be the envy of all her
friends. Camille was going to rock Frankie's world tonight
to express her gratitude. She loved it when her husband
spoiled her like this. "You look great, Toya," Camille said.
"You must've lost weight or something." Toya did look
wonderful. She had always had a small waist and a big ass,
and that hadn't changed. But her body was much more
toned as a result of her crush on her personal trainer at the
gym she belonged to.

"Thanks," she said, noticing that Camille had put on a
few pounds since the last time they'd seen each other. She
was still a lovely woman, but Toya felt that Camille's figure
couldn't afford the big hunk of cake she was devouring.
Back in the day, the two of them had been the most sought-
after girls in their age group. Camille had been a new girl in
their circle, since she was from Staten Island and had attended high school in Brooklyn at the illustrious Brooklyn
Tech. While Toya had the appeal of being a typical Brooklyn bombshell, Camille's unique appeal had been that she

was someone unfamiliar to them. All the guys from around the way wanted them, and all the girls wanted to be like them. Toya enjoyed her status as the center of attention and had always ensured that she looked flawless wherever she went. So had Camille. Toya hated to think that Camille might be letting herself go. But she kept her mouth shut. After all, today was Camille's birthday and she had a right to enjoy her own damn cake.

Toya scanned the room, watching everyone getting liquored up and having a good time. She spotted Frankie across the room standing with a stunning woman with long hair and frowned.

"Camille, who's the bitch that's been chilling with your husband all night?" Toya asked, nodding in Frankie's direction. "Every time I see him, she's never far away. She ain't trying to give him no breathing room at all!"

Camille looked over and waved her hand as if it were no big deal. "That's Frankie's best friend, Gillian. They work together." Gillian was Doug Nobles's daughter—Baron Nobles's younger sister from a different mother.

Silence shrouded the table as the women digested this information. "Wait a minute," Toya said. "Your husband's best friend . . . Gillian, the one you're always talking about . . . is a female?"

Camille nodded. "Yup. She's cool."

"Oh, *hell no*!" Toya bellowed, setting her glass down heavily on the table. "Cool, my ass! I thought Gillian was a guy the way that you talk about him—her. 'Gillian came and got Frankie and they went golfing.' Or 'Frankie and Gillian just got back from out of town.' You were talking about a female all that time?"

Camille smirked and sipped her drink. She couldn't help being amused by how worked up Toya was getting. "Yes, Toya. Gillian's a female."

Toya shook her head and reached for her own drink. "I would never go for that shit. That woman is beautiful, Camille."

Camille smiled. "Well, so am I, Toya."

Toya nodded, agreeing. "Yes. Yes, you are." Camille *was* beautiful. She had the type of face that was so flawless people often caught themselves staring at her. Her impeccable style didn't hurt, either. But Toya couldn't help noticing that Gillian was *strikingly* beautiful. She looked like Alicia Keys, with a body like a Coke bottle. Camille's weight gain seemed even more tragic now that Toya knew that Frankie was keeping time with America's Next Top Model. Judging from how Frankie was hanging on her every word, Gillian appeared to be a very intoxicating woman. "But what's the saying? 'The only thing better than pussy is *new* pussy.' As long as you and Frankie have been together, you can't tell me that he don't wanna sample something different from time to time. And you're cool with him being that close with a chick like *that*?" Toya looked at Gillian's hourglass figure in a short red jersey dress. Her hair was perfectly coifed, and her shapely legs were accentuated by four-inch Gucci heels.

"I trust my husband," Camille said simply. She shoveled a forkful of cake in her mouth and washed it down with a swig of champagne. Gillian and Frankie were like brother and sister. Their families were intertwined in a way that Toya could never understand.

"Really? You *really* trust that he has never sampled that?"

Camille nodded as she struggled to keep her game face

on. Inwardly, she was seething that Toya was making such a big deal of the fact that Gillian had been so close by her husband's side all night. He never gave Camille any reason to doubt that his relationship with Gillian was anything but platonic. Gillian had been around for as long as Camille could remember, so her presence just sort of came with the territory.

In truth, Camille wasn't necessarily thrilled about Frankie's friendship with such an attractive woman. But she didn't make a fuss over it. Frankie was a good man who didn't ask for much from his wife. After all, she was the one with his last name, the allure of being married to the hottest hustler in the game. And tonight he had thrown her a lavish party to show the world how much she meant to him. True, she secretly resented Gillian's presence there; resented the way she had Frankie hanging on her every word even at this moment. But Camille would never let these bitches know that. Camille's insecurities were her best-kept secret.

Toya looked at her for a long time. "Hmmm!" she muttered. "*She* probably picked out your necklace."

"I doubt that, Toya." Camille sighed, trying not to show her annoyance.

"Look at him over there Chi-town stepping with her. Hmmm! Not me, honey!" Toya shook her head in disbelief as she looked at the stunning woman Frankie was dancing with.

Camille waved her hand at her friend as if to say, *Please!* "Gillian has a man. She's been dating some stockbroker guy for a while now."

"*Iiiiiiiiiii* wouldn't give a damn. She still wouldn't be two-stepping with my husband!" Toya took another swig of her drink. She was growing agitated the more she thought about it. She wondered if Camille was naive or just plain dumb.

Dominique was feeling the effects of her Long Island iced tea and she liked it. She, too, thought that Camille was crazy to let her husband gallivant around town with someone like that. But it was Camille's business. Besides, surely there must be more to the story. "Well, maybe Camille has a male best friend to keep her company when Frankie's out with his female best friend." She smiled at Camille. "Do you?"

Camille shook her head vehemently and laughed. "No, nothing like that."

Toya looked at Camille with mischief in her eyes. "You've *never* cheated on him?"

"Never." Camille was proud of that. She was committed to her husband.

"Do you think he's ever cheated on *you*?" Toya sipped from her glass and looked at Camille over the rim of it. The question was a test to see how dumb Camille really was.

Camille laughed. "No, I don't. Frankie loves me." She made up her mind that Toya was just jealous. Camille had learned that women will often try to fill your head with doubt about your man when they wish he was *their* man instead. She shook her head at Toya and changed the subject. "So where do you live, Dominique?"

Toya noticed the shift in topic and smirked. Camille was the ultimate dumb bitch! But she was her friend, so she dropped it.

"I have the most fabulous apartment on the Upper East Side, thanks to the best real estate agent in the world!" Dominique clinked glasses with Toya, who appreciated the compliment. "That's how I met Toya. A coworker of mine told me about her and I gave her a call. We became instant friends."

Toya waved her hand. "Please. If it wasn't for me, she'd still be living in small-town Staten Island hanging around with a bunch of chickenheads."

Dominique laughed. But Toya was right. When the two of them met, Dominique had been surrounded by a bunch of so-called friends who hated on her. She was the single mother of a thirteen-year-old daughter she had given birth to while just a senior in high school. Dominique hadn't let that deter her. While many had written her off as just another baby having a baby, she had gone to school part-time while interning at radio stations and record labels in order to get her foot in the door of the entertainment industry. With her father's help she'd made it, graduating with a degree in communications from the College of Staten Island while he babysat her daughter, Octavia. Today she was a top A&R at Def Jam and working her way up the ranks. Octavia was now an eighth-grader at an exclusive prep school scoring straight Bs and playing in the school symphony to boot.

Because she was so young and had climbed the ladder to success so rapidly, Dominique had little time to form new friendships. She had resigned herself to hanging out with the same girls she'd been friends with since grade school—girls who were stuck in dead-end jobs and shitty relationships. They envied Dominique, who rubbed elbows with all the hottest stars and traveled to exotic locations constantly. When she met Toya—a successful real estate broker who lived life to the fullest—Dominique had found her first friend who had success equivalent to hers. It felt good to be able to eat dinner at the finest New York City restaurants with a girlfriend who could also afford it due to her own hard work and perseverance. Hanging out with Toya was one of the few occasions when Dominique neither had to hide nor be apologetic for the wealth she had amassed over the years.

"But Toya underestimated me at first," Dominique said, sipping her drink once again.

Toya looked confused. "I did not."

"Yes, you did." Dominique laughed and looked at Camille. "After I closed on my house, Toya and I agreed to keep in touch since we hit it off so well. So one Friday night I had tickets to a Mary J. Blige concert at the Garden."

"Oh, damn!" Toya began to laugh as she realized which story Dominique was about to tell.

Dominique laughed, too, and Camille was more eager than ever to hear the rest.

"So I invited Toya. I told her that I had two tickets—floor seats—and I had no one to go with. But Toya already had a ticket to the show that night. I suggested that she sell her ticket and take my spare one so that we could enjoy the show together. And what did you say?" Dominique asked, looking at Toya, smiling.

Toya shook her head, laughing. "I said, 'Excuse me? My seats are in the thirteenth row. Where are *yours*?'" She spoke in the same stuck-up tone of voice she'd used that night before the concert.

Dominique nodded. "So I explained that I hadn't picked my tickets up from my coworker yet, so I wasn't sure. All I knew was that he promised me they were excellent seats."

Toya sighed. "So I declined." She stirred her drink, then shrugged her shoulders and shook her head. "Uh-uh, I wasn't giving up my row-thirteen seats for some unknown section just to sit next to Dominique."

Dominique laughed. "See how she is?"

Camille laughed, too. "I know exactly how Toya is. She hasn't changed a bit since high school."

They all chuckled and Dominique finished the story. "So we agreed to meet for drinks before the show. I gave my spare ticket to a friend of mine and we all met at a T.G.I. Friday's near the Garden. We had drinks and finger food and then headed to the concert. When we got inside, the usher came over to show us to our seats. He took Toya to her row, then he turned to me and my friend and told us to follow him."

"I was waiting to see where their seats were, and he started leading them closer and closer to the stage. I was pissed already!" Toya was laughing at the memory.

"We just kept going farther and farther," Dominique re-iterated. "We kept walking, and my friend turned to me and asked what kind of seats I had. I still had no idea. The tickets only said section A, seats seven and eight. We were walking down, closer and closer—till we got to the front row! I could not believe that we were in the first row at a Mary concert at the fuckin' Garden! Me and my friend started jumping up and down. We were so excited! Then we heard a voice from the thirteenth row yell out—"

"Oh, *hell no!*" Toya finished the sentence for her. All three friends laughed till their stomachs hurt. "I was so mad! These two bitches were sitting front and center and all of a sudden my seat felt like it was all the way up in the fuckin' balcony. I was heated!" Toya paused to compose herself after so much laughter. "During intermission I went down there to talk to them and I turned my nose up. I said, 'Ain't nobody in the front row tonight but hoodrats.' Dominique's friend said, 'We may be hoodrats. But we're in the front

row!' I had to watch the whole show with them right at
Mary's feet and me all the way back in row thirteen. I was
furious!" Toya chuckled.

Dominique laughed. "Taught her not to underestimate
my connections. She should have just snatched up the ticket
I offered to her, but no. Miss Thing had to be a diva till the
end."

Camille had tears in her eyes from laughing so hard.
Toya had been the same way in high school. She was always
bossy, always boisterous, but she was also always the life of
the party. As long as she could have a drink in her hand and
be snapping her fingers, Toya was happy.

A petite young lady with the baddest haircut on earth
approached the table grinning. "This table is having too
much fun," she said.

Camille looked at the young woman and smiled. "Toya,
remember her?" Toya looked confused. Camille laughed.
"Dominique, this is my little sister, Misa."

Toya's smile broadened. "Oh, my goodness, I haven't
seen you in years! You're gorgeous!" she yelled. Toya could
see the resemblance between the sisters and felt silly for not
guessing who this was. Both of them shared smooth, flawless, dark chocolate skin, striking eyes, and full lips. But
Misa was clearly younger and about fifteen pounds lighter
than Camille. "Misa, sit down and join us." Toya remembered her as a nappy-headed little brat who tagged along
with Camille every once in a while in their teenage years.
Now she was very much a young lady—at least by the looks
of it.

Misa smiled, liking her sister's friend already. Compliments were a surefire way to get on Misa's good side. She
didn't remember Toya, but it seemed that she was a friend of

Camille's from way back. Already she was more interesting
than any of the desperate housewives in Camille's usual
circle of friends. Misa and Camille were native Staten Is-
landers who grew up in the borough's gritty Stapleton
projects. Their mother raised them as a single parent on
welfare, and their upbringing had been rough. Those days
were long gone now that Camille was married to one of the
most powerful men on the streets of New York. Now their
mother lived in a split-level home on Long Island that Camille paid for. Misa contributed to their mother's living expenses, but not much. She figured that Camille could afford
to do it all, so why should she do more than necessary? But
while Misa still maintained friendships with the girls she'd
grown up with in the projects, Camille's friends these days
were very far removed from the life they'd once lived. Toya
was a breath of fresh air to Misa. "Don't mind if I do," she
said, pulling up a chair and sitting beside Toya.

"So you're what . . . twenty-one or twenty-two?" Toya
guessed, noticing that Misa had a flair for fashion. Tonight
Camille was reserved in a black sheath dress, while her
edgier sister wore patterned black leggings with a red minidress and heels.

Misa shook her head. "I'm twenty-four. Freshly divorced
and ready to take over the world!"

Camille rolled her eyes as Toya slapped her sister a high
five. *Take over the world.* Camille would have been happy
if Misa just took over paying her own car note!

"You're on the right track," Toya observed, building her
up before tearing her down again. "But you're only twenty-
four. And you're fierce! Why would you get married so
young in the first place?"

Camille frowned. She felt that Misa had let a good guy

get away. Marriage and children were supposed to be sacred things . . . gifts. "I don't think age matters."

"Of course you don't! You got married early and it worked for you." Toya managed to bite her tongue but was fiending to point out that her marriage might not be working out as well as she thought, with Gillian in the picture. She decided not to rub it in Camille's face on her birthday. "But most of the young ladies in Misa's age group aren't ready for marriage and kids, and neither are the *boys* they're marrying."

Misa had to agree. "That's true. You live and you learn. I was looking for a fairy tale and it didn't work out. I got pregnant with my son, and his father asked me to marry him. I wanted to have the whole family for my son—father, mother, child, white picket fence. All that bullshit." Misa poured herself a glass of the champagne sitting on the table.

Dominique leaned in Misa's direction. "I had my daughter when I was young, too. You can still be a success story even though you're a single parent. This is only the beginning."

Misa clinked glasses with Dominique. "My aunt told me that women marry for love the first time, and the second time it's for the money. That's my way of thinking these days. But I'm in no rush. I'm having fun being single!" Misa was determined to come back to the single life, better than ever.

"I like you," Toya said, relieved that at least Camille's sister seemed to have some hope. Toya didn't believe in soul mates, happily ever after, or any of that bullshit. In her mind, that nonsense didn't exist. The sooner women figured that out, the better off they'd be.

"Thanks," Misa said, smiling.

Dominique snapped her fingers to the beat of the music. "Did your brother-in-law ask you to help him plan this party?" she asked Misa. Dominique was having a blast!

Misa shook her head. "Frankie did all this on his own. If I would've planned it, the budget would've been a lot smaller!"

Camille and Misa shared a laugh at that one. But deep inside, Camille knew that her sister meant that sincerely.

"Well, he sure pulled out all the stops," Dominique observed. "All this food, the deejay is excellent, we got Hennessy, Patrón, Absolut, Jack Daniel's . . . chicken! What more could black people ask for?"

Misa laughed. It was about time Camille found some real friends! She liked Toya's bold personality and Dominique's sense of humor. She crossed her legs and sipped her drink. Then she nudged her sister playfully. "Camille, introduce me to some of Frankie's friends," she coaxed. "There's some ballers in here tonight."

Camille rolled her eyes, chuckling slightly. "Frankie's friends are all married or living with somebody. They're family men."

"And?" Misa asked. "What's your point?"

"Those be the worst ones, honey," Toya cosigned, looking pointedly at Camille.

Dominique was really feeling tipsy now. She looked around the room at all the people and spotted a tall, slender, gorgeous man with a perfectly groomed goatee and the sexiest green eyes she'd ever seen. He seemed to command the attention of everyone around him, and she was in awe.

"Who is *that*?" she asked Camille, discreetly pointing in the mystery man's direction.

Misa smiled, licked her lips. "That's Baron, girl."

Camille smiled, too, because he *was* a beautiful man.

"That's Gillian's half brother, Baron Nobles. He works with Frankie, too. He's engaged to a sweet young lady named Angie."

"*Really?*" Toya was intrigued.

Camille nodded. "Baron and Gillian have the same father but different mothers. Baron's mother is a beautiful black woman. She's so regal, just a really cultured Southern woman. Very Diahann Carroll. She was Nobles's first wife and she had divorced him years before he got sick."

"Sick?" Dominique interrupted.

"He's in a wheelchair. Multiple sclerosis, or something like that. He was only diagnosed within the past year or so. But he remarried right after he divorced Baron's mother. Gillian's mother is a Cuban woman. I don't know much about her, except that she's still married to Doug Nobles."

Dominique was hypnotized by how handsome Baron was. He had to be about six-three, with broad shoulders and an amazing smile. He had mocha-colored flawless skin, the diamond watch on his wrist only making him glow even more. Best of all, he had a commanding presence that just screamed "swagger." Dominique was impressed.

"He's so sexy," she said, finally prying her eyes away from him.

Toya smiled. "Excellent! Go over there and invite him back to your place. Let him fuck you all night long. That way you can forget about the fucking convict once and for all!"

Dominique shook her head. "I'm not cheating on Jamel, no matter how fine Baron is."

Toya frowned. "Dumb! Just *so* dumb!"

Misa smiled. "Jamel is your man, I assume."

Dominique nodded. "Yes, he is. He's out of town for a little while—"

"The bastard is locked up. He's in jail for selling drugs." Toya wasn't going to let Dominique get away with saying her so-called man was just "out of town."

Camille seemed surprised, and Misa laughed. Dominique was annoyed.

"Don't you think I would have told them that myself if I wanted them to know, Toya?" Dominique demanded. She had just met Camille and Misa and didn't want them to make up their minds about the type of people she and Jamel were based on Toya's already biased opinions.

Toya shrugged. "Oh, please! We done got all up in Camille's business tonight." Camille chuckled in agreement. "We all know each other now. Just tell it like it is. That loser is locked up. He's going to come home and be jobless, broke, unmotivated, and he's going to disappoint you. Meanwhile, you're out here being faithful to that *loser*, when you're only thirty years old with a shitload of men at your beck and call." Toya looked Dominique in the eye as if challenging her to deny any of her claims.

Camille intervened. "Is this guy your child's father?"

"No," both Toya and Dominique answered.

Camille was trying to put a positive spin on the situation, but she came up empty. "Well, make sure he's worth your time if you decide to put your life on hold for him."

Toya shook her head. "Ain't no man worth that!"

Frankie and Baron walked by their table and greeted the ladies as they made their rounds. Misa and Dominique looked like they were falling under Baron's spell as he flashed them his megawatt smile. Frankie caressed his wife's cheek and smiled at her. He was happy to see that she was enjoying herself. After all, he owed it to Camille. This party was the least he could do to ensure that she knew she was appreciated. He stood behind her, rubbing her shoulders as he made small talk with her friends. Toya noticed, but was still convinced that he was caressing Gillian as well. She was impressed, though, by the quality of the lavish birthday celebration he had surprised Camille with. It was clear that Frankie loved Camille, and that he threw one hell of a party. And for that reason, she was happy for her friend.

After a few moments of light banter, Frankie and his friend drifted away to mix and mingle. Looking at Baron's long, athletic physique, Dominique decided to correct Toya's last statement.

"Okay, maybe that one might be worth it," she said, admiring Baron's exquisite features.

The ladies laughed, shared a few more drinks, got their dance on, and celebrated Camille's thirtieth birthday until the party came to an end. By the time the night was over, they had formed a new clique, and it was the beginning of a beautiful friendship.

Too Much, Too Little, Too Late

Misa snuggled closer to Cyrus and rested her head on his chest. He had to resist the urge to push her away. They had been seeing each other for less than two months, and already she was smothering him. She called him several times a day, e-mailed him, texted him, and tonight she had shown up at his house unannounced. When he saw she was at the door, his first impulse had been to tell her off and send her away. He didn't appreciate her popping in on him uninvited. But when he swung the door open, Misa had greeted him looking sexier than ever wearing a red belted trench coat and four-inch stilettos. She wore a pair of designer sunglasses and a bright smile, and she soon revealed that was *all* she was wearing. Misa was naked as a newborn child underneath her coat, and when she untied the knot, Cyrus's frown had spread into a broad smile. He had ushered her inside and they had a passionate and fiery sex session followed by a shower together.

After that she had offered to cook for him, which he declined. Then she'd told him about a dream she'd had about the two of them getting married. And now she was all over him, her leg slung across his as her head lay on his chest. He just wanted her to go away.

"So I was thinking," Misa purred.

"Oh, God," Cyrus sighed under his breath.

Misa giggled and hit him playfully. "Seriously," she said. "Maybe we should move in together."

"What?" Cyrus couldn't believe his ears. This bitch must be crazy.

"I mean, my place is awfully big for just me and Shane. And rent nowadays is sky-high. We could save money *and* spend more time together." Misa was sick of living such a boring life in comparison to her sister's. Misa worked as a receptionist at an insurance company, and it was a very mundane job. She made a decent salary and lived in a nice two-bedroom town house in Staten Island's Graniteville section. It was a humble home compared to Camille's, but still an upgrade from how the sisters had grown up.

Cyrus lay there in silence and wondered how best to say what was on his mind.

"What do you think?" Misa pressed him.

"Nah," he said. "It's too soon for all that."

Misa looked at him to see if he was serious. "Too soon for what?" Cyrus was a mailman. He had a sexy physique, a competitive salary, and the aura of a real man. Misa had met him at a lounge on a Friday night and had fallen fast. Since he had all the makings of a good husband, she was wasting no time making sure that he knew how she felt.

Cyrus gently pushed her off him and sat up in bed. "It's too soon for us to be talking about moving in together. We just met."

Misa was outraged. "We did not! It's been months. And

you sure didn't think it was too soon for you to fuck me. So what are you saying, exactly?"

"Calm down," Cyrus said. "I'm not trying to play you, sweetheart. I'm just saying that living together . . . it's too soon for that. We're both grown. Sex is what grown people do. So don't make it sound like I took advantage of you or whatever."

She looked at Cyrus blankly. "Well, I just figured I'd mention it to you," she said, sounding dejected. "But that's not what you want, so . . . forget it." She got up and reached for her trench coat. Cyrus rolled his eyes, feeling like the whole situation had suddenly flipped and now he was the bad guy.

He reached for her. "Don't be like that, ma. I wasn't trying to hurt your feelings."

Misa shrugged him off and slipped her feet into her heels. "You didn't hurt my feelings," she lied. "It's all good. I'll call you tomorrow." She winked at him on her way out and headed for the door, feeling like a fool once again.

Toya was breathless. She had never had so many orgasms in one session. She lay there, staring at Alex, the Tupac lookalike with six-pack abs and what Toya liked to refer to as the "V," where the man's abs met his private parts in a very well-toned V shape. It was like an arrow pointing to the Promised Land, and Toya loved it! Alex was chocolate brown with thick luscious lips and a dick game like no other.

She watched him roll over and scoop up the blunt he had abandoned close to an hour ago. Toya smiled, loving just to look at him. He was a beautiful man, an electrician who immigrated to America from Jamaica when he was barely eighteen. He'd arrived in this country with twenty dollars and a prayer and was now a contractor with a house, a car, and money that was legit. Again, a great example of how hard work and determination paid off. Toya liked men who didn't hide behind excuses.

She had met Alex in Home Depot, and his thick Jamaican accent intoxicated her almost immediately. Toya was sprung from the first night they spent together. The trouble with Alex was that he smoked weed religiously and never wanted to go anywhere or do anything. His entire life consisted of working hard and smoking constantly. To Toya, life was a party. She was always on the go. And Alex was content to sit in his bedroom, in the dark, getting high while watching *Forensic Files* or the History Channel. Toya's patience was wearing thin with him. But the sex was out of this world.

He puffed away, lying back against the bevy of pillows on her bed. He reached for the remote and flicked the TV on. When he immediately turned to the History Channel, Toya shook her head.

"Uh-uh, son." She had little energy after the atomic orgasm she'd just had, but she managed to sit up. "I'm not doing this again. It's Saturday night. It's only ten forty-eight, and I'm not lying here in the dark all night with you watching this shit. We do this every weekend." Toya had pulled out all the stops tonight. She had put on sexy see-through lingerie and cooked a Southern feast for Alex. And when he was full and satisfied, she'd given him head that had blown his mind. After a powerful fuckfest and a few moments of basking in the afterglow, the last thing she wanted to do was watch television.

Alex laughed a little, then spoke again in his Jamaican accent. "Why do you always have to go, go, all the time, go?"

He shook his head. "You should be still sometime. Be quiet. Chill."

"Fuck that." Toya snatched the remote from him and turned the TV off. "Go chill at your house, then. I'm going out."

Alex looked at her in silence, trying to figure out if she was serious. He puffed his L once again. "You ain't going nowhere. Stop fronting."

She climbed out of her platform bed and handed him his boots. "Call me tomorrow."

Alex stared at her, then reluctantly took his boots and got dressed. He shook his head as he headed for the door. "You are something else, Toya."

"Bye!" She locked up after him, then went upstairs and lay across her bed once again. She was still drained after the brief moment of ecstasy that she'd experienced that evening, so her eyes slowly closed. As she drifted off to sleep, she wondered what it would take for her to find the perfect man. It seemed to her that no one could keep up with her. Toya dated several men, though she took none of them seriously. And it was times like these that she was happy to have other men in her arsenal. As she slipped into a nap, she decided that when she woke up she would go out and have some fun. Alex wasn't about to mess up her entire evening.

Toya woke from her blissful slumber to hear her cell phone ringing. She frowned and reached over to answer it. She could hear raindrops drumming relentlessly on her windowpane.

"Hello?"

"Hello." The male voice sounded familiar, but in her sleepy haze, Toya didn't recognize it right away. "How are you, Latoya?"

She froze and felt like she was still asleep and this was a
bad dream. There weren't many people who called Toya by
her full first name. And there was only one who said it in a
way that made her skin crawl. "Who is this?" she asked
through clenched teeth.

"You know who it is."

She did. She found herself speechless for the first time in
years. She could feel her adrenaline rush instantly, and she
gripped the phone tighter.

Then he spoke again. "I was thinking about you." He
paused as if he knew that she was not at all happy to hear
from him. "I only called because—"

Toya hung up the phone before he could explain himself.
Then she turned it off and fought to get her breathing under
control. She lay there in shock for several moments before
she ran off to the bathroom, fighting back tears.

"Hi, Camille. It's Gillian. Can I speak to Frankie?"

Camille looked at the bedside clock and saw that it was
3:14 A.M. The nerve of this bitch, to be calling at such a late
hour to speak to her husband! Gillian was in a relationship
of her own. So Camille tried not to believe that anything
was going on between her and Frankie. Still, calls like this
at all hours of the night were beginning to wear on her patience. "Is everything all right?" she asked.

"Yeah," Gillian said, simply.

"It's late," Camille reminded her.

"I know. I'm sorry if I woke you." Gillian offered no
explanation for the call, and after several moments of silence, Camille roused her husband and passed him the
phone.

"It's Gillian," she told him, her voice heavy with aggravation.

Frankie took the phone and sat up in bed. "Hey," he said. "Nah, it's all good. She's not upset." He pulled the sheet back and swung his feet around to the floor. To Camille's surprise, he took the phone down the hall and continued his conversation in the privacy of the guest room. She lay there in their king-size mahogany bed, snug in eight-hundred-thread-count Egyptian cotton sheets, and wondered why she was so annoyed.

She had a fabulous life with Frankie. They lived in a lavish, custom-built home in Staten Island's Annadale section. The four-bedroom, five-bathroom house sat on a half acre of land on the edge of Blue Heron Park and boasted such amenities as a twenty-one-foot ceiling, twin waterfalls in the foyer, granite flooring, and hand-etched windows. She drove a Range Rover some days and a SL600 on others. Frankie alternated between an Escalade day to day and a Bentley he brought out only on special occasions. Frankie's assortment of legitimate businesses served as a front for the extravagant lifestyle they enjoyed. They had worked hard to have the life they lived. Surely, Frankie would never take that for granted. Gillian was innocuous, Camille told herself. Just a woman Frankie did business with. But she *was* an incredibly attractive woman with a body that made every man pant. Truthfully, it made Camille uneasy to think of the two of them spending so much time together. But she trusted her husband, and whenever those thoughts entered her mind, she quickly dismissed them.

"She's harmless," Camille reassured herself. She pulled the covers up to her chin, turned over, and tried to fall back asleep. "Harmless."

"What's harmless?" Frankie asked, coming back into the bedroom and returning the cordless phone to its cradle.

Camille turned to look at him, embarrassed that she'd been caught talking out loud to herself. She ignored his question and asked, "What did Gillian want?"

Frankie crawled back in bed beside his wife and wrapped his arms around her body, pulling her closer to him. "She's upset 'cuz she broke up with Safari or whatever his name is."

Camille looked at him curiously. "Sadiq, Frankie."

"Yeah, him. They had a fight."

"And she called *you*?"

Frankie noticed the frown on Camille's face and shrugged his shoulders. "Yeah. It's no big deal."

Camille pulled back slightly from her husband's embrace. "She's breaking up with her man and that's no big deal?"

Frankie sighed. "She's just a little upset about it, and she called me to get some shit off her chest. She caught him cheating again. It ain't the first time, so she'll probably take him back just like last time."

Camille looked at her husband like he was crazy. "It's still a big deal, Frankie!"

He resisted the urge to get defensive. Lately, he felt that he was defending his friendship with Gillian more than ever before. He was starting to feel like his wife didn't trust him the way she once had. "I don't think it is. We're friends."

"I know that. But you're such good friends that she would call you in the middle of the night to tell you that she broke up with her man?" Camille searched Frankie's eyes for the truth.

He met her gaze and stared into her eyes. "Yeah," he said. "You know that, so why are you acting surprised all of a sudden? Gillian is like a sister to me, always has been and always will be."

Camille looked at Frankie, wondering if he would ever stand for her having a male best friend who called to speak to her at three o'clock in the morning. "I just don't see why she had to call you of all people at this hour of night to discuss her love life."

Frankie shrugged his shoulders. "I probably spend more time with her during the week than I do with you, considering all the time we spend getting money. She runs a lot of her father's shit these days, and you know I do a lot of business with them. When you work with somebody that much, you get to know each other. So we talk about our relationships sometimes, our families. You should ask her how much I talk about you." He gave her his most sincere expression. "I guess she wanted to talk to somebody who already knew the story so that she wouldn't have to start at the beginning. I've known for a while that they were having problems. So she called me. Like I said, it's no big deal."

"Doesn't she have *girlfriends* she can call at a time like this?"

Frankie looked at Camille and frowned. "Not every woman has a group of nosy chicks she has dinner with every Friday night to talk shit about the men in their lives, like you do," he teased.

Camille wasn't laughing, and she was done talking. She turned over and closed her eyes as if she were going back to sleep. In her heart, she hoped that Frankie would continue to plead his case so that she wouldn't go to sleep angry at him. But to her chagrin, he turned over also and fell asleep before she did. She lay there in the dark and silently cried herself to sleep.

Family Matters

Dominique's black stiletto Mary Janes mashed the gas in her MKX as she zipped down the FDR on her way to drop her daughter, Octavia, off at her prestigious private school. She was late, and that was never a good thing. Not only did Octavia's school frown upon tardiness, but today Dominique had a long list of tasks ahead of her at work. It would be another long night, which meant that Dominique's dad would be "babysitting" thirteen-year-old Octavia. Normally, she and Octavia rode the train together each morning as they set out for their separate destinations. But since they had gotten off to a late start (the result of Dominique hitting the snooze button on her alarm clock one too many times), today she was navigating the busy streets of Manhattan.

"Make sure you go straight to your granddad's house after school. You don't have dance class today so it should only take you twenty minutes to—"

"Ma, I know!" Octavia turned toward the passenger-side window and rolled her eyes. Her mother got on her nerves sometimes. Octavia loved her mother, but she hated the way Dominique constantly smothered her. Octavia's every move was supervised and mapped out for her ahead of time. And Dominique kept close tabs on her daughter's movements—calling and texting periodically throughout the day to make sure that she was safe. Octavia took tap and modern dance classes after school three days a week, and even those had been coordinated to coincide with the days her grandfather attended kidney dialysis. Octavia was sick of being treated like a little kid.

She glanced at her mother and lightened up. Dominique was such a pretty young mom, unlike the old, wrinkly white parents of most of the students at her elite all-girls school. Today, with her hair blowing in the breeze of the open sun-roof and her D&G shades perched on her nose, Dominique looked lovely, and her daughter softened slightly.

"Ma, I get sick of going to Granddad's house all the time after school," Octavia admitted. "All the other kids hang out at the park across the street or at the pizzeria down the block, and I'm never there." Even on weekends, Octavia spent most of her time at her grandfather's house while Dominique traveled upstate to visit her jailbird boyfriend. Octavia was sick of it.

Dominique was grateful for the sunglasses she wore because they masked the fed-up expression on her face. She was so sick of her child yearning to be ordinary when she was such an extraordinary young lady. "Octavia, you should think before you speak." Dominique glanced at her daughter briefly and then turned back to the road ahead. "You have the nerve to say you're sick of going to your grandfather's house . . . do you know how much he does for you?"

"Yeah."

"I don't think you do, baby girl. The time he spends with you after school is more valuable than anything you could learn from those rich white kids at the pizzeria."

Octavia got defensive. "It's not just the white kids. You always say that. There's black kids in my school, too. Spanish ones, Indian ones, even Asians. Segregation is over."

Dominique pressed her lips together and gripped the steering wheel tighter. Her reflex was to pop her smart-ass daughter in the mouth for the sarcastic tone in her voice. But that urge was overpowered by the pride she felt that her daughter was obviously getting a great education at her stuck-up school. That was all that Dominique wanted—for her child to have a great education and excel in every possible way.

"Just take your behind to your grandfather's house after school. No detours." She drove in silence for a few minutes, thinking about how ungrateful her daughter was. On days like this, when her schedule was so overcrowded, Dominique often got home in the wee hours of the morning. Her father was a godsend, not just on these occasions but every day. He looked out for Octavia when Dominique's hectic schedule forced her to be elsewhere.

Her mother had passed away when Dominique was only seven years old. She had suffered a fatal and unexpected heart attack, which devastated the entire family. Dominique had an older sister, Whitney, who was fourteen at the time, and the loss of their mother had changed things dramatically. Somehow their dad had managed to make ends meet. When he was laid off from his job at an auto body shop, he took every civil service exam until he scored high enough to be hired by the City of New York Parks Department. It was a meager living, which meant that there was little room for extras. But what he lacked in legitimate salary, he made up for in his side hustles—running numbers, gambling, shit like that. He kept food on the table and clean and stylish clothes on their backs, and he did the best he could to keep them from falling prey to the bullshit that awaited them in New York City's mean streets. When Whitney turned eighteen, she went away to school and never looked back. But Dominique's road to success hadn't been so smoothly paved. Because she had Octavia while she was in high school, she had been forced to stay close to home in order to continue her education. Her father, in fact, still lived in the same project apartment in Mariners Harbor in which he had raised his daughters. Despite the success that Whitney and Dominique enjoyed, he was happy staying in his humble apartment, surrounded by neighbors who loved him and familiar faces in all the neighborhood stores. Dominique loved her father and had inherited his desire to stay close to their humble roots. Bill was definitely a huge influence on her. Without her father's help, she had no idea how she would have made it.

She pulled up now in front of the school and looked over at her daughter, the ingrate. Dominique shook her head, trying to recall if she had taken things for granted as much when she was that age. "Call me when you get home," she said. She gave Octavia a kiss and watched as she climbed out of her car.

Octavia shut the car door, wishing she could slam it and get away with it. Knowing that her mother was not above opening a can of whoop ass right in front of her prep school friends, Octavia decided against it and stormed off to class, late and pissed off.

Dominique arrived at work thirty minutes late for her

meeting with a new girl group called StarTrak. She was excited about these four young ladies with heavenly voices; she had big plans for them to be the next Pussycat Dolls or Danity Kane. After apologizing for her tardiness, she got down to business, laying out her vision for the ladies' success. By the time she was done, they were sold on her ideas, and Dominique had to admit that she had impressed herself.

She returned to her office and began checking her e-mails, throwing her hands up in exasperation when she read one from her boss. He needed her to travel out of town this weekend, when she had hoped to visit Jamel instead. She started composing a response to her boss to explain that she had other plans for the weekend. But as she prepared to send it, she thought of her coworker and arch-nemesis, Lizz Robbins, who was doing her best to take Dominique's shine. If Dominique didn't go on the trip her boss had laid out for her, Lizz surely would. She discarded her e-mail and sat back in her seat, frustrated. No matter how much she missed her man, he wasn't worth losing her coveted job over. Jamel would have to wait another week.

"Good morning." Gillian said, smiling. She held the door open and ushered Frankie inside as the rain poured down around him. With raindrops drumming a steady beat on the massive house, Frankie stepped into the foyer, towering over her. Water dripped from his jacket, and Greta, the maid, appeared out of nowhere to remove it from him. She scurried away with it as suddenly as she'd appeared, causing Frankie and Gillian to laugh.

"She takes her job so seriously," Frankie said.

Gillian nodded. "She better, for what my father pays

her." She couldn't help noticing how good Frankie looked standing there, wet from the storm outside. His long eyelashes contrasted with the rugged, chiseled features of his handsome brown face. Gillian's gaze rested on Frankie's lips before she caught herself staring and snapped herself out of her momentary daze. "Come on. He's in the living room waiting for you," she said, before leading the way to her father.

Frankie followed, watching Gillian's ass the whole way. She was wearing a body-hugging pair of Guess jeans, and each sway of her hips was like a pendulum rocking Frankie into a blissful trance. When they got to the grand living room, he watched as Gillian crossed to where her father sat dozing off in his recliner and kissed him on his forehead. "Daddy, Frankie's here."

Nobles opened his eyes and smiled at his beautiful daughter, nodding. Nobles himself still looked good for a man who had to be at least seventy years old. He was bald and clean shaven, and today he wore a pair of black leather house slippers, baggy black pants, and a wifebeater—all that beneath a plush navy blue bathrobe. He sat up in his seat and gestured for Frankie to sit on the couch across from him. Frankie crossed the room and sat down, stretching his long legs out and getting comfortable. Nobles poured himself a drink from the bottle of cognac on the table beside him, looking at his young protégé. Frankie noticed that today Gillian didn't leave them alone for their weekly discussions as she normally did. Instead, she took a seat beside him on the sofa, crossed her legs, and folded her hands in her lap in anticipation of what her father was about to say.

"Frankie, I got a situation I need your help with," Nobles said, wasting no time in getting to the point.

Frankie nodded slowly. "Whatever it is, you know I got you." He meant it. There was not very much that Frankie wouldn't do for this man.

Nobles smiled. He loved Frankie's loyalty, something that was hard to come by these days. "It has to do with my son." Nobles sipped his drink and exhaled.

Now Frankie wanted to eat his words. He had been careful over the years not to interfere in family matters. He made sure never to cross the line. Despite her flawless looks, Frankie had never been more than friends with Gillian—not because he didn't have the opportunity to be more than that, but because he never wanted to complicate the delicate tightrope he walked each day with her family. He knew that Nobles trusted Frankie with his daughter. That meant a lot to him, because Nobles rarely trusted anybody with shit. At times Frankie wondered if Nobles was testing him, putting gorgeous Gillian in his care on numerous occasions to see if he would take the bait. And he never did.

His relationship with Baron was no different. There was a line that Frankie didn't cross with him as well. Baron was one of his only true friends. In fact, their relationship was deeper than friendship because of their mutual respect for the man who sat before him.

Nobles had been a father to Frankie when his own was nowhere around. And, in turn, Frankie had looked out for Baron like a brother would. Still, Frankie never lost sight of the fact that he wasn't really family to Baron, or to Nobles, for that matter. He steered clear of interfering in family politics. So he wondered what Nobles had in mind.

As he watched the aging hustler sip his drink, Frankie smiled. Nobles was the last of a dying breed—a true OG who got paper back in the day with the best of them, did time, came out wiser, and flipped the script. He did nearly twelve years for murder and came home and never got his hands dirty again. Instead, Nobles had groomed his son, Baron, to follow in his footsteps, a move that he was often criticized for. But few could argue the fact that the enterprise they'd built was one of the only criminal organizations still thriving in tough economic times. They had so far managed to remain under the radar. And that was due to Nobles's guiding hand over both Baron and Frankie.

Nobles leaned his head to the side and looked Frankie in the eye. "I need you to convince Baron to take a break."

Frankie frowned. "Take a break from what?"

"From being in charge."

"Why?" Frankie asked, confused. He noticed Gillian playing with her hands.

"He's getting a little ahead of himself." Nobles shifted slightly in his seat.

"That's nothing new."

It was true. Baron handled all of the family businesses— drugs, guns, credit cards. It was a lot for any man to juggle. Gillian helped out, but not nearly on the same scale as her brother. And Frankie and everyone else knew that Baron was a young man drunk off power and understandably arrogant. But that had always been the case. He wondered what was so different this time.

Nobles laughed. It certainly wasn't new. But lately his son's antics were costing him money and more. "Tell me about the situation with Dusty and Jojo."

Frankie froze, stunned that news had traveled back to Nobles so quickly. Frankie had personally helped Baron see to it that everything was handled swiftly and kept quiet.

Then he looked at Gillian. "Damn," he said out loud, realizing that she had told her father something. Was she ratting out her own brother?

"Tell me what happened," Nobles repeated.

Frankie was still staring at Gillian. She stared right back. "Baron's doing a good job for you," Frankie said, turning to face Nobles at last.

"But he's not listening to good advice, is he?" Nobles sat his drink down on the table. "Back to Dusty."

Frankie shook his head. "Gillian already told you," he said, shrugging his shoulders and looking at her again. She stared back, so Frankie turned his eyes away from her before she could lock him in her gaze again. He looked at Nobles instead. But Nobles didn't respond. Gillian did.

"I think he wants to hear *your* side of the story, Frankie." She tried to make eye contact, to no avail. "I already told him my side."

Frankie was stunned speechless. She didn't even deny it. He was still confused, but he knew Nobles wanted to hear something. "Me and Baron got ourselves in a tight situation."

Gillian sucked her teeth. "You had nothing to do with—"

"You said you told your side already." Frankie cut a glance at Gillian out of the corner of his eyes. He cleared his throat and continued. "Couple of days ago, we ran into Dusty and some other character at Roseland. Dusty was talking real reckless and Baron was talking back. It got out of hand. You know the rest."

Nobles sipped his drink. "Continue." It didn't sound like a request.

Frankie felt uncomfortable. "That clown threw a drink in Baron's face, on some bitch shit," he explained. "So Baron cracked a bottle over his head. Things escalated and it spilled outside. We left then and I got Baron home and everything got squashed. I haven't heard from him in a few days, but when I left him, he was out of harm's way." He exhaled. "That's it."

"And what happened to Dusty?"

Frankie looked at Gillian. He wondered how much she'd actually told her father. The truth was, he and Baron *had* squashed things that night. But they had caught up with Dusty two days later and Baron had shot him. They had disposed of Dusty's car in the wee hours of the morning, and it had been Gillian who picked them up from the remote location at the very tip of Brooklyn, surrounded by woods and weeds, where they'd dumped Dusty's remains. The spot was one they'd used before in situations like this. Times when Baron's temper had gotten the best of him and Frankie, true to form, had been on point and cleaned up the mess. This time it was a fool with a mouth just as loud as Baron's and a point to prove. Baron had mirked him. And now Frankie looked at the beauty before him and wondered if she had really been tainted against her brother all along.

"I don't know," he said.

"Gillian told me something different." Nobles watched Frankie's reaction, and noticed that he was careful not to show any clues of what he was thinking. "She said that you all went to the party and everybody was having fun. She said Baron threw a drink in Dusty's face. Not the other way around. That Baron broke a bottle on the muthafucka's skull. Gillian said that you tried to calm the situation, tried to get my son to leave quietly. But he kept talking shit. Then it spilled outside."

"That's when I left," Gillian said quickly. She looked at Frankie, hoping again to make eye contact.

Nobles watched the exchange between his "son" and his beloved daughter and cleared his throat. "Don't cover for him, Frankie. Tell me the truth."

Frankie said nothing.

"I think you know exactly what Baron did." Nobles was hoping he could coax Frankie to tell him everything. But part of him admired the man's obvious loyalty to Baron. It made him respect Frankie even more.

"I dropped Baron off at home that night. And Dusty was still breathing the last time I saw him." Frankie was looking at his hands now.

"So neither one of you knows what happened?"

Frankie looked at Nobles and breathed a quiet sigh of relief. So she *hadn't* told him everything. When he looked at Gillian again, he could read the expression on her face. With her eyes, she was saying, *Follow my lead this time.*

Frankie spoke up at last. "I'm telling you what I know, Pops. They did have a fight, and we all got tossed out. Once we got outside the party, we squashed it and everybody drove off peacefully. I got Baron to let me drive him home. Gillian left right before we did."

Nobles drank some more in silence. Several long moments passed this way, with both Frankie and Gillian sitting in anticipation before him. "Dusty's missing. That's the word on the street." Nobles was eyeing Frankie.

"Baron didn't have nothing to do with that." Frankie could feel sweat forming on his brow. He hated lying to this man.

Nobles was no dummy. "I don't believe that. And Dusty is major. He's high profile. It's not like nobody's gonna notice he's missing. Jojo is losing his mind, searching for his brother. What the fuck was y'all thinking?"

"Baron's all right. That's all that matters." Frankie was walking a thin line between dry snitching and being honest with the man he loved like a father. The truth was, Baron was out of fucking control. He was doing too much, too fast, and he was beginning to feel invincible. It was working against him, and in turn it was working against the family. Baron had another dead body on his hands, and ultimately it would be Nobles who would have to make this whole thing go away. But Frankie didn't want to get caught up in all this. All he wanted to do was make money and enjoy spending it.

"I want Gillian to take over." Nobles laid his case out flatly. "I'm getting old, this disease is kicking my ass, and I know I can't live forever." He sipped his drink. "When I'm gone, I don't want to have to worry that Baron fucked up everything I worked hard for. He's gonna have to scale back, and I already know he's not gonna like that. He's cocky just like me, and when he realizes that Gillian wants in, he's gonna fight that. I need you to help him listen to reason."

"What?" Frankie sat forward in his seat. "How?"

"Make it happen," Nobles said.

Frankie looked at Gillian. So that's what this was about. Gillian was making a power move and using Frankie to accomplish it.

"I want to split everything three ways when I die."

"Don't talk like that," Frankie said, waving his hand dismissively. "You still got a lot of living to do."

"The reality of the situation is that I'm getting older. I'm not gonna live forever. And when I'm gone, I want each one of you to take an equal piece. Baron, Gillian, and you," the old man stated.

Frankie felt both honored and guilty. "I don't deserve that."

"You deserve it the most."

Frankie could feel Gillian's gaze on the side of his face as she watched the exchange between two men she loved so much. She uncrossed her legs and sat up, growing animated. "I love my brother to death. You know that."

Frankie nodded. "He loves you, too, Gillian. And you know he listens to you. So you could talk to him yourself and leave me out of it." Gillian was the one person, besides Nobles himself, who could ever get through to Baron whenever he went over the edge.

"I know, Frankie. But he won't listen to me when it comes to this. He thinks I'm not cut out for this life. But what it's really about is that he doesn't want to share the spotlight. You know that my brother respects you. If you make him see that it's a good idea, maybe Baron will change his mind."

"So what am I supposed to do to make him feel better about it?" Frankie asked, confused.

After several silent moments, Gillian shrugged. "Baron needs help, Frankie. He's making big mistakes, and it's gonna backfire. You know it's true. I only told Daddy about the fight at the bar because I knew eventually somebody else would tell him. We owe it to Daddy to bring family business to him before the streets get to him first. That's how I feel." She looked at her father. She was telling the truth. She loved Baron, but her loyalty was to her father first and foremost.

She looked at Frankie again. "I don't know what happened after the party," she lied. "But Baron is putting us in the spotlight, and that's the last thing we need. Even if he didn't have nothing to do with Dusty's disappearance, it looks bad. The last time anybody really saw him, he was beefing with Baron. That puts the focus on us whether we're involved in it or not."

Frankie was noticing several things. For one, Gillian was smarter than he gave her credit for. This was clearly a power move, designed to give her more control of the family business than she'd ever had while endearing her to her father more than ever. He also noticed that suddenly she was using the words "we" and "us" very liberally in relation to family business. And Nobles wasn't correcting her. She had figured out a way to convince her father to let her get deeper in the game. Now she was trying to reel Frankie in as well.

"I taught Baron maybe a little *too* well." The liquor was making Nobles introspective. "I taught him all about the game, taught him how to get money. But I didn't teach him how to appreciate the power that comes with all of that. You have to have something or someone that you love more than the money. Baron doesn't have that. He has no life outside of this one. All he knows is this family."

Frankie shook his head. "So what's the problem?" He held his hands up as if in surrender. "That's what any organization wants in their leader. One hundred percent dedication. You have that in Baron." He looked at Gillian with new eyes. No longer was she his platonic best friend with the phat ass, the one who was like family to him due to the fact that her father had practically raised Frankie. She was now a grown woman, ready to contend for her share of the family business. With a brother as ruthless and addicted to power as Baron was, that was brave, to say the very least. "Can you be one hundred percent dedicated to this shit, Gigi?"

Gillian looked at him, happy that he was still calling her

by the nickname he alone had given her. Calling her Gigi
was the first sign that Frankie still felt some endearment toward her. "Baron is just like Daddy. He likes to handle
everything by himself. But I've been learning the ropes by
watching my brother, my father, and *you*." She flashed her
pearly whites as she said this. "I know I can do it." She didn't
verbalize it, but she knew that in order to get Baron to let her
take over with no hard feelings, she needed Frankie's help.

"I'm not thrilled about this, either." Nobles spoke up.

"Like father, like son," Gillian observed, smiling.

Nobles smiled back at his beloved daughter, who knew
him so well. "I don't want my baby girl to get hurt." Nobles
shrugged his shoulders. "But I worry about Baron, too. I
don't want him to wind up fucked up like I am." He pointed
to his wheelchair, which was leaning against the wall. He
had been confined to it since being diagnosed with multiple
sclerosis eight months prior. "All that work and stress, long
hours and endless days catches up with you. And if that
doesn't do it, haters in the street will do you in. I always
said that having one head of the family is stupid. When I got
sent up north, we could have lost everything if Baron wasn't
ready to step into my shoes. Now that he's in control, who
will be ready to take his place when and if the time comes?
If my son isn't careful, he's gonna be an easy mark for some
young cat trying to make a name for himself. And where
does that leave the rest of the family?"

Frankie nodded. He understood where Nobles was
coming from. Still, he couldn't see why he had to stick his
nose into what amounted to family business. "Why do you
need me to explain that to him? You could tell all that to
Baron yourself."

Gillian smirked and shook her head. Nobles took another sip of his drink before answering.

"Well, Frankie," he said. "It's not just about Baron. Don't get me wrong. I don't want Baron to think I'm playing favorites. He has to think it's his idea. But there's another reason why I need you. I told Gillian that the only way I trust her getting deeper in this business is if you go in by her side. That way I'll know that she's being kept out of harm's way."

Frankie frowned again. "What are you talking about? Baron would look out for her. She's his sister."

Nobles drained his glass. "Baron looks out for Baron." He set his glass down on the table and sat back. "Make no mistake about that." Nobles sounded so sincere.

Frankie shook his head. "So, let me get this straight. You want me to convince Baron to step down and let Gillian take over. Plus you want me to walk her through that transition. Baron's gonna flip the fuck out when he hears that. It sounds like a takeover, and I'm not trying to get caught up in all that."

Gillian touched Frankie's leg ever so briefly. "Please," she said, softly. "I need to do this. We could lose everything unless we stop Baron from messing it all up. Daddy and I think you can make Baron see it your way."

"My way?" Frankie asked. "Or yours?"

Gillian ignored the question, batting her long curly lashes instead. "You have a way of suggesting things to people and making them feel like the whole thing was their idea."

Frankie laughed. "Do I really?"

Gillian smiled. "Yeah. You do. So just suggest it to him and make him think it was his idea from the get-go."

Frankie laughed again. "You give me too much credit."

Nobles shook his head. "No, she's right." He looked at Frankie. "You're like a son to me, Frankie. You know that. You probably don't realize how valuable to this family you really are."

Frankie felt good hearing his father figure say such nice things about him. But he was still hesitant to get involved in Nobles family business. He shrugged.

"What is Baron supposed to do while Gillian's taking over and I'm helping her take over? He's supposed to sit around and watch from the sidelines, playing video games or some shit? And you think something that I can say will make him feel better about that? That don't even sound logical."

Their discussion was interrupted when Nobles's wife, Mayra, breezed into the room. Wearing a long silk bathrobe cinched tightly at the waist, she excused herself. "Sorry to interrupt," she said as she smiled at Frankie before turning her attention to her husband. "Baby, don't take too long in here. Remember we have that party tonight and we don't want to be late. You still have to decide which suit you're wearing."

Frankie had known the family since he was a young boy. He remembered meeting Mayra for the first time and thinking she was the most beautiful woman he'd ever see in his lifetime. Baron was eight years old when his father divorced his mother and married Gillian's mother in the same year. Baron's mother—Celia Parker-Nobles—was a well-educated woman from a proud lineage. She'd lowered herself, according to her family's standards, by marrying Doug Nobles, who was in and out of prison as a result of his criminal activity. She took it understandably hard when her husband of twelve years left her and their son, and married his deceased best friend's widow.

Mayra Leon was a beautiful Cuban woman with milky pale skin and long flowing dark hair. She had been married to Harvey Leon, one of Nobles's dearest friends. When Harvey was murdered in a robbery, it wasn't long before Nobles began an affair with her. That affair turned into love, and he left his wife alone with their son in their New Jersey estate and moved into a huge Westchester mansion with his new young bride.

Gillian was born a year later. Mayra went all out, buying the most expensive strollers and baby clothes, having the most elaborate christening party, decking out the nursery in their opulent home with designer trimmings. Celia, meanwhile, faded into the background and never complained or made waves. Nobles continued to pay all of her bills and expenses. In return, Celia never moved another man into her home to play father to his son. Celia was a dignified woman who saved her money for her son, invested wisely, and lived a life of quiet luxury. Gillian's mother was the total opposite. She lived for the limelight, the glitz and glamour. Everyone warned Nobles that he would go broke trying to keep up with her. But he loved her anyway and let her do as she pleased. To this day, she spent like there was no end to her husband's wealth, and Nobles didn't utter a word. All he had ever cared about was that she made him happy. As long as she did that, she could have whatever she wanted. Meanwhile, Nobles saw to it that his children—his yin and his yang—grew up side by side.

Now Nobles nodded and smiled at his beautiful wife. She still made him weak after so many years. Mayra kept her body in excellent shape and wore the most expensive clothes to show it off. "I'll be there in a few minutes."

Satisfied, Mayra smiled and winked at her husband. "Frankie, it's good to see you," she said. "Will you be there with Gillian tonight?"

Frankie looked caught off guard, and Gillian frowned since she had already told her mother that she wasn't inviting Frankie to the party. It was moments like these that she wanted to slap her mother for starting shit all the time.

"Ma, I told you I'm going alone." Gillian spoke through nearly clenched teeth. "Frankie's busy."

Frankie noticed the tension between the mother and daughter, so he decided not to point out the fact that he wasn't busy at all that night. In fact, he had planned to go home and spend a rare night alone with his wife. But since there was a party going on, he would have much preferred to spend the evening there instead of watching Lifetime movies with Camille. Plus, he had some questions for Gillian. What was she trying to do? He wanted to know exactly what had prompted her to tell Nobles about her brother's altercation with Dusty.

"I see." Mayra smiled. "Well, next time then," she said to Frankie before leaving to prepare for the evening's big bash.

When she was gone, Frankie looked at Gillian and noticed that her posture had stiffened considerably since Mayra had mentioned the party. Gillian wasn't about to spend a night being interrogated by Frankie. She knew that he would want answers about why she had filled her father in on the beef between Baron and Dusty. The truth was that it was clear in Gillian's mind that her brother was headed to either prison or a cemetery. He was living dangerously. And she had learned too much from the men in her life to let her family's hard work go up in smoke because of Baron's foolishness. Gillian had felt for years that Frankie was her father's true heir apparent. And she knew Frankie well enough to know that he felt ambushed by her and her father. Gillian wasn't ready to face his many questions. Not tonight.

Nobles noticed the tension in the room as Gillian fiddled with the rings on her hands while Frankie stole glances at her every few moments. Nobles could see clearly what was happening between the two young people who sat across from him. They were falling in love, and doing everything they could to fight it. He thought the whole thing was very amusing. He certainly could not have chosen a better husband for his precious baby girl than Frankie. The problem was that Frankie was already married. And even though Nobles loved Frankie like a son, he would kill him if he ever broke his daughter's heart.

He cleared his throat, ending the silence that had engulfed them. "Well, you two, I'm going to get myself together for tonight. Frankie, don't forget what I said. Baron listens to you. Make it happen."

Frankie nodded. "I'll try."

He retrieved Nobles's wheelchair and assisted him into it. Greta appeared again and wheeled the old man to his bedroom while Gillian and Frankie were left standing alone in the expansive living room.

"So you know I'm not busy tonight, right?" Frankie asked, his hands tucked in his pockets.

Gillian was stuck. "Oh," she said. "I just assumed that you'd be with Camille. You haven't spent a night at home in weeks." Gillian really didn't give a damn whether Frankie spent time with Camille or not. She was really just trying to avoid his inevitable questions. "Besides, it's just my aunt Serena's birthday party. You'd probably be bored."

Frankie nodded. "Yeah," he said. "You're right." He wondered why he resented the notion of being with his own wife as opposed to spending the evening in Gillian's presence. He shook it off. "So you wanna tell me what all this was about today?"

She looked at him sheepishly. "Not now, Frankie. I gotta go get ready for this party."

He knew she was just stalling, but he decided not to push it. After all, she hadn't told her father *everything*. So this conversation could wait one more day. Still, he wondered why she seemed to be pushing him toward the door faster than usual. A thought occurred to Frankie. Was Gillian expecting company?

"You're going to the party with that Wall Street clown, ain't you?" The look on his face was a mixture of suspicion and disappointment. Gillian hadn't even admitted it yet, and already he knew her well enough to suspect that she was back together with Sasquatch, or whatever his name was.

Gillian had to suppress a smile. Frankie was clearly jealous of her relationship with the stockbroker. "He may come. Depends on whether or not he has to work late."

Frankie nodded, secretly pissed that Gillian's bourgeois boy toy would be with her that night. Knowing that he had no right to be jealous, he shrugged it off. "Call me later, after the party. I'll be at home."

Gillian nodded, following Frankie to the door. As he stepped back out into the chilly rain, Frankie put his hood on, then bid Gillian farewell and trotted off to his car parked in the driveway. She watched him jog away, missing him before he even reached his car. As he started it, backed up, and drove off, she continued to watch him—all the way down the long and winding driveway that led to their estate. Even as his car faded from sight, she found herself staring after it, the scent of him still lingering in the foyer he'd stood in only moments prior. Finally, Greta shuffled by, snapping Gillian out of her reverie, and she shut the door at last.

Fed Up

"This muthafucka thinks I'm playing!"

Misa threw her cell phone into her purse and shoved two twelve-packs of toilet tissue in her shopping cart. Her ex-husband, Louis, had just canceled on her for the third time in a row. That meant that she would have to tell her poor son, Shane, that once again, Daddy wasn't coming for him. It also meant that, without a babysitter, she couldn't go out tonight as she had planned. She seethed as she turned into the next aisle.

Camille could see the rage burning in her sister's eyes after her conversation with her ex. She followed Misa at a safe distance, knowing that she would talk about it when she was ready. Camille quietly perused the shelves at BJ's, a wholesale store just over the bridge in New Jersey. Coming to this "low-budget" warehouse was beneath her, but she'd come along with Misa anyway. The plan was for them to do some school shopping for Shane before he and his mother headed home to meet Louis for his weekend visitation. Camille seldom turned down an opportunity to shop, so she had happily tagged along. Stopping off at this superstore wasn't on her agenda, though. She walked behind her sister, hoping that she was almost done shopping, and breathed a sigh of relief when she saw Misa heading for the cash registers.

They stood on line, and finally Misa filled the silence. "That son of a bitch is so selfish, Camille." Misa looked at the floor and shook her head. She was truly hurting for her child, who was always disappointed by his no-good father.

Camille wished there was something she could do to make it easier on her sister. She couldn't imagine how it must feel to have a rat-bastard husband abandon you. "Misa, Shane is loved. With or without Louis's dumb ass." They moved forward slightly in the line. "You don't need him. If you want to go out this weekend, I'll keep Shane."

Misa brightened a little. That meant that she wouldn't have to cancel her plans with the guy she had met at Almond earlier in the week. "Thank you, Camille," she said. "But that's not the point. Louis should want to spend time with his son. I shouldn't have to argue with him to get him to do that. And he should be man enough to step away from that bitch he's living with so that he can build a relationship with Shane. I'm sick of him, for real." Misa took a deep breath. Her eyes seemed almost sorrowful. "I don't want to wind up like Mama, living alone, struggling to get by. This single-mother thing is so hard!"

Camille wanted to hug her younger sister and assure her that things would get easier. But they were next in line, and so instead she helped Misa load her laundry detergent, toilet tissue, and paper towels—enough to stock most homes for an entire season—onto the conveyor belt. Misa handed over her store card and then foraged through her purse for her credit card. Coming up empty, she leaned against the shopping cart and rifled through her bag in search of enough cash to pay the $87.46 total.

As she saw her sister struggling to come up with the money, Camille came to the rescue, handing over her own credit card to pay for it.

"Thank you," Misa said again, smiling slightly. "I mean that, Camille. I'm just gonna go home, pick up Shane, and stay home this weekend. I'll go shopping one day after work next week, since I forgot my wallet at home."

Camille helped Misa load her bags into the shopping cart, and they headed for the parking lot. On the way, Camille stopped her. "Let's still go shopping," she suggested. "My treat. We'll get Shane whatever he needs for school, and we'll get a little something for ourselves, too. Whatcha think?"

Misa lit up. "Wow, Camille." She shook her head and shrugged her shoulders. "Okay. I guess that'll take my mind off of Louis's dumb ass."

They laughed and walked to the car, ready for some retail therapy.

Toya was on her way to her car after locking up her home. As she shut her gate, she saw her neighbor from across the street strolling over in her direction. She had only seen this character on a few occasions, exiting and entering his house. He always had a smile and a wave for her, and she would barely acknowledge him before scurrying inside her own plush surroundings. She unlocked her car and opened the door, tossing her Chanel bag onto the passenger seat as she prepared to climb inside.

"Excuse me," her neighbor said as he approached her car. "Can I talk to you for a minute?"

Toya turned around and got a good look at her neighbor up close for the first time. He was average height with a muscular build and a deep voice. But that face! Toya recoiled slightly, thinking that he had to be the ugliest man she'd seen since meeting Flavor Flav back in the nineties at a Brooklyn rally for Tawana Brawley.

"What's up?" she asked curtly, eager to get away from this ugly bastard. "I'm in a rush right now."

He nodded. "I understand. I just wanted to introduce myself. We live across the street from each other but I don't think we've ever been formally introduced." He held his hand out. "My name is Russell."

She took his hand and shook it lightly. "Toya," she said, before she turned and got behind the wheel of her car. She pulled the door, hoping to shut it right in this ugly dude's face, but he put his arm out and stopped the door from closing. She looked at him, taking in his Southpole jeans and plaid shirt. He had no flavor and he was ugly as sin. She glared at him icily.

"Okay, Toya," he said, smiling. Toya couldn't help noticing that smiling only made the situation worse. He looked like a monster! "Well, I noticed that you're single."

"You noticed that, huh?" she said sarcastically. She hated neighbors who were so aware of her comings and goings. Most of the homes on her residential block were occupied by families—husbands with wives who watched Toya like a hawk, insecure around the single femme fatale who could afford to live in their tony neighborhood without the luxury of a husband. Now she was finding out that this beast was watching her as well.

He nodded. "Yes, I did. So I was hoping that you'd let me take you out sometime. Maybe go to dinner or—"

Toya was immediately offended. "Why would *I* go out with *you*?" Her face expressed her disgust and complete amazement that a man this hideous would ever think he had a chance with a woman like her.

The beast seemed taken aback. "Well . . ."

"Sorry," Toya cut him off. "I gotta go." She pulled her car door shut and started her car, then peeled away, leaving her dejected neighbor staring off after her. She glanced at him again in her rearview mirror and shuddered. "Ugh! The nerve!"

Octavia sat on the train heading to her dance class after a tough day at school. It was Friday afternoon, and that meant that her grandfather was attending kidney dialysis.

Bill Storms's kidneys had begun to fail six years ago, and he opted not to have a kidney transplant. The list for a donor kidney was incredibly long, and the odds of him getting one before his own kidneys completely shut down were small. When he broke the news to his daughters, their responses had been as different as they were. Whitney, his eldest child, told him that she would do research to aid him in his search for a kidney—even going so far as to suggest that they could buy one with all the clout and connections she had. She knew that in foreign countries there were channels through which these things could be done for a reasonable fee. Bill had declined, though he thanked Whitney for her offer.

Dominique, on the other hand, had a different response altogether. "You can have one of mine, Daddy," she'd said.

"You only need one to survive. And I'm young and healthy. Let's get tested to see if I'm a match." Bill had been extremely touched by that. Within a week, Dominique had gone with him for a battery of tests to determine if she was a viable kidney donor for her dad. As it turned out, she was a perfect match. Still, Bill refused to take her kidney.

After the results came back, he had sat his daughter down and explained why he was opting for dialysis as opposed to a transplant. "What if I take your kidney, and then something goes wrong? I saw a segment on *Dateline* where a man got his son's kidney and the son died during the operation. I couldn't live with myself if that happened to you."

Dominique had laughed. "Daddy, that's not gonna happen."

Bill had shaken his head. "Well, if it did, they might as well bury me, too. 'Cuz it would kill me. I'm going on dialysis. It's no big deal. Just three days a week for three hours. It ain't like I got a whole lot of other stuff to do."

Reluctantly, Dominique had acquiesced. Through the years since then, Bill had become a favorite patient of the staff at the dialysis clinic he attended. In a way, he enjoyed the three days a week when he could go in and flirt with nurses and techs who were half his age. The other two days of the week, he looked after Dominique's daughter, which was another highlight for him. He loved his granddaughter and enjoyed the time he spent with her. Octavia enjoyed it, too, although she wished that just once she'd have the opportunity to do whatever she wanted with her afterschool time.

Today, she had a modern dance class scheduled for four o'clock, and as usual, her mother would be picking her up afterward. She felt trapped and babied, while all the other kids her age seemed to be enjoying freedom and privileges that Octavia only dreamed about.

As she sat on the train with her long legs crossed, a young man got on with an iPod in his hand. He sat across from Octavia and smiled at her. She smiled back. He was cute! He looked like he was from the same tribe as Kobe Bryant. He was tall, dark, and handsome, and he seemed to only have eyes for Octavia.

The boy checked her out and smiled again, liking what he saw. Her prep school uniform looked sexy as hell to him. Her long bare legs were on display in the pale blue skirt she had hiked up higher than she wore it at school. Octavia had rolled the skirt up at the waist and folded it over in order to shorten it to about midthigh. On her feet she wore a pair of ballet flats, and her crisp white blouse was unbuttoned nearly halfway, her red bra visible beneath the fabric. She had a North Face book bag sitting on the seat beside her, and he wondered if she was a stuck-up private school chick. He decided to find out.

Taking the headphones out of his ears, he leaned toward her. "How you doing? My name is Dashawn."

Octavia felt like she was in a movie. Guys never seemed to notice her—at least, not the ones she found attractive. The boys at her school were either white boys from wealthy families or black boys who wished that they were white boys from wealthy families. Octavia's type was the athletic, rap-music-listening, basketball-dribbling category that Dashawn seemed to fit into.

She smiled back. "Hi," she said. "My name is Octavia. Nice to meet you."

Dashawn thought she sounded very proper, unlike the

girls who lived uptown near him in Harlem. "You got a boyfriend, Octavia?"

She shook her head. "Nope." She was enjoying flirting with a handsome stranger on the train this way. "How old are you?" she asked.

"Sixteen," Dashawn said. "How about you?"

"Fourteen," she lied, though she rationalized that it was only a little white lie. She would be fourteen in a couple of months.

"That's wassup," Dashawn said. "So can I get your phone number so I can call you and get to know you?"

Octavia nodded and exchanged phone numbers with the handsome stranger. When her stop came, she waved goodbye to him and sauntered off the train as if she were strolling down the catwalk. She knew that Dashawn was watching her and she wanted to give him a show. As she went to dance class and changed into her leotard, she suddenly felt more grown up. And she liked it.

Frankie walked into his house and found it empty. Breathing a sigh of relief, he tossed his keys on the coffee table and headed straight for the kitchen. On the counter he found a note his wife had scribbled for him on her way out the door. It read,

> Baby, I went with Misa to do some school shopping for Shane. I'll be home soon. There's a dinner plate in the microwave for you. I love you.
>
> Camille

Frankie was glad that she wasn't there. As much as he loved Camille, she had been smothering him with attention lately and he was tired of it. She woke him up with breakfast in bed, came into the shower while he was in there so that she could wash his back, walked him to the door when he left, called him several times throughout the day, and was standing there when his car pulled into the driveway most nights. His dinner was always ready, his laundry and dry cleaning were always done, the house was always spotless. And while Frankie appreciated the fact that he had a good wife who loved him without question, lately he found himself wishing that she had some interests other than him to keep her occupied. In fact, he wished she had more interests so that she could be more interesting to him! She was so predictable, and it was beginning to bore him. He sincerely loved Camille, but lately he wondered if love was enough.

He took a bottle of water out of the fridge and went upstairs to his bedroom. Stepping into the huge room covered wall to wall in plush carpet, he kicked off his Timbs. Camille was an impeccable housekeeper, and Frankie appreciated that because he was a neat freak. Growing up in a strict household, he and his brother had been treated like soldiers. Cleanliness and organization were things that were ingrained in him from early on, and they were qualities that he still valued. He flipped on the TV and watched the news while he stepped out of his jeans and peeled off his sweater. After turning on the shower in his big adjoining bathroom, he looked at his reflection in the mirror. He admired his good looks with a smile and then left the bathroom to allow the water to get piping hot, the way he liked it. Now clad in just a wifebeater, boxers, and a pair of black socks, he sat on the edge of his California king–size bed and watched a story about a brazen bank robbery in South Ozone in which two people had been shot. The robbers had escaped with an undisclosed amount of cash, but the whole scene was captured on surveillance cameras. Frankie shook his head, thinking that it was just a matter of time before the guys who did it were caught. Bank robberies had too much potential to go wrong. Dye packs, silent alarms, armed guards . . . there were bound to be casualties.

He didn't liken the casualties of the bank robbery on the news to the casualties of the life he lived as part of the Nobles crime family. Frankie had little sympathy for those who played the drug game and lost. He did, however, hate to hear of innocent bystanders, people who were just in the wrong place at the wrong time because a gang of young fools got some guns and played with them as if they were toys. He had seen many innocent people fall victim over the years, and it fueled his belief that the game had changed forever.

Back when Frankie came into the life, there had been three or four top hustlers, each of whom controlled a crew of soldiers, all of whom made money. There were guns, and there were also violence and casualties. But not on the scale that existed today. In Frankie's opinion, once guns had become available to young knuckleheads in the hood who had no leaders to follow, the whole game changed. It became a free-for-all instead of the grown man's game that it once was.

His cell phone rang, and he reached for it. Glancing at the caller ID, he had to suppress a smile.

"Hello?"

"Hey," Gillian said softly. She sat on a stool before her vanity mirror, her makeup all laid out before her and her hair pinned up in curlers. She looked at her reflection and hated how her heart rate sped up when she heard his voice. She was in her old bedroom at her parents' home. It was a place where she had pined for Frankie in silence for years before she'd grown up and gotten over it. Even though she was four years younger than Frankie, Gillian had had a secret crush on him from the very beginning. When Frankie married Camille, Gillian had suffered in silence. She had hoped that Frankie would see her as more than a "lil sis." Unfortunately, he had only had eyes for Camille back then. Gillian often wondered what might have been.

Sitting in her old bedroom brought back tons of old memories of the days when she had yearned for him. The party was just an hour away, so she'd opted to get dressed there as opposed to going all the way home. After Frankie left, as she sat there in the familiar surroundings of her childhood, she had felt the need to come clean with him. The last thing she wanted was for Frankie to go to bed that night thinking that Gillian was a snake. "Are you busy? I wanted to explain what happened earlier," she said.

Frankie walked into the steamy bathroom and turned off the shower, then sat back down on his bed. "I'm listening."

Gillian sighed. She tweezed her eyebrows as she spoke. "Besides you, Baron is my best friend."

Frankie didn't bother to fight the urge to smile this time. The bond between the two of them was often an unspoken one, so it was nice to hear her express the fact that he was special to her.

"We didn't grow up in the same house, but we were as close as possible under the circumstances. I look up to him. You know that."

"So why did you tell Pops about the shit with Dusty?" Frankie asked, turning the volume on the TV down.

Gillian stopped midpluck and stared at her reflection in the mirror. She searched her own eyes as if she were searching her soul for the true answer to that question. " 'Cuz I can't watch this shit fall apart right in front of my father's eyes, Frankie. It would kill him." Gillian found herself choking back tears. Struggling to keep her voice under control, she continued. "Daddy spent his *whole life* building this business. All of the connections he's made over the years, all the time he spent on the grind, and all those years he spent in jail while me and my brother grew up . . . he paid his dues and he put this together. And when he came home he gave it all to Baron. I respect that. In fact, I think it would be great if my dad could retire for real, Frankie. Really hand this shit over to his firstborn and kick back somewhere in retirement. I could go legit. Every opportunity to go straight is available to me. But Baron is squandering this shit. He's been doing it for years. The parties, the fucking payoffs, the gambling, all the losses we suffered, all because of Baron spiraling out of control. You know it and I know it. But Daddy doesn't know. He thinks he knows, but he really has no idea."

Frankie frowned. "Yes, he does, Gigi. Don't get it twisted. Pops is not out of touch with what's going on with Baron."

"He doesn't know the half," Gillian said, tweezing again. She began to tell Frankie the whole truth. "My brother came to me a few months ago for money. He said he wanted to take some money out of the restaurant and invest it on some bullshit—"

"Wait a minute," Frankie interrupted. "Baron took money

out of Conga? Who let him do that? Your mother?" Conga was the upscale Cuban restaurant in Harlem that Nobles had opened for his wife. Mayra ran the day-to-day operations, and both Baron and Frankie held meetings there from time to time. It was the family restaurant in more ways than one. But Baron had always assumed that Mayra was in control of the finances for the successful venue.

"She runs it, but Daddy was handling the financial aspect of everything. And it was going well. Mommy was happy, the restaurant was getting great reviews, a few celebrities stop through from time to time, all that. But you know that Daddy's getting old."

Frankie was the one who let out a sigh now. He hated to acknowledge the fact that Nobles was aging. Lately, he was forgetting things, and that had never been like him. The multiple sclerosis was definitely taking its toll on Nobles. "Yeah. And?"

"He's too proud to tell his son that he can't handle some things. I think he's too proud to tell you, too. You know you're like a son to him. I think it's some man thing. Like a pride thing." Gillian peeked over her shoulder to make sure no one was listening. She turned back to the mirror and began applying her smoky eye shadow. "Anyway, he called me into his study and told me that he wanted me to take over my mother's books at Conga. You know that I was a business major at Columbia, so it was no big deal for me. But I noticed little errors here and there. Shit that Daddy would have normally never missed. I saw that he was starting to forget things and it was costing us. So it was good that I took over. Then he let it slip to Baron in a conversation that I was doing the books at the restaurant."

"He forgot that Baron didn't know?" Frankie was aware that Nobles's memory had suffered as a result of the MS.

"Exactly. And once Baron found out, he didn't make a big deal out of it. After all, it is my mother's business and I'm her child. It's natural that when Daddy was ready to pass on responsibility for it, that it would go to me. The thing is, right after he found out about that, he came to me for a loan."

"A loan? Against the restaurant." Frankie was shaking his head. That could only mean one thing. That Baron had exhausted all or most of his own cash and was desperate. That's the only reason Frankie could imagine for Baron to go crawling to his sister for money.

"Exactly. Talking some bullshit about an investment. I saw right through it so I made him tell me the truth. He owes Jojo money."

Frankie frowned. "Baron owes him money?" He thought about the beef between Baron and Dusty at the club recently. Frankie had been on the dance floor with Gillian, having a great time, when all of a sudden there was a fracas at the bar. Frankie wondered now if that argument had erupted as a result of the money Baron owed Dusty's brother, Jojo. And if that was the case, Frankie no longer felt that Baron was right for murdering Dusty. This meant that the beef with Jojo would inevitably escalate to heights none of them wanted.

"Yes," Gillian said. "His gambling is out of control, and he messed around and wound up owing Jojo a lot of paper. He's my brother, so I gave it to him." Gillian moved on to the other eye, switching her BlackBerry to her other hand.

"How much?" Frankie asked.

"Fifty-five grand."

Frankie's eyebrows raised. "Seriously?"

"Unfortunately, yes." She shook her head. "I gave it to him with the promise that he would get it back to me in thirty days. Well, I still haven't gotten that money back, Frankie, and that was almost three months ago. I know he's losing money elsewhere. He has to be. And I'm not gonna sit by and let him fuck up what our father built through so much blood, sweat, and tears."

"I don't understand," Frankie said. "Baron doesn't seem like he's suffering. He's still dealing with me on the same scale that he always was." Baron was one of Frankie's most consistent customers in his drug-distribution business. So far, he hadn't scaled back on the quantity of his purchases, so this new revelation of Baron being in debt surprised Frankie. Baron was known for having the flashiest cars and the biggest chains, and for buying expensive things that no one else could afford. "He's still buying out the bar when we go out. Shit don't seem to be that bad for son. Maybe he's just doing that shit to you because you're his little sister. You know what I'm saying? He feels like he doesn't have to pay you back because you're lil sis."

Gillian shook her head and frowned, hating to be dismissed as weak for any reason. "It's not that, Frankie. I'm telling you that Baron is about to fuck it all up. He never paid Jojo back the money he owed him. And now he's responsible for Dusty's murder. This shit is gonna draw too much attention to us, Frankie. That's why I need to take over. I need for Baron to back off and let us salvage whatever is still left of our business."

"I hear you, Gigi." Frankie lay back on the bed, staring at the ceiling. He thought about all that Gillian had told him.

"Baron is on the verge of ruining everything. He's out there making some real enemies for this family. We don't need that right now. Not with Daddy in a wheelchair and me living alone uptown and Baron out in the middle of the woods in New Jersey by himself. This is not the way shit is supposed to be, with us looking over our shoulders for Jojo because nobody has the heart to tell Daddy that Baron has real beef out there. We need the goons at everybody's houses right now. Baron should be making sure that happens. But he's not. He's out drinking and partying and carrying on like nothing is wrong. And I can't call the shots. Not until my father puts the stamp of approval on me." She paused as she pulled out her mascara. "But *you* already have Daddy's stamp of approval."

Frankie smirked. "So you're using me."

She smiled as well. "I knew you would say that." She finished her makeup and began to take the rollers out of her hair. "I'm not using you, Frankie. But I do need you. I'm not ashamed to admit that."

Frankie was momentarily breathless. "What do you need me for, Gigi?"

She placed the last roller on the dresser and looked at her reflection in the mirror. Oh, if only he knew. "I need you to help me ease the reins out of my brother's hands. I need you to help me run this when that happens. And I need you to be patient with me while I'm learning."

Frankie was nodding, although Gillian couldn't see that through the phone. He wondered if there was more that she needed, more that she was leaving out.

"So will you help me?" she asked, as she slipped on her plum-colored BCBG minidress.

Frankie sat up and scratched his head. He rubbed his hand across his face and took a deep breath. "Yeah," he said. "You know I can't say no to you."

Gillian smiled, wishing that Frankie were going with her to tonight's party after all. But then she figured it was for the best. Everything happened for a reason. She knew that the more time she spent with her "best friend" Frankie, the deeper she was falling for him. She slipped her feet into her A.B.S. heels and retrieved her diamonds from a velvet satchel in her purse, then put on her earrings and bracelet, opting not to wear the necklace that night. She didn't want to steal the spotlight from her aunt. And, looking in the mirror, she realized that she was flawless without the necklace. She left it lying on her dresser and began to fill her purse with the usual contents. "Thanks, Frankie. I appreciate you so much."

"Yeah, yeah, yeah." Frankie laughed. "Why did you call me before the party instead of after, like I said? You didn't want me to know what time you wrapped things up with ole boy?" Frankie couldn't help prying.

Gillian laughed. "Is that why you told me to call you *after* the party? So you could check up on me and see what time I was getting home from my night out with Sadiq?"

Frankie was stuck for a minute. "Never answer a question with a question."

Gillian laughed, and Frankie pictured her face. He loved the way she looked when she laughed. "I gotta go now. I don't feel like hearing my mother's mouth tonight about me being late."

Frankie reluctantly agreed. "Have fun," he said. "Call me af—"

"In the morning," she finished his sentence for him, smiling. "Good night." Gillian hung up the phone and Frankie chuckled to himself.

He walked to the bathroom, turned the shower back on, and undressed completely. As he climbed inside and let the steam engulf him, he couldn't erase the image of Gillian's radiant, smiling face from his memory.

Meanwhile, Gillian was breathing a sigh of relief. She was happy to know that Frankie had her back as she prepared to pry the family business out of the hands of her reckless brother. It gave her a sense of security to know that Frankie was within close reach at a time like this. Her boyfriend, Sadiq, never dabbled in her family business. And Gillian would never share the intricate details of her family with him. Sadiq represented everything that was legitimate in her world. He was straight-laced, successful, wealthy, and he was safe in a different way than Frankie was. Frankie represented a familiar safety. He knew all that there was to know about her life as heiress to a large criminal empire. There were things that didn't need to be explained to him about how she felt and what she was dealing with day to day. Sadiq, on the other hand, was safe in the sense that she didn't have to worry about cops and feds while she was with him. He was different from what she was accustomed to.

As she headed out the door, she smiled to herself, thinking about how lucky she was. She was surrounded by strong men who treated her like a princess. And she was about to take her place at the head of the family where she belonged—with Frankie right by her side.

Food for Thought

"Damn! *This* is how you throw a cookout!" Toya was having a ball. She stood peering at the table brimming with burgers, sausages, hot dogs, chicken, ribs, salads, corn on the cob, and even shrimp skewers. A nearby table was filled with bottles of all kinds, while a cooler held nonalcoholic drinks for the kids and nondrinkers.

Camille was busily playing hostess to a large crowd of her and Frankie's family and friends. It was Labor Day weekend, and Frankie had convinced her to host a barbecue at their huge home. Normally, Camille loved opportunities like this when she could show off a little and enjoy one of her favorite pastimes—eating. But today their usual intimate gathering had turned into a big extravaganza. Frankie was using this event as an opportunity to network and to introduce Gillian to some of the movers and shakers in the business whom she had never gotten the chance to meet before. It was his way of slowly increasing her visibility and status in the crew.

Nobles, Mayra, Gillian, Baron, and the entire crew were there, along with many folks Camille was meeting for the first time. She had no idea what her husband's motives were for having a gathering this large, but she went along with the program and tried her best to make him proud. Camille's family was there also—Misa, little Shane, and their mother, Lily, were in attendance along with a few of Camille's cousins. But the overwhelming majority of the attendees were Frankie's peeps, and Camille was working overtime to impress them.

She smiled at Toya and told her to enjoy herself. Dominique stood glaring at her daughter, who was clad in a white bikini and denim shorts over by the pool. She had peeled off her T-shirt the moment they arrived. Dominique hated that Octavia had worn that outfit, but she had promised her daughter that she could wear whatever she wanted on the weekends since she was forced to wear a school uniform five days a week. With all the men present today, Dominique was regretting that promise more than ever.

Camille invited the ladies to help themselves to whatever they wanted. Then she glanced over at Frankie. He was sitting at a table playing spades with Baron, Misa, and Gillian, surrounded by a crowd of people both familiar and unfamiliar to Camille. Toya saw her friend looking forlornly in her husband's direction and couldn't resist. "Damn! She's even his spades partner?"

Camille rolled her eyes at Toya and walked to the drink table to pour herself a stiff one. Dominique nudged Toya and frowned at her. "Would you cut it out? Stop rubbing salt in her wounds. At least for today. She looks so stressed out trying to make sure everything's perfect."

Toya shrugged and led the way over to a table not far from the card game. The two of them sat down and dug in to their meals. Dominique watched as Camille made her rounds, greeting neighbors and shooing kids away from the hot grill. She stopped at the table where Nobles sat with his wife, and flashed a smile as she ensured that they were comfortable and had everything they needed to enjoy themselves. Next, Camille walked past the huge in-ground swimming pool to make sure that the children were playing safely under the supervision of Frankie's brother, Steven. Steven was living in their one-bedroom rental at the rear of their property. He had been laid off from his job and eventually ran out of money to pay his rent. When he was finally evicted, he showed up on Camille and Frankie's doorstep and they had taken him in. That had been nine months ago, and Steven still had no job and no job prospects. Camille was losing patience, but Frankie seemed not to notice that his brother was freeloading. Steven ate up all the food, ran up the electric bill, and slept all damn day. When he woke up, he lounged around watching talk shows and smoking weed. Camille tried not to complain to Frankie about it, though, since she didn't want him to think that she was intolerant of his family.

She spotted Dominique's daughter, Octavia, splashing through the water in her teeny bikini. Camille noticed a few men who should have known better than to ogle such a young girl standing around and watching her. She shook her head and kept it moving. After all, Octavia was Dominique's problem. She had her hands full as it was, trying to keep tabs on Frankie. Finally, she headed over to the grill and thanked her cousin Peanut for doing such a great job with the food. She looked around and saw her mother stepping in the name of love with one of Frankie's crew members as the song blared from the deejay's speakers. Camille shook her head and kept on walking.

Satisfied that everything was running smoothly, she made her way over to the table where Toya and Dominique were devouring the delicious ribs. Camille was holding a big cup of Absolut in one hand and a beer in the other, and she looked genuinely bothered by all the pressure she was under to keep the party going.

Dominique decided to break the ice. "Camille, this is a great barbecue. Everybody is having fun."

Camille swigged the Absolut and swallowed hard. "Thanks." She looked around and noticed Frankie and Gillian slapping each other five after a good hand in their card game. "I'll be glad when it's over," she said.

Dominique laughed. But Camille seemed dead serious.

"Misa," Camille called to her sister. Misa put her cards down and looked in Camille's direction. "Where is Shane? I haven't seen him."

Misa waved her hand as if Camille was being overprotective. "He's running around here with all the rest of the kids. He's okay. Steven said he was keeping an eye on him." Misa went back to concentrating on her card game.

Dominique sipped her beer. "Who is Steven? Is that Misa's boyfriend?"

Camille shook her head. "No. Misa doesn't have a boyfriend. Steven is Frankie's brother, the parasite who takes up space in the guest house and pays nothing. He's a fucking bum." Camille said it so matter-of-factly that both of her friends were surprised.

Toya cocked her head to the side in amazement. "Mrs. Bingham? Are you cursing and using unladylike language?" she teased.

Camille shrugged her shoulders. "He is! That son of a bitch sits around all day long doing nothing. He has no job, no hobbies, no motivation whatsoever. He's a bum."

Toya smirked. "Cool. He can hang with Jamel when he gets home from Sing Sing," she joked. "He won't be doing a damn thing with his time, either."

Dominique stopped midchew and shot an evil look at Toya.

Camille couldn't help but laugh. "See, Toya. That's why I love you. Even though you can be mean sometimes, you never fail to cheer me up."

Toya was happy to hear that. She smiled at Camille. "With a house this grand, honey, you shouldn't need cheering up. If you ever want to sell it, I will get you the sun, moon, and stars for a home this magnificent."

Camille nodded. "It *is* a beautiful place." She took a deep breath and looked around at her lovely home, grateful for all that she took for granted sometimes. "Frankie and I bought it when we were young and just starting out. My mother used to work as a home health aide on this side of the island, and at the time all the homeowners in this area were white."

"They still are," Toya observed. "I peeped that while I was parking my car out front. You gotta be the only black family on this block."

Camille nodded. "We are. But there's an Indian family that moved in a few doors down. That wasn't how it was back then. When I was a kid, you wouldn't see a brown face living anywhere near this side of the island. Sometimes I would come with my mother to visit the old lady that she cared for. When we would pass this house, I swear I would feel goose bumps. Even as a little girl, I knew that I wanted to own this house one day. I remember back when I started dating Frankie and we got married, he was working so hard that I rarely saw him. But he was making money . . . so much money. And one day, he came home and told me that he was sick of living in our small apartment and it was time for us to get a house. Well, all I could think of was this place. I told him about it and he said that he would get it for me because he could tell that it would truly make me happy. And wouldn't you know it, the previous owner was some Mafia type who got sent to prison, and the wife could no longer afford it on her own. It was priced way out of our range, but we made an offer anyway. The next thing we knew, they accepted our offer and we've been here ever since. It was like divine intervention."

Dominique smiled at her friend. Camille seemed to glow as she described the good old days when she and Frankie were just starting out. "It seems like your life is a fairy tale, Camille. You've got the man you wanted, the house you always dreamed of, cars, clothes, diamonds . . . you're very blessed."

"Amen!" Misa chimed in, joining them at their table. "Plus a loving sister like me to share it all with. Who could ask for anything more?"

Camille sucked her teeth and smiled. "Finished with your card game?" She looked over and saw that Frankie and Gillian were headed over to Nobles's table.

Misa frowned. "Yeah. Baron was my partner and he kept reneging. Frankie and Gillian beat us like we stole something."

The ladies laughed, while Camille noticed Toya shoot a look in her direction that said, *Told you so.* She ignored it and watched as Frankie and a few other guys went to refill their plates. Gillian stood talking to her father and sipping on a Corona.

Dominique was checking out sexy Baron. He stood next to his sister with his hands in his pockets as he talked to his family.

"That man is *gorgeous!*" she proclaimed.

Misa nodded vigorously in agreement. "Yes, he is! And I bet he's hung like a horse, too!"

Camille gasped and took Misa's drink away from her. "No more for you!"

Misa frowned and looked at Camille like she was crazy. "What are you, the tipsy police?" She snatched her drink back from her sister. "You can't tell me when to drink and when not to." Misa was feeling buzzed, but wasn't about to let Camille treat her like a little kid.

Camille shook her head disapprovingly. "You should go and check on your son," she suggested.

Misa blew her off. "He's fine, warden! Shit, I thought this was a barbecue. He's having fun, Camille. And so was I until I came and sat over here."

"Yeah, Camille, lighten up," Toya urged, snapping her fingers and dancing to the Biggie hits the deejay was playing. "Seems like everyone is having fun but you."

Camille rolled her eyes and scanned the yard for her husband. She saw him standing with his crew downing shots of Patrón. She shook her head. "He's gonna be drunk if he keeps that up," she said out loud without realizing it.

Misa threw her hands up. "Let him! Hell, you should get drunk, too. That way you guys can have wild, kinky sex tonight. With your uptight ass!" Everyone laughed, except for Camille. Misa pulled out a deck of cards from the pocket of her shorts. "Let's play some cards, y'all."

The ladies played two rounds of spades before calling it quits. Camille and Misa were no match for Toya and Dominique. As kids, while Misa and Camille had been braiding each other's hair and playing with dolls, Toya and Dominique had been playing cee-lo and poker with Brooklyn thugs. The sisters had been defeated badly, and Camille was sick of hearing Toya teasing them constantly that they were "in the hooooooooooole!" She had had enough for one day.

"I'm gonna get going," Toya said. "Got a date tonight with pussy-eating Jameson." She downed the rest of her iced tea and set her cup back on the table.

As Toya rose to leave, Dominique joined her. "I have to go, too. Octavia has a test on Tuesday and I need her to get some studying done." She scanned the yard for her daughter and spotted her talking to one of Frankie's younger crew members. Dominique shuddered, more determined than ever to get the scantily clad Octavia home before this fool sunk his claws into her.

"Thanks for coming, ladies. I hope you enjoyed yourselves." Camille walked them to their cars and hugged them before they made their exit. She returned to the yard and saw Misa heading toward her with their mom in tow.

"Mama's tired," Misa explained. "She's gonna stay at my house tonight, so we're gonna bounce."

Lily smiled at both of her daughters, proud of the young ladies she'd raised to be such wonderful women. "Camille, I think this is the best barbecue I've ever been to. You outdid yourself." She kissed her daughter and squeezed her tightly before she and Misa headed home for the night.

Once her mother, sister, and nephew were gone, Camille looked around for her husband. At first she couldn't find him, and she began to wonder what the hell he was up to.

But then she spotted him staggering up the stairs leading to the house with Gillian and Baron supporting his drunken steps. She started toward them but was stopped en route by Nobles's wife, Mayra.

"Camille, I have got to get your recipe for that macaroni salad. It was delicious! I thought you had this all catered, but Frankie was bragging to everybody about how you did all this by yourself. I'm amazed!"

Camille smiled, grateful for the compliment, but kept an eye on Frankie as he disappeared into the house with Gillian and Baron. "Thanks, Mayra," she said, turning her attention back to the lovely older woman. "I'm not the most domestic person in the world, but I know my way around a kitchen. Events like this are the only times I really get to show off my skills."

Mayra chatted on and on about how good the food was, and Camille only half listened. When she saw Baron come back out of the house alone, she couldn't take it anymore. "Excuse me, Mayra," Camille said, having to cut her off in midsentence. "I'll be right back."

Camille crossed the yard and climbed the stairs to her house. Once inside, she found scores of people milling around and watching television. Frankie and Gillian were nowhere in sight. She climbed the stairs leading to the bedrooms and vowed that she would kill them both if anything inappropriate was going on. As she neared her bedroom, she could feel her heart pounding. Looking in, she found no one. When she continued down the hall, she could hear low voices coming from the guest bedroom, and she tiptoed closer and stood outside the door undetected. She peeked inside and saw Frankie sprawled across the queen-size bed, lying on his stomach, and Gillian sitting beside him, rubbing his back.

Frankie's speech was slurred as he spoke. "I'm fucked up, Gigi. Word."

Gillian chuckled. "I told you not to try to keep up with Baron. My brother drinks like a fish, and you should know that by now."

"I could hang with Ba— With Baron." Frankie hiccupped. "Fuck that."

Gillian shook her head. "Apparently not." She sighed. "Get some sleep. That's what you need. Close your eyes and relax."

Frankie took her advice and shut his eyes as Gillian stroked his back. "I . . . love you . . . Gigi. Word." Frankie hiccupped again, causing Gillian to giggle.

"Yeah, yeah, yeah. I love you, too. Now go to sleep."

Outside the door, Camille fumed. She stood there feeling a mixture of jealousy and anger, and then at last she stepped into the room and cleared her throat.

Upon seeing Frankie's wife, Gillian didn't seem fazed. "Hey, Camille. Looks like our boy has had too much to drink."

Camille didn't return Gillian's smile, nor did she appreciate her referring to Frankie as "our boy." She stared at Gillian and spoke flatly. "I'll take care of my husband from here. Thank you."

Gillian caught the tone in Camille's voice and smirked slightly. Camille was so clearly insecure, and Gillian thought it was pathetic.

She stood up, picked up her purse from the nightstand, and walked toward the door. "Great barbecue," she said. "Tell Frankie to call me tomorrow."

Camille stood with her hands clenched together. "I'll do that."

Gillian walked out and Camille stared at her sleeping husband with contempt. She had heard what he said to Gillian, but told herself not to overreact. Surely, Frankie meant that he loved Gillian the way a man loves his best friend. Not the way that he loved his wife. She walked over and sat down beside Frankie. He stirred from his sleep, still inebriated, and burped. Camille patted him on his back comfortingly, and Frankie smiled. "Love you, Gigi." He fell back asleep within moments. Meanwhile, Camille sat there and continued stroking his back, with her emotions knotted like a ball in her chest.

Ice Queen

Toya stretched out on the massage table and stuck her face inside the donut hole at the front. She could not wait for Max to get started on her full-body massage. It had been a whole two weeks since her last one and she was fiending. Especially after the unexpected (and unwanted) phone call she'd gotten the other day. She needed Max more than ever right now!

Toya's time on the massage table was her chance to relax, think things through, and clear her mind of all the negativity she dealt with each week. As a professional, single, career-minded black woman, she had her share of bad days. Still, she wouldn't have traded her life for that of any other woman. Toya knew she was a bad bitch, and often referred to herself that way. Camille had asked her the other day why she used the word "bitch" so often and pronounced it with so much venom. " 'Cuz you have to let a bitch know that you mean what you're saying, *bitch*!" They'd laughed about it, but in actuality, Toya really didn't care who disapproved. She didn't take anybody's bullshit. She didn't hesitate to speak her mind. She was confident, a bit conceited,

and convinced that there was no badder bitch on the planet
than Latoya Blake.

She had, however, been shaken to the core by the phone
call she'd received the other night. She shrugged away the
thought of it, shuddering just a little at the memory of his
disgusting voice in her ear. Finally, Max came in to start her
massage. She closed her eyes, as he pointed out that she was
feeling tense in the shoulders again. She hadn't always been
so tough. Like any typical little girl, she had enjoyed her
dolls and dressing up in her mother's clothes. She grew up
with four brothers and she was the only girl. That was what
made her strong. Toya was ridiculed and teased so often
that it seemed like they took turns making her cry. But then
she realized that her crying only gave her brothers more
satisfaction. So she developed a thick skin and began to
hone her verbal skills by tearing her brothers apart with her
words. When they called her ugly, she called them faggots.
When they made fun of her hairstyles, she made fun of their
cheap sneakers. Times were hard back then, and this was
their entertainment. With five kids to raise, a no-good, alcoholic husband, and the mean streets of Brooklyn waiting
to eat her family alive, Toya's mother held things together
as best she could. Mrs. Blake was college educated, as were
all the elders in her family. But she'd fallen for a smooth
talker, gotten married, and had a whole bunch of his ba-
bies. Her teaching job didn't pay much and her husband,
Nathaniel, never kept a job. The tough economic conditions
of the eighties only magnified the misery in their household
even more.

For entertainment Toya talked shit, while her brothers
played pranks on her. One time they told her to turn the
light on in the bathroom. When she pulled the string, a dead

mouse was hanging from it. They laughed as she screamed and cried, and she was distraught for a long time. But that night she lay in bed, plotting her revenge. The next morning she put dead roaches in all of their cereal bowls, and waited until her eldest brother—the one who had urged her the strongest to turn on the bathroom light—had shoved a whole spoonful into his mouth before she spoke up. He spit it out all over the kitchen table, the floor, and his brothers. Toya got her ass beat for that one. But she learned to hold her own and eventually became so adept at giving her brothers a taste of their own medicine that she earned their respect. This only emboldened her, giving her the cockiness she needed to pick fights at school and in their neighborhood. Soon she became known as the loudmouth chick that all the guys respected and all the other chicks were afraid of.

As she grew older, Toya's relationship with her brother Derrick grew stronger than her relationships with her three other brothers. She and Derrick were the closest in age and had the most in common personality-wise. Her eldest brother became a police officer, and the two brothers in the middle were successful in the corporate world. Derrick had been a hustler from the start. He got caught up in the lifestyle and was gone. Toya was well aware of what her brother was into, and she didn't judge him. She had her own flaws, after all. Eventually, Derrick got bagged in a buy-and-bust. Toya was the one member of their family who stood by Derrick when he was sent away for three years at the age of twenty-one. Toya mailed him packages and even made the trek upstate for a visit or two. She encouraged her brother to come home and get his life together, and she promised to help him. Derrick assured her that when he came home he was going to turn his life around.

And he kept his word. When he had been released from prison five years prior, he married his daughter's mother and settled into a quiet life as Mr. Mom, working the early shift at the hospital as an orderly so that he could be home in time to greet their daughter as she returned home from school. To Toya, it was remarkable that Derrick had changed his life so drastically. He had gone from a block hugger to a homebody, and she admired him for it. And that meant that if he could do it, there was no excuse for the countless losers who hid behind felony convictions as an excuse for why they couldn't change their ways. Particularly Dominique's man, Jamel.

Toya thought about Dominique's relationship with "the convict" as she lay on the table enjoying the feeling of Max's fingers working magic on her lower body. She felt that Dominique was suffering from chronic low self-esteem. Why else, she reasoned, would a single woman pulling down a six-figure salary and working in a high-profile career in the music industry ever settle for a lame who never had a real job in his life? She wondered why Dominique couldn't see what a stupid mistake she was making by spending time and money on a man like Jamel. In Toya's eyes, he was a fucking loser.

She also had her opinions about Camille's man, Frankie B. So what if he was making some money? He was a criminal, and he was using Camille as his trophy wife, Toya reasoned. Camille was blindly allowing her husband to spend tons of time with a gorgeous female "friend," all because she was living in a mansion and getting pricey gifts. How pathetic! Toya had her own money and success, not that of a man who could snatch it from her grasp at any moment. The lifestyle was attractive, but only if it was *your* shit and not somebody else's.

Toya dated several men, but each of them served a differ-

ent purpose. In addition to Alex, there was Larry, who Toya
knew the longest and was most familiar with. They had been
drinking buddies on Friday and Saturday nights for years.
He had a long, picture-perfect penis and stamina like a man
half his age. But he also had a live-in girlfriend and a son at
home. He and Toya were friends with benefits, and neither
of them ever tried to complicate that arrangement by in-
volving feelings in the equation. Larry would come through
with a bottle of Hennessy on a Saturday night, and it would
be on and popping.

Last, there was Jameson Bartlett, an executive at Google
who lived on the same block as Toya. His house was the big,
sprawling one on the corner with the lawn that wrapped
around from front to back and with four levels of luxury
amenities. The house had been left to him and his older sister by their grandparents. His sister and her four-year-old
daughter lived in the upstairs apartment. To Toya, he was
nothing to stare at. In fact, they'd only struck up a conversation because he worked her nerves while riding the Long
Island Rail Road to Midtown Manhattan one morning. The
train had been crowded, and Jameson had sat next to Toya,
squeezing his long six-four frame into the seat. Toya had
given him a look of pure disgust as she was forced to put her
Louis bag on her lap. Jameson had laughed, amused by how
clearly her emotions were conveyed in her facial expressions. He loved black women and their bullshit. She hadn't
said a word, but there was no doubt in his mind that she was
cursing him out in her head.

Jameson had apologized to Toya for inconveniencing
her, and she had nodded. He struck up light conversation
and that was when he impressed her. He was well spoken,
using proper English and big words. And he seemed to have

amassed a considerable amount of success, considering the fact that he was only in his midthirties. Toya sized him up during their discussion, and couldn't believe her eyes. True, it was Friday. Many companies allowed "casual Fridays." Still, Toya couldn't get past his pants, which were too short for his long-legged frame. Or his beady black sweater with SEAN JOHN screaming across the front of it. All of it was accentuated by his jacked-up haircut. She didn't even dare to look at his shoes to see what he was working with. She could already tell that he was not the kind of guy she could ever be seen in public with. Her brother Derrick and her friends would have laughed her off the planet, especially with her high-maintenance ways. But his credentials impressed her. Before she knew it, she was accepting his invitation for dinner, except that she invited him to her house instead of going to some fancy, high-profile restaurant. She shuddered now at the very thought.

For their first date, Toya had him over on a Saturday night and she cooked a seafood feast. After dinner, she let Jameson feast on her, and she had never had her pussy eaten so well. He was a pro, no question about it. She couldn't help the noises that escaped her lips as he licked and sucked her with perfection. She was sold. From that point on, every now and then, when the streetlights came on and the neighbors had gone to bed, she would invite Jameson over and command him to take her to ecstasy. She treated him like a slave, and he loved it.

Toya smiled and sighed as she thought about how wonderful her life was. She took no bullshit, she lived life on her own terms, and she was sitting pretty. Who could ask for anything more? Now if only she could get her hopelessly romantic friends to see things her way.

She drifted into bliss as Max massaged her stress away. She thought about her phone conversation with Dominique the night before. Dominique had been complaining that Toya was too condescending, too demeaning with her criticisms of her friends and their life choices. Toya knew that she often came across as mean or unapproachable. And she really didn't intend to be that way. Still, she couldn't help feeling that she had things all figured out and that everyone else should follow her program. She had explained to Dominique that she wasn't trying to hurt her feelings when she pointed out that she was a "dumb bitch" for the hundredth time. She was only trying to get her friend to see that she was too good to be putting up with the likes of Jamel. But Toya had done something she rarely did—she apologized. She told Dominique that she would try to tone down her criticism of her love life. "From now on, I won't say shit about the convict. Not a single word." She knew it was bullshit. But it had made Dominique feel better, so the white lie was worth it.

When her spa session was over, Toya stepped out into the crisp autumn air and took a deep breath. Instead of heading for the subway, she decided to treat herself and she hailed a taxi. "Third Street, Park Slope," she called to the driver as she climbed into the backseat. While heading for her home in Brooklyn, she gave Jameson a call. She pulled out her iPhone and dialed his number. He answered on the first ring.

"Hey, sexy," he said.

"Hello," Toya replied, crossing her legs and getting comfortable in the backseat of the cab. "Come over to my house at seven."

Jameson chuckled, tickled that she was ordering him

around. As a high-powered exec, he was the one calling the shots most of the time. But this sex kitten Toya was happy only when *she* was the one in control. Jameson loved it. He was happy to let her be her usual dominant self.

"Okay. For what?" he asked.

She looked out the window as they crossed the bridge. "So you can eat my pussy," she said.

The driver looked at her through the rearview mirror, stunned. Toya ignored him and acted as if he didn't even exist.

"I'll leave the door open," she continued. "Just come on in."

"That sounds good. I—"

"When you get there, don't say shit! Just come in and find me, get on your knees, and eat my pussy." She knew the cab driver was listening, so she decided to have him drop her off at the liquor store a block from her house just to be on the safe side. That way his nosy ass wouldn't know where she lived.

Jameson was aroused already. "Okay," he said simply. "See you at seven."

Toya hung up the phone and smiled. There wasn't a single aspect of her life that she would want to change. Her love life, her career, her life as a single, successful New York City woman—she controlled it all. Her destiny was in her own hands. She wouldn't have it any other way.

Camille watched Frankie pace the floor and couldn't help but notice how beautiful her husband was. Dressed in just a wifebeater and a pair of Antik jeans, he walked back and forth across the bedroom floor with the phone in one hand and a cigar in the other. To Camille, he had never looked sexier.

"I can't wait till next week, son. I need it now. I'm agreeing to take less than what you owe me, even though we both know that's bad business. The least you can do is get the shit to me when I need it. Friday. No later than Friday, four o'clock."

Camille smiled as Frankie closed his mystery deal. It was times like these that she felt so lucky that he was her husband. He exuded power and strength. She loved him so much. Lately, things between them had been a little tense. Camille was longing for children, and Frankie was seldom home long enough to make any. All he did was grind, and she appreciated that. After all, they were living in very plush surroundings while many of their friends were struggling to make ends meet. Still, Camille longed for the old days when they just had to be near each other. They'd been inseparable once. And she would do anything in the world to get that back.

Ever since the barbecue, Camille had been determined to put the spark back in her marriage. Hearing Frankie tell another woman that he loved her, no matter how innocently he may have meant it, caused Camille to feel more insecure than ever. Whether she wanted to or not, she couldn't help thinking about the things Toya had said. What if Frankie had begun to see Gillian as more than just a friend? She had made love to Frankie that night, and many nights thereafter, with a passion that he hadn't seen from her in a long time. And things had gotten better between them in the weeks since then, but Camille was still hoping to change Frankie's mind about making a baby.

But whenever Camille talked about this, Frankie couldn't help wondering if her yearning for children was the only thing that fueled her passion for him each night. The thought of having a child scared him, though Camille couldn't seem to get that through her head.

He hung up the phone and walked over to the ashtray sitting on top of the dresser. He snuffed out his half-finished cigar and came and sat beside her on the bed.

"Is everything okay?" she asked. Frankie never divulged any details of his business to her. He said it was for her own good. The less she knew, the better. And Camille rarely pressed him for details that he didn't volunteer.

True to form, he didn't tell her much. "Yeah. Gillian put me on to this dude and he's playing games. It's all good. Nothing to worry about." He kissed her and she pulled him on top of her. Frankie ran his fingers through her long hair, and Camille was ready for him to take her to paradise.

But Frankie pulled back and sat up. "I'm going out," he said. "There's a poker game at Mikey's house and I can't miss it."

Camille sighed and couldn't hide the look of disappointment on her face. It was only six o'clock, and already he was leaving her. "Come on, Frankie," she moaned. "You've been out every night this week. I miss you."

He smiled at her. "I know." He saw the sad expression on his wife's face and playfully tapped her. "Don't be like that. I'll spend more time at home after this. I don't mean to neglect you, ma."

Camille shook her head. "It's not just that," she said. "You won't even discuss the baby thing anymore. We're getting older, Frankie. I'm ready for a baby and I think you should at least talk about it with me." Camille was kinda pissed. If she had known that Frankie was going out again, she could have accepted Toya's invitation to join her for a massage at one of the best spas in the city. Instead, she'd be spending another night alone.

Frankie was annoyed that she was back on her baby shit. "Really . . ." He sat down on the bed and leaned in close to her. She smiled, thinking he had changed his mind about going out. That wasn't the case at all. "Why do you keep bringing up this baby shit, Camille? Seriously."

The look on his face was so menacing that Camille felt her heart pause.

"You think having a kid is gonna make everything perfect?" Frankie was looking at her like she disgusted him.

Camille seemed shocked by the question. She shook her head. "Everything is perfect now."

Frankie nodded. "So what do we need a baby for?"

She responded meekly. "I'm just saying—"

"I understand what you're saying. I'll cut back and spend more time at home. But I'm getting tired of you constantly talking about kids. That's not what I want right now. All right?"

Camille felt like she should apologize, but she knew it wouldn't do any good. She should have never said anything to begin with. "All right," she said, hoping that she hadn't pissed him off too badly. She wished she had just kept her big mouth shut.

Camille never wanted to fight with Frankie out of fear that she could easily be replaced. She lived a life of luxury. No working, no school, no responsibilities other than to make her man happy and to represent him well. While most of the other women she knew had to work long hours and live by strict budgets to get by, Camille was living without those obligations and boundaries. The last thing she wanted was to be replaced with the next bitch.

"I just love you, that's all." Her voice was barely above a whisper.

He kissed her on the forehead and stood up. "I love you, too." Picking his shirt up off the chair, he retrieved his cigar and headed out the door, leaving Camille praying that she hadn't rocked the boat.

Manhunt

Toya sat up in bed and lit a cigarette. She glanced over at Jameson and wondered how a man who was such a cornball could eat her pussy like such a champ. "You're the type of guy who'll make a bitch pass out, Jameson." She exhaled the smoke. "I like that."

He laughed. "I know you like it." He clasped his hands behind his head, closed his eyes, and got comfortable in her big beautiful bed. Toya watched him get cozy and frowned. The last thing she wanted was for him to think that he could make himself at home in her sprawling Brooklyn brownstone. This was no long-term relationship. Jameson was her jump-off, no more, no less. He worked for Google and lived in a house that made Toya's swanky home look modest. Still, she wasn't impressed enough by that to let this son of a bitch spend the night.

"I don't like it that much, muthafucka. Don't get all comfortable in my bed!"

Jameson opened one eye and looked to see if she was serious. "What do you mean?" he asked. "I can't spend the night?"

"No!" Toya took another toke of her Newport. "There will be none of that!"

Jameson propped himself up on one elbow. "Why not?"

Toya put her cigarette out and stood up. Her bathrobe was wide open, revealing her big breasts, flat stomach, and perfectly trimmed bush. "Because I said so." She picked up his clothes and set them on the edge of the bed. "I don't do sleepovers."

Jameson was offended. "Damn!" he said. "It's like that?" He sat up in bed and waited for her to say that she was only joking. But he knew her well enough to know that she wasn't playing. Toya was a woman who spoke her mind freely regardless of the circumstances. They had met a year earlier. Their relationship wasn't serious—no dates, no long phone calls, and no "I love you's." Instead, it was simple. They called each other when they needed a sexual fix, and that was that. Hearing Jameson question their arrangement made Toya wonder what was wrong with him.

"Call me tomorrow. Maybe we can get together when I get back from the gym." Toya walked out of the room, leaving Jameson to get dressed by himself. She went down to the kitchen and poured herself a glass of Bacardi and gave a doggy treat to her cute Pomeranian, Ginger. Jameson climbed out of her bed in silence, feeling slightly rejected. This was an unwelcome change of pace.

Part of Jameson was intrigued by her. Toya was a sexy, successful, independent woman with a sex drive like a horny teenager's. And he liked these things about her. She never stressed him out, never called him off the hook, never tried to take their relationship to the next level. There was no pressure for him to define their relationship, no expectation of flowers on Valentine's Day or presents at Christmas. It made Jameson *want* to see her, made him want to crack her tough outer shell. But Toya wasn't having that. Every time Jameson tried to get closer to her, she resisted. He didn't know why he even cared, since Toya obviously didn't. As he got dressed, he couldn't help feeling dismissed. But he swallowed his pride, put on his clothes, and went downstairs. He peeked into the kitchen, where he found Toya sipping on a drink and marinating a steak for dinner the next day.

"I'm out," he said.

"See ya!" Toya called out, not even bothering to glance over her shoulder. "Call me tomorrow."

Jameson left with his pride slightly wounded, while Toya sang along with the song on the radio.

Misa and her girlfriends were holding court at the bar at one of New York City's legendary parties thrown by Gator Productions. These parties were always fantastic, packed to capacity with wannabe ballers blowing their rent money and car notes just to floss in front of the half-naked beauties in attendance. Misa and her friends hadn't bought a single drink all night and they were having a blast. They were all searching for Mr. Right, or at the very least, Mr. Right Now. Misa had given up on Cyrus. She could tell that he wasn't the settling-down type, and she had no time to waste. She was looking for her come up. Instead of dwelling on the chemistry she lacked with Cyrus, she took it as a lesson learned. Next time, she wouldn't rush it. She knew that her aggression had scared Cyrus off, and she was determined not to make that mistake again. Still, Misa was in no way laid-back.

"Look at this bitch!" her friend Bobbi said, gesturing

toward a light-skinned girl wearing a pair of stilettos with straps that wrapped around her legs, a miniskirt that stopped just below her crotch, and a bra top that was spilling over with her huge breasts. "When I start dressing like a two-bit whore, please slap me!"

Misa and Jennifer laughed and agreed to do just that. All three of them were dressed sexily, though neither of them looked as slutty as the young lady Bobbi was now scowling at. Their laughter was interrupted by a deep voice behind Misa.

"Ain't it past your curfew, sweetheart?"

Misa turned around and beamed when she saw Baron Nobles standing behind her, accompanied by a few of his friends. "Hey!" she said, her smile showcasing her newly whitened teeth. "I should be asking you that, Baron. You're the one with a fiancée waiting patiently at home."

Baron smiled and shook his head. "Not anymore. We broke up."

Misa had to resist the urge to jump for joy, but her smile spread wider as she heard this bit of news. "Sorry to hear that," she lied. She noticed Baron's friends checking out her friends, so she introduced them.

Baron's eyes were fixated on Misa as his friends were introduced. Misa was wearing a tight blue dress with a plunging neckline and a short hem. Her thick legs looked shiny and soft in the light of the nightclub, and he was tempted to touch them. He had known Misa for years, but only as Camille's baby sister. During the time that they'd known each other, Misa had been married with a child and Baron had been in a relationship with a woman he truly loved. So despite the fact that he always thought she looked good, Baron had never pushed up on her. But Frankie had mentioned that Misa was divorced now. And that was perfect timing as far as newly single Baron was concerned.

He summoned the bartender, who came right away, much to the chagrin of the other people at the bar who were eager for his attention. The bartender knew who Baron was and immediately gave the generous tipper his undivided attention. "Let me get another round of drinks for the ladies and two bottles of Cris." The bartender scurried off to get the bottles of champagne and to refill the ladies' empty glasses. Meanwhile, Baron leaned on the bar, looking at Misa like she was the most exquisite woman he'd ever seen.

"How's your son?" he asked. "Frankie talks about him all the time." Baron smiled. Frankie complained about Misa's son all the time.

Misa was surprised. Shane never mentioned Frankie whenever he came back from Camille's house. He always talked about what a great time he had with Aunt "Tamille" and all the games he played with Frankie's good-for-nothing brother, Steven. But he never mentioned Frankie. "Really? I always thought Frankie hated kids."

Baron laughed because it was true.

"My son is at Frankie and Camille's house now, as a matter of fact," Misa pointed out. She frowned. "Frankie's not here with you, is he?" When Misa had dropped Shane off, Frankie had allegedly been out handling business. She looked around, wondering if Frankie was really lying to her sister. If so, she was definitely snitching.

Baron saw her scan the club for her brother-in-law and smiled, musing that women sure did stick together. "Nah," he said. "Not at all." He didn't elaborate, instead opting to leave out the fact that Frankie was once again out with his sister, Gillian.

Misa turned her attention to the fresh drinks the bartender sat before her and her friends. As Baron's cohorts took their bottles and headed back to their table, Baron looked at Misa and flashed his most disarming smile. "Wanna join us?"

Bobbi was off the barstool before Misa could even accept Baron's invitation. The ladies followed him back to his table next to the dance floor and noticed the wicked glances from jealous bitches who had been trying to get sexy Baron's attention all night. One of his friends asked Bobbi to dance and she disappeared with him. Jennifer was engrossed in conversation with another of his friends. Misa sat down, crossed her legs, and set her purse on the table, smiling at Baron.

"Well, damn," she said. "I've known you for years and the only thing I really know about you is that you suck at playing spades." Baron had always been a handsome mystery to her.

He laughed. "I know. I'm working on that."

"Good."

Baron flashed his sexy smile. "Plus, I had to wait for you to get divorced before I could try to get to know you. I didn't want your man to kick my ass for talking to wifey."

Misa laughed, imagining punk-ass Louis being bold enough to step to Baron, the live wire. "Please! Somehow I doubt that."

Baron grinned. "I always noticed you, though. Sometimes you come to the family functions with Camille. But she sits on the sidelines and you're always on the dance floor."

She nodded. "True. Camille is shy and reserved."

"And you're . . . what? Bold?"

Misa smirked, not sure she knew how to answer that. She thought about it. "Yeah. I guess you can say that."

He nodded. "That's a good look," he said. "I like women who ain't afraid to speak their mind."

Misa smiled hard. Baron was fine! And he was giving her his undivided attention, much to the chagrin of the chicks surrounding their table, dancing to the music as if they were putting on a show for Baron alone. "So what happened with you and your fiancée? Why did you break up?"

He shrugged his broad shoulders. Baron still loved his ex-fiancée, Angie, because she had proven time and time again that she loved him for who he was as a man, just as much as she loved the life he lived. But the relationship had run its course. "Well," he said, sitting back in his seat. "I tried to help her understand the nature of my business, you know what I'm saying? Why I need to be on the move constantly, traveling in and out of town and all that. But she got fed up with it. She was insecure about the time we spent apart. And I got tired of bending over backward to get her used to it."

"So you dumped her?" Misa asked.

Baron shook his head. "Nah," he admitted. "She walked out on me."

Misa raised an eyebrow. "Really?" *What a dumb bitch!* Misa thought. "Did you try to stop her, try to get her to take you back?"

Baron shook his head. "Nope. I had to let her go." He sipped his Cristal. "I figured if it was meant to be, she'd come back. But she didn't. So fuck it."

Misa soaked it all up, and read between the lines. Despite his tough-guy talk, she could tell that he still loved the girl he had only recently ended his engagement to. Baron had dated Angie for close to four years. She knew firsthand that getting over something so serious was never easy.

"Well, it's her loss," she said.

Baron smiled, but didn't let Misa's compliment go to his head. After all, he was used to women behaving this way around him. He attracted women's attention wherever he went. Whether he wanted it or not, women gave him the red-carpet treatment in every way. He was charismatic and charming, handsome, tall, and toned. And he was unapologetic. He knew that he was a good-looking man, that he exuded power and strength. That was exactly how he wanted it.

Misa was drunk, but still maintained her composure. Baron could tell that she was feeling the effects of the alcohol, though. He calmly poured her a glass of champagne and continued their conversation. "So what about you?" he asked. "You still got feelings for your ex-husband?"

Misa looked at Baron like he was crazy. "Hell no!" She sipped her champagne as Baron laughed. "The only good thing that came out of that relationship was my son."

"I hear you."

She took another swig. "Do you want kids?"

He nodded. "Someday, yeah. But when I have my kids I want to stay with the mother for life. Have like a hood version of the Huxtables or some shit."

Misa laughed. She thought Baron was the perfect candidate for the family she had in mind. He was paid, handsome, powerful, and had family values. She touched his leg as she leaned into him. "I think that's sweet."

Baron could tell that she was twisted. Her seductive smile was turning him on, and he smiled back. "You gotta pick up your son when you leave here?"

She shook her head. "No, Shane is staying the night at my sister's house."

"Wanna get outta here?" he asked, licking his lips.

Misa nodded quicker than she meant to. "Just let me tell my friends that I'm leaving."

Baron noticed that Misa's friend Jennifer was letting one of his boys rub her legs as he whispered in her ear. He glanced at the dance floor and saw that her friend Bobbi was grinding seductively on his other friend, and he chuckled. Looked like all his boys would be fucking tonight.

Misa turned to Jennifer, talking in her ear over the sound of the booming music. Jennifer nodded and then Misa turned her attention back to Baron. "Ready when you are."

He took her by the hand and led her out of the packed club. Misa was radiant as she watched the jealous women eating their hearts out. She liked the way this felt, being on the arm of the most wanted man in the room. And as they headed to the parking lot, she made up her mind that she would do whatever it took to solidify a permanent position at Baron's side.

As they waited for the parking attendant to bring Baron's Maybach to them, Baron watched the devil in a blue dress at his side puffing on a cigarette. "You got a real nice body, sweetheart," he observed. Her four-inch heels accentuated her toned legs and thick thighs. And her dress was clinging to her, revealing a flawless figure. Maybe it was the alcohol, but right now Misa was looking delicious.

Misa smiled at the compliment. "Thanks." Baron's car rolled out, causing all the other customers' heads to turn. His black Maybach gleamed in the light, and Misa pretended not to be impressed. She wanted Baron to think she was accustomed to things this luxurious. And in a way she was. She had ridden in Frankie's Bentley before, so she knew what it was to ride in the finest cars. But this life had never been *hers*. Instead, she had been borrowing from pieces of Camille's. Baron held the passenger-side door open for her, and once she was safely inside, he strolled over to the driver's side, aware that all eyes were on him—as usual.

They peeled out and headed for the Lincoln Tunnel. Misa didn't question where they were going, since she had done her homework and knew that Baron lived in his family's suburban New Jersey estate. They listened to Jay-Z's *Blueprint* CD as they drove, Misa impressing Baron by rapping along with Jigga's lyrics. He smiled at her, then reached in his ashtray for a half-smoked blunt. He lit it, took a long puff, and passed it to Misa. She happily accepted it and took a couple of tokes before passing it back to Baron. With weed smoke wafting through the air, they zipped through traffic and were soon pulling up in front of Baron's huge home.

This time, Misa didn't bother to pretend that she wasn't impressed. Big, sprawling oak trees shielded the enormous house from the other homes on the long and winding road that connected them. Misa admired the lush garden out front, with perfectly pruned bushes and flowers of every shape and color.

"This is beautiful!" she exclaimed, as she climbed out of the luxury car. "My God! You live here by yourself?"

Baron smiled, proud of his massive home. "Yeah." He ushered her up the stairs and inside the huge oak doors and watched her take it all in. "This house was a gift from my father to my mother for their first anniversary."

"You're kidding." Misa was astounded. Cathedral ceilings, marble floors, floor-to-ceiling windows, priceless paintings, and awe-inspiring chandeliers peppered the space. She was breezing from room to room, starting in the foyer and proceeding to the expansive living room and neighboring den.

Each room was more beautiful than the last. "*This* is what he gave her for their first anniversary?"

Baron nodded, smiling. "Yeah. This is where I grew up. But ever since my mother moved to Charlotte to be closer to her sister, this place is barely lived in anymore. I'm always traveling and paper chasing." There was always something occupying Baron's time and making him the center of attention. It was as if he couldn't sit still for long or he'd die of boredom.

Misa was stunned speechless. She couldn't imagine living in a house like this. True, Frankie and Camille had a beautiful home as well. But it was nothing compared to this estate. She felt almost inadequate as she realized that her entire modest town house could fit easily into Baron's living room!

As she looked around, she wondered how it was possible for a guy this fine and this paid to be single and have no kids. And she made up her mind that she was going to be the queen of this castle, no matter what she had to do to make that happen.

Baron pulled her close to him and snapped her out of her trance. She smiled, thrilled that she was here with this beautiful man in this beautiful home with no one to interrupt them. As he kissed her, she felt the effects of the alcohol and the weed as her head spun wildly. She lost all of her inhibitions and knew that this night would be her chance to gain entry into the exclusive club of the rich and powerful. Their tongues dancing together, Misa happily let Baron undress her and didn't protest as his hands hungrily roamed her body. With her dress in a pool at her feet, she let him lead her by the hand to his bedroom. She stepped into the sprawling master suite wearing nothing but her Manolos, and Baron smiled seductively.

"I'm gonna fuck you real good," he said, looking her up and down and admiring her flawless body.

"Promise?" Misa grinned.

He laughed and pulled her onto the bed beside him. As he sucked and fucked her, Misa was glad that his neighbors lived so far down the road. That way they couldn't hear her screaming in a mixture of pleasure and pain as the night slowly faded into morning.

Great Expectations

"I have a collect call from Jamel, an inmate at Marcy Correctional Facility—a New York State correctional facility. To hear the cost of this call, dial two. To accept and pay for this call, dial three. To reject this call and block future calls of this nature, dial four."

Dominique pressed three, as she always did, and waited breathlessly for her man's voice to fill her ear. Finally, she heard Jamel's sexy bass say, "Hello?"

"Hi, baby!" Dominique could barely contain her excitement. Jamel called her often, and she anticipated each call as if she hadn't heard from him in decades. Her telephone bills were astronomical, flooded with collect calls from the state penitentiary. But Dominique never complained. She happily paid each exorbitant bill, grateful for the calls that gave her access to her beloved for thirty precious minutes at a time.

"Hey, baby girl. I love you."

Dominique's smile broadened. "I love you, too, baby. I'm counting down the days till you get home."

Jamel smiled. He was counting down as well. Just six more months to go on his three-year sentence and he could get back to the life he'd left behind. He missed his son, missed the block, and missed his lady.

Jamel was Dominique's one true love. She met him while she was in college. Her daughter had been two or three years old at that time, and her daughter's father was long gone. He had enlisted in the Army and only sent checks home to his kid on her birthday. As a young single mother going to school full time, Dominique had little time to chill. So meeting men was not her priority back then. While her girlfriends were partying and dating, Dominique had been focused on being a mother and solidifying the career she'd always dreamed of. That's why it seemed like divine intervention when she met Jamel at a card game. It was a cold night in December, and Dominique was on break from school. Octavia was asleep at home, where Dominique's father was happy to babysit. On that night, after a grueling week of finals and papers to hand in, Dominique was getting the chance to go out and let her hair down for once.

Jamel had stepped to her almost immediately, playing her close while the spades game was going down. She was flattered, and eager for some male attention. It had been a long time, after all. That night they flirted, got a little tipsy (Dominique was careful not to drink too much or be too off point), and exchanged phone numbers. Jamel called almost immediately, and soon they were caught up in a hot, sweaty, hood love affair. Dominique resumed her studies during the week, and Jamel invited her over and caressed her walls each Saturday night. While it started out as little more than a convenient physical relationship, over time that began to change. Without warning, their steamy sex sessions were followed by conversations. And it was during those conversations that the two of them connected. Jamel was caught off guard, having developed strong feelings for this woman whose life was so starkly different from his own.

When they met, Dominique had been a naive young girl, unfamiliar with the streets and the elements within them. Jamel had been a drug dealer with a ruthless personality who was determined to get money by any means. He had a son with a girl he swore was nothing more than the mother of his child, and Dominique was fine with that. He was, after all, such a doting father, and it was hard not to find that sexy. They were from completely different worlds. Dominique was a good girl taking college courses while getting her feet wet as an intern in the music industry. Jamel was a hustler graduating from selling dimes to selling weight. Despite their differences, the sex was incredible, and, surprisingly, their conversations were more stimulating to Dominique than any of the discussions she had with her collegiate peers. Even though she was in no rush to introduce him to Octavia, she was certain that they would all mesh as a family someday. She convinced herself that he was the man she'd dreamed of all her life.

On the flip side, Jamel wasn't head over heels right away. To him, Dominique represented all the cute, prissy girls with an education who didn't give him the time of day. He wasn't college educated, but he was smart and he knew it. Jamel had seduced Dominique with his looks, his sex, and his conversation as well as his intellect. And fucking her had been like gaining access to an exclusive club that had denied him entry on countless occasions. He knew she was open and that she fell for him rather quickly. He kept his emotions in check at first, basking instead in the fact that he had her eating out of the palm of his hand.

The trouble with Dominique Storms was that she was a

rare mix of two completely different worlds. On one hand she was a well-educated, driven, and career-minded young lady who came from a stable household and never got into too much trouble. On the other hand, she was a young black woman from the projects who enjoyed rap music and an occasional blunt, and could toss back a bottle of Hennessy with the best of them. Unlike her bourgeois sister, Whitney, Dominique was an educated round-the-way girl with a weakness for guys like Jamel.

She was aware of the fact that she was among the few in her demographic who had a future ahead of them. She loved her humble yet stable upbringing and was as comfortable in a project apartment as she was in a penthouse suite. And she believed that Jamel was not the average hustler. He read *The New York Times* religiously at a time when most guys on the block were barely reading *XXL*. He was well versed on everything from sociopolitical matters to stock-market indexes. Dominique believed if Jamel were given access to boardrooms in corporate America, he could hold his own with the best businessmen. She felt that all he needed was a chance. It seemed that they were destined to be together.

Then he was arrested after making a sale to an undercover, and the exchange was caught on tape. Jamel was sent to prison for five to ten years under a plea deal. Dominique had been devastated but was determined to stand by her man. She made trips upstate to visit him twice a month; accepted every collect call (and he called every single day); sent packages, cigarettes, money, and books; and wrote him letters. Repeatedly, Jamel swore that when he came home he was going to marry her, that nothing would ever come between them. He was going to quit the game and get a job, and Dominique vowed to help him every step of the way.

She had even lined up potential interviews for him, using her own valuable connections to help Jamel get a new lease on life. He told her that he was ready to start over, and Dominique believed him—she believed *in* him.

As she listened to her man fill her in on the details of his day—the group meeting he had to take part in and the usual bullshit the COs put him through—Dominique thought about her friend Toya. Toya always lectured Dominique about her relationship with "the convict," which was how Toya referred to Jamel. "Why are you wasting your time with that fool when it's clear that he's going nowhere?!" she'd ask. And all that Dominique could do was tell the truth.

"I love him," she'd tell her friend, simply. And that was all that mattered to her. Dominique's family also thought she was crazy. Particularly her father, who couldn't fathom how a young lady with so much going for herself would lower her standards by spending time with a career criminal. He saw the drive his daughter possessed, and for the life of him he couldn't figure out why she wasted time with a hoodlum like Jamel. But Dominique saw something her friends and family didn't see. Jamel was more than just his rap sheet. He was a smart man, an excellent father, and she believed that he would make a great husband. He and Octavia would eventually form a close relationship, she reasoned, and that was a major part of it. She wanted her daughter to have a father figure, which she felt was lacking in her life. She knew that, in time, everyone would see what she had seen in Jamel all along. Potential.

After hanging up the phone, Jamel sidled back to his cube. His small area in the prison dorm was in no way glamorous, but thanks to Dominique he still had all the comforts of home. His twin bunk bed had flannel sheets on it to keep him warm in the cold, dank jail. He wore a sweat suit, crisp new Nike socks, and a pair of Nike sandals. His locker resembled a food pantry stuffed with tuna fish, iced tea mix, coffee cakes, Doritos, Lay's potato chips, Vienna sausages, bread, and all kinds of other snacks that kept him from having to eat the slop they served at the mess hall. Dominique sent him a food package each month weighing the thirty-five pounds allowed under the facility regulations. He realized how lucky he was to have her in his corner. She did her best to make the situation he was in easier to deal with. Each day at mail call, Jamel heard his name. He would look forward to it because he was never let down. There was always an envelope with his name written in Dominique's perfect penmanship. Many of his fellow inmates never got packages, letters, visits, phone calls, or the multitude of other perks that his lady lavished on him regularly. Jamel was thankful that he was among the lucky ones.

His boy Skills came over and asked if he had a cigarette. Dominique had just sent him a fresh new carton of Newports, so Jamel retrieved them from his locker. Instead of giving Skills the one cigarette he had asked for, Jamel stretched his hand out to give him an entire unopened pack. Skills frowned as if confused.

"You got it like that? You giving away packs now? Let me find out your shorty got you balling like that."

Jamel laughed. "Please! Ain't no giveaways, son."

Skills's smile turned into a frown. He held his hands up and shook his head. "I ain't got nothing to trade you for, son. I got a total of eighty-four cents in my commissary."

Jamel waved his hand at his boy and handed him the

pack of Newports. "All I want is for you to draw something nice for Dominique. Her birthday is coming up and I want to send her something special."

Skills smiled. "No doubt!" He took the cigarettes and gave Jamel a pound.

Skills got his nickname from the drug game. But the true skill he possessed was the ability to draw like a real artist. In jail, that talent had allowed him to barter with the other inmates for things that he couldn't buy with the few spare dollars his mother managed to send him from time to time.

He smiled now at Jamel. "You a real lucky man, Jamel. Got you a lady with a corporate job. You get to call home whenever you want 'cuz she pays for it. She sends you all this stuff, writes you letters all the time, *and* comes to visit you on the regular. Seems like you got a real good girl on your hands."

Jamel smiled. "Word. She's good to me. And when I get home, I'm gonna be good to her, too."

Skills nodded. "You better." He went back to his own cube, leaving Jamel alone with his thoughts.

The truth was, as his release date neared, Jamel was getting increasingly nervous. He was scared to death that he wouldn't fit into Dominique's neat and proper world. After all, he was a thug with a long criminal record and a penchant for finding trouble. As much as he loved Dominique and believed her when she swore that she wasn't fazed by the negativity her friends and family spewed concerning her relationship with him, he had his doubts. She loved him, and that was all that mattered. That was what she kept assuring him. And Jamel loved Dominique as well. Still, there was an uneasiness in the pit of his stomach at the thought of changing his life at the midway point. He hoped he could live up to her expectations. The last thing he wanted to do was disappoint Dominique.

Russell rang Toya's doorbell and waited. He hadn't stopped thinking about her in the time since their last encounter. He really had a thing for Toya, having watched her come and go and seen how she appeared to be a sexy, smart, independent woman. Tonight was his birthday, and he had an offer that he prayed she wouldn't refuse. He heard her little miniature dog barking as if it were a pit bull and there was an intruder on the premises. Russell laughed, thinking that all it would take was one kick and that Pomeranian would be finished. Despite its incessant yapping, he knew that he was safe.

Finally, he saw Toya peer through her screen door. She looked at him like he was crazy to stop by her house unannounced. It seemed for a moment that she had no intention of opening the door. But, finally, he watched as she undid the latch, swung the door open, and stood there with the most adorable frown on her face.

"Can I help you?" she asked, as if he didn't live across the street. Her greeting seemed more appropriate for a salesman or Jehovah's Witness.

"Hello, Toya." Russell smiled in an attempt to garner the same from her. He had no such luck. Her expression remained as icy as ever. "Sorry if I'm disturbing you."

Toya's Pomeranian, Ginger, was growling at the unwelcome stranger, and Toya didn't bother to try and calm her. She was tempted to sic the dog on this beast.

Russell cleared his throat. "Anyway, today is my birthday. I'm having a little get-together at my house, and I was hoping that you would stop by. I'm not having a lot of people over. Just a few of my boys and—"

"I'm busy." Toya cut him off and offered no further explanation. She didn't owe him anything, she reasoned. And he had a lot of nerve even thinking that she would be bothered with the likes of him.

Russell's disappointment was visible on his face. He let out a long sigh. "I'm sorry to hear that." He stuck his hands in his pockets. "Can I ask you a question?"

Toya shrugged her shoulders. This dude had about ninety seconds left before she slammed the door in his face.

"Are you seeing anybody? I mean . . . you got a man? Last time we talked I told you that I noticed that you were single. But that was kind of presumptuous. I never asked you if you're already spoken for." He was wondering if another man was to blame for the fact that she was dismissing him constantly.

"That's really none of your business."

"I don't mean to get in your business. It's just that I see you coming and going on the regular. But I don't really see you with anybody, and I was just wondering if you're single."

"Let me ask *you* a question," Toya said, folding her arms across her chest. "How do you have so much time to watch me? And why are you checking to see who's coming and going and what the fuck I'm doing with my life in my house?"

Russell was caught off guard, but managed to recover quickly. "I'm not stalking you or nothing like that—"

"That's what it sounds like."

"Well, that's not what it is at all. I like you, Toya."

"You don't even know me."

"I'm trying to change that. I just want the chance to take

you out and get to know you. I'm not asking for a miracle. But I like what I see so far and I was hoping you'd give me a shot." His smile was slowly fading and his hopes were diminishing the longer he stood there explaining himself.

Toya was thoroughly entertained watching Russell squirm. "I already told you that I'm busy."

Russell nodded. "Okay. Maybe some other time?"

Toya scooped her dog up into her arms, aware that Ginger was still growling. Once she was face-to-face with Russell, Ginger began to bark aggressively. "I gotta go." Without another word, she stepped back and shut the door right in Russell's face. Stroking her dog gently, she said, "I know, Ginger. He's so ugly that he scared you!" She chuckled to herself as she carried Ginger back upstairs to her bedroom, where she'd been watching Puffy's latest reality show.

Russell was disappointed and embarrassed. What Toya hadn't known was that his boys—friends of his who had grown up with him back in Jamaica, Queens—were watching from across the street. From the moment he laid eyes on her, he thought she was sexy as hell. But he wasn't the handsomest man, and his boys had suggested that she was out of his league. Still, he was persistent, hoping that he could persuade her to come over to his place for his birthday gathering. His friends had bet him that a guy like him could never get with a woman like that. And Toya had just proved them right. Russell sulked back across the street with his tail between his legs. She hadn't even bothered to say "happy birthday."

Brotherly Love

Frankie rang the doorbell and waited with his hands in his pockets. It was mid-October and he could feel a chill in the air already. He looked up and down the quiet block and was tempted to sell his own beautiful house in exchange for a home like this one in Kearny, New Jersey. The house was big, and the land surrounding it was vast. The grounds were perfectly manicured and he could hear the faint sound of birds singing in the otherwise silent autumn air. Finally, Baron came to the door and ushered Frankie inside. Stepping into the open foyer, Frankie greeted his host with a hood handshake before following him into the living room.

It seemed as if Baron had been lounging around on the sofa all day, evidenced by the rumpled blanket and pillow lying across it. His T-shirt was wrinkled and his basketball shorts hung low. Baron's size 13 Nike sandals sat empty beneath the coffee table, while he shuffled around on the sparkling hardwood floors barefoot except for a pair of black ankle socks. He was unshaven and looked sleepy, but he still went to the refrigerator and retrieved a Corona.

"Want one?" he asked.

Frankie declined, shaking his head and taking a seat on the recliner. "I thought you were leaving for Vegas later on today," he said, confused. "Don't look like you packed anything."

Baron plopped down on the sofa in the same spot he'd been lying in before Frankie's arrival. His long legs stretched out before him, he sipped his beer and sighed. "I ain't going. I'm tired, son. Every weekend for like three months straight I've been traveling, partying, driving, flying, drinking, smoking . . . that shit took its toll on me, for real. I'm staying home this weekend. Sitting right here on this couch like this." Baron gestured with the remote in his hand and his posture completely relaxed. "I got all this house and I'm never home to live in it."

Frankie looked around and nodded. It was true. Baron was a workaholic and a professional party animal, just like his father had been in his youth. This huge house often sat empty, with Baron traveling most of the time or lying up at the home of some random chick. There was always something occupying Baron's time and making him the center of attention. It was as if he couldn't sit still for long or he'd die of boredom. Lately, he had taken more trips, made more money, and taken bigger risks than ever before.

"That's true," Frankie observed, still nodding. "These days, you should be keeping a lower profile anyway."

Baron glanced at him. "Yeah?" he asked, taking a swig of his beer. "You think so, huh?"

Frankie didn't miss the tone in Baron's voice and knew that he had touched a nerve. Baron hated being told what to do, even when it was clear that he should heed the unwanted advice. He looked at his friend, his voice and gaze unwavering. "Yeah. I think so."

Baron smirked. "Why's that?"

Frankie chose his words carefully as he answered. "Well," he sighed. "You said yourself that you're tired. You're doing too much. Besides, you know there's a situation right now. It would be smart to keep a low profile."

"So I should hide 'cuz of Jojo, Frankie?" Baron's face was twisted into a grimace as he asked him.

Frankie shook his head. "That's not what I'm saying."

"That's exactly what you're saying."

"No, it's not. Hiding is one thing. I would never tell you to run and take cover like a bitch over some shit you started." Frankie took the gloves off now.

"Some shit I started, huh?" Baron laughed at Frankie's audacity in placing all the blame on him.

"Yeah." Frankie frowned as if there was no question as to whose fault the beef with Jojo was. "That shit with you and Dusty is what started everything, and now he's dead. His family is looking for him, his mother is crying in the street, all of Brooklyn wants payback. Jojo's out there talking all his shit and he got his heart set on killing you. Shit is real right now, but I'm not telling you to hide. Keeping a lower profile is different. It's not about being scared. It's about being smart, and recognizing that Jojo's not the most dangerous nigga alive, but he's mad right now. His brother is missing. And I understand his fury 'cuz it would be the same way if it was you that was missing instead of Dusty." Frankie looked at Baron. "If it was my brother, I would want war, too."

The tension in Baron's jaw slackened slightly. Although he didn't agree with everything that Frankie was saying, he appreciated the fact that Frankie loved him like a brother. After all, the two of them had been practically raised together under Doug Nobles's tutelage. He knew that Frankie wasn't just criticizing him for the hell of it. He was family. "I can't keep too low of a profile," Baron said. He took a sip of his beer. "I got work out there that needs to be taken care of. So I can't lay low, son. That's not an option."

Frankie looked around at the mess in the living room. Baron had recently ended an engagement to a woman he had dated for close to four years. She couldn't adapt to his jet-set lifestyle, no matter how hard she tried. This big house, in which he'd grown up, was supposed to be the home where he would start his family. But now that he was a bachelor again, the place was a mess. Clothes hung over the stairway banister, and an empty takeout food container sat open on the coffee table. Doritos rested beside a half-empty bottle of orange Fanta.

"Get the maid in here, B." Frankie picked up the Styrofoam container and tossed it back on the table for emphasis. "Maria don't come no more?"

"Magdalena, son. And nah, she don't come no more. She got deported."

Frankie shook his head and looked at his friend sympathetically. "That's why you should apologize to Angie."

"Fuck Angie." Baron took a swig of his beer and wiped his mouth with the back of his hand.

Frankie sat back and got comfortable. "That's what you say, but you know you love that girl."

Baron didn't respond right away. He seemed to ponder Frankie's last statement. He knew that most women were enticed by his good looks, his lifestyle, his money, and his power. But Baron had found something deeper than that with Angie—until he fucked it all up.

He genuinely loved Angie. But things had taken an ugly turn in their relationship toward the end. Baron had a problem with his hands, and found himself taking out his frustrations on Angie when things didn't go his way in the streets. He had beaten her with increasing intensity over the years, leaving her with bruises, black eyes, busted lips, and even a broken wrist once. She had urged him to seek help, but Baron refused to admit that he had a problem. When Angie walked away at last, Baron had only reluctantly let her go. While he was out of town on a trip to Miami, Angie had moved her things out of the New Jersey mansion they'd shared for years. When Baron returned, he searched high and low until he found her seeking refuge at the home of her best friend. Demanding that she come home, he had tried to intimidate her into coming back. She threatened to tell his family about the abuse she had suffered in silence if he continued to pursue her. The last thing Baron wanted was for his parents to know the demons that lurked behind the facade he showed them daily. He feared that his father might strip him of his power as a result, and he knew that his mother—a woman who exuded an air of royalty—would have never forgiven him. As much as he hated to relinquish control over Angie, he had.

Finally, he said, "No doubt. I'm always gonna love her. But I don't love arguing all the time, attitudes and tension. I don't miss that shit. And I'm not gonna apologize for the life I live. This is me. It ain't changing. Angie can't deal with it. So fuck it. I'd rather be by myself."

"You said yourself that you're tired of partying, drinking, and all that. Face it, son, you're getting old just like the rest of us. Time to settle down. Find that one good woman."

Baron laughed. He knew better than anybody that Frankie didn't think married life was all that. "For what? So she could sit around all day spending up the money I make? No good."

Frankie felt sucker punched, but Baron didn't notice. He was too busy turning to a rerun of *Law & Order*. Frankie thought about Camille sitting at home all day looking like Kimora in a Baby Phat ad, just for being his wife. Meanwhile, a woman like Gillian was itching to get in the game with the big boys and make her own moves. He had to admit that Baron had a point.

"Like my pops and Gillian's moms," Baron explained. "He did all that work to get established in the game. Robbed hustlers, killed 'em, lied, cheated. He clawed his way to the top, paid all his dues. And all she had to do was marry him and she got the keys to the kingdom. I don't want no female getting ahold of what I work hard for unless she truly deserves it." He watched the scene on TV until it went to commercial, then picked the conversation back up where he'd left off. "You're right, though." Baron licked his lips, dry from a long night of drinking and weed smoking. "I am getting old. I'm tired as hell, Frankie. I used to do this all night and still be on point all day." Baron held up the beer bottle for emphasis. "I need to start taking vitamins or something. Get in the gym."

Frankie shook his head. "What you need to do is to take a break and enjoy what you work hard for. Then you can get back at it with your head on straight. Reevaluate everything."

Baron stared at Frankie. Swigged his beer again. "Why? So you can take my place?"

Frankie laughed. "You know damn well that I don't want your spot." Frankie looked at Baron to see if he was serious. He was glad to see that Baron had a smirk on his face. But years in the streets had taught him that a smirk could mask a thousand emotions. "If I wanted your spot, I'd have it already," he said.

Baron's smirk spread into a smile. "Always talking that shit." He knew that Frankie meant what he said. Still, he also knew that Frankie had his back, if only on the strength of his father. Baron shook his head and stared off blankly. "I know I got us into a lot of trouble with that Dusty shit."

Frankie nodded. "You sure did. Now you gotta worry about Jojo getting at you. It's time to lay low, I'm telling you."

Baron's jaw clenched. "Ain't nobody fuckin' scared of Jojo! Let him come and get me. I'll bury him right next to his fuckin' brother."

"See? That's what I'm talking about, son. That shit has to stop. That's not the way to deal with everybody all the time."

"Why not?"

Frankie shook his head. Today, he didn't have the energy to go down this road again with his friend. "Bottom line is, the last time Dusty was seen, he was beefing with us. That was weeks ago; nobody has heard from him since. Jojo wants blood, and he's making that known. Just watch your back. I'm damn sure watching mine." Frankie saw Baron think about it. He let him soak up the severity of the situation before saying, "You need to step out of the spotlight for a minute. Take a break, Baron."

Baron looked at Frankie and shrugged. "I already told you. There's only one person besides me that Pops would trust to run all this shit. That's you. So if you don't want it, how can I take a break?"

Frankie thought back to his conversation in Nobles's living room not so long ago and shrugged. "You got a point, you know what I'm saying." He stared off as if deep in thought. "You got Gillian."

Baron thought about it, but quickly shook his head.
"She's not ready."

"That's not what you said before. We were at Camille's
birthday party and you were talking to me about how much
you loved Angie. How you wanted to settle down, start a
family with her and all that. But she was in your ear about
leaving the game alone, scaling back on all the shit you're
into. And you said the only person you felt you might ever
trust with what your father built was Gillian."

Baron looked at Frankie and nodded. "I remember saying that. But I wasn't talking about now. I was talking about
if I ever got to the point that I couldn't hold my own. Like
how Pops is."

Frankie nodded. He didn't want to seem too eager to
champion Gillian's cause.

"She wants it," Baron said, swigging his beer again. "I
know that for sure. But Gillian ain't ready."

Frankie shrugged. "She might not be. But you and I both
know she won't ever be ready unless you show her the ropes
yourself. Start grooming her for the business so that if you
ever get to that point—God forbid—you'll know that Gillian is ready to step into your shoes."

Baron thought about it. Frankie might be right. He loved
his sister and was very protective of her. But she had been
soaking up the game for years. Maybe it was time for him to
truly take her under his wing. Baron looked at Frankie and
wondered if he should admit the truth. He trusted Frankie,
so he leveled with him.

"I don't have a problem with giving Gillian some play. My
problem is with her mother. Mayra doesn't love my father as
much as he loves her. And sometimes I wonder if she's the
reason why Gillian stays so caught up in this life instead of

being legit. Like . . . is she trying to push my sister into this shit so that she can see as much of the Nobles family money as me and my moms?"

Frankie realized immediately why Nobles had asked him to speak to Baron, rather than doing it himself. It was no secret that Celia—Baron's mother—harbored resentment toward Mayra. The woman had basically stolen Nobles right out from under Celia's nose, after all. And while Celia had been a dutiful, demure, and respectful wife, Mayra was pampered, extravagant, and spoiled rotten with Nobles's money and power. Despite the fact that the two women were cordial in each other's presence, they were in silent competition with one another—using their children as pawns in their twisted game of chess. Frankie had watched Nobles gracefully sidestep the simmering drama between his first and second wives. Nobles had managed to remain friendly with his ex-wife—he still paid all the bills and doled out cash whenever she needed it—while enjoying a happy marriage with his sexy, younger second wife. Frankie understood now that he had to be the one to get Baron to let his sister in the game, since Nobles suggesting it would have seemed like playing favorites.

"But it's not about Mayra. Pops is the one who laid the foundation with Gillian. He taught her the basics because he don't want her to settle for being one of those wives you were talking about before. Sitting around waiting for her husband to come home and lavish her with shit. He wants her to have her own, not somebody else's. And he taught her well, too. She has that going for her."

Baron nodded, staring blankly at the TV. "She does have this shit down pat."

"Exactly," Frankie cosigned. "What she needs now is her

big brother to take her under his wing and show her the shit up close and personal. The same way I've watched you scoop these young fools off the block and show them how to really get money, you can show Gillian how to do what you do so that you can finally take that break you deserve. I think that's the solution right there."

Baron thought about it. Frankie was right. He did have a knack for taking the most hopeless of prospects and turning them into real contenders. If he could do the same thing with Gillian, he could keep the money in the family while giving himself the time to live a little. They had grown up closely, and Baron had protected and catered to Gillian as much as their father had. Being almost ten years older than his sister, he had schooled her and helped to mold her into the queen she was now.

But, truthfully, the one thing he had over his sister was his seat at the helm of the family. His position was what he believed endeared him in the heart of his father. The last thing he wanted was to relinquish that spot to his sister, for fear that she would do just as good a job—if not better. As much as he loved Gillian, there still existed a sibling rivalry of sorts for the admiration and respect of their father.

"I hear you, Frankie." Baron nodded. "But I can't walk away from this shit now. That's not an option for me. This is my life." He seemed to think about it for several long, silent moments. He sat there as if entranced, until a KFC commercial snapped him out of it. He picked up the remote and turned the channel. "Eventually, when I'm ready to stop, Gillian can have the business and all the headaches that come with it. Then I can spend more time watching *Maury* and shit." He flipped past the paternity-test episode as he said it.

Frankie was disappointed. Convincing Baron to step

down would be harder than he'd thought it would be. "Gillian won't let you down. You know she's respected, she's smart. You should have given her the shot a long time ago."

Baron smirked and looked at Frankie questioningly. "Yeah?" He laughed. "I would expect you to say that. She got you wrapped around her finger."

Frankie laughed. "Gillian ain't got me wrapped around nothing."

Baron was smiling. He loved his sister, but she was cunning as hell. He suspected that she had probably sold Frankie on the idea of her taking over long ago. Nobles, too. Frankie, in Baron's opinion, was being teased into submission. Baron watched his sister like a hawk, so he didn't believe that she had ever been intimate with Frankie. Baron thought back to a conversation he and Gillian had years prior concerning her feelings for Frankie. Their discussion about Frankie's upcoming wedding somehow turned into Gillian ranting about her disdain for Frankie's soon-to-be wife. She believed that Camille was undeserving of the life she was marrying into. After listening to her bash Camille for a while, Baron had asked Gillian point blank if she had feelings for Frankie. Gillian admitted that she did. Baron had allowed that Frankie was a good man, and he really didn't mind the idea of having him as a brother-in-law. But he also pointed out that Frankie seemed to really love Camille. Baron had advised his sister that if Frankie actually went through with the wedding, she should let go of any feelings she may have for him. She had taken his advice so far, and Frankie was really like part of the family. But Baron was not blind to the fact that his sister was a beautiful woman. He suspected that Frankie might have a crush on Gillian. He was sweet to her, thoughtful and patient. Gillian had their father eating out of the palm of her

hand the same way. She was cultured, refined, and sassy at
the same time. And when she wanted something—especially
from a man—she tended to get it. As a daddy's girl, she'd
been spoiled rotten. True, she was down to go to a football
game. But trust that she'd be watching from the skybox with
a bird's-eye view. She did everything big, expensive, over the
top—just like her mother.

In fact, it had been Gillian who suggested (if not insisted)
that the family put more of their money and manpower behind Frankie. Frankie was one of Nobles's soldiers and had
made a name for himself and all that. But he had not been a
major player in the game as far as Baron was concerned.
Nobles loved Frankie like a son, and Baron was aware of
that. At one time he had resented their relationship, wondering if Nobles's love for Frankie signaled that Baron
wasn't enough of a son to satisfy him. Not that he had anything against Frankie; quite the contrary. Baron admired
Frankie's hustle and his drive. And he had come to love him
like a brother over time. He just hadn't been sure in the
early days that Frankie was worthy of the faith that Gillian
and their father had in him. But Gillian had convinced
Baron to give Frankie his full support. It was a decision he
had never regretted. Frankie had proven to be trustworthy
and consistent, and he continued to be a surrogate member
of the Nobles family. Baron had watched Gillian's friendship with Frankie blossom from then on, so it came as no
surprise to him now that Frankie offered his endorsement
of her.

"Yeah," he said, sipping his Corona again. "She got you
wrapped around her finger for real."

Frankie grinned. "Yeah, aiight. Call it what you want, but

you know I'm right. She has what it takes to be more hands-on. Plus you need the break, so in my opinion it's win/win."

Baron knew it was true. He needed to take a break, if only to get some much-needed rest. His cousin was having a bachelor party in Las Vegas that night and Baron had no intention of going. Anyone who knew him well would have been surprised to find the notorious party animal opting for a spot on the sofa instead of a wild night in Vegas.

Frankie's grin faded as he thought about Gillian. "What's up with your sister and that suit-and-tie lame?" he asked.

Baron took his eyes off the TV for a moment and glanced at Frankie. He didn't know whether or not Gillian had told Frankie about her recent reconciliation with Sadiq. Baron shrugged. "Gillian don't know what she wants. One minute she's saying she hates his guts, and the next she's going with him to a Broadway play. Whenever dude fucks up, he stops by Harry Winston or whatever and it's all good. You feel me? Gillian and her moms are a lot alike in that respect."

Frankie nodded. He knew that Gillian was a sucker for designer labels and costly things. What he admired about her was her ability to get those things for herself. True, she expected them from her man as well. But, unlike Camille or Mayra, she was capable of having those luxurious things with or without a man.

"I just want to make sure she's not getting played," Frankie said, looking truly concerned. "If she's happy, she's happy. If not, I wanna do something about it."

Baron nodded, wondering when Frankie and Gillian would stop bullshitting about their true feelings for one another. Clearly, there was more between them than the friendship they hid behind. "Pops likes this dude she's seeing.

He told her that she would be smart to hold on to this one. And you know how much of a daddy's girl Gillian is. She's probably staying with this guy out of some twisted need to please my father."

Frankie nodded. Nobles had mentioned that he admired Gillian's latest boyfriend. He was a successful Wall Street type who had all kinds of degrees. Still, Frankie couldn't help worrying that Gillian was being blinded by this man with money and credentials. There had to be more to the guy than it seemed.

"So, you wanna get your ass whipped at Madden or what?" Baron picked up the Xbox control and looked challengingly at Frankie.

Frankie smirked and stopped thinking about Gillian for the time being. "Quit talking shit and let's go." Frankie grabbed the other control and got ready for war.

Secret Society

"Camille, can you pick Shane up from the babysitter for me today? Baron asked me to go out with him after work." Misa was ecstatic about the invitation. It would be the first time that Baron was taking her somewhere public. In the weeks since they started their sexual relationship, all they'd ever done was spend lusty nights in his beautiful home. Baron was more aggressive than she had expected. He choked her during sex, slapped her, and even spit on her. Misa didn't really like all that, but she willingly allowed it, eager for a permanent position in the life Baron was living. It was a small price to pay, in her opinion, for the opulence of the Nobles family circle.

Camille sighed and shook her head. "You can't keep asking me to do this for you, Misa." Camille loved her younger sister with all her heart. But she was sick of picking her nephew up, dropping him off, and of being asked to babysit weekend after weekend. Camille was happy that her sister was moving on with her life after a heartbreaking divorce from her cheating husband. But lately she was seeing more of her nephew than ever before, and having less time to herself.

Meanwhile, Misa was having a grand old time. "I have a life of my own, you know?"

Misa rolled her eyes. Please! Camille had no life. All she had were fabulous things, a beautiful home, and the status of being Frankie B's wife. She had no job to report to each day, no class she had to pass, no worries. Misa felt that her sister had no interests other than redecorating her home or buying something expensive, and no better way to spend her evening than caring for her nephew, as far as Misa was concerned. She didn't feel like hearing this shit right now. She knew that Camille would give in to her. No matter how much she complained, Camille never said no. That was why Misa called on her so often. "Come on, sis. You know I got you. Name your price."

"For what, Misa? You can't pay it. You already owe me five thousand dollars." Camille was sick of feeling used.

"I know that," Misa said, with an attitude. She had to resist the urge to suck her teeth. "And I'm gonna pay you your money, Camille. Don't make me feel worse than I already do. I hate having to ask you for help. But you know that Louis ain't helping me much with Shane. He hardly ever picks him up or even calls to talk to him. The little bit of child support I get—"

"I know, Misa." Camille sighed again. She felt guilty for lecturing her sister. She didn't want to throw anything in Misa's face; she was well aware that her sister's ex did nothing to help out with little Shane. And Camille was glad that at twenty-four years old, Misa was getting a chance to enjoy her youth. "I'll pick him up for you. Have fun."

"Thank you!" Camille could hear the smile on her sister's face. "I really appreciate it. I'll pick him up in the morning on my way to work."

Camille frowned. "Wait a minute! Why can't you come and get him tonight?" she asked. "How long are you planning to be out tonight?"

"Well . . . all night. I'll probably go home with Baron, Camille."

Camille shook her head. Her sister was something else. Camille was tempted to warn Misa that Baron was a notorious playboy and that she shouldn't put her heart into him. But the last thing she wanted was to put a damper on her sister's joy. "Fine. But don't make me late for my yoga class like you did last time. Pick him up *early*, Misa. I'm not playing!"

"Thank youuuuu!" Misa sang. She hung up, thrilled that she had the night to herself once again.

Camille, meanwhile, was wondering how she always managed to get suckered into shit like this. She finished making dinner and headed out to get Shane. In the car on her way to the babysitter's house, Camille thought about her life. She felt so unappreciated—not just by Misa, but by Frankie as well. From the outside they looked like a perfect family. But behind closed doors, things were anything but perfect.

She picked her nephew up and headed home, stopping to get a few things at the supermarket. By the time she pulled her car into the driveway it was after seven P.M. She walked into the house and found Steven sitting on the couch watching television.

"Hey, Shane!" Steven smiled at the kid.

"Hi." Shane shyly hid behind his aunt.

Camille was instantly annoyed. "Something wrong with the TV in the rental unit?" she asked.

"Nah," Steven said, his eyes droopy from getting high. "I just wanted to watch the plasma." He knew that Camille was sick of him being there, and Steven didn't give a fuck.

His brother was in charge, not her. As if on cue, Frankie came in through the back door and frowned when he saw Shane standing behind Camille.

"Hey," he said, walking in and giving Camille a kiss. "You're watching Shane *again*?"

Camille could hear the annoyance in her husband's voice and tried to ignore it. She was tempted to remind Frankie that Shane was there from time to time but Steven was there *all* the time. She decided against it.

Innocently unaware of his uncle's unwelcoming tone, Shane smiled when he saw Frankie. "Hi, Uncle Frankie."

Frankie gave the little rugrat a pound and looked at his wife for her explanation.

"Misa had to work late, so I'm keeping him tonight," she lied.

Frankie nodded, but said nothing as he headed to the kitchen. Camille followed. He took a Heineken out of the fridge and opened the drawer in search of the bottle opener. "You might as well take custody of your nephew, Camille. Misa never has her own kid."

Camille looked at Frankie. "It's not that bad. Misa's young and trying to have fun, that's all." She felt sometimes that Frankie became annoyed whenever he saw the kid enjoying the luxuries in their home. If Shane was playing video games, Frankie felt that he should be doing chores of some sort. If Shane was watching TV in the living room on the high-definition flat-screen plasma, Frankie tried to get him to watch the nineteen-inch TV in the spare bedroom instead. Meanwhile, Frankie seemed to have no problem with Steven's grown ass enjoying the same luxuries. Camille noticed his behavior, but did her best to appease her husband in order to keep the peace. Maybe he was sick of seeing Misa walk all over her, Camille reasoned. Maybe Frankie was so concerned about her well-being that he didn't notice his own brother's freeloading.

"I'm going to the Knicks game tonight. They play the Cavaliers and I got money on this game." He walked back into the living room, leaving Camille standing alone. She raised an eyebrow. More and more, Frankie had "money on this game" or "money on this fight." His gambling had started out harmlessly, but lately, he was out gambling every night, if what he told her was true. Not wanting to rock the boat, Camille didn't call Frankie out.

More than anything, she wanted peace in her household. She wanted everyone to coexist with the least amount of conflict possible. But that was beginning to feel like wishful thinking. Camille was playing referee between her husband and her nephew, tolerating an unwanted tenant in her home, and being taken advantage of by her younger sister. And she was almost single-handedly supporting her mother since Misa so seldom had any extra money to contribute toward their mom's living expenses. Camille felt like she was a ticking time bomb waiting to explode.

She went upstairs and got Shane situated in front of the TV in one of the spare bedrooms. While he watched a DVD featuring Piggley Winks, Camille went to her room and found Frankie dressing to go out. She thought about asking him to stay. She was lonely, and no matter how beautiful their home was, it wasn't the same without Frankie being there with her. She sometimes felt that Frankie worked so hard while she was the only one who got to enjoy it. But Camille decided not to say anything. She didn't want to set him off again. Instead, she poured herself a shot of Patrón—a nightly ritual these days—and watched her husband walk out the door.

Misa took a long, hot shower and spritzed on her favorite perfume. She did her hair and makeup and stepped into a black Norma Kamali dress she'd borrowed from Camille. Tonight, she was hitting the town on the arm of Baron Nobles, and she was eager to really let her hair down. They were going to a show at B.B. King's—a popular nightclub in Times Square where music acts performed in a cozy and intimate setting. It was a birthday celebration for one of Baron's friends, and she was honored that he had chosen her to accompany him.

Misa felt better than ever. She'd gotten her hair and nails done, plus a pedicure and eyebrow wax for good measure. She was treating herself well these days as a new divorcée. And having a sister like Camille, who could never say no and mean it, was an asset at a time like this. Misa had her sister's money at her disposal plus the luxury of a great babysitter. What could be better than that?

Not that Misa didn't love her son. Shane was the best son a mother could hope for. He was adorable, well mannered, and pretty laid-back for a three-year-old. Misa adored Shane, but was finally getting the chance to live the free-spirited lifestyle she'd forfeited when she became a wife and mother at such a young age. She was grateful for and perhaps a bit jealous of Camille. Camille had no children to weigh her down, and a life of lavish spending and big pimping, courtesy of her role as Frankie B's wife. If Misa had been lucky enough to stumble into a life like the one her sister enjoyed—a life that was child-free and glamorous—

she would have been partying, traveling, and living it up! But not Camille. She was content to sit at home and look like a porcelain doll as she waited for her beloved husband to return home to her each night. Shit, it was only right that Camille babysit, Misa believed. What else did she have to occupy her time?

As she climbed behind the wheel of her brand-new Camry (a pity present from her sister and Frankie B after her rough divorce), Misa thought about her ex-husband, Louis. What a fuckin' loser. Five years she'd spent with him, and they'd never had a car—let alone a Maybach, like Baron had. Never had their bills been paid on time as Louis struggled to make ends meet. Misa had never wanted to work. She didn't feel she should ever have to. Camille never did. Misa wanted to live that same type of life, and Louis had been fine with that. After all, the last thing he wanted was Misa squeezing her juicy ass in some business suit and setting off to meet some man who made more money than him. He also didn't want *her* to make more money than him. He was happy with her decision to be a stay-at-home mom and care for their son. But, as it turned out, *he'd* been the one to upgrade, leaving Misa and their son to move in with a woman he met at work. She was a senior executive at a brokerage firm and he was the security guard who worked in the building lobby. When their flirtation turned physical, sparks flew. And it wasn't long before Misa and Shane got pushed to the background as Louis enjoyed lavish vacations and luxury cars for the first time in his sorry life. He was so caught up in the unexpected invitation to his mistress's life-style that he forgot all about the vows he'd taken as a husband and his responsibilities as a father.

Meanwhile, Misa sank into a deep depression. She hadn't

counted on being abandoned. She had always expected her
marriage to work, and when it didn't, she fell apart. Camille
had been there for her, bringing over ice cream and chick
flicks and comforting her sister through the storm. And Misa
appreciated and loved her sister more because of that. She had
leaned on Camille, and today she was stronger than ever.

Now that Misa was over that loser, she noticed that the
difference between her miserable marriage and her sister's
happy one was money. Money was what helped Camille
turn the other way and pretend to be sleeping when Frankie
B crept in late at night. It was what kept her wearing designer labels and pricey baubles when everyone else was
complaining about their tight budgets. Misa assumed that
money was what kept NBA and NFL wives happy in their
marriages. Money, power, million-dollar mansions. That's
what made the difference between a nagging wife—which
Misa had sadly become to Louis before they parted ways—
and one who knew that her sole job was to be arm candy and
to tend to the home and the children. Misa wanted that—the
glitz and the glamour. And she figured she'd spend as much
time chasing money-makers like Baron as she could until
she landed a gold mine just like her sister had.

Misa pulled up in front of Baron's home and parked her
car. She called him on her cell phone and told him that she
was outside. Then she checked her makeup in the mirror one
last time. He emerged from the house and trotted down the
stairs, wearing a pair of True Religion jeans, a white button
up, and a dark blue blazer. She noticed the crisp white Nikes
on his feet and the sparkling diamonds in his watch and
smiled. He had a fresh haircut, and when he got close, she
could smell his intoxicating cologne. Misa was falling hard.
Baron greeted her with a kiss on the cheek and then led the

way to his car. Misa locked her own car, which she would
retrieve after their night on the town, and they headed for
Manhattan. She was through mourning the promises that
she and Louis had made to stay together till death parted
them. Instead, she was making her own promises to herself.
Never again would she settle for less or put her heart before
her head. From now on she was going for the money. Happiness would surely follow.

Crash

Toya's shoes clicked on the pavement as she trotted toward her brownstone with bags from Lord & Taylor in hand. She took her keys out of her pocket and unlocked her front door. Once inside, she turned to lock her screen door and saw a figure coming toward her through her yard. She quickly locked it, then reached behind the sofa cushion for the gat she kept on hand just in case of shit like this. She waited for the stranger to come closer in the dark.

Knowing her as well as he did, Nate knew what she had been scurrying for and smiled proudly. He had taught her well. "You don't need that, Latoya," he said, standing at a safe distance just in case she started firing.

She cocked the gun anyway. She could hear the smirk in his voice and it only infuriated her more. Her nine-millimeter gripped tightly in her hand, she was tempted to kill him and say it was an accident. Instead, she waited to see what he would say or do next. The nerve of this bastard to show up at her house! How had he found her? And did he really think she would hesitate to shoot him for all the times in the past when she hadn't had the means to do it?

"Calm down and let me talk to you, baby. That's the only reason I came over here. I just wanna talk to you about some things."

"I don't have shit to say to you. And I don't want to hear shit you have to say. So turn around and get the fuck away from here. Don't ever come back here again." She shook her head in fury, fighting the tears that threatened to burst forth. "You're dead to me, and if you ever come back here, I'll kill you!"

Nate waited. He wasn't sure what he was waiting for. Perhaps to see if she would really do it. He didn't even care if she did it at this point. Or maybe he was waiting to see if she'd change her mind, unlock the door, and give him a chance to speak his piece. After all, she owed him that much. Despite the fact that their relationship had always been tumultuous, he did love her. More than he had ever loved anyone else in his lifetime. Sometimes he loved her too hard, he reasoned. And if she could just get that through her head, maybe she could give him one more chance.

"*Ten seconds, muthafucka, and you better be the fuck outta here!*" Toya's voice bellowed enough to convince Nate that tonight was not the night to try and persuade her. He turned and walked swiftly away, disappearing into the night just as suddenly as he'd appeared.

Toya locked her doors and sat down on the couch with her gun still in her hand. She squeezed her eyes shut, blocking out the memories of what she'd endured with him for so long. Finally, she opened her eyes and slowly looked down at the gun in her hands, wishing she had done them both a favor and killed his bitch ass.

"You having fun?" Baron asked, nudging Misa playfully.

She was. They were waiting along with about six or seven of Baron's friends and their dates for the rapper Common to take the stage. Drinks were flowing, and they were all laughing and having a good time. Misa was enjoying being part of Baron's inner circle and was satisfied that she looked better than all the other bitches in attendance. Baron was the center of attention, and Misa felt like the queen bee. They had arrived after everyone else, making a grand entrance just as she'd hoped. And now they were seated at a table filled with bottles and food, and the mood was festive. They were celebrating the birthday of Tremaine—a member of the Nobles crew whom Misa had seen at many of their functions. Now that she was with Baron, she felt that she had been given access to a very exclusive club, and she couldn't imagine why Camille chose to be a homebody when she could be living like this on a regular basis.

As her mind drifted to her sister, she leaned in close to Baron so that he could hear her over the music. "Didn't you say Frankie was going to the Knicks game tonight?" she asked. "I thought he was close to Tremaine, too."

Baron nodded toward the crowd. "Here he comes. He wouldn't miss this."

Misa looked up and saw Frankie coming through the crowd, and she smiled at her approaching brother-in-law. Her smile faded when she noticed that Gillian was right behind him. Everyone at their table erupted in loud greetings and handshakes as Frankie arrived. Misa smiled again, although she couldn't help wondering if Camille knew that her husband was out with Gillian while she was at home alone again.

Frankie scanned the table and was surprised to see Misa sitting beside Baron. He smiled and greeted her with a kiss on the cheek. "I thought you were working late," he said, remembering the excuse that Camille had given him for Shane being at their house yet again.

"I thought you were at a basketball game," she countered, looking at Gillian, who was resplendent in a black halter top, jeans, and a pair of Louboutin ankle booties. Gillian's well-toned arms were on display as she peeled out of her beautiful white fox fur jacket, revealing iced-out diamond bangles on her wrists. Her hair was pulled up into a neat bun on top of her head, and her baby hair lined her delicate face. With Gillian's makeup so flawless and her earlobes glistening with diamond-and-platinum hoops, Misa suddenly felt like the spotlight had shifted off of her.

"We just came from the game," Frankie explained. "The Knicks lost. What else is new?"

Gillian glanced at Misa and smiled weakly. She had seen Camille's sister around before, but she wondered what the hell she was doing here tonight, when Camille was nowhere in sight. Frankie cleared his throat and leaned over to whisper to Baron.

"What's Misa doing here?"

Baron frowned slightly. "I been kicking it with shorty, that's all. So I invited her."

Frankie looked at Baron. "That's wifey now?" he asked, surprised.

Baron laughed. "Nah, son. I'm just hitting that."

Frankie laughed, too, although he was still uneasy about

Misa being there. It felt strange to have his sister-in-law present, even though he really had nothing to hide. He couldn't help wondering if Camille was using her sister to spy on him.

Common took to the stage and the crowd went crazy. As he performed one hit after another, their whole table rapped and sang along and everyone was having fun. Misa thought Common was sexy as hell, and she wasn't the only one.

"Damn! He's so beautiful," Gillian said, smiling.

Misa had to laugh in agreement. "He sure is!"

Frankie, Baron, and the rest of the males at the table groaned in protest. "He ain't all that."

"Y'all wouldn't even look twice at him if he wasn't famous," Tremaine said.

Gillian shook her head, smiling. "Don't hate, guys. He's handsome. End of story."

"Exactly," Misa agreed.

Gillian slapped Misa five and Baron looked at Misa like she was crazy.

"You think he looks better than me?" he asked, grinning.

Misa laughed. "No, baby. He definitely don't look better than you."

Gillian put her finger in her mouth as if she was making herself throw up. Frankie laughed and so did everybody else. Gillian looked at Baron. "Misa is only saying what you want to hear." She looked at Misa and winked. "Smart move, girl. My brother loves to have his ego stroked."

Baron tossed a napkin at his sister playfully and said, "I prefer having something else stroked, but my ego will do for now."

The men laughed while Gillian, Misa, and the other young ladies at the table made disapproving faces and shook their heads. "You're so nasty," Gillian teased. She looked at Misa. "You're too classy to waste your time with him."

Misa smiled at the compliment, and shrugged. "I'm only keeping him around until I get backstage to meet Common."

Gillian burst out laughing and Baron did, too. "Damn," he said, shaking his head at Misa. "That's cold."

Misa was having a good time, and she softened a little toward Gillian. Maybe she wasn't so bad, after all. As the show went on, she watched Frankie whisper in Gillian's ear from time to time, and vice versa. They sat closely together and laughed at their own private jokes. If she didn't know any better, she might have thought they were a couple. Still, she didn't see anything out of the ordinary. The way they acted around each other tonight was no different than the way she'd seen them act on countless other occasions when Camille was present. She figured maybe she was just being territorial on behalf of Camille.

When Common was done with his performance, the crowd lingered as they danced to the music the deejay was spinning. Gillian felt like getting her two-step on, so she took Frankie by the hand and led him to the dance floor. He didn't protest, following behind her as they made their way through the crowd.

Misa noticed, and kept an eye on them as they danced. She tried to recall the last time she'd seen Frankie dance with Camille. In fact, she wondered if her sister even knew that Frankie was here with Gillian tonight. She excused herself from the table and stepped outside. She waited until her BlackBerry got a good signal and then dialed Camille's phone number.

"Hello?" Camille asked, sounding as if she were asleep despite the fact that it was only eleven thirty on a Thursday night.

"Camille, wake up," Misa urged. "I'm at this party with Baron and Frankie's here—with Gillian."

Camille's eyes widened, and she propped herself up on her elbow in her bed. "What party?" she asked.

"Tremaine's birthday party," Misa explained. "We're at B.B. King's in Manhattan. Frankie and Gillian came here after the game, and I just wanted to know if you knew they were here together."

Camille tried not to sound upset that she knew nothing about Tremaine's birthday party. "Well, he didn't mention a party. But I don't need to know Frankie's every movement," she said nonchalantly. "He probably forgot about the party until after the game and so he stopped by afterward. It's no big deal."

Misa felt that her sister was as blind as a bat. "So you knew he was with Gillian?" she asked, for clarification.

"Yeah," Camille lied. "They're just friends, Misa. Don't start acting like Toya."

Misa sucked her teeth. "Whatever. I'm just trying to look out for you, like any real sister would."

"Yeah, thanks," Camille said. "I'm going back to sleep." She hung up the phone, leaving Misa to question why she had even bothered.

She went back inside and found Baron on the dance floor with some Latina. She strolled over boldly and interrupted, tapping the unknown woman on the shoulder. "Thanks for keeping him company," she said. "I'll take it from here." Then she stood between the two of them and fell right into step.

He laughed as the Spanish woman stormed off, talking shit. "You got a lotta nerve, baby girl."

"I sure do." She turned and grinded her ample ass against his crotch as the music pulsated around them. She could feel him rise to attention and smiled. Spotting Frankie and Gillian across the dance floor, dancing close and smiling at each other, she shook her head. If Camille didn't care that her husband was slipping through her fingers, neither did she.

Reasons

After her sister's phone call Camille got out of bed. Trying to sleep was pointless. She went downstairs and poured herself a glass of Grey Goose and cranberry juice. Moonlight peeked through the bay window above her kitchen sink, and she stood there in the glow of it, a thousand thoughts swarming in her head.

Frankie was at Tremaine's birthday party—a party he had conveniently neglected to mention to her—with Gillian. Jealousy blanketed Camille. She took a long sip of her drink and closed her eyes as she swallowed. She asked herself how the hell she'd gone from a sought-after model to a desperate housewife sitting home with nothing to keep her company but a fully stocked bar. Shaking her head, she took her drink into the living room and opened up a large trunk in the corner. Pulling out two leather-bound photo albums, she sat down on the sofa and opened them up. A magazine clipping fluttered to the floor and Camille picked it up. She smiled, recalling her glory days in the fashion industry. That had been the happiest time of her life.

Camille had struggled with low self-esteem early in her

career as she watched thinner, lighter girls get jobs she felt that she was perfect for. Back when she was in high school, Camille had been proud of her beautiful brown skin. She and Toya were the most sought-after girls in their school, and neither of them was light. It wasn't until she entered the fashion industry that her complexion became an issue. It gave her a bit of a complex. But when she met the man she would eventually marry, Camille's poor self-image became a thing of the past. Frankie had wooed her with an intensity that swept her off her feet. As fine as he was, and with all the clout he had in the streets, it seemed that he only had eyes for Camille.

Looking down at the photo in her hand, she smiled again. It was part of an ad campaign she'd done for Gap back in the nineties. Camille sat back, sipping her cocktail as she flipped through the album and remembered the love she shared with Frankie in those days. He would accompany her to photo shoots and watch from the wings as she pivoted and posed. He seemed almost in awe of her, admiring her every move. From time to time, he would buy the clothes she modeled. He knew her size in everything from apparel to shoes in those days and would surprise her with beautiful things all the time. Camille had been told that she was pretty. But Frankie made her feel sexier, more beautiful, and more interesting to him than any of the other women he knew.

Camille had lost herself in him. She realized that now. As she turned the pages of the photo album, she felt as though she were leafing through the archives of her life, catching glimpses of her former self. There she was, smiling, long-legged, radiant, posing in one amazing picture after another. It occurred to her that she hadn't smiled that hard in a long time.

She flipped to a picture of Frankie holding her in his arms

on the beach in Saint-Tropez. In the photo, Camille wore a tiny white string bikini and not an ounce of excess body fat was visible. She felt disgusted with herself now as she glanced down at her stomach lapping over her panties and her flabby upper arms glowing in the moonlight. She swigged the rest of her drink and went to pour herself another.

Camille returned to the living room with the entire bottle of vodka. She sat back down and refreshed her drink, then picked up the second photo album. Opening it to the first page, she stopped suddenly and her eyes instantly blurred with tears.

"Jesus," she whispered.

She gazed down at a picture of her and Frankie on their wedding day. The two of them were beaming with joy, the sun setting in the distance. Frankie stood behind his wife, his hand placed affectionately on her belly. Camille remembered the very moment that photograph was taken. It was the end of their romantic wedding day and Misa had asked for one last shot of the newlyweds. When Frankie had held her that way, cradling her small waist delicately in his large hand, Camille found herself imagining the day when their child would be growing in her belly. She imagined Frankie's strong embrace protecting both of them just this way. But that hadn't happened. Frankie didn't want any children, and Camille felt abandoned in a relationship that had fizzled into a boring routine in a big, lonely house.

She wiped the tears that fell from her eyes. This was not how she hoped her life would turn out, and she couldn't seem to do anything to change it. When she paid more attention to Frankie than ever, he seemed to feel smothered by the attention. When she gave him space and stopped complaining, she sat home alone and drank until she passed out while Frankie danced the night away with Gillian. She had always felt special because she was the woman Frankie loved, the one he gave the keys to his kingdom. That role had made her the envy of many women and a role model for others. But she was starting to wonder how long it would be before her horse-drawn carriage turned into a pumpkin. Her intuition was nagging at her, telling her that she was in danger of being replaced. That just couldn't happen. Camille was too accustomed to the finer things in life to surrender it all to someone else. Frankie couldn't leave her. If her marriage failed, not only would she be terribly hurt, she would be embarrassed. Camille wasn't having that.

She went back to the trunk and pulled out boxes of old photos. She went back to the couch and sat there for several hours sifting through one memory after another. In the last box, she sighed when she saw a picture of Frankie, Gillian, and Baron taken at Great Adventure. The sepia-colored photo featured the trio dressed as Wild West outlaws, guns and all. As Camille gazed at the picture, the smirk on Gillian's face irked her. She noticed that one of the straps on the thin, pale top Gillian wore had fallen provocatively, revealing her bare shoulder. Frankie and Baron flanked her, both of them looking ready to do anything it took to protect her. Camille tossed the picture across the room and guzzled the rest of her drink before staggering down the long hallway toward the staircase. She was tipsy, and she tripped a little as she made her way up to her bedroom.

Tumbling onto her bed, Camille sighed deeply. She looked at the clock, and saw that it was after four o'clock in the morning. Frankie still wasn't home. As she drifted to sleep, she couldn't shake the image of Gillian's smirking face staring back at her from that sepia print, while Frankie stood by her side.

Temptations

Octavia rushed out of school on a Wednesday afternoon. Since this was one of her grandfather's dialysis days, she was supposed to be heading to her dance class. But today she was going to do her own thing. For once, she was determined to break a rule after a lifetime of following them to the letter.

Octavia had always been well behaved to the point of being downright predictable. Because she was the only child, her mother lavished her with things and expected her to work hard in return. Good grades, a clean room, respect, and obedience were all that Dominique asked of her. Octavia had no problem with any of that. She loved her mother and was grateful for all the wonderful things and opportunities she'd been given. But lately she was beginning to think that, in a lot of ways, her mother was a hypocrite.

Octavia wasn't allowed to date yet. At thirteen, she was supposedly too immature to handle a steady boyfriend and all the emotions that relationships entailed. Yet Dominique had snuck around and dated when she was a teenager. Octavia's grandfather had regaled her with the stories of her mother's teenage rebellion and it had surprised her. She had always believed that Dominique was a Goody Two-shoes teenager who got suckered into giving it up too soon. But Bill's version of the story was slightly different. He had described his daughter's carefree spirit—smoking weed in the staircase with other neighborhood kids, missing her curfew, and cutting class—and it had made Octavia question her own obedience. What could possibly be wrong with breaking a rule every now and then?

She rushed nervously down the Upper East Side block, feeling butterflies in her stomach at the thought of seeing Dashawn again. When she spotted him standing on the corner, leaning against a wall with his backpack slung over one shoulder, she smiled instantly. He looked good, just as she had expected him to. He walked toward her with a smile on his face and a single rose in his hand.

"Hey, beautiful," he said, handing her the bright red bloom. "This is for you."

Octavia was beaming. "Thank you! Oh my God. This is so sweet." She was nervous, but tried her best to act as if this weren't unusual for her—hanging out with a boy she liked. Truthfully, she was new to this. She wasn't allowed to date, despite the fact that all of her friends had boyfriends. Octavia felt that her mother was too strict and was out of touch with reality. It was almost as if Dominique was doing her absolute best to ensure that her daughter had the least amount of fun possible. Octavia had to use her girlfriends' tales about the guys they dated as a blueprint for how she should act around Dashawn today. "So," she said softly. "Where are we going?"

Dashawn smiled. "You hungry?"

Octavia nodded. "Starving. I went to my counselor's office during my lunch break so that I could figure out which specialized high schools to apply to. So I haven't eaten yet."

Dashawn raised his eyebrows. Not only had he managed to get the attention of some prissy prep school broad, but she was articulate, and focused enough to skip lunch in order to further herself. He was impressed, since lunch was his favorite part of the program at his school. "Cool. Let's go get some pizza. Then we can chill at my house until it's time for you to go home."

Octavia hesitated. She wasn't sure that going back to his house was a smart idea. Her grandfather Bill had warned her on numerous occasions that boys only wanted one thing from girls when they were her age. Since she was still a virgin and unwilling to change that, going to Dashawn's place wasn't sounding like a good idea. "Well," she said, then bit her lower lip. "I don't think that's a good idea."

"Why not?" he asked.

"I'm just not sure that I should do that. We've talked on the phone and stuff, but I don't know you well enough to go home with you." Octavia was almost embarrassed to admit that she was too scared of what might happen if she followed him back to his apartment in the Harlem River Houses projects.

"Let me find out you're scared of the hood." He laughed. He was only half joking, though. He wondered if Octavia thought she was too good to hang out at his place.

"No!" she assured him. "I'm not scared at all. My grandfather lives in the projects, and I'm there all the time. Don't let this uniform fool you." Dashawn laughed. "I just don't want to rush anything."

"Okay. We don't have to go there. But just so you know, I wouldn't rush you to do anything that you didn't want to do. I just want to go somewhere with you so we can talk without a whole bunch of people in our faces, being nosy. You said that you have to be home by six thirty, so that doesn't give us too much time to chill. And it's too cold out to sit in the park. But whatever you want to do is cool with me."

Octavia thought about it. Dashawn was standing there looking so good and being such a gentleman. She sniffed the rose in her hand and saw him smile at her. And she melted. "I guess we can go to your house. Just don't try to take advantage of me."

Dashawn laughed. "I won't. I promise." He reached for her hand and she gladly gave it. As they walked to the pizzeria, Octavia prayed that she could really trust him. There was only one way to find out.

Gillian impatiently tapped her L.A.M.B. heels on the floor, waiting for Frankie to arrive. She was sitting at a table in B. Smith's, a popular restaurant in Manhattan. She had been waiting for half an hour for Frankie to show up, and as she glanced at her iced-out Cartier watch, she sighed in exasperation.

As if on cue, Frankie glided through the door and scanned the room for his friend. When he spotted her, he couldn't help noticing the pissed-off expression on her face. He knew that Gillian hated to be kept waiting.

"Before you start beefing, let me explain," Frankie started as soon as he reached the table. He slid into his seat and sat back, looking Gillian in her catlike eyes. "I fell asleep on the couch this afternoon 'cuz I was still hungover from last night." Frankie and Gillian had gone out the night before to a show at Webster Hall featuring a bunch of eighties hip-hop artists. Along with a few other members of the Nobles crew, they had downed bottle after bottle of liquor and champagne, and he had suffered a massive hangover as a result.

"When Camille saw me sleeping she left me alone and I didn't wake up till my brother shook me at like five o'clock." Frankie summoned the waitress over and she held up one finger, signaling that she'd be with him in just a second. "Anyway, by the time I got dressed and left my house, I ran right into rush-hour traffic. I got here as fast as I could."

Gillian tried to stay pissed, but it was useless. She could never stay mad at Frankie. "All I'm saying is you could call when you're gonna be late," she said. "I hate sitting at a table for two by myself. It's embarrassing."

Frankie nodded. "You're right. Won't happen again." He smiled. "But if I saw a woman like you sitting alone at a table for two, I would take that as my cue to go holla at her. None of these men in here had the guts to approach you, huh?"

Gillian smiled reluctantly. "Flattery will get you nowhere."

The waitress finally stopped by their table and took their orders. When she walked away, Frankie smiled at Gillian. "You look nice today," he said.

She shrugged. "I look nice every day." She sipped her margarita and Frankie laughed.

"Conceited, aren't we?"

"No, just honest. Won't catch me letting myself go, no matter how old I get!" Gillian was telling the truth. She worked out five days a week, ate healthy, and pampered herself with facials, waxing, manicures, pedicures, and all the things that came along with ensuring that she looked picture perfect at all times.

Frankie admired that about Gillian, and couldn't help pondering the fact that Camille had put on a few pounds over the past few months. It seemed that she was always eating, especially late at night. And with Shane over at their house more and more often, Camille was going to the gym less frequently. She was starting to let herself go.

"That's why I hang around with you," Frankie said. "You make me look good."

Gillian chuckled, knowing that wasn't the only reason Frankie hung around with her. The two had been friends for many years and were as close as two friends could be. They told each other everything and spoke to each other every day. So she knew that he was getting bored with Camille. Gillian, for one, had been bored with Frankie and Camille's relationship since the day it began. She had wondered how long it would take for Frankie to see that Camille was no longer the driven top-model wannabe that he fell in love with. She was, in Gillian's eyes, just a pretty girl who had gotten lucky and snagged a man with drive and ambition. And Gillian was counting the days until Frankie kicked Camille to the curb.

Gillian and her stockbroker boyfriend had a tumultuous on-again, off-again relationship that was never without its share of drama. With her schedule more open, she and Frankie had been spending lots of time together. Once content to go to a Knicks game together or to play a few holes of golf on a Sunday afternoon, these days the two of them were spending more time enjoying intimate dinners, like the one they were having tonight.

Gillian had accepted the fact that Frankie was off-limits as anything more than her friend. As much as she liked him, she wouldn't date a married man because she'd been raised to know that she deserved more than just to be some man's mistress.

Frankie, on the other hand, was beginning to realize he was happier spending time with Gillian than he was with his own wife. In his heart, he knew that he was falling for Gillian and he was falling fast. He was also beginning to notice that his relationship with Gillian was becoming unbearable to Camille. He recalled coming home late one night and finding pictures and photo albums strewn across the living room floor. Thinking nothing of it at first, he had assumed that Camille had been feeling nostalgic. But one photo in particular was on the far side of the room, almost as if it was tossed there angrily. When he picked it up, he was surprised to see an old shot of him, Gillian, and Baron at an amusement park. He could tell that Camille was getting sick of his affiliation with the Nobles family.

Camille was a lady in every sense of the word. She got dressed up all the time, her makeup was always flawless, her hair was never out of place, and she didn't do anything that might cause her to break a nail. Frankie liked that about her, especially in the beginning. She turned heads when they went out together, and she was always impeccably coifed. She made him proud to be her man. But after so many years together, he wanted more than just arm candy. He wanted a companion he could relate to on his level once in a while. Camille seemed reluctant to do so. If Frankie suggested that she go fishing with him, she would turn up her nose in disgust. If he suggested that they go to a football game, he spent so much time explaining the game to her that he couldn't enjoy himself. Gillian, on the other hand, balanced her stunning sex appeal and superstar looks with a love for the rougher side of life. To Frankie, Gillian was like one of the guys. She was a Cowboys fan, had season tickets during NBA season at the Garden, and played pool better than most of the men he knew. These things—along with his love for her father and respect for her brother—gave Frankie tremendous admiration for Gillian. Plus, she understood his business. She was a part of that life herself, so she had a deeper understanding of who Frankie truly was. She was indeed his best friend. But lately, he had begun to realize that she was becoming more than that.

Their food arrived, and they discussed business while they ate. Her cell phone rang during dinner, and Gillian glanced at it. Apologetically, she explained to Frankie that she had to answer it, and he waved his hand as if it was no problem.

"Hey, baby," Gillian purred. "What's up?"

Frankie immediately stopped chewing his steak and looked at her. Was she talking to that Wall Street lame?

"Well, I'm in the middle of dinner, so I'll call you back and let you know. Okay. Bye." Gillian hung up the phone and flung it back into her bag. She noticed Frankie staring at her and frowned. "What?"

"Who was that?" he asked.

"Why?"

"*Why?*" he asked, as if she had no right to ask that.

Gillian grinned. "Yeah. Why? What are you, jealous?"

Frankie finally finished chewing his food and took a sip of his cognac. "Nah, jealous of what?" He took another bite and thought about it. Swallowing, he said, "I just don't know why you keep getting back with that corny muthafucka."

Gillian laughed. "Corny?"

"Yeah. Saddam, or whatever his name is."

She could hardly control her laughter now. "Sadiq! Not Saddam. And he is not corny."

Frankie sat back and wiped his mouth with his napkin.

"He corny as hell. What, does he work on Wall Street or some shit like that? Corny."

She laughed. "Don't be like that. He's a good man."

"So why are you always mad at him, then?"

Gillian looked at Frankie. She sipped her drink. "I hate his wandering eye."

Frankie chuckled a little, and then shook his head. "He's an idiot for cheating on you."

Gillian shook her head. "Not everybody can be as perfect as you, Frankie B."

Frankie smiled. "Flattery will get you nowhere," he quoted her.

Gillian smiled back and ordered another drink as the waitress came to clear their plates. Frankie ordered one, too, and he looked at Gillian across the table. Damn, she looked good tonight! She wore a tight linen Michael Kors dress that was sexy as hell, and her long hair was pulled back from her face in a neat chignon. He wanted to take her somewhere, rip her out of her conservative outfit, let her hair fall down around her shoulders, and fuck her till she screamed his name.

"What you thinking about?" she asked.

He was busted. Trying to come up with something to say, he stammered for a few seconds. "I don't know."

"Tell the truth," she asserted, realizing that he was trying to come up with some bullshit to say rather than what he was really thinking.

Their drinks came, and he contemplated telling her what had been on his mind. But by the time the waitress was gone, he had thought better of it. "I was just thinking that this dude better be worth your time. Don't make me act like your big brother and fuck him up."

She smiled. "I already have a big brother. Baron is enough. I don't need any more brothers."

"What do you need, then?" Frankie asked, the cognac speaking for him now.

She looked at him, wondering if he was ready for the truth. She went for it. "I need you to hurry up and divorce that wife of yours so I can get with a real man and stop wasting time with these lames." She smiled, and he wondered if she meant it.

Frankie was quiet for several moments. "What would your brother say if he heard you talking like that?" he asked, not really giving a fuck what Baron thought. At this point, he was just happy that she was talking this way. There had been such an unspoken chemistry between them for so long that he was relieved to be finally airing it out.

Gillian shrugged, smiling. "Baron gave you his stamp of approval long ago."

Frankie was shocked. "You talked to your brother about getting with me before?"

Gillian nodded.

"Yeah, right! When?" Frankie asked, flattered.

"Years ago, when you were about to marry Camille. I was gonna profess my lust for you back then. My brother told me that you were a good dude and that he wouldn't object if me and you got together."

Frankie smiled, flattered that beautiful Gillian had wanted him for so long. "Lust, not love, huh?"

She shrugged again. "It's a start, ain't it?"

He stared at her, looking so beautiful in the candlelight. "Damn. I wish I woulda known that."

She sipped her wine and looked him dead in the eyes. "What would be different if you had known?"

He thought about it. "I might not have made it down the aisle in that case."

Gillian licked her lips and stared at him. "Well, I should have spoken up sooner," she said softly.

He looked at her. "It's not too late, you know." Frankie could feel his dick getting hard and was glad that the table-cloth shielded it.

Gillian raised an eyebrow. "You getting a divorce soon?" she asked.

Frankie laughed. "I might get one tonight if you keep talking like this!"

Gillian laughed, too. She knew that Frankie didn't mean it. He wasn't divorcing Camille anytime soon. But she was happy that they'd finally addressed what they'd both known all along—that they had love for each other as more than just friends.

They enjoyed two more rounds of drinks and ate dessert before they spilled out of the restaurant into the brisk autumn air. The wind caused a loose strand of her hair to dance in the breeze and Frankie had to resist the urge to reach for it. The sounds of New York City surrounded them as sirens blared and taxis honked their horns. Music blasted out of a nearby bar, and the sound of the patrons' laughter mixed with that of the city in motion. They were both feel-ing the effects of all the alcohol consumption, and the night air only magnified it. Without warning, Frankie pulled Gil-lian close to him. She was visibly caught off guard, but didn't protest as he held her face in his hands and kissed her softly on her lips.

Gillian was swept up in the moment and couldn't believe how good it felt to be lost in Frankie's kiss, paralyzed by his strong embrace. She returned his kiss with a passion that surprised her. Soon their tongues were intertwined and their bodies were pressed together so closely that Gillian could feel heat between her thighs, and a moan escaped her lips. She pulled away from Frankie and stepped back, lightly touching her lips as if she couldn't believe they'd been pressed against his only moments ago.

Frankie reached for her, but she pulled away.

"This ain't right," she said softly. "You're married, Frankie."

Frankie hung his head, ashamed of the truth in her statement. He loved his wife. But, shit! Gillian was making him want to give it all up.

"I'm not happy with my wife anymore," he said, realizing how true that statement was as the words left his mouth. "I haven't been happy with her for a long time. That's why I'm never home."

Gillian looked at him, and then looked away. She knew that he was telling the truth. She'd known it for some time now. And she had to admit that it felt good to hear him say it out loud. But part of her felt guilty for wanting another woman's husband so badly. "Then tell her that. Until then, we can't cross that line, Frankie. That's not how I want to do things."

He sighed, then nodded, understanding how she felt. "So I guess I can't come home with you tonight." He smiled innocently at her. Frankie wanted so badly to be between her legs until the sun came up.

Gillian shook her head and smiled. "Guess not." She hailed a taxi to take her uptown to her East Ninety-sixth Street town house and blew a kiss to Frankie as she climbed inside.

"I'll call you tomorrow," she called over her shoulder.

Her taxi pulled away slowly, leaving Frankie standing on the curb still tasting her sweet lips. He walked to the parking garage, feeling somewhat lost. He loved Camille. She was, after all, his wife. But these days he had a longing for Gillian that was growing harder to control with each moment that passed. He drove home carefully, aware that he was definitely driving under the influence, and finally made it back home safely. He pulled his car into the garage and entered the dark house quietly, intending to slip into bed beside Camille and rouse her for a quickie. Since he couldn't have Gillian, he'd settle for his wife.

As he entered his spacious bedroom, though, he stopped in his tracks and sighed. Camille was sprawled out across their big bed with little Shane snoring softly beside her. Frankie couldn't help noticing that Shane's little ass was on *his* side of the bed. Frustrated, he turned and went to sleep alone in one of the guest rooms. As he settled into the unfamiliar bed, he thought about Gillian, wondered if she was making love to that wack-ass stockbroker at that very moment. The thought of it pissed him off even more than the thought of Shane sleeping in his spot. Annoyed with everyone and everything, Frankie fell asleep hoping for a sweet dream in order to escape his disappointing reality.

Ladies' Night

"You's a dumb bitch!" Toya sipped her red wine and shook her head in disgust. The ladies had gathered together for what had become a weekly ritual—dinner and drinks at one of New York's fabulous hot spots. Tonight it was the famed Buddakan, an upscale Asian-inspired restaurant in Manhattan's Meatpacking District.

"Will you help me or not?" Dominique demanded as she sliced her steak and looked at Toya.

Toya frowned and shook her head. "No, I will not. I'm not about to call some girl and question her about her relationship with your 'man,' if that's what you want to call this muthafucka. You know why I'm not gonna call some girl and question her? Because that's stupid and it's childish. It's immature, it's a sign of low self-esteem, it's—"

"Fine!" Dominique cut her off. "Camille, will you do it for me?"

Camille almost choked on her food. "Me? No way! I would mess that up completely."

Dominique rolled her eyes. "Not if I'm right there with you, telling you what to say."

Camille shook her head. Misa spoke up. "Don't even look at me, 'cuz I don't play phone games with chicks. You're on your own, sweetie."

"Come on, y'all. I need you right now."

Toya sucked her teeth. "No, what you need is a damn psychiatrist. I can't believe you!"

Dominique tossed her fork onto her plate and sat back with her arms thrust in the air in exasperation. "Why am I the one who needs a psychiatrist when I'm the one being cheated on?" Dominique's diamond earrings sparkled by the light of the candle burning in the center of their table.

"So what!" Camille hissed, causing some of the other diners to glance uncomfortably in their direction. "You're not the first woman to be cheated on, Dominique. And you won't be the last. This is not how you deal with things." Camille could feel her blood pressure rising and wasn't sure why she was so upset.

Toya shook her head. "Listen to yourself," she said. She looked at Dominique and tried to reason with her friend. "You do realize that Jamel's broke ass is in jail right now, don't you? He's in *jail*, Dominique! And you're worried about whether or not another female is going up to the jail to visit him. Listen to yourself, you dumb bitch." Toya shoved more salad in her mouth, wondering why she wasted time with this hardheaded friend of hers.

"The CO told me that another girl was up there visiting him the weekend that I couldn't make it, and I think it was his son's mother. I can't call her and ask her myself, 'cuz then she'll tell him and he'll probably get mad at me. You know how men try to flip shit around all the time. So all I need is for one of you to call like you're a prison official and ask if she was there to visit him recently."

"The muthafucka is a convict," Toya reminded her.

"Jesus!" Dominique folded her arms across her chest as if Toya's comment had made her lose her appetite.

Toya ignored Dominique and continued. "*Yet*, you keep acting like he's God's gift to women. You must be out your mind if you think that I would *ever* waste my time trying to find out if his bum ass is creeping on you. The CO said another bitch was up there. That should be it! What more do you need?"

"I need to know for sure. I need to hear *her* say that she was up there visiting him."

"Does that even sound logical to you?" Camille asked. "You're not making sense."

Dominique nodded quickly. "It makes perfect sense to me," she said. "Jamel is a good catch. I recognize it and so does his baby mama, and that's why she won't leave him alone. I need to let her know that I exist. But I don't want to risk losing him because I went and called his ex. So I need one of you to do this for me. This is the type of shit that friends are for."

Misa laughed. "That's not what friends are for. Friends are for telling you when you're wrong and keeping it real with you. And the truth is, your ass is crazy, Dominique. He's not worth all this." Misa was happier than she had ever been now that she was carrying on a lusty romance with Baron. He hadn't taken her out on the town much, but they had spent several passion-filled evenings holed up in his New Jersey mansion. It was enough to make her feel grown and sexy like never before.

"You don't even know him," Dominique said, looking at Misa as if she had offended her.

"I know enough. He's not the good catch that you think he is." Misa shook her head.

Camille ordered dessert from the passing waitress.

"All right, just forget it," Dominique sighed, exasperated, and resumed eating. "I should've known that none of you would help me."

Camille sat back and looked at her friend. Dominique could be so wild sometimes. But it was one of the things Camille loved most about her. They all had their distinctions, which was what made their friendship special. In the months since Camille's surprise party, they had all established a close friendship. They met for dinner and drinks every Friday night. Each woman brought something unique to the mix.

"Dominique, you know we got your back. But you gotta listen to reason sometimes." Misa signaled the waitress for another drink.

"Well, moving on . . ." Toya shot a look at Dominique to let her know that her request for their help was out of the question. "Alex is taking me to Brazil for my birthday," she announced with a nonchalant tone in her voice. "We're leaving the Friday before my birthday and we'll be back a week later." Now that he realized how fed up Toya was with his lack of energy and fun, Alex was stepping up his game. Toya smiled to herself, happy that her relationship with him was finally taking a turn for the better.

Dominique exhaled loudly. "Why do you always find the ones who pay for trips and buy you nice shit, while I get stuck with the two-timing losers?"

Toya laughed. "'Cuz, honey, I would never give a loser

the time of day. I don't play that shit. If a man can't do for me, what do I need him for? He better know how to fix something, or be able to buy me something, or he better have connections to someone or something that interests me. Otherwise, I don't need the muthafucka!"

Misa gave her a high five and Dominique shook her head. "That's not what love is supposed to be about, Toya. What if you fall in love with a man who treats you like a queen but doesn't have a lot of money?"

Toya shook her head, frowning. "Dominique, who said anything about love?" She took a sip of her margarita and continued. "Love is nothing but fucking trouble. I'm not looking for love. All I need is a stiff dick and some perks."

Everyone laughed, and Toya smiled, looking intently at Dominique. "Take notes, bitch. I don't do relationships and neither should you. You're too young, and you got everything going for you. Why would you want to settle down with one lame when there's a whole city full of sexy men out there waiting to be tried out?"

Dominique shrugged and stirred her drink, still disappointed that none of her friends would help her in her plight with Jamel.

Camille looked confused. "But that outlook can't last forever, Toya. Relationships aren't always so bad."

Toya frowned at Camille and set her drink down. "Just because you're living the boring married life doesn't mean that we all need to settle, too."

"Hey!" Camille objected. "Who ever said that I was bored or settling? I love Frankie. It *is* possible to be happily married."

"You sound like you're trying to convince yourself," Toya suggested.

"No. I'm trying to convince *you* so that you'll stop putting crazy ideas like that in Dominique's head."

"Well, let me ask you this," Toya responded, leaning forward slightly. "How much time do you spend doing the things that you like to do? Aside from our Friday nights out, what do you do for yourself to make *you* happy?"

Camille gave the question some thought.

"Exactly," Toya said. "I rest my case."

Misa nodded. "She's right, Camille."

"You didn't even give me a chance to think of an answer," Camille protested.

"You shouldn't need to think about that. I can tell you right now what I do to make myself happy. I go out when the fuck I want. I go home when the fuck I want. I get monthly facials, weekly manicures and pedicures. I get my hair done. I get massages. I go on shopping sprees whenever the mood strikes me. And I don't need to ask anybody's permission to do none of that shit! I don't have to hide my bags in the back of the closet 'cuz some *husband* wants to make me feel guilty about what I spend. I don't have to pick up after a messy muthafucka. And best of all, when I'm done cumming, he can get the fuck out."

Camille shook her head. "You can be so crazy sometimes." She laughed, but couldn't help thinking about what Toya was saying. She had to admit that Toya's life sounded much more appealing than hers did at the moment. "I go to the gym," she said. "I go shopping whenever I want and I redecorate the house. I have things to do to make myself happy."

Toya could tell that Camille was trying to convince herself that her life was fine the way it was. But she knew the truth. "Those things don't make you happy. They keep you distracted so that you don't realize how unhappy you really are."

Camille thought about what Toya had said and disagreed completely. To Camille, nothing in the world was better than being married. "I love my husband, Toya. I know Frankie's good traits and his bad ones. I know who I'm going to bed with at night and who I'm waking up to in the morning. I don't have to wonder about anything. I already know who I've got and what he's about and I don't miss the dating scene at all!" Camille looked at each of her friends sincerely. "I worry about you out there living the single life. There's all kinds of shit out there. STDs, downlow men . . . you never know what you're gonna get. It's like playing Russian roulette. I swear, I'm so glad that I'm married."

Toya scrunched up her lips in disbelief. "Please! You ain't fooling nobody with that shit."

Camille laughed. "I'm not trying to fool anybody. I'm happy with Frankie."

Toya waved her hand and said, "You're only happy 'cuz you've convinced yourself that your life is some fairy tale. You're one of those women who believe that you can't be happy without a man. You like being able to say 'my husband,' as if that makes you sound more accomplished or something." Toya laughed as if it were a ridiculous notion. "Being happy that you're a wife doesn't necessarily mean that you're happy with Frankie. In fact, you hardly ever get to *see* Frankie because he's always out there grinding. Am I right?"

Camille was frowning. "Yeah, but—"

"You hardly see the man. So it's not about you being so happy with him. It's about you being happy with the thought of being married."

Camille stared back at Toya and shook her head. "You're wrong."

"Whatever." Toya gulped down the rest of her drink and signaled for another one. She knew that she had hit a nerve with Camille. But Toya didn't care. She hated Camille's stance on marriage. Toya was well aware that everything wasn't as sunny in the Bingham household as Camille made it out to be. Toya knew all about Frankie's close relationship with Gillian. Frankie's long hours away from home, his frequent "business trips," the mysterious charges for dinners for two on his credit card statement; Camille had shared it all with Toya. So it made her feel almost sick to her stomach to hear Camille talk so condescendingly to the single ladies.

Misa stayed quiet while Toya read her sister like a book. She, too, was sick of hearing Camille brag about her marriage, when everybody knew that it was anything but picture perfect.

When they'd all gotten another round of drinks, Dominique decided to break the ice. "Toya, why don't we go shopping for your trip to Brazil. You know I have the inside track to all the hot new stylists. Let me set up some appointments and see if we can get you some free shit," she suggested, smiling.

Toya's face lit up. "If it's free, it's for me, bitch!" She beamed with joy and raised her glass tipsily. "A toast," she said. "To being fuckin' happy!"

They all cheered, clinked glasses, enjoyed their drinks, and shared Camille's dessert. It was nights like these that solidified their friendship. Despite their differences, they had one another's backs. And that would prove to be more important than any of them knew at that moment.

Stepping-stone

Misa lay on her side in Baron's bed, her back facing the doorway. She was in so much pain that she dared not move. She had finally positioned her bruised body in a way that gave her some relief from the throbbing aches. Baron had done a number on her this time. He had erupted in a fury so violent, Misa had been caught off guard.

Baron appeared in the doorway and saw her lying in the fetal position. He felt guilty for taking his frustrations out on Misa the way he had. They had been having one of their usual hot sex sessions and, as he'd done countless times before, Baron was choking Misa. This time, he had to admit, he may have been more aggressive about it as he thrust himself in and out of her, squeezing her throat with one hand while watching her try in vain to gasp for air. He had been strangely turned on by her inability to breathe, felt a power that he thoroughly enjoyed. As he got caught up in that feeling, Misa was struggling for air and she had reached up and clawed at his face, scratching him and drawing blood. Angry, Baron had slapped her hard across her face. Misa had hit him back and before he knew it, Baron had reacted viciously. He had punched and kicked Misa until she began to cry and beg him to stop. Instead of feeling sorry for her, Baron was aroused and laughed at her sinisterly as he forced her into a prone position and violently entered her from behind. Misa had howled in pain as he pummeled her anally, and the more brutal he was, the louder she screamed. When he was finally done with her, he'd coldly left her crying in a heap of messy sheets and pillows while he got up, got dressed, and walked out the front door. Misa had lain there for hours this way, wondering what to make of the man she wanted so badly to be Mr. Right.

Now, as he reentered the bedroom and saw her there, he shook his head. This was the kind of behavior that had caused him to lose Angie. Here he was doing it again, taking his anger and frustrations out on a woman. He walked over to the bed and touched Misa's rumpled hair. She cringed, partly out of fear that he was back to hurt her some more and partly because her head was sore where he touched her. He sat down beside her and cleared his throat.

"Look at me."

Misa bit her lip hard as she turned slowly to face Baron, her head throbbing the entire time.

He looked at her and shook his head. "I'm sorry," he said flatly. "I spazzed out 'cuz you never should have scratched me like that."

Misa was stunned. Was he blaming her for this? "You were choking me," she said softly, not wanting to set him off again. "I couldn't breathe."

Looking at her bruises, he shook his head. He could never let Camille see her like this. Frankie would kill him. "Well, like I said, I'm sorry." His voice was emotionless, but he was smiling at Misa so she relaxed slightly. "I want you to stay here with me for a couple days. I'm sure Camille will look after your son. It's Columbus Day weekend, anyway, so she won't mind."

Misa shook her head, still in pain. "No. I need to get home to Shane." She really wanted to get the hell away from Baron after what he had done to her.

He took a deep breath and looked at her. There was no way he was letting her go home to Staten Island looking like Tina Turner after one of her fights with Ike. He reached into his jacket pocket and pulled out two jewelry boxes, one larger than the other.

Misa couldn't help but smile. "For me?"

He nodded. "I saw these and I couldn't decide which one was beautiful enough for you. So I just bought them both." He smiled back at Misa, and handed the boxes to her.

Misa reached for the bigger box first. Opening it, she gasped. Two brilliant diamond bangles sparkled back at her and her smile spread even wider.

"Oh my God, Baron! These are gorgeous." Misa was nearly breathless as she eyed them.

Baron was happy that his apology was working so far. "Open this one."

Misa took the smaller box and slowly opened it. She peered inside and looked at Baron questioningly. "What is this?" she asked, pulling the diamond ring out of the box. Her heart jumped as she wondered whether Baron was proposing to her.

"It's a ring," he said. "Just a ring. Don't get excited."

It was too late for that. Misa was already excited as she put it on. "What does it mean?"

He shrugged. "Just means that you're special. And I care about you."

The ring was stunning and Misa didn't care if it wasn't a proposal of marriage. "I love it."

Baron kissed her softly. "Good. I'm glad." He paused for a moment, looked in her puffy eyes. "You sure you don't want to stay for the weekend?"

Misa thought about it. She looked at the ring on her finger and the bangles and shrugged. She had to admit that she wanted to stay. Baron was *fine*! He was paid, powerful, and as long as she was on his arm, she would be paid and powerful, too. She could give Shane the life she hadn't had growing up. She could stop sponging off Camille and make her own way, have her own money and respect. But right now she was still very afraid of Baron. "I think I need to leave," she said. "I need to go home and take care of Shane."

Baron looked at her, his green eyes seeming to plead with her. "Call Camille," he said. "Ask her to watch him for you. I want to take you with me to Miami for a few days."

Misa would have jumped up and down had she not been so sore. "Miami?" she asked, fighting the urge to smile. She pictured them on a beach together, coupled up. Her and fine-ass Baron! She cleared her throat. "I've never been there before."

Baron smiled. "Good. Let me take you there for a few days. Get you a massage, some rest, and we can get to know each other a little better." His smile faded. He looked down at his hands and then back at her. "I'm not a monster, you know."

Misa didn't move. She didn't dare respond, either, out of fear that he might snap again.

"I didn't mean to hurt you like this, Misa. And I won't put my hands on you again. I promise."

Misa wanted so badly to believe him. She thought again about the idea of flying away with Baron for a little while. "Okay."

"Call Camille and then come and take a bath with me."
Baron left the bedroom and Misa's heart raced with excitement. She thought about what happened as she called her sister. True, Baron had gone too far. But he had made up for it
with the beautiful gifts he'd given her. Plus he'd said that she
was special, that he cared about her, and now they were flying
off to Miami. This was the type of shit she'd dreamed about.
Misa figured that maybe she shouldn't have scratched him;
maybe she should never have let him start choking her in the
first place. She rationalized that she may have been partly to
blame for how Baron had reacted. And she forgave him. After
all, he was Baron fucking Nobles, and that meant that she and
Shane were on the verge of a wonderful life. Baron was the
key to her happiness. If she could get him to settle down with
her, Shane could go to the best schools and they could move
out of her humble home and into this opulent one. *Shit*, she
decided, Camille wasn't the only one deserving of a fairy tale.

Camille knew that she'd been drinking too much lately. Last
night, she'd passed out after downing an entire bottle of
Hennessey White she'd brought home from some long-ago
trip to Jamaica. Shane had awakened bright and early the
next morning as he usually did. But Camille had been snoring away in a drunken stupor. Thank goodness Steven had
come over early and had given Shane some cereal and turned
on his favorite cartoons. When Camille had finally shuffled
downstairs feeling like a heap of shit, she'd found Steven
playing hide-and-go-seek with a giggling Shane.

"Thanks, Steven," Camille mumbled. She pulled her
robe tighter around her bulging frame and wished she could
just crawl back into bed. Damn Misa! She was off frolicking

in Florida while Camille was left to care for her kid. "I'll take over from here."

Steven looked at his sister-in-law and laughed a little. Miss Goody Two-shoes was really starting to break down. He had noticed that Camille was spending most of her nights hitting the bottle and listening to sad songs. While his brother, Frankie, was out doing his thing, his wife was falling apart at home. Steven felt kind of vindicated. Frankie had reached a level of success that Steven knew he would never reach. Frankie had gotten out early, escaped the cruel punishments their father had dished out at whim. Frankie was the man, everybody knew that. So, Steven rode his brother's coattails. He knew that someday the façade of his brother's "perfect" life would come crashing down around him. On the surface Frankie B had the perfect looks, the perfect wife, home, cars, and connections. Steven suspected that it wouldn't always be that way, and those suspicions were starting to ring true. Not that he wanted his brother to fail. Steven had a lot of love for Frankie. But growing up in his shadow had been far from easy. Plus, Steven had his own demons to deal with. And somehow living in the splendor of Frankie's home seemed to make those demons easier to battle.

"You look like you need to sleep some more," he said to Camille. "Frankie went to Nobles' house. He said he'll be home in time for dinner."

Camille looked crestfallen. "Frankie was home? He left?"

"Yeah. He's gonna wanna eat when he gets home. What you making?"

Camille felt sick at the very thought of food.

Steven laughed. "That's what I thought. Go lay down and I'll order food from the Italian spot we like."

Camille noticed that Steven was becoming more and more comfortable in their home instead of utilizing the guest house. *The Italian spot* we *like*. Steven was starting to become too much of a fixture in her personal space. She didn't care that their home was large and lavish. It was hers to share with Frankie—*alone*—until the day when they decided to have children.

But as her stomach went topsy-turvy, she looked at Shane. He was jumping up and down in the middle of the floor, yelling, "Come and find me, Unca Steben!" The child was bubbling over with energy and Steven seemed to finally have something productive to contribute to Camille's life.

She nodded. "Okay. Wake me up at three." She shuffled back upstairs to bed and was asleep the moment her head hit the pillow.

Three days later, Misa came home and she couldn't wait to see Shane. It had only been a few days since she'd dropped him off and headed for Miami, but she missed her son like crazy. She put her Louis Vuitton luggage in her bedroom and plopped down on the couch to call Camille.

As the phone rang, she couldn't help but marvel at all the things Baron had bought for her. In addition to the diamonds and the luggage, he had purchased an entire wardrobe of beautiful clothes for her, since she hadn't had an opportunity to go home and pack anything. They had stayed at a lovely beach resort on Collins Avenue and Baron had been gentle and kind toward her. She was feeling brand new and ready to begin a deeper, more meaningful relationship with him.

Steven answered the phone and Misa frowned. "Hi. Put my sister on the phone," she said, hurriedly.

"Your sister is asleep," Steven said. "You wanna talk to Shane?"

"Asleep?" Misa frowned. It was well after one o'clock in the afternoon. It wasn't like her sister to lounge around this late. She reminded herself that Shane could be a handful, and shrugged. "Okay . . . well . . . I'll be by there to pick him up in about an hour." She hung up and began to unpack. Before she went back to being a mommy she wanted to bask in the glow of being Baron's wifey for a little while longer.

She pulled out a negligee she'd worn on their second night in Miami. Misa smiled as she recalled the way that Baron had looked at her when she emerged from the bathroom wearing the short lace nightgown. He'd been so gentle with Misa while they were away, and had toned down his violent tendencies during their sex sessions. True, his anger had resurfaced when he was dealing with some Spanish drug dealers on their first night in Florida. Baron had grabbed one of the men by the throat during a heated argument over money in their hotel lobby. Misa had felt oddly proud watching Baron menace the men in their own hometown. She had never witnessed anything like it, and when he got his way and the men delivered what Baron wanted, he had spent the rest of their trip lavishing her with clothes, cash, and jewelry. His mood had changed for the better, and she was hopeful that it would stay that way.

Now that they were home, Misa wondered how things would be between them going forward. She had visions of being one big happy family—her, Baron, and Shane—and she was willing to do whatever it took to make that dream a reality.

The Fabulous Life

"Check this out," Lexy said, handing Toya a Nanette Lepore blouse. Alexis "Lexy" Lassiter was one of New York City's top celebrity stylists. She worked with all the A-listers, and was in such high demand that Dominique had had to pull every string she had in order to get this appointment with her. Toya's trip was a week away and they had no time to waste. They had already picked out a Tracy Reese dress, Tory Burch sandals, and a pair of Bottega Veneta sunglasses. But they still had a lot of work to do.

"I like this!" Toya proclaimed, holding the canary-colored fabric in her hands. "What else you got?"

Lexy pulled out a Cavalli dress, which Toya snatched up as well. After grabbing a pair of Moschino jeans, an Allen Schwartz minidress, and a Marc Jacobs sheath, they were finally done. Toya couldn't believe that all of this shit was free! All Dominique had to do to get it was agree to use Lexy solely as the stylist for the new "it" R & B sensation Kiara. It was days like this that Dominique loved her job. After securing a Dolce&Gabbana dress and Versace pantsuit for herself, they were done. They felt high as they stepped out onto Fifth Avenue and hailed a cab.

Once inside, they giggled like schoolgirls. "That was *fun*!" Toya exclaimed. "You do that shit all the time?"

Dominique shook her head. "Not really. I try not to take advantage of my position too much. But every now and then if I need something for a special occasion or for a special trip, hell yeah!"

"Damn, you're lucky! I just walked out of there with like eight thousand dollars' worth of clothes, and we didn't come out of pocket at all! I'm not used to shit like that."

Dominique smiled, happy that Toya was pleased. It was hard to impress Toya. She already had a fabulous wardrobe, drove a luxury car, and lived in a beautiful brownstone. As a high-end real estate agent, she was accustomed to the finer things in life. But paying for expensive things and getting them for free were two entirely different things. Dominique was happy to share her good fortune with her friend. As they pulled up at Waverly Inn, an exclusive New York City eatery, both women were euphoric. There was nothing as satisfying as retail therapy.

They were seated right away, since the place was relatively empty on a Wednesday afternoon. They ordered and sat back, and Dominique felt strange. "It feels weird being here without Misa and Camille," she said.

Toya rolled her eyes. "Oh, Lord." She waved her hand, dismissing her. "Not to me. I'm sick of hearing Camille's naive ass talking about how Frankie is so wonderful, being married is so wonderful, and how she feels so fuckin' sorry for us. Please!"

Dominique waited until the waitress set their drinks

down on the table and left before responding. "You think Frankie's cheating on her?"

Toya looked at Dominique like she was crazy. "You can't be serious. He's definitely fucking Gillian, and Camille is too dumb to see it. Personally, I don't think she cares. In her heart of hearts, that bitch knows he's cheating. But would you say a muthafuckin' word if you were living in that house and sleeping with that sexy son of a bitch and you had a Bentley parked in your four-car garage? You would play dumb, too."

Dominique laughed. "Ya damn right I would! He could fuck that bitch on the bed next to me and I wouldn't say shit."

Toya laughed. "That's 'cuz you don't love him. And if I were Camille, I wouldn't love his ass, either. I would never love a guy like that. When you're dealing with a man of Frankie's caliber, you can never get your feelings involved. Never. That's rule number muthafuckin' one."

Dominique nodded, cosigning. "True. But women can't turn their emotions on and off like that."

Toya almost spit her drink out in her haste to respond. "Who can't?" She shook her head. "I don't deal with emotions at *all*! Those days are over."

Dominique smirked. She knew that Toya liked to come across as rough and tough. But she suspected that underneath that steely exterior lay a soft and pink side. "You can't help who you love," she said.

Toya wanted to throw up, but resisted the urge. "You have so much to learn."

"Seriously, Toya. I love Jamel. And I can't even help it. I try to tell myself to put the brakes on and try to slow down and not get too serious about him. But that doesn't work. When I'm with him I feel complete. I know he's the one, so why should I fight it?"

Toya wasn't sure if she should slap her friend or put her in a straitjacket. She stared at Dominique intently for a long time before she spoke. Finally, she said, "You know what, Dominique? I worry about you. All this time that we've been friends . . . all this time . . . you've been watching how I get down. So even if you were a dumb bitch before you met me, by now you should know better. What the hell do you mean, 'you can't help who you love'? What the fuck part of the game is that?"

"I'm saying—"

"You ain't saying shit! That's the problem."

" 'Cuz you won't let me get a word in, Toya!"

"For what? So you can say some more dumb shit?" Toya saw a look of hurt pass over Dominique's face and felt slightly guilty. Dominique *was* saying dumb shit, but Toya knew that she needed to have more patience with her friend. But times like this and statements like that made it hard for Toya to keep her mouth shut.

"All I'm saying is, don't sell yourself short, girl. You're trying so hard to lock this fool down as if he was 50 Cent or somebody. You might love him, fine. But not so much that you should be fiending for him. He ain't even that cute!"

"Cute isn't everything."

"But it's something, bitch! At least if he's cute, you can rationalize losing your mind over him. But Jamel is very average, and I'm being generous! Why would you sacrifice your pride for a man like that?"

"You're just mean, that's what it is." Dominique smirked and sat back as the waitress brought their lunch to the table.

When she was gone again, she said, "I don't want to grow old by myself, Toya. So if I find a man and he's a good catch— like Jamel is—I'm gonna hold on to him. I don't care what you say."

Toya looked at Dominique and shook her head. "You's a dumb bitch!" Toya proclaimed, slipping into her Ebonics. "And I mean that shit, Dominique. You're too young to be worrying about growing old by yourself. You haven't been listening to me at all. 'Cuz if you were, you'd know that you can't force a man to want you. If Jamel thought you were as good of a catch as you think he is, there wouldn't be any miscellaneous bitches on his visiting log."

"See?" Dominique said, chewing her salad. "That's why I can't tell you shit. Every time I share my feelings, you make me regret it."

Toya smirked. "Don't be mad at me 'cuz I tell it like it is." She picked at her salad.

"I'm not mad," Dominique clarified. "I actually enjoy your honesty most of the time. But friends are supposed to be able to listen to each other without judging. You can't ever do that."

"I don't judge you, Dominique," Toya lied. She thought about the ton of clothes she'd just gotten for free on the strength of her silly friend and decided to soften her approach. "Look, if you wanna be a dummy all your life, then go for it. I won't say another word. You and Camille can make whatever decisions you want about the men you love. I still love y'all the same. Just don't come crying to me when the bastard breaks your heart. 'Cuz all I'm gonna do is remind you of what I told you." She sipped her water and looked at Dominique seriously. "Until then, I won't utter another negative word."

Dominique rolled her eyes and ate her lunch in silence, knowing that Toya keeping her mouth shut was wishful thinking. It was just a matter of time before Toya would be offering her brutal opinion once again.

Gillian sat with her toes in the nail dryer on the floor and her fingers carefully perched in the hand dryer in front of her. She was happy with her manicure/pedicure, and in love with the new shade of red she'd found at the Chanel counter. It made her nails look inviting without seeming trashy. Her Cole Haan bag sat on the seat beside her, and she watched *Access Hollywood* on the plasma TV hanging on the wall. Britney Spears was making another comeback, by the looks of it.

She heard the clerk greet a client who had just arrived, but she didn't bother to look away from the television. Not until she heard a voice say, "Hi, Gillian. I didn't expect to see you here."

Gillian looked up to see Camille Bingham standing next to her wearing a Diane von Furstenberg wrap dress, sparkling diamonds, and a phony smile. Gillian's smile was equally fake as she greeted Frankie's wife. "Camille, how are you?"

"Great," Camille replied. "And you?"

Gillian nodded. "Fine." She noticed that Camille had her hair pulled back today, revealing the beginnings of a double chin. The diamond sparklers in her ears did little to detract attention from the extra skin hanging beneath them, Gillian silently mused. "You come all the way to Midtown to get your nails done?" She couldn't understand why she had to run into Frankie's Stepford wife at her favorite day spa when they lived boroughs apart.

Camille shrugged. "I had a free day, so I decided to try out this place because my friend Toya came here and bragged about it. I'm making a full day of it. Mani/pedi, massage, the works." Camille smiled again, phonier than before. She was battling her growing feelings of jealousy toward Frankie's beautiful best friend. But it was hard, especially at times like this when Gillian was looking so lovely and smiling so fake.

Gillian nodded. "Have I met your friend?" she asked, trying to recall if she had ever heard of Camille even having friends. It had always seemed to her that Camille lived so much in Frankie's world that she had abandoned her own.

"I think so. Yes, at my birthday party."

Gillian nodded, still not recalling Camille's friend. An uncomfortable hush fell between them, and both women searched for ways to fill it. "So," Camille said, playing with her hands awkwardly. "I hear that my sister has been spending time with your brother, Baron. Who would've predicted that?"

Gillian smiled, her pearly white teeth sparkling brighter than her lip gloss. "Yeah, you're right. Who knows? Maybe she'll get him to settle down." Gillian doubted it. She hoped that Camille and Misa were aware that Baron wasn't the settling-down type. Misa was by no means the only chick that Baron was involved with.

"Well, what about you? Don't you want the same for yourself?" Camille smiled. "To settle down, I mean."

Gillian wasn't sure how to answer that question. She was tempted to tell Camille that the only man she could imagine having such a life with was already married—to her. She nodded slowly. "Yeah. I do want that. I'm just not in a rush to find it."

Camille nodded. "Are you still seeing the stockbroker?"

Gillian smiled, since Frankie had obviously been discussing her love life with his wife. Camille had never had a conversation with Sadiq, so there was no other way she could have known his occupation. "Yes, we're still dating. He's a nice guy. But like I said, I'm in no rush to get serious."

Camille was sorry to hear that. She wanted Gillian married and pregnant so that she could stop monopolizing Frankie's time. "Well, I know that your mother would plan the wedding of the century for you."

Gillian laughed and nodded. "She sure would. She loves to throw a huge party."

"Speaking of which, Frankie told me that your parents are having a big anniversary party soon. You must be excited." Camille wasn't looking forward to another Nobles family function, but Frankie was insisting on being there. She certainly wasn't letting him go alone, so she was searching frantically for something to wear as the date of the event neared.

"Yes," Gillian nodded. "Twenty-eight years of wedded bliss." She slipped her feet out of the nail dryer and watched as the nail technician ensured that they were indeed dry. Turning her attention back to Camille, she asked, "You're coming, right?"

"Of course," Camille answered, fingering the platinum necklace she wore. "Wouldn't miss it." She watched Gillian slip her feet into her shoes and slide a tip to the lady who had serviced her. Gillian stood up and Camille smiled, taking it all in. Gillian's curves were legendary, and the jeans she wore only highlighted that fact. Her ass looked bigger than ever. The tight blouse and Gucci belt she wore accentuated her tiny waist. Camille fought the urge to hate.

"Great," Gillian said, smiling. "I'll see you there. Take care."

"Bye." Camille watched as Gillian sashayed out the door, donning her designer shades as soon as she stepped into the sunlight. Camille sat down to begin her manicure, wondering why she was hearing Toya's voice in her head, urging her to wake the fuck up.

On the Prowl

Misa and Camille walked into the house with little Shane in tow, only to find Steven sitting on the couch once again. For the life of her, Camille couldn't understand why Frankie allowed his brother to take advantage of them the way that he did. Steven was twenty-five, had no children, no debt, and no motivation to do anything with his life. He had been living in the rental unit (though he paid no rent) at the rear of their property for close to a year. Camille felt that he was lazy, while Frankie insisted that Steven was a little slow. In Camille's opinion, Steven wasn't slow. He was a fucking user.

Steven and Camille were cordial to each other, but that was as good as it got. Camille didn't appreciate Steven sponging off Frankie. To Steven, Camille was a bourgeois, stuck-up housewife who hid behind her husband's success to mask the fact that she had none of her own. Steven knew that Camille would love to see him move out. But as long as Frankie said that it was all right to be there, Steven had no intention of budging. In his opinion, Camille had no say-so in the matter. She was merely a tenant, just like he was.

"Steven," Camille greeted him simply as she headed to the kitchen with grocery bags.

"Camille," he answered, laughing to himself at her obvious attitude. He looked at Camille's sister and smiled. Misa was very pretty. She reminded him of an actress he'd seen in a bad Tyrese movie one time, but her name didn't come to mind. Misa was dark brown with lush lips and eyes that made him want to look deeper. Her hair was pulled away from her face, and her earlobes bore big hoop earrings with her name in the center. She had on a pair of tight jeans, a fitted I LOVE NY T-shirt, and a pair of Steve Madden boots. And Steven couldn't keep his eyes off her phat ass.

"Hi, Misa," he said, still smiling.

"Hi." She waved at him over her shoulder and kept it moving, joining her sister in the kitchen. Shane had pulled up a stool at the breakfast nook and was already munching on a pear. Misa smiled at him and started helping Camille unpack the groceries.

To Camille's disappointment, Steven followed them into the kitchen. He walked over to Misa and asked, "Need any help?"

Misa looked at Steven and smirked. "Nah, I got it. Thanks." She knew that Steven had a crush on her. But she never gave him a second look. He was blessed with the same tall, dark, and handsome looks as his brother, Frankie, but Steven wasn't in the same league as his brother. While Frankie had money, power, and respect, Steven had little more than a few bucks in his pocket. And even that had most likely been given to him by his brother. Misa was through getting involved with losers like Steven. She had her sights set on bigger and better men than him. Men like Baron Nobles. The only problem was that Baron hadn't called her in days, and she was beginning to wonder if he had already moved on to a new chick.

"Steven, did Frankie say where he was going?" Camille asked. When they'd left for the supermarket earlier that afternoon, Frankie had been taking a much-needed nap on the chaise lounge. Camille had intended to prepare him his favorite meal, even though he had come home in the wee hours of the morning. Things had been tense between them over the past few days, and she felt that it was time to make amends. But she'd noticed that his car wasn't in the garage anymore, and he hadn't mentioned going out. She couldn't help feeling annoyed that he was not at home with her yet again.

Steven shook his head. "No. When I woke up and came over here to watch TV he was already gone.

"Wassup, Shane?" Steven greeted the youngster by giving him five, and Misa smiled. Shane was tearing that pear up! "You spending the night again while Mommy goes out?"

Camille shot a look at Misa, wondering if that was what she had in mind.

Misa gave her sister an innocent look. "What?" she asked. "I mean, if you're offering to watch him . . ."

"I'm not." Camille kept unpacking groceries, and Misa put on her sad face.

"Camille, please. You're home for the night, so what's the problem? I just want to go out for a few hours to let off some steam." Misa hoped that she could convince her sister to watch Shane so that she could try to get in touch with Baron. She didn't want to stalk him, but she was sick of him sending her repeated phone calls to his voice mail.

Camille ignored Misa, hoping she'd take the hint and go away. She didn't.

"Please?"

Shane watched his mother beg and spoke up. "I'll be good, Aunt Tamille."

Camille melted and smiled at her nephew. "I know you will, baby. And of course you can stay tonight." She shot a wicked look at her sister. "But your mommy has to remember that sometimes you want to be at your house, too."

Shane shook his head. "Nuh-uh! I *always* like to be at your house, Aunt Tamille!" Shane was smiling, showing all his teeth.

Steven laughed. "I know how you feel, son!" He gave Shane five again, and Camille rolled her eyes at Steven's comment. Misa kissed Shane on his forehead and wiped his sticky hands off. Grabbing her purse, she smiled coyly at Camille.

"Thanks, sis," she said, scampering toward the door.

"You're pushing it!" Camille called after her sister, who was already at the front door.

Steven was hot on Misa's heels. "You think I can tag along with you?" he asked. "I get sick of sitting in this house all the time."

Misa looked Steven's broke ass up and down and frowned. "Get a job then," she said. She turned around and sauntered out of the house, leaving Steven standing speechless in her wake.

Baron glanced at his cell phone and saw Misa's name on the caller ID for the hundredth time. He pressed Ignore and kept right on driving.

His female friend Trina sat in the passenger seat of Baron's car, feeling a buzz from the weed she was smoking. They were on their way to her Bushwick, Brooklyn, apartment, and she couldn't wait to get there. It had been weeks since she'd last seen Baron. He was staying away from Brooklyn these days, since he had beef with Jojo and Brooklyn was where Jojo held court. Trina had heard all about it, since the streets were abuzz with the scandal of Dusty's disappearance and Jojo's thirst for revenge. She had called Baron to tell him that she was in need of his good loving and was thrilled when he agreed to pick her up from her job at LensCrafters in Fulton Mall.

"I missed you," Trina said, passing the blunt to Baron.

"Yeah?" he asked, smiling. "When we get to your house you can show me how much."

Trina smiled back. "Turn here," she said, pointing to the next intersection. "It's faster this way."

Baron did as she instructed and turned the corner, anxious for the chance to be alone with her. They pulled up at a red light and Baron reached over and touched her thigh. Trina was a pretty light-skinned girl with sandy brown hair and green eyes. She had been his chick on the side for years, playing her position and never wanting more than their occasional rendezvous. He was eager to get her home so that he could dig her out.

A minivan pulled up alongside them at the traffic light, and Trina looked over at it. Distracted by trying to relight the blunt in his hand, Baron had his head bowed and didn't notice the events unfolding around him. The minivan was on Trina's side of the car, and she watched as the van's side door slid open. Suddenly, Baron saw a hasty movement out of the corner of his eye, and, before he could react, gunfire tore through the Brooklyn air. Baron's car was hit, and the rear window shattered into smithereens. Baron could hear screams from the passersby as they scrambled for safety. As the gunman climbed out of the minivan and kept firing at Baron's car, Trina opened the passenger door and got out. The gunman ignored her and kept advancing on the car, shooting all the while. Baron managed to hit the gas and peeled off as the gunman scurried back inside the van to follow him.

Baron sped down the street and sharply turned the next two corners, checking his rearview mirror for his would-be assassins. Blood poured from his shoulder and his heart pounded in his chest. He knew that Jojo was behind the attempt on his life, and he chastised himself for being in Brooklyn alone in the midst of Brooklyn beef. It was a dumb move, all in a quest to get some pussy. He looked again in his rearview and was relieved to see that it appeared he had lost his assailants.

He kept driving and pulled out his cell phone. Baron called Frankie and was glad when he answered right away. "Yo, son. These muthafuckas shot at me. I'm on my way to Pops's house. Meet me there."

Frankie was confused. "Somebody shot at you?"

"Word."

"Where are you?"

"Bushwick."

"Brooklyn?" Frankie asked, shocked.

"Yeah, son."

"What the fuck are you doing out there?" Frankie asked, thinking Baron had to be the most foolish muthafucka he knew.

"Listen," Baron said, still checking behind him for the shooters. "Just meet me at Pops's house!" He tossed his phone down and kept driving, noticing that his clothes were stained with blood and flecked with broken glass. Baron was shaken. He had to get the fuck out of Brooklyn.

Stripped

Frankie's Escalade screeched to a halt in front of Nobles's house and he leaped out, taking the stairs leading to the sprawling home's entrance two at a time. Before he could ring the doorbell, Gillian pulled up behind him and parked her Benz. She got out of her car and scampered up the stairs until she stood at Frankie's side. She greeted him and they proceeded inside as Greta opened the door.

"Everyone is in the dining room," Greta said, her thick Spanish accent slicing through the awkward silence.

Frankie could see that Gillian was upset, and he pulled her close and hugged her. "He's okay," Frankie reassured her. "Baron is fine."

She nodded, though she was still shaken up. They walked together to the dining room, where they found Nobles and Baron sitting at opposite ends of the long table, with Mayra sitting in the middle. Baron looked dazed as he sat with his arm in a sling and a big bandage on his right shoulder. Gillian ran to her brother and threw her arms around him.

"Are you okay?" she asked, tears flowing.

Baron patted Gillian's back and tried to calm her. "Shhhh. Don't cry. I'm all right. One of the bullets just grazed me."

"He's a fucking fool!" Nobles was furious, and, for the first time, Frankie noticed the tension in the air. Mayra looked as if she'd been playing referee, and Baron looked like a kid who'd gotten a note sent home from his teacher.

Mayra stood up and greeted her daughter and Frankie. She walked over to Nobles and kissed him on his forehead. "Calm down, baby. He's okay. That's all that matters."

Mayra walked out, leaving them to discuss business privately.

"Tell me what happened," Frankie said, sitting down near Nobles. Gillian took a seat near her brother, holding his hand in hers.

Baron had a captive audience as he relayed the events that led to the shooting. Gillian, for one, was hanging on his every word. As Baron spoke, Nobles puffed on a cigar, looking disgusted by his firstborn and the beef that was boiling over between Baron and Jojo.

"She set you up," Gillian said, sitting back like she had just solved a mystery on *Forensic Files*.

"Trina?" Baron asked. "I thought about that. But it doesn't make sense. She's been riding with me for years now. Why would she flip?"

Gillian shook her head, thinking that her father was right. Baron was a fucking fool. "Who knows why? She could've known Jojo for longer than she's known you, Baron. She could be his jump-off and he got her to set you up. Bottom line is that she rolled out of the car during a drive-by! Who does that? She must've known that they wouldn't shoot her. Otherwise, she would've just ducked down and tried to hide under the dashboard or something. She probably knew what was about to go down, and she moved out of the line of fire."

Baron thought about it, contemplating whether or not Trina was capable of betraying him like that. "Well, whether she set me up or not, Jojo was behind it."

Nobles shook his head, seeming terribly disappointed in his son. "All because of that shit with Dusty."

Baron looked caught off guard and Gillian looked away. "What shit with Dusty?" he asked, feigning ignorance.

"Don't play stupid!" Nobles was furious. "The streets talk, and I might be old, but I'm not too old to listen. You got in a fight with Dusty a while ago. He hasn't been heard from in weeks. And with Dusty's big mouth, you know damn well that he's dead, otherwise everybody would've heard from him by now. He could never be quiet this long. And you're behind it. You know it, I know it, and Jojo knows it. Now you brought war to this family."

Baron shook his head. "Pops—"

"Pops, my ass! You're gonna fall back, Baron." Nobles pointed at his son.

"Fall back?" Baron was frowning.

"You heard me. *Fall back!*" Nobles leaned forward, his booming voice echoing in everyone's ears. "You're gonna pass off your responsibilities to Gillian and Frankie—"

"Fuck that!" Baron pounded his fist on the table. "That's bullshit, Pops!"

"No, *this* is bullshit, Baron! You're out there every fucking night calling attention to yourself. The parties, the bitches, the fights, this beef . . . you're out of control. And I'm tired of it. I worked hard to get this family where we are, and you're fucking it up. You could have been killed today!"

Gillian tried to intervene. "Daddy, calm down."

Nobles tuned her out and continued to set his sights on his son. "You're gonna lay low from now on. Keep your stubborn ass in the house, stay out of the fucking spotlight, and for the time being, Gillian and Frankie—"

"This is fucked-up, Pops." Baron looked like he was near tears.

"Baron, they're trying to kill you. Don't you think it's a good time for you to be easy?" Gillian spoke softly.

"Yo, mind your business," Baron hissed.

Nobles threw his ashtray at his son, sending the heavy crystal dish hurling toward Baron's head. Baron ducked in the nick of time and jumped to his feet defensively. Frankie could tell by the look on Nobles's face that if he were able to, he would have kicked Baron's ass. Frankie put his hand on his mentor's shoulder in an effort to calm him down.

"Okay, relax."

He looked at Nobles breathing hard, his chest heaving with rage. Then Frankie looked at Baron, who was still standing. "If they would've got you today, it would've killed all of us in this room. Your father is worried about you. We all are. This dude ain't playing with you, Baron. He tried to kill you today, and if I'm right, he's gonna try again. I agree with Pops. You need to lay low for now. It's as simple as that."

Baron looked around the room. Frankie looked at him sincerely, hoping that his friend would listen to reason. Gillian looked worried, while Nobles looked just plain pissed.

"Pops . . . it's like you're punishing me for being shot at. I didn't do nothing wrong today. I'm the fucking victim, and everybody's telling me to go hide like a bitch."

Nobles shook his head. Baron just didn't get it. "I ain't never tell you to hide." He rubbed his head as if stressed from the day's events. "I'm only gonna say this one more time. Gillian is taking over. Frankie will help her. You'll lay low until I tell you otherwise."

Silence filled the room, and Frankie fidgeted slightly, feeling awkward.

Baron shook his head, shrugged his one good shoulder, and walked out of the room. Frankie didn't know how to feel. But one feeling was unquestioned: relief. At least now he wouldn't have to be the one to break it to Baron that his reign at the top of the Nobles family was over.

Baron sat in his huge living room in the dark, drinking straight from a bottle of Veuve Cliquot. He was already drunk, but still he swigged the chilled contents in an effort to numb both his physical and mental pain. He couldn't believe that his father had so easily stripped him of his position. And he was resentful that Gillian had been chosen as his successor. He genuinely loved his sister, but couldn't help feeling passed over. Frankie, too, was being given the keys to the kingdom, and Baron was expected to stand idly by and let that happen.

As he sat there, he replayed the events that led up to the shooting. Six hours had passed since it all happened, and Trina hadn't called him once. He concluded that Gillian was right. Obviously, Trina was involved and had set him up to be shot. He recalled that she had told him to go down an unfamiliar street, claiming that it was a shortcut. And he thought about how she'd escaped from the car, seemingly unfazed by the fact that she was exiting right where the shooters were standing. Now he felt stupid for having fallen for such a clear setup.

Baron hated being made a fool of. And the shooting had

cost him his spot in the family. He wasn't going to take this lying down. Staggering to his feet, he grabbed his car keys off the coffee table and headed for Brooklyn once again. This time, he wasn't going alone.

It was three o'clock in the morning and it had been hours since Jojo's crew had ambushed Baron. Jojo was restless because the ambush had been botched. Baron had gotten away and shaken the men pursuing him. Now Jojo had no idea whether Baron had survived the attempt on his life. He lay awake, wondering if his enemy had even been hit.

Jojo knew that Baron was behind the disappearance of his younger brother, Dusty. He had known the Nobles family for years, and had even done business with them from time to time. But Jojo's main hustle wasn't drugs. He ran a gambling ring that held high-stakes card games as well as a loan-sharking business that brought in the bulk of his cash. And it had been a big surprise to him when Baron had come to him months ago for a loan. Despite the fact that Baron had participated in several of Jojo's card games and lost a great deal of money at times, Jojo never expected that things had gotten so bad for Baron that he would come to him for help. Apparently, Baron had been taking out large sums of money from the coffers of the Nobles family businesses and needed to put it back before anyone got wind of it. Jojo had looked out for him and loaned him fifty-five grand, with the promise that it would be repaid within a week or two. But that hadn't happened.

Instead, Baron had avoided him and continued to spend money around town as if he wasn't indebted at all to Jojo. It was blatantly disrespectful, and both Jojo and Dusty were furious. When Baron and Dusty ran into each other in a club a few weeks ago, Dusty had approached Baron and confronted him about the money that he owed. Rather than being apologetic or even humble, Baron had cracked a bottle over Dusty's head, and then a fight had broken out between Baron's crew and Dusty's. When Dusty disappeared days later, there was not a doubt in Jojo's mind that Baron was behind it.

Jojo lay there, wide awake, with a million thoughts running through his head. No matter how frustrating it was, Jojo wouldn't rest until Baron came up missing as well.

"**911, what is** your emergency?"

"I think that someone is trying to break into my apartment," Trina whispered into her telephone. It was the middle of the night and she had just recently drifted off to sleep, only to be awakened by the sound of movement outside her front door.

"Ma'am, what is your address?"

Trina kept her eye on her front door as she recited her address to the 911 operator. "I can hear them outside," she said. "Please hurry up!"

"Okay, keep the door locked and stay on the phone with me. We're sending a unit over to—"

The operator was interrupted by the sound of breaking glass as the intruder shattered the glass panel on the front door. Trina's screams drowned out the operator's words as she called out, "Ma'am . . . ma'am!"

"*Help me!*" Trina screamed as the camouflage-clad intruders pounced on her, slapping and punching her in her lovely face. One of the goons gun-butted her in the head and knocked her unconscious. They dragged her limp body out to a waiting stolen car and drove off into the night with her bound in the backseat.

Hours passed before she came to. She awoke to find herself seated in an uncomfortable chair, her hands bound behind her naked body and her feet tied to the chair with heavy ropes. Her whole body ached, and she knew immediately that these bastards had raped her. Her vagina and ass were painfully sore, and she could feel the wetness between her legs and smell the musky scent of the unfamiliar men all over her. Trina began to cry, realizing that this was no fucking game. She foggily recalled them taking turns with her as she faded in and out of consciousness, and she momentarily squeezed her eyes shut to block out the memory and the pain she was feeling in her pounding head. She could see her captors leering at her from behind ski masks. She was still in a fog, and her head was throbbing from being knocked senseless. But she was able to make out the fact that she was in what seemed to be a cheap and seedy motel room, though she had no idea if she was still in Brooklyn, or even in New York at all, for that matter. Sunlight peeked through the musty old curtains hanging over the windows, and she knew that she had been unconscious for some time. Trina counted five men in the room, four dressed in camouflage gear and ski masks and one dressed in black with his arm in a sling. When the odd one out turned around to face her, she moaned in horror. It was Baron.

He smiled at her and moved toward her. "Tsk, tsk, tsk," he teased. "Trina, baby. What happened? I thought you were on my side."

She screamed at the top of her lungs, hoping that someone in a neighboring room would hear her and rescue her from what she now believed was a sure death. She had set Baron up and now the tables were turned. The goon closest to her slapped her so hard that her teeth clicked and she bit her tongue, wincing in pain. She stopped screaming, but it didn't matter. Another of the mysterious goons taped her mouth shut with duct tape and then pulled her head back by her hair so that she was peering into Baron's menacing face. Baron stood before her, wearing a sinister sneer.

"So," Baron said, looming over her. "You set me up, huh?"

She shook her head vehemently and tried to wriggle free of the ropes that tied her hands and feet. She had to figure a way out or she was certain she would be killed. She kept shaking her head no, pleading with her eyes for mercy. She tried to say something, but the tape prevented her from making any sense.

Baron stepped back slightly and looked at her. Her toes were freshly polished. Her smooth yellow skin was silky and supple, and his gaze traveled upward to her perfectly groomed bush. She was a lovely girl with some good pussy. It was a shame that she had to be dealt with so harshly. He shook his head slowly and then reached forward and squeezed one of her nipples, lightly at first and then with increasing pressure until she was whimpering in pain.

"Aww," he said, releasing his grip at last. "I thought you liked it rough." His goons laughed and gawked at the sight of Baron's naked jump-off. Trina was a sexy woman, and they had all taken turns using her voluptuous body.

Baron pulled a chair up and sat close to her. He pulled out his Glock and looked at her seriously. "I'm going to take the tape off and I don't want you to scream. Okay?"

She nodded quickly.

"If you do, I'm gonna shoot you in that pretty face of yours. Understand?"

Again she nodded.

"Good girl," he said. He peeled the tape off slowly and kept the gun trained on her the whole time. "Now," he said, sitting back in his chair and resting the gun on his thigh. "Who put you up to it?"

Trina looked at Baron, then at the four other men in the room. All eyes were on her. She shook her head, deciding to try to convince Baron that she had been a victim just like him. "I didn't set you up, Baron."

He cocked his gun and stood up as if that was not the answer he was looking for. Trina panicked and began to cry. "Okay, okay!" She was hysterical, and Baron sat back down and looked at her.

"Who set me up?"

She knew that it didn't matter at this point. If she lied, he was going to kill her. If she told the truth, he might still do that. But she figured the smartest move would be to take her chances that he might have mercy on her if she leveled with him. In a voice barely above a whisper, she answered, "Jojo."

Baron nodded. "That's what I thought." He sat back and looked at her again. "You been fucking him, too?"

"No!" She knew that he didn't want to know the answer to that question. If she admitted that she had been sleeping with Jojo for as long as she'd been involved with Baron, he would definitely flip out. Trina was money hungry. And while Baron was generous, Jojo was a lot more forthcoming with both money and time. He paid more attention to Trina than Baron ever had, so she had begun to fall for Jojo. When he confided in her about the disappearance of his brother, she had lost a lot of respect for Baron. Dusty was like family to her, since she'd gone to school with him and had practically grown up side by side with him. Hearing that Baron was behind his disappearance was enough for her to offer to help Jojo set him up—for a small fee, of course. But things hadn't gone as planned. She hadn't gotten paid, Baron hadn't gotten killed, and now she was bound to a chair, naked before a room full of masked men like a sheep among wolves.

Baron looked like he didn't believe her. He shrugged his shoulders and sat forward in his seat. Then he reached in his pocket, and when he pulled his hand out, Trina flinched, expecting the worst. Instead, he handed her her own cell phone, which they had taken from her house. "Call him," he demanded.

"I don't know his num—"

Baron punched her in the mouth, and she tasted blood immediately. She could tell that he had knocked her tooth loose, and she cried out in pain.

"Shut the fuck up!" one of the goons roared. "Call that muthafucka."

Trina felt like pointing out to these idiots that her hands were tied and she couldn't dial Jojo's number if she wanted to. As if reading her mind, Baron smirked. "What's the number?"

Reluctantly, Trina recited it. Baron dialed it and activated the speaker phone.

Jojo answered on the third ring. "Wassup, Trina?"

"Jojo!" she cried out.

Before he could answer her, Baron let off a shot and the bullet whizzed past her head. Trina was crying hard now, begging for her life, and Jojo was listening to it all unfolding.

"Trina!" he yelled into the phone. "What the fuck?"

Baron laughed. "Okay, nigga, I got this bitch and she told me that you set me up. So now, how should I handle this?"

Jojo frowned, realizing that it was Baron on the phone and that he had Trina. "Fuck you," he said.

"Fuck me, huh?" Baron laughed, as did his boys in the room. "Nah, son. Fuck you. Next time, send some real killers after me. That shit yesterday was sloppy. Now I gotta bury this bitch next to your bitch-ass brother." Baron pointed his gun at Trina's head and looked into her eyes.

"No, Baron! *Pleeeease!!* No!" she cried. "I'm sorry!"

Boom! Boom! Boom!

The line went dead and Jojo tossed his phone across the room in a fury. He was upset about Trina. But what shook him to his core was the fact that Baron had admitted killing Dusty. Suspicions were one thing. But as far as Jojo was concerned, Baron's admission that he had killed his brother would be his death sentence. Baron was a dead man.

The Beginning of the End

Deep Inside

November 15, 2007

Baron stepped out of his house and looked around cautiously. He unlocked his Range Rover and got inside, careful to check his backseat for enemies creeping. Once he was certain that the coast was clear, he got behind the wheel and started it up. As he backed out of his driveway, he felt his phone vibrate in his jacket pocket. Once he pulled out onto the main highway, he glanced at his phone and saw a missed call from his sister.

He dialed her back and activated his Bluetooth. She didn't take long to answer.

"Hey, Baron," she said. "You're coming to Thanksgiving at Daddy's house next week, right?" His ongoing problems with Jojo made it necessary for Baron to stay close to home, where he was safe amid the calm and quiet of his Kearny, New Jersey, estate. But she hoped that he still intended to come to Thanksgiving dinner as he always had.

He sighed. "Nah, not this year. I'm going down to Charlotte to spend Thanksgiving with my moms." The last thing he wanted to do was to spend the holiday at the family home, where he would be the black sheep on display for everyone to judge. He was aware that the streets were abuzz with news of Trina's disappearance. Her frantic 911 call had been played on nightly newscasts for weeks, with authorities unable to figure out who had brutally kidnapped Trina Samuels. Her family had plastered pictures of her throughout Brooklyn, and all the local newspapers covered the story as well. Sometimes, for kicks, Baron would read the nonstop coverage of the case. The whole situation was amusing to him. All that Trina had ever been good for was sex, and the media was acting as if one of the community's stars had fallen. None of the news fazed him. They would never catch him. Baron was two steps ahead of all of them—at least in his own mind.

The problem was that his father didn't see it that way. Nobles, Frankie, Gillian—everyone in their crew—believed that Baron was behind Trina's disappearance. They knew that he suspected her of setting him up, and they all assumed that Baron had done it. Despite these suspicions, though, the goons who assisted him in the kidnapping and murder of the young lady knew better than to cross him. They kept their mouths shut and feigned ignorance of Baron's deeds. He was bitter about everything. It seemed to Baron that all the years that he had spent keeping the businesses running, of making sure that nothing came back to incriminate them for any major crimes, meant nothing. Baron felt that his father had made up his mind that he was a failure.

Gillian frowned. "When did you decide to go down there?" The family tradition had always been for Baron and Gillian to spend Thanksgiving and Christmas at their father's home. Baron's mom usually came up for the holidays and stayed with her son at the house she had raised him in. Celia would arrive right before Thanksgiving and stay until a few days after Christmas before returning to her home in North Carolina. It had been that way for many years, so Gillian knew that Baron was leaving town on purpose this year in order to avoid their father.

"I just decided it. I'm on my way to the airport now." He pulled the sun visor down to block out the blinding rays. "I'm gonna stay down there until after Christmas."

Gillian suddenly had a headache. "That's gonna break Daddy's heart, Baron."

Baron sucked his teeth. "Please, Gillian. As long as you're there and Frankie's there, he'll be all right."

"That's bullshit!"

"Listen, you're the one who was agreeing with Pops that I should lay low. What's lower than down South?" Baron wasn't dealing well with the notion of Gillian being on top. He seldom visited his father at the Westchester estate anymore. A line had been drawn in the family and Baron felt like no one was on his side. Frankie and Gillian stopped by often in order to seek his advice on things. They wanted Baron to know that he was still included despite his absence from the family's day-to-day dealings. Baron reluctantly cooperated, but Frankie and Gillian both suspected that he was feeling slighted after the way things were handled by his father.

Gillian was torn between being happy that her brother was keeping a low profile and being angry that he was ostracizing himself from the rest of the family. It seemed that since the fateful night in Brooklyn, Baron had kept himself isolated, opting to sit at home and wallow in self-pity most of the time. "Did you even tell Daddy that you're leaving?" she asked.

"Nope," Baron answered. "You can do the honors."

"Wow." Gillian shook her head in frustration, holding the phone but not knowing what to say.

Baron was done talking. "I'll call you when I get back." He hung up his phone and tossed it in the seat beside him. He felt a momentary twinge of guilt. This would be the first holiday season that he didn't spend with Pops. He shrugged the feeling off and decided that it was time for a change. Time to do what he needed to do for himself, since as far as he was concerned, himself was all he had.

Frankie whipped his Escalade through the streets of Jamaica, Queens, with Gillian riding shotgun. He was still getting used to the idea of her being his equal in the game. He wasn't sure if he was feeling it, but he had to admit that it felt good to have her around so much. Even though they worked together a lot over the years, her new position increased their time together significantly.

They stopped at a red light and Frankie looked at Gillian. He thought she was the most beautiful woman he had ever laid eyes on. He reached over and smoothed a stray piece of hair out of her face, tucking it behind her ear. Gillian looked at him and smiled shyly. She knew that he had overheard her conversation with her brother. He could tell that she was stressed out, and wished that he could take all her stress away. He hated seeing her like this.

"He's not coming, huh?"

She shook her head. "He's going to Charlotte to spend the holidays with his mother."

Frankie nodded. "That might not be such a bad thing. It keeps him out of trouble, at least for a little while."

She nodded. "I know. But this is just a bad situation all around, Frankie."

"What you mean?" He glanced at her.

"If I would have known that me taking over would cost me my brother and cost my father his son, I wouldn't have done it."

"That's not how it is, Gigi."

"Sure it is. I know Baron."

Frankie didn't know how to respond to her. Truthfully, he knew that Baron was upset about the way things had changed. Frankie just didn't want Gillian blaming herself for her brother's selfishness.

After several silent moments, she reached forward and turned the volume up on the radio. She couldn't help noticing the song that was playing: "teachme" by Musiq. She listened to the lyrics. *"Show me the way to surrender my heart."* She couldn't help feeling like that's what Frankie was doing for her. Even though they weren't more than friends, she felt things for Frankie that she had never felt for any man. With the few guys Gillian had gotten involved with, she had always kept things in perspective and had never been the kind of woman to sweat someone. Instead, she was the one who held all the cards, and she liked it that way.

Gillian had always been with a man who was legit—a fellow student at Columbia, a contractor who worked on her mother's restaurant, and now a stockbroker. None of them had dabbled in the illegal activities that had made her family rich. They knew about the Nobles legacy, but never asked too many questions or in any way interfered in the politics of the business. With Frankie, she felt comfortable being her whole self. She didn't have to watch what she said or keep any secrets. He made her feel protected, understood—and even loved. Only a fool could miss the unmistakable chemistry between her and Frankie. Lately, she wondered where it was going. But deep down she knew that she had already fallen.

Frankie knew that he was playing himself. He was married, and Camille hadn't done anything specific to turn him off. Still, he found himself making excuses for the time he spent with Gillian even though he knew that it was excessive.

They pulled up on a residential street lined with neat brick homes. Frankie expertly parallel parked and they headed toward a house surrounded by a small black wrought-iron fence. Together they climbed the stairs and rang the bell.

A young girl who appeared to be about nineteen or twenty years old came to the door. She had on a tiny T-shirt and sweatpants that hung tight on her wide hips, exposing a small portion of her midriff. She had an ass so big that Gillian noticed it from the front. She was short and stacked, with big brown eyes and a smile that lit up the foyer as she ushered them inside.

"Hello, Frankie," she almost sang. "Come on in."

Frankie and Gillian followed her inside.

"My name is Angelle," she said, extending her hand to Gillian. "You must be Baron's sister."

Gillian nodded. "Yes. Nice to meet you. I'm Gillian."

Angelle smiled. "Come on in," she sang again. She offered to take their coats, but Frankie and Gillian declined. Neither of them expected this to take very long.

Gillian noticed that Angelle wore a chunky iced-out bracelet on her right arm, and it was gorgeous. Looking around, she also noted the huge flat-screen TV and the Bose stereo system. Seemed like her job as a medical receptionist had proven very lucrative. Gillian also observed the familiar way in which Angelle lightly touched Frankie as she laughed at his jokes. She wondered what the story was behind the pretty young lady smiling so brightly across from her.

Angelle sat with one leg tucked beneath her on the sofa. She looked at Frankie and toyed with her bracelet. "So, Baron told me that things are changing," she said. She turned her attention to Gillian. "You're coming in the game on some Queen Pen–style shit, huh?"

Gillian simply smiled.

"Shit must be going real good in your life, girl," Angelle pressed. "Hanging out with sexy Frankie all day *and* making money? That's a win/win."

Gillian's jaw tensed and Frankie noticed. He decided to try and break the ice a little. "Seems like shit is good for you, too, ma. I saw you at the party last week looking like Beyoncé." Angelle was a girl he and Baron had known for years. Just a typical round-the-way girl from the projects in Brooklyn where Frankie grew up, she had graduated high school, unlike the rest of them. Angelle went on to land one job after another, while managing to keep hustling the way she'd learned in the streets of Brooklyn. She always had a hookup or a get-money scheme, and she often shared these with Frankie and Baron. In return, they hit her off with money, and, as an added perk, Baron hit it every now and then. She wasn't wifey material, but Frankie and Baron both still admired her go-getter mentality.

Angelle lit up at the compliment. "Well, I try to keep it sexy," she purred. Angelle had always thought that Frankie was fine, but since she'd met and started screwing Baron first, she never had the chance to sample his friend. Turning her attention to Gillian, she said, "I've seen you before, with Frankie. But we were never introduced."

Gillian nodded. Angelle didn't look familiar, though.

She looked like just another one of the girls who hung on Frankie's and Baron's every word, trying to be the next wifey.

"So let's go over what you wanted to talk to us about," Gillian said, getting to the point of their visit. "Baron said that you wanted to make some changes of your own."

Angelle nodded. "I've been working at Dr. Tatum's office for close to two years now. I'm taking a risk forging so many prescriptions, 'cuz if I get caught I could get in mad trouble."

Gillian stared at her blankly. "How would they find out? You've been doing this for a while now, and nothing has gone wrong. So what's the problem?"

Angelle batted her long eyelashes. "My point is that I'm taking a big risk. And for what I'm getting out of it, it's not worth that risk for me anymore." She shrugged.

"So you want more money?" Gillian asked.

Angelle looked at Gillian questioningly. "Who *doesn't* want more money?"

Angelle and Frankie laughed. Gillian didn't.

"But besides that, there's so many people popping pills these days that there's no reason why we can't keep getting money. Shit, everything from the foundation to the roof of this place was made possible by the business I do with your family."

Frankie smiled. "That's a two-way street. Having you work with us has made a lot of things possible. Word. We definitely wanna keep doing what we been doing. How much more money you need?"

Gillian noticed that Frankie seemed enamored of Angelle. He looked at her sidelong with a half smirk on his face. Gillian hated seeing him look at another woman that way. It seemed too familiar, and she could tell purely from their body language that they were close. She couldn't understand why Frankie was so quick to start talking money when this chick wasn't even giving them any reason to entertain that request.

"I just want to be able to do what I can to help my family out. You know my brother is locked up and all that." Angelle touched Frankie's leg again.

Gillian cleared her throat. She tried not to show how uncomfortable and pissed off she was. She was supposed to be able to keep her emotions in check. "We all have problems."

Frankie saw the look on Gillian's face and could tell that she wasn't feeling Angelle. But he didn't want to get involved in the cattiness of females. What he was focused on was maintaining the lucrative connection he had without it cutting into his profit too greatly. He knew that everything came down to money with Angelle. The more she could get, the more cooperative she became. "Keep going," he urged.

"I was telling Baron that I wanna step it up a notch."

Frankie had to resist the urge to laugh, since he suspected that she hadn't been explaining anything between thrusts and moans other than how good it felt. As "brothers," they discussed their more memorable trysts, and Baron had told Frankie about how wild the sex was with this one.

Angelle continued. "The doctor's brother-in-law owns the pharmaceutical-supply company that he does business with. The man is disgusting—pale, old, still trying to act young. But he likes me. Every time I see him, he says something fresh or asks me out. I can get shit straight from him, probably. But I'd have to fuck him. And that's gonna cost you."

Frankie laughed, but Gillian was disgusted by this slut

sitting next to him. She felt so uneasy. Gillian had no respect for women who loosely slept around with men just for money or personal gain. She had been raised to understand the meaning of being a woman, and the virtues of being a lady. So this part of the business was new to her—dealing with women like Angelle who didn't care about selling their bodies or their souls for material things.

"If you want to talk figures, I'm listening," Angelle said. She rubbed her hands together in anticipation. Frankie sat forward in his seat.

Gillian cleared her throat. It seemed to her that her brother's and Frankie's familiarity with Angelle was clouding their better judgment. In her opinion, they shouldn't even be entertaining this conversation at all. "We shouldn't talk figures until you make sure you can get the product directly from the brother-in-law. Just because he wants to hit it, doesn't mean he's willing to risk going to jail to do that."

"He'll do it." Angelle seemed surer now.

"Then go for it. If you feel like using sex to get it, go for it. But that's your investment. Not ours. There's no bonus for giving up ass. That's just part of *your* hustle."

Gillian heard Angelle suck her teeth softly, but she ignored it. "By dealing with him one on one, you should be able to increase everything that you're supplying us with. If he'll do it, come back to us with figures. That's when we'll talk numbers. Not the other way around." Gillian rose to leave and Frankie followed suit. She extended her hand limply to Angelle, and smiled. "It was nice to meet you, Angelle. I'll follow up with you in a few days."

Angelle's smile was vague, her attitude clearly conveyed despite it. "Great."

As they left, Frankie looked at Gillian questioningly. It was obvious that the two women didn't like each other. And Gillian had ended the meeting so abruptly that he was completely confused. Frankie got into the Escalade and looked at her again.

"You shut her down," he observed. "What was that all about?"

She smirked. "I just want to keep it professional. I can see that she's your friend. But I'm not gonna let her rape us just because she's cool with you."

Frankie was caught off guard. If he didn't know better, he'd have thought Gillian sounded jealous. "Ain't nobody raping me."

Gillian shot him a look that warned him to tread carefully.

Frankie smiled. "I feel you," he said. "But before you jump in with your eyes closed, you should get the background on the situation."

Gillian grinned. "You're right. Why don't you fill me in?" She folded her arms across her chest and leaned back.

"Angelle is a chick who always gets money. She gets down like the big boys. Always has. You could learn a lot from her."

Gillian frowned. "You think I could learn a lot from a chick who would fuck a man she has no attraction to for money? That's what I should aspire to?"

Frankie shook his head. "You know that's not what I'm saying. She didn't even mean that shit," he said, waving his hand dismissively. "Angelle is cool."

She shook her head. "I'm not concerned about how cool she is. This is about getting money, right?"

"Yeah, it is." Frankie nodded. "But part of getting money is knowing how to deal with people and keep them on your team."

Gillian sucked her teeth. "So that's why you flirt with her? To keep her on the team?"

Frankie wanted to laugh, but didn't. He could see now why she had such a nasty attitude toward poor Angelle. She was definitely jealous. He shrugged his shoulders, not sure what he should say. "You call it flirting. But I'm just being nice to that girl."

Gillian looked away. "I'll deal with her directly from now on so that you and my brother don't keep getting business and pleasure confused."

Frankie smirked as Gillian folded her arms across her chest like a spoiled brat. He started the car and pulled off, looking at her out of the corner of his eyes. "You're so pretty when you pout."

Gillian fought unsuccessfully to suppress a smile. "Flattery will get you nowhere."

Blinded

Dominique sat at the table in the prison visiting room, anxiously waiting for Jamel to walk in. She could hardly wait to see him again! It had been three whole weeks since the last time she'd made the seven-hour bus trip from Manhattan to upstate New York, and Dominique was practically bubbling over with anticipation.

She glanced around the room at all the women and children who, like Dominique, had made the long trek from their homes in the middle of the night to arrive at the facility in order to be searched and barked at first thing in the morning. The visitors were frowned at, were spoken down to, and had their clothing examined to determine whether or not their wardrobe violated any of the prison's rules. The corrections officers were rude and condescending, which made the whole experience even more demeaning for the visitors. All of this, just to enjoy the privilege of sitting across a table from the men they loved, while under the watchful eye of corrections officers who could decide to terminate the visit at any time.

Her mind wandered back to the conversation she had

had the evening before with her father. She had dropped
Octavia off at her grandfather's apartment. Bill Storms had
asked his daughter why she was wasting her time on a con-
victed felon who never finished high school and had no
hopes of ever making as much money as she did.

"Here you go traveling all them hours upstate to visit
some thug doing time."

"Daddy . . ."

"You're a smart girl, Mimi. Intelligent, got a good job,
nice home, money in the bank. Lucky for you, you look just
like your daddy, so you're pretty."

Dominique had laughed at that. Bill Storms knew he
was a good-looking man.

"Seriously, you got a lot going for yourself. People in the
entertainment industry know your name. They respect
and admire you. And even with all that, you insist on being
with a hoodlum like Jamel. He ain't got no job . . . probably
never had one. What kind of contribution can he make to
your lifestyle?"

"It's not all about money, Daddy," Dominique had
explained. "I'm not one of those women who dates a guy
based on his net worth or the title he holds at his job. If I
like a man and he treats me right, makes me laugh and gives
me good conversation . . . I'm fine with that. Financially, I
can take care of me. I don't need a man to do it."

Her father had nodded. "I think that's good, Mimi. But,
damn. Date somebody with some potential. You work
around all those producers, music execs, and . . . professional
men. Why waste your time with a damn drug dealer?" Bill
had laughed as if the thought of it was absurd to him.

Dominique understood how her father felt. And what he
was saying was absolutely right. But what he (and everyone

else, for that matter) failed to realize was that she was in love with Jamel. There was history between them that few could understand. They knew each other well, and their conversations were great. What Jamel lacked in credentials he made up for in chemistry. And that was enough for her.

As two little boys who couldn't have been older than seven or eight years old began chasing each other around the visiting room, one red-faced, scowling officer yelled, "Please keep your Future Felons of America under control! There is no running in here. Make them sit down or your visit will be over before it starts."

Dominique, as well as several other visitors, was absolutely outraged by the officer's remarks. "Did he just say 'Future Felons of America'?" she asked a woman at the table next to her.

The woman nodded. "They say whatever they want because they get away with it. They see all of us as one big pit of niggers. It's as simple as that."

Dumbfounded, Dominique watched as the boys' young mother told them to sit down and be quiet until their daddy came out. Finally, the inmates began to enter the room one by one. Each one walked over to the corrections officers' desk first, where they were instructed to stay on the opposite side of the table from their visitor and to refrain from excessive touching or kissing. The inmates then proceeded to their assigned tables, where each one was greeted with hugs and smiles from the visitors who waited for them.

Dominique sat waiting patiently for Jamel to come out. Each time the door swung open, she hoped that he would be the young black man in green prison garb who emerged. But so far, each prisoner who entered was headed for another table. Finally, she watched as the door opened and Jamel stepped confidently into the room. He walked so gracefully and with such pride that it commanded attention. Dominique caught a couple other girls watching Jamel as well, and it only made her prouder that he was headed her way.

She stood to greet him and kissed him deeply. The kiss was shorter than she wanted it to be, since the COs had their eyes on them. They sat at opposite sides of the table and held hands as they stared at each other, smiling.

"Hey, you!" Dominique was ecstatic to be here with her boo. She missed him like crazy.

Jamel thought she looked so pretty. She had gotten her hair done, and she looked nice. She couldn't stop smiling at him. Her skin seemed to glow with happiness, and he was honored that a woman of her caliber was this visibly excited to see him.

"Wassup, baby girl? You look good."

Jamel smiled, and his deep dimples made Dominique's heart race. To her, Jamel was so sexy. As she talked to him about her trip up north and about all the new developments in her life since they'd last spoken on the telephone (the night before), she couldn't help longing for the day when she wouldn't need to sit on a prison bus to come and see him. She wanted to wake up beside him each morning, to fall asleep in his arms each night, and to spend all the time in between in his presence. She was so in love with Jamel.

They talked about everything from the times they spent together before he'd come to jail to the times they planned to spend together when he came home. As the conversation switched from what they'd done in their past to their plans for the future, Dominique couldn't hide the troubled expression on her face.

"What's the matter?" Jamel asked her.

She looked around the room at all the families there. Some were baby mamas bringing a bunch of little kids to see their fathers. Some were mothers and grandmothers coming to see their sons. Some, like Dominique, were ride-or-die chicks standing by their men. But they all had one thing in common: They shared the misery and degradation that the penal system put their loved ones through, and they all wanted it to be over. Dominique was sick of leaving her beautiful home in the middle of the night only to travel for hours to reach this dungeon. She was sick of having to defend her relationship against the naysayers. And, truthfully, she was sick of missing Jamel. All her friends had the warmth of a man to snuggle up to in the coming winter months, while the man she loved was locked behind gates, walls, and barbed wire.

Dominique finally shrugged. "It gets harder and harder to come up here," she said. "Seeing these cops treat these women and kids like this. One of those bastards called those two little boys over there 'Future Felons of America' before you came out. They're so disrespectful and so rude to everybody." She shook her head as she thought about the indignities she'd seen many visitors suffer over the years since Jamel had gone to prison. "When you get out of here, Jamel, you have to swear that you'll never come back. I don't want to be bringing our kids up here to visit you, having to deal with some asshole talking to them crazy or looking down on them."

Jamel nodded. He understood how she felt; he also suffered indignities at the hands of the modern-day overseers. "I promise," he said. "I'm never coming back here."

Dominique nodded, feeling somewhat reassured. There was another issue pressing her, and she cleared her throat and finally brought it up. "Did your son's mother come up here to see you?"

Jamel looked caught off guard by the question, but tried to recover quickly. He debated whether or not to lie about it, but then figured that he may as well tell the truth. After all, if she was asking she must already know something. "Yeah," he said. "Shonda came up here and brought my son to see me."

Dominique watched him sit back in his chair and stroke his chin, his eyes shifting from her to the little girl at the table next to them. His sudden interest in the toddler only confirmed for Dominique that he was uneasy with the direction of the conversation. She pressed further.

"When?"

"Last month, I think it was." He licked his lips as if they were suddenly dry.

"You *think* it was last month?" It was a rhetorical question. Dominique didn't really expect an answer, so she wasn't surprised when she got none. "Why didn't you tell me?"

" 'Cuz I thought you'd be upset like you are now. That's why."

Dominique smirked. She had to hand it to him. He was crafty when it came to shifting blame. "Why would I be upset that you had a visit with your son? What would upset me about that?"

Jamel shrugged. "All I know is you got the same look in your eye as the prosecutor in the courtroom. I feel like I'm being interrogated, cross-examined or whatever. It's not like I lied to you. I just didn't mention it 'cuz I didn't want to bring no drama between us. I get enough of that from Shonda."

She said nothing for several moments. "What did you and Shonda talk about?" she asked.

Jamel shrugged again. "We didn't really talk much. I was just chilling with little Anthony the whole time."

Dominique had to resist the urge to laugh. "Anthony is six years old. What did you talk to him about for five hours?"

"See what I'm saying?" Jamel gestured with his hands. "Interrogation."

Dominique was done listening to him. Her mind had already begun to imagine what Jamel and his baby mama had discussed during their secret visit. She could only assume that there was more going on between Jamel and Shonda than he was willing to admit.

"So now you're gonna sit there quietly?"

She looked at him and his handsome, rugged features and loved and hated him simultaneously. "What can I say?"

He smiled coyly. "You can say that you love me."

This time, she was the one who shrugged. "You already know that," she said. Choosing to drop the subject, she walked to the vending machine and got a pack of donuts for herself and a bag of Dipsy Doodles for Jamel. She understood that there was history and possibly even love between him and Shonda. But she was determined to keep him focused on their future together, and in order to do that he had to let Shonda go. Dominique wondered what she could do to help ensure that happened.

She returned to the table and sat across from Jamel. She watched him sizing her up and was confident that she was the flyest chick in the room. She hoped he knew how lucky he was to have her. Deciding not to ruin the visit by dwelling on the situation with Shonda, Dominique allowed Jamel to change the subject. For the remainder of the day, they held hands, kissed, talked, and laughed, and before they knew it, the time had sped by. As the CO happily announced that the visits were over, Dominique and Jamel stood together and embraced strongly. He was going to miss her, but part of him was relieved to see her go. Even though she had dropped the subject, Dominique knew about Shonda's visit. How had she found out and what else did she know? he wondered.

She walked toward the exit along with all the other visitors, casting a longing glance over her shoulder at Jamel as she left. Once back on the bus, she leaned her head against the window, feeling emotionally drained. This part of visiting Jamel was by far the worst—leaving him. Especially when there were unresolved issues between them. She had mixed emotions, on one hand feeling elated that she'd spent an entire afternoon with the man she loved, but on the other hand feeling distraught that she was having to deal with Shonda being part of Jamel's life whether Dominique liked it or not. Finally, she drifted off to sleep, dreaming of the day when he would finally come home and be back in her arms where he belonged.

Octavia was nervous as hell. She lay beside Dashawn in the bedroom of his fifth-floor apartment that he shared with his brother. They were home alone, and Octavia had become quite familiar with this room, this apartment, and this boy she had been spending much of her time with in the past couple of months.

They had a ritual that had become the highlight of her week. Each Monday, Wednesday, and Friday, when she was supposed to be attending dance classes, Octavia instead spent the afternoon with Dashawn. His mother was seldom at home, and even when she was she didn't ask questions. As the mother of two boys, she didn't mind them having girls over. With that in mind, Octavia and Dashawn would go back to his apartment and spend time holed up in his room, kissing and touching and exploring each other's bodies. It made Octavia feel so grown up, so sexy and desired. They would carefully watch the clock to ensure that she left in time to make it to the dance studio, where she'd stand out front and wait for her mother to pick her up. With the demands of her job, the time she spent writing letters, sending packages, and talking on the phone to Jamel, and the Friday nights she spent with her girlfriends, Dominique hadn't even noticed that anything was different with her child.

Just the other night, Octavia had gone into her mother's bedroom and lay across her bed as she watched Dominique load up two boxes of food for Jamel. While Dominique struggled to fit a fourth box of coffee cakes into the care package, Octavia had propped herself up on the huge mound of pillows and asked a question.

"Ma, why do you do all of this for a guy like Jamel?"

Dominique had paused and looked at her daughter as if the question was unexpected. "What do you mean, 'a guy like Jamel'?" she asked.

Octavia had shrugged. "I don't know. The jail thing. He's a drug dealer, right?"

Dominique had set the box aside and sat on the foot of her bed, facing her daughter. "Well, Octavia," she began. "Everyone makes mistakes in their lives. Sometimes good people make bad decisions. I've known Jamel for a long time, so I know that he's a good person. He was living dangerously and it caught up with him. Now he's paying the price for the bad decisions he made. And once he's done paying his debt to society, I think he deserves a chance to get it right again."

Octavia had nodded, impressed by her mother's explanation. She liked how Dominique made it sound so simple. Octavia decided to apply the same philosophy to Dashawn. He had made some questionable decisions as well, like his recent choice to drop out of school. He hated school and felt that he had already learned enough to pass his GED. Octavia had been struggling over whether or not to dump him. Her mother and her grandfather had always told her not to waste her time with idiots who weren't going anywhere in life. But hearing Dominique express hope for Jamel's future had given Octavia reason to be optimistic about Dashawn's.

Today, Octavia and Dashawn had decided that it was time for her to lose her virginity. She was nervous but excited at the same time. She was about to go from being a little girl who was babied all the time to a young woman who was making adult decisions of her own. And no one or nothing could stop her.

As he kissed her, she tried to push the thought of the pain out of her mind. Her friends at school had told her that the first time was painful, and she was most nervous about that. But she wasn't about to turn back now. Dashawn climbed on top of her. She spread her legs, closed her eyes, and held her breath as he entered her.

Thankful

It was Thanksgiving Day and Camille had the dining room filled to capacity with food. Turkey, ham, greens, corn-bread stuffing, candied yams, macaroni and cheese, cranberry sauce, and assorted breads adorned the long mahogany table. Frankie sat at the head of the table flanked by Steven and Lily, Camille's mother. Misa, Shane, and Camille filled in the rest of the seats, and everyone bowed their heads as Lily said grace.

"Dear Lord, please bless this beautiful meal that is laid before us on this Thanksgiving Day. Bless the hands that prepared it with love and bless this family as a whole, O Lord. Father, we come to you with grateful hearts, thankful for the roof over our heads, the clothes on our backs, the cars that we drive, and the air that we breathe. We know that without you, none of this is possible. Thank you, Lord. We ask that you look down upon us and root out those things that are not pleasing in your sight. Replace those things with the fruits of the spirit and give us all a desire to seek a closer walk with you. These, and all things, we ask in Jesus' name. Amen."

"Amen," everyone chimed in. Misa and Camille exchanged knowing glances and suppressed their laughter as their mother helped Shane with his napkin. Each year, at Easter, Thanksgiving, and Christmas, Lily launched into a prayer worthy of an evangelist. But aside from these three days, she cursed, gossiped, smoked, and drank more than anyone. It was an inside joke between the two sisters that they had shared since they were kids growing up. As Frankie carved up the turkey, Camille sliced the ham, and everyone began to dig in to all the trimmings.

"This looks delicious, baby," Frankie complimented his wife. "It gets better every year."

Camille glowed from the compliment, and her smile lit up the room. "Just make sure that you all save room for dessert. Mama made a cheesecake, a German chocolate cake, *and* banana pudding!"

"Wow!" Steven said, excitedly rubbing his hands together. Camille had to resist the urge to roll her eyes. Instead, she reminded herself that this was Thanksgiving and Steven was part of the family. Regardless of the fact that he freeloaded all year long, on this day he got a pass.

Misa frowned. "How come you didn't announce my carrot cake, Camille? I was part of the culinary team, too, this year." Misa smiled at Frankie, Steven, and little Shane. "It is so moist and delicious, if I must say so myself. Make sure you try it."

"I didn't announce it because you didn't bake it—you bought it from Alfonso's!" Camille shook her head and chuckled. Misa considered stopping by her favorite bakery to be her contribution to the feast. She slyly gave Camille the finger without their mother noticing, and heaped some more macaroni and cheese onto her plate.

"Misa, next year we're gonna have Thanksgiving at your house," Frankie teased. "I want to see if you know your way around a kitchen."

She smiled. "Frankie, I can cook. Don't listen to Camille. My baby has survived for three years and he's growing tall and strong. Must be my good cooking."

Camille sucked her teeth. "Please. Shane is growing tall and strong because he eats dinner over here every night."

Frankie laughed because it was true. He saw more of the little rugrat than ever before now that Misa was divorced and living the single life. At times, Frankie was amazed that Shane even knew who his mother really was.

"Whatever," she said, loading a bunch of collard greens into her mouth and closing her eyes to relish the taste. "These greens are excellent!"

Now Lily beamed. "That's my old Mississippi recipe, honey. Don't nobody make greens like a Southern woman. I don't care what you city girls say."

Everyone ate, drank, and got so full that they were stuffed. Lily and Misa managed to find the strength to help Camille clear the table while Frankie and Steven retired to the living room to watch the football game. Shane went with them, although he knew nothing about the sport. Steven and Frankie had insisted that it was never too soon for him to learn about the game they both loved so much.

As they loaded the dishwasher and tidied up the kitchen, Misa looked at her sister sheepishly. "Hey, sis. Feel like watching your nephew tonight?" She flashed her most brilliant smile at Camille, in hopes that it would persuade her to do what Misa wanted.

Camille dropped the sponge into the sink and whipped around to glare at her sister. "No, Misa! Not today. It's

Thanksgiving, for God's sake! You act like the only reason
I get out of bed each day is so that I can drop off Shane, pick
up Shane, or babysit Shane. He's *your* son, Misa. Don't you
think he wants to see *you* sometimes? You think he might
want to play with his toys in his room at his house? Fall
asleep in his bed for once? Why would you leave your son
on a holiday to go run the streets?"

Misa frowned and put her hands on her hips. "Okay,
Camille. All you had to say was no. You don't have to question me as a parent. Just no, and that's it. I'll find somebody
else to watch him." She spun around and snatched a couple
dirty glasses off the counter, then loaded them into the dishwasher.

Camille shook her head in disbelief. "So that's your solution, Misa? Pawn Shane off on somebody else instead of
staying home with him?"

Misa looked up at the ceiling as if the Lord himself was
perched on it. She took a deep breath and then glared at her
sister. "First of all, it's one of the biggest party weekends of
the year, and I intend to go to at least a few of them. Just
because you like to sit around here playing Suzie Home-
maker doesn't mean that I want to do the same thing. Second
of all, I don't pawn my son off on anybody. Most people
enjoy Shane. He's a good kid. You act like he's a demon
child, Camille. Like I'm asking somebody to babysit Chucky
or Damien! He's quiet and well behaved, he has manners,
and he doesn't ask for much from you. So why are you making it sound like that?" She sucked her teeth, then bent over
and continued to load the dishwasher. Misa didn't see why
she was being criticized for wanting to go out and get her
mind off the fact that she still hadn't heard from Baron.

Camille was still shaking her head at her pitiful sister. "I never said that he was bad. That's not even the point. The point is that you can't seem to stay home and spend any quality time with your own kid, Misa. He's over here all the time. And when he's not here, he's with one of your girlfriends. I'm talking about you, not Shane. Why are you so selfish that you can't take time to spend with your own son?"

Misa stood up and stared her sister down. "Selfish?" she asked in amazement. "Selfish, Camille? I get up every single day and go to work. I get Shane up, get him dressed, pack his lunch, and bring him to school. Then I go to that office and I sit at that desk, answering phones and running around like a slave for eight hours. What do you do with your day? Do you have to punch a clock, Camille, or jump when some executive tells you to? You got a lot of nerve calling me selfish when all you ever have to worry about is yourself."

"You done lost your damn mind!" Camille said in wide-eyed amazement. "I'm selfish because I've been blessed enough to have this life I'm living? I'm selfish because my husband doesn't require me to work and because I don't have any kids of my own? Are you serious?" She cocked her head to the side, as if looking at Misa from a different angle might make her more understandable. "Misa, how about after you work those eight hours? Huh? What then? Do you rush home to pick up your son and spend time with him before he goes to bed? Do you read him a bedtime story and tuck him in and remind him to say his prayers? Or are you calling me and asking me to pick him up so that you can go run around town like a tramp?"

"I got your tramp!" Misa moved toward her sister, but finally their mother stepped between them. "Y'all oughta be ashamed of yourselves, arguing like this on Thanksgiving! Today is supposed to be a day when you reflect on all the blessings in your life—your family being one of the biggest blessings! Instead, you're in here at each other's throats."

Misa pointed at Camille. "All I asked is if she wanted to watch Shane tonight, and she went off to left field with it." Misa looked hurt, and she scowled at her sister. "It's nice to see how you really feel, though."

Lily looked at her baby girl and folded her arms across her chest. "Camille is right, Misa. You are never with Shane. Every time I call here, your son is here and you're nowhere to be found. You probably never stopped to think about it because you're having so much fun out there at all them parties and whatnot. But you better get back to parenting your son before he forgets that you're his mother. Pretty soon he's gonna start calling Camille 'Mama,' and then your feelings are gonna be hurt."

Misa could hardly believe her ears. Her mother was turning on her for no good reason. "Mama, I'm wrong to want to live my life? I'm supposed to just curl up in a ball and die because Louis left me to start over? That's supposed to be the end of my happiness?" Misa had tears falling from her eyes, but her facial expression conveyed anger rather than the hurt that was audible in her voice.

Lily shook her head. "No, no. Ain't nobody telling you to let life pass you by. Just because Louis doesn't have sense enough to spend time with Shane doesn't give you the right to neglect him, too."

"I do not neglect my son!"

"Yes, you do," Lily asserted. "You buy him designer clothes and expensive toys. And you make sure that he eats well and has a roof over his head. But there's more to being a mother than that. You have to put that time in, Misa. And running around from party to party ain't benefiting Shane."

Misa wiped her tears away angrily, and sniffled. "Well, I had no idea that you two think I'm such a bad mother." She looked at Camille. "And I had no idea that Shane was all in your way."

"Misa, I didn't say that." Camille felt guilty.

Misa held her hand up as if to quiet her sister. "It's all good. I won't ask you to watch him for me anymore. But all I was trying to do was find some happiness of my own for once." She looked at her mother then. "It just doesn't seem fair, you know? Louis walks off, pretends that he never got married or started a family, and he gets to just start over. He has a new woman in his life, he can go out and travel whenever he wants to, and he doesn't have a second thought about Shane. I try to carve out a little time for myself and I'm the worst mother in the world. I just think that's a double standard." Misa closed the dishwasher and wiped her hands on a nearby towel. She looked so sad as she reflected on the way in which Louis had abandoned her and Shane that it tugged at Camille's conscience.

"I'll keep Shane tonight, Misa. But you're gonna have to start spending more time with him. Seriously."

Frankie came into the kitchen just then and cleared his throat. "Excuse me, ladies. Sorry to interrupt." He looked at Camille. "I'm gonna step out for a little while, baby. I'll be back."

Camille frowned slightly. "Where are you going?"

"Over to Pops's house. Baron's out of town and I think Pops might feel bad about that. It's the first time he hasn't spent Thanksgiving with the rest of the family."

Camille was tempted to point out that *that* family

shouldn't be Frankie's concern. She wanted him to focus more on the family he had under his own roof. "I see," she said simply.

"I'm gonna jump in the shower real quick. I'll stop in to give you a kiss before I leave," he said. "Dinner was perfect!" And then he was gone.

Lily looked at both of her daughters and wondered where she'd gone wrong with them. One was so busy gallivanting around town that she was abandoning her three-year-old in the process. The other was so blinded that she couldn't see her husband slipping through her fingers.

"Misa, Shane can come home with me," she said. "He has all this time off from school and I don't have nothing to do. Might as well let him come and hang out with his grandma for the weekend. This way you can party tonight, tomorrow, and Saturday. Pick him up on Sunday and get that baby ready for school."

Misa smiled. "Thanks, Mama. I think Shane will like that." Misa couldn't imagine what she would do with herself with all those days to do as she pleased.

Lily turned her attention to Camille. "In the meantime, *you* better go with your husband over to them people's house. Every time I call you, Frankie is out with that woman. I know they're friends, but you better watch that. If it's all on the up and up, then there's no reason why you can't go with him." Lily handed Camille her sister's store-bought carrot cake. "Take this over there and keep the good eye on your husband."

Camille agreed reluctantly. She had hoped to spend the day in the comfort of her own home, surrounded by her own family. Dessert hadn't even been served yet and already Misa was headed out the door, her mother was heading back to Long Island with Shane, and now she was having to follow Frankie over to the Nobles' house in Westchester. This was not how she had envisioned spending Thanksgiving.

When Frankie came down from his shower, he looked and smelled better than ever. His hair was filled with perfect waves and he had trimmed his facial hair to perfection. He wore a black button up and a pair of dark jeans and black shoes. His Rolex gleamed on his wrist and his cologne wafted directly to Camille's nostrils. He saw her standing at the door with her mother and Shane, both of whom were bundled up in their coats and scarves.

"Why are you guys leaving so soon?" he asked, kissing her mother on the cheek as she bid him farewell.

"Well, Frankie, Shane is coming home with me for the weekend because Misa went to hang out. So this works out, because now you and Camille can spend the holiday together like a family is supposed to." Lily winked at her daughter. "I'll see you guys soon. Have a good time at the Nobles' house."

Frankie seemed caught off guard, but he managed a smile. Once Lily and Shane had gone, he looked at his wife. "You're coming with me?" he asked, surprised. Camille very rarely accompanied him to any of the Nobles family functions.

Camille nodded. "Yeah. I mean . . . if that's okay."

Frankie was thinking that it wasn't okay. He had been looking forward to spending the day with Gillian without having to watch what he said or did. Camille was throwing a monkey wrench in his plans.

"Yeah, that's cool," he lied. He saw no way out of it. He

grabbed his car keys off the table and they headed out the door.

Mayra rushed to answer the doorbell and realized how much she missed Greta. They had given their housekeeper the holiday weekend off, since she did have a family of her own, after all. But since it was Thanksgiving, the doorbell hadn't stopped ringing all day. She opened the door and smiled when she saw Frankie, looking more handsome than ever. Her smile waned a little when she saw that his wife was in tow. Camille had only been to their house a handful of times over the years, and Mayra often wondered if Camille thought that she was too good to come there. Seeing her now came as a big surprise—and a big disappointment. Mayra had always hoped that Frankie would end up with her daughter. She knew that Gillian didn't feel for her boyfriend the way that she felt about Frankie, and reasoned that if Frankie were single again, Gillian would end her relationship of convenience. If only Camille would disappear.

"Hello, Frankie!" Mayra kissed him on his cheek and took his coat. "Camille," she sang. "What a surprise!"

Camille smiled and stepped inside. "Happy Thanksgiving." She peeled out of her coat and handed it to her hostess.

Mayra managed to keep the smile frozen on her face as she ushered them into the house. Music was playing—a medley of seventies and eighties hits—and the volume increased as they got closer to the living room. Mayra turned around to face them with a smile on her face. "The whole crew is here, Frankie. Everybody showed up! They all ate at home with their own families and then came here. So it's a party. Help yourself to the food that's in the kitchen and

make yourself at home. You know how we do it every year."
It was true. Each year, there was a gathering of at least
twenty people. But as they entered the living room, Frankie
could see that today there was easily double that number in
attendance. Frankie smiled and began greeting each of the
familiar faces with a handshake or a hug. There were many
members of Nobles's organization there with their wives or
girlfriends. Frankie knew that all these people were there to
make up for Baron not being there. His heart was filled with
gratitude that they had so much love for the man.

Camille stood off to the side watching her husband work
the room, and she couldn't help thinking that this holiday
celebration was in very stark contrast to the one she'd
hosted at home. She noticed Nobles seated in his beloved
recliner with Mayra standing right by his side. Several other
couples peppered the area, and a few people were dancing in
the center of the huge room. She wondered if this festive
spirit was one of the reasons that Frankie opted to spend so
much time in the presence of this family instead of at home
building a family of their own. Finally, her eyes rested on
Gillian, who sat on the sofa like a queen perched on her
throne, staring directly at Camille.

Gillian was glaring at Camille, since for the life of her
she couldn't figure out why the hell Frankie had brought
this bourgeois bitch with him. She rolled her eyes and
looked away, then scowled at Frankie when he glanced her
way. The last thing she expected was to have Camille rain
on her parade. With Baron spending Thanksgiving in Charlotte, all Gillian had had to look forward to all day was the
moment Frankie arrived to keep her company. That moment was now clouded by Camille's presence.

Tremaine, one of Frankie's boys, came over to where

Camille was standing. He gave her a kiss on the cheek and a bright smile, a welcome sight since she was feeling so uncomfortable with Gillian eyeing her the way she was.

"Hey, Camille!" Tremaine was clearly tipsy already. "I can't believe you came. You never come to Thanksgiving over here."

Camille was already feeling awkward, and Tremaine reminding her that she was the odd one out only made her feel more discomfited. "Well, there's a first time for everything," she said.

"True, true." Tremaine nodded. "Here," he said, handing her a glass of Alizé. "You gotta drink while you're here. It's mandatory."

Camille took it and laughed. "Okay, no problem." Things were suddenly looking up. With Frankie away from home more often than ever, alcohol had been her only company besides her three-year-old nephew.

Tremaine gave her a thumbs-up and pointed to the bar. "There's more where that came from, so don't be shy." He left her standing alone again, and she watched him take part in the Soul Train line that had formed in the center of the room. She stood there, laughing and enjoying the spectacle, until her drink was drained. Looking at her empty glass and seeing Frankie seated beside Nobles laughing hard at some unknown joke, she decided to go and refill her drink, and strode over to the bar. By the time the Soul Train line was over, she had downed two more glasses of Alizé and was nursing another one.

Frankie watched his wife at the bar and shook his head. He sat down next to Gillian on the sofa and nudged her playfully. "Hey, gorgeous," he said. "You've been awfully quiet tonight."

Gillian shrugged. "Didn't want to piss your little wife off, that's all."

Frankie sighed, aware that Gillian was upset that Camille was there. "She tagged along. I didn't invite her."

"Really?" Gillian looked at Camille at the bar putting a dent in the liquor supply. "Looks like she's having a blast," she observed sarcastically.

Frankie shook his head again. "That's all she does anymore. Every day she downs a pint of something. She's gonna fuck around and become an alcoholic," he said.

Gillian laughed. "Not Miss Perfect!"

Frankie looked at her. "She's far from perfect. Not perfect for me, anyway."

Gillian looked at him. She was tempted to tell him that she was the only woman who was perfect for him. She liked to think of them as Bonnie and Clyde, although they had only gone so far as to flirt with one another thus far. She had fallen in love with Frankie. It was obvious. "I tried to tell you that years ago, but you wouldn't listen."

Frankie laughed. "You didn't try to tell me shit!"

Gillian laughed, too. She wished she had been bold enough back then to tell Frankie not to walk down the aisle and marry Camille. But there was no sense trying to change the past. "Too late now," she said.

Camille saw Frankie sitting next to Gillian on the couch and felt a surge of resentment. He seemed to have forgotten all about her. She watched as Gillian leaned against Frankie while they laughed at another private joke that Camille wasn't in on. She was getting sick of this, tired of feeling like she was an outcast in this separate world in which her husband existed.

Mayra interrupted the conversation between the two

would-be lovebirds. "Frankie, did you taste the peach cobbler? It's Doug's favorite, and I made extra this year."

Frankie rubbed his stomach in anticipation. "I haven't had any yet, but I'm about to go address that now."

Mayra reached for his hand. "Well, come on. I'll get you a plate."

Frankie headed to the kitchen with Mayra. He looked in Camille's direction and waved, happy that she had kept her distance all night even though she was holding court at the bar like a lush. She waved back, but as soon as he went into the kitchen, her smile faded. She was miserable, and the alcohol in her system was giving her some much-needed liquid courage. Camille grabbed her drink and headed over to the couch where Gillian was seated.

Camille plopped down on the sofa right next to Gillian and seemed to catch her by surprise. "Well, hello, Gillian." Camille had a grin on her face like the cat who ate the canary. "I've seen you sitting over here all night, but we haven't had a chance to talk."

Gillian smirked at Frankie's wife, wondering why she was there. "I was just surprised to see that you came," she said honestly. "This is a first."

Camille nodded, crossed her legs, and tried to fix her shirt to disguise the belly fat that was spilling over the top of her jeans. Gillian's flawless figure never ceased to intimidate Camille. "I just couldn't stand to not be around Frankie on Thanksgiving." Camille thought she saw Gillian roll her eyes, but she wasn't sure. Since she had been drinking, she didn't want to jump to conclusions and cause a scene. So she overlooked it. "I hardly get to see him anymore since he's always with you."

Gillian looked directly at Camille and had to admire her straightforwardness. For several moments she didn't know what to say. Unexpectedly speechless, she smiled at Camille. Finally, she managed to ask, "How was Thanksgiving at your house?"

Camille sipped her drink. "It was nothing like this." She watched as Tremaine staggered through the living room, and shook her head.

Gillian looked at Frankie's wife as if she was crazy. Was this stuck-up bitch looking down her nose at them? "Really? Well, Frankie seems to be enjoying himself." Gillian gestured toward the center of the room, where Frankie was battling Mikey to see who could do the robot the best. Mayra stood close by, holding Frankie's plate of cobbler and egging them on.

Camille had to admit that she hadn't seen her husband have this much fun at home in months. She stared at him so long that she forgot that Gillian was sitting beside her until she spoke again.

"You're a very lucky woman, Camille. Frankie's a good man."

Camille wanted to throw her drink in the bitch's face. "I know that."

Frankie appeared suddenly, and could sense the tension between the two women immediately. He wondered what had possessed Camille to strike up a conversation with Gillian. The sight of the two of them seated side by side made him cringe. "Hey," he said. "What y'all talking about?"

Gillian grinned. "We were just talking about you, actually. I think Mikey's robot was better than yours."

Frankie laughed. "Whatever!"

Camille didn't say a word and instead sipped some more of her drink. The doorbell rang and Gillian rose to answer it. Frankie sat beside Camille and smiled. "Having fun?"

"Yeah. This is a real experience."

Frankie sensed the sarcasm in her voice and shook his head. "You could've stayed home, you know. This ain't really your scene."

Camille's feelings were hurt. She felt that Frankie didn't want her there. Before she could respond, Gillian came back into the room with her boyfriend, Sadiq, in tow. He greeted Nobles and Mayra and then came over to where Frankie sat on the couch.

"Mr. Bingham. How are you?" Sadiq had a big smile on his face as if he and Frankie were old friends. Frankie had to battle the urge to punch him in his mouth.

"Happy Thanksgiving," he said instead. "You're getting here kinda late, aren't you?"

Sadiq sighed and looked at Gillian. "I had to spend the day with my mother. I'm her only son, so I couldn't get around it."

Gillian scrunched her lips up at Sadiq's excuse. "I told him to invite his mother over here, but he chose not to," she said.

Sadiq shook his head. "She likes to spend the holidays close to home." He looked at Frankie and Camille. "My mother lives all the way out in South Jersey." The truth was that Sadiq's uppity mother refused to come to the home of a drug lord for the holiday. They were an upper-middle-class family, and the criminal aspect of the Nobles family didn't sit well with her. Sadiq enjoyed spending time with Gillian, but his mother was waiting for the day when he'd find a woman who was better suited to their lifestyle.

Camille chimed in. "I can understand her wanting to be

closer to home. I'm the same way. But Frankie wanted to come over here, so . . . here we are." She sipped her drink again.

Frankie cut a glance at his wife, and Gillian watched the exchange. Clearly, there was trouble in paradise.

"Okay, guys. I think Sadiq and I are gonna head home now," she said.

"Home?" Frankie asked, as if that was the last thing he wanted. "Everybody's just getting started. Why would you leave?"

Gillian looked Frankie in the eye and then looked down at his wife still seated on the couch. She turned back to Frankie. "I'm tired. I'm sure Sadiq is, too." Sadiq nodded in agreement. "It's been a long day."

"Sure has!" Camille agreed.

Gillian bit her lip to keep from saying something slick. "Frankie, call me tomorrow." Gillian smiled at Camille. "Have a good night."

"You, too." Camille managed a fake smile and watched as Gillian and Sadiq said good night to her parents and to the guests scattered around the opulent home. Camille was thrilled to see her go and hoped that Frankie would be ready to go soon as well. She was sick of this whole scene and anxious to get back to the comforts of her own home.

Frankie sat and watched as Gillian sauntered out of the house with Sadiq. He thought about what she had said—that she had known all along that Camille wasn't right for him. As he watched Gillian leave and then glanced at Camille, he wished that he had figured that out a long time ago.

Daddy's Girl

"Blake Realty," Toya answered her desk phone as she composed an e-mail to a prospective home buyer. She had just returned from out of town. First, she'd gone to Brazil with Alex to celebrate her thirtieth birthday. Then she'd come back to the States and gone directly to Atlanta to spend Thanksgiving with her mother and her brothers. Now that she was back in New York, she was exhausted, but had a ton of work to get to. She cradled the phone on her shoulder as she typed away.

"Don't hang up this time, Latoya."

That voice was back again—that same voice that terrorized her in nightmares when she slept and in her worst memories when she was awake. With her teeth clenched, she hissed, "How the hell did you get this phone number?"

Nate took a deep breath. "I called your mother and—"

Toya hung up on him in midsentence and immediately dialed her mother in Atlanta. When she answered, Toya wasted no time getting to the point.

"Ma, why the hell would you give Nate my phone number?" Normally, Toya would have never spoken to her mother, Jeanie, this way. But today's circumstances were exceptional.

Jeanie sighed. "Toya, he's your father—"

"That crazy bastard ain't shit to me!" She was furious. "Are you kidding me right now?"

Jeanie's voice rose. "Now, listen here! I'm your mother, Toya. I don't care how grown you are."

"Exactly! And as my mother, you should understand why I don't want to talk to him."

"There are things you don't know about your father, Toya. You should listen to what he has to say."

Toya felt like she was in *The Twilight Zone*. "Are you hearing yourself? What could he possibly have to say to me? In fact, why are *you* talking to him? Don't you remember what he did to this family? How could you listen to anything he has to say? And how dare you give him my information? I was wondering how that bastard got my cell phone number when he called me a few weeks ago. Now you done gave him my office number, too? He came to my house! You must be crazy if you think I'm gonna talk to him."

Jeanie had known that her daughter would react this way. She closed her eyes and shook her head. "I know how you feel, Toya."

"Obviously, you don't! 'Cuz if you did, you never would have betrayed me like this."

"Betrayed you? You're overreacting."

"I don't have nothing else to say to you right now. Call me back when you come to your senses and, until then, *stop giving my phone number out!*" Toya slammed the phone down, irate that her mother was being such a sucker. Toya vowed that she would never forgive her father, regardless of what he or anyone else had to say about it.

She paced her office, feeling frustrated, angry, and disgusted by both of her parents. Her father for the ways he'd hurt her in her lifetime, and her mother for being such a damn sucker for love.

Dominique was seated at her desk when she got a call on her cell phone. She didn't recognize the phone number, but answered it anyway. What she heard on the other end made her heart stand still.

"This is Diane, Mr. Bill Storms's dialysis nurse. Is this Dominique Storms?"

"Yes." Dominique was on the edge of her seat.

"I'm afraid there's been an accident. I'll need you to come to the emergency room at Staten Island University Hospital immediately."

Dominique hurriedly turned her computer off and within seconds was racing down the corridor headed for the elevator. "What happened?" she asked, panicking. "What happened to my father?"

"Dominique, the graft in your father's arm where we hook him up to the dialysis machine was compromised. Your father has gone into cardiac arrest. Please hurry. It's very serious."

Dominique quickly ended the call, jumped on the elevator, got in her car, and sped off to Staten Island in tears. In the car, her legs trembled as she drove, her hands gripped the wheel tightly, and her vision was blurred by tears. All she could think about were the words the nurse had said—"cardiac arrest," "serious." She felt like traffic was at a complete standstill even though she was zipping up the FDR Drive at seventy miles per hour. It occurred to her that it was a Monday and that Octavia would be expecting her to pick her up from dance class. While maintaining her speed, she dialed her daughter's cell phone number and got her voice mail. She left a frantic message explaining that Bill was at the hospital and that Dominique would send someone else to pick her up. Next, Dominique called Toya at work.

"Blake Realty, how may I help you?"

"Toya, my father was rushed to the emergency room from dialysis and I'm on my way to the hospital now."

"Oh my God!" Toya could hear the urgency in Dominique's voice and could tell that this was serious. "You need me to come there?"

Dominique switched lanes. "No. But I was wondering if you could pick Octavia up from her dance class on Eighty-sixth Street for me?"

"Of course," Toya said. "Give me her cell phone number and I'll pick her up and keep her with me until you get home."

Dominique recited the information for Toya as she neared the tunnel. "Toya, thank you so much for doing this."

"Girl, please! This is what friends do. I got you. Just go see about your father. And calm down. You don't need to be frantic while you're driving. Be careful and call me and let me know what's going on."

Dominique hung up and sped through the tunnel, her heartbeat racing just as fast as the car she was in. Every mile seemed longer than the last. She kept thinking about her father and the things they'd been through as a team throughout her lifetime.

She recalled the day she told him that she was pregnant at the age of seventeen. Whitney had called her dumb, crazy, and every other negative adjective she could think of. She had urged her sister to "get rid of it" and shaken her head at her stupidity when Dominique refused. Dominique had known that it wouldn't be easy being a young mother. She knew that the odds were stacked against her and that her dreams may have to be deferred because of the decision she was making. But more than anything, she was afraid of being the recipient of her father's disappointment. She was scared to death it would change the way he felt about her. But Bill had listened as she laid out her reasons for not wanting to abort her child. He listened as Whitney berated her sister, and then he spoke at last.

"Leave her alone, Whitney," he had said. "She's keeping the baby. That's it." Looking at Dominique, he had smiled. "It's okay, baby. I got your back. We'll figure it out and everything is gonna be all right. You know that Daddy loves you."

Dominique had burst into tears, relieved that her father was still on her side, that he still loved her and that he was supporting her decision. Throughout the months that followed, as her belly swelled more and more, Bill hadn't hidden his head in shame as the neighbors stared and whispered about his child. And he hadn't allowed Dominique to hide her head in shame, either. Each day, he'd walk with her to the store in their neighborhood, walk her to the bus stop on her way to school each morning, and smile at the nosy neighbors who stared at them. "You see?" he would say to them. "I'm about to be a grandfather for the first time! I hope it's a boy!" His support of Dominique had helped to erase some of the shame she felt as a young lady with a baby face and a baby on the way. And that was typical of Bill Storms. No matter what mistakes or missteps his children made in their lives, he was supportive and didn't judge them harshly for it.

Even now, as Dominique saved her love for a man doing time for drug offenses, though Bill had clearly expressed his disapproval of the man she'd chosen to give her heart to, he never withdrew his support of her. He happily cared for her daughter while Dominique visited Jamel in prison. Although he would shake his head in amazement, questioning the wisdom of giving her all to a career criminal, he still supported her decision. "Be careful, Mimi," he would say. "I don't want to see you get your heart broken. But just remember this. If for whatever reason it doesn't work out, just know that it's his loss. Not yours. He may wind up right back in jail again after he's released. When men go to jail, they'll tell a woman whatever she needs to hear in order to get what they want from her. They'll promise you the world. So don't feel like it's your fault if he doesn't live up to what he promised you."

She thought about her struggles over the years as a single mother. Despite having Octavia at such a young age, Dominique had graduated on time, gone on to college, and carved out a remarkable career for herself. And while earning her high school diploma and her degree had been a great source of pride for her, Bill was most proud of the mother she had become. He watched the way that his daughter cared for Octavia and how his granddaughter thrived. Bill constantly told Dominique that she was a good mother, that she was a great daughter, and there had never been a doubt in her mind that she was loved. Even though her mother had been gone for most of her life, Dominique had never felt in any way deprived thanks to the wonderful father she'd been blessed with.

When she finally reached the emergency room, she parked her car and ran inside, stopping at the security desk outside the ER to explain who she was and why she was there. They had been expecting her, and the security guard ushered her inside, where a doctor greeted her as she entered.

"Miss Storms, my name is Dr. Yang." He extended his hand to her and she shook it, eager for more information on her dad's condition.

"Hello."

He led her into a small room. "Your father is in a coma right now."

A sob escaped Dominique's lips. "How did this happen?"

"One of the new technicians at the clinic had been using the graft in your father's arm to hook him up to the dialysis machine despite the fact that there was a clog in the graft. Normally, there's very little bleeding as a result of a clog like that. What they'll usually do in such a situation is bandage the site and use extra caution when hooking the patient up to the machine in order to avoid compromising the graft. Unfortunately, what happened today was that the tech removed the bandage from your father's arm in order to prepare to begin the process. But when the bandage was removed, the graft came out of his arm, which caused a massive flow of blood from both the main artery and a vein in your father's arm."

Dominique was trembling and shaking her head in disbelief.

"Before the nurses were able to stop the bleeding, your father went into cardiac arrest and his heart stopped."

"Oh my God!"

"They managed to revive him, and we got him here in the ER and repaired the site where the graft had been. We gave him three bags of blood, and we'll give him some more soon. That will, hopefully, bring his blood pressure up. However, he hasn't regained consciousness at this point."

"Where is he?" Dominique's eyes scanned the room full of gurneys as she searched for her father.

The doctor led her to a bed in the far corner of the room, where she saw a figure lying beneath a white sheet. Machines beeped and buzzed, and a myriad of tubes ran from those machines to the patient. Dominique stood at the foot of the bed, refusing at first to believe that the slight, frail figure lying there was her father—the man whom she'd seen as larger than life for so many years. She slowly inched forward, and tears flowed heavily once she gazed down at her father's face. Bill was unconscious, with tubes in his nose, probes on his chest, and a respirator breathing for him.

"Oh, Daddy . . ." She moved to the side of the bed and touched his face, praying that he would wake up at the sound of her voice. She looked at all the machines, listened to all the beeping and buzzing, and squeezed her father's hand. "Daddy, what happened?"

The doctor stood nearby, watching her crying and feeling extremely sympathetic toward her. It was clear that this was a daughter who adored her father, and as she dissolved into sobs that shook her to her core, he stepped forward and patted her on the back to comfort her.

She rubbed her father's hand, stroked his face, and spoke in a soft voice. "Daddy, it's me . . . Mimi. I'm here. I got here as fast as I could. I need you to open your eyes now. Please. Open your eyes or squeeze my hand. Come on."

The doctor cleared his throat. "Miss Storms, I want to talk to you about signing a DNR."

Dominique looked at the doctor and shook her head. "What is that?"

"DNR stands for 'do not resuscitate,' and what that means, basically, is that if your father should suffer cardiac arrest again, we would make no effort to revive him."

Dominique looked at Dr. Yang like he had lost his mind. "Why wouldn't I want you to revive him?" she asked, shocked. "This is my father."

"I understand that—"

"I want you to do everything possible to keep him alive."

"Miss Storms, with the amount of blood that your father has lost and the fact that he has not responded to any stimuli—verbal, physical, or otherwise—the likelihood that he will regain consciousness is very slim. His pupils are fixed." The doctor stepped in and pulled one of Bill's eyelids up, flashing a small flashlight in his eye. Bill's pupils didn't respond at all. "Most patients who come in here having lost the amount of blood your father has don't make it. I'm afraid that, in my opinion, he will not make it through the night."

She shook her head. "I don't care about most patients, Dr. Yang. This is my father. And I want you to do whatever you need to do to keep him alive. I'm not signing any DNR."

Dr. Yang nodded, although he still believed that it was wishful thinking to expect much improvement. "I'll let you have some time with your dad," he said. Touching Dominique lightly on her arm, he paused. "Many experts believe that comatose patients can hear you talking to them, even though they are unable to respond. So keep talking to him. I'm sure he's aware that you're here."

As the doctor walked away, she thought about what he said. The thought of her father dying so soon shattered her resolve and she openly wept, her tears dropping steadily onto his hand. Realizing that this might be the last opportunity she had to say all the things she never had the chance to tell her father, she pulled up a chair and leaned close to her father's ear as she spoke.

"Daddy . . ." She fought to keep her voice under control. "I really love you. I know that you can hear me, so please fight. Wake up and prove these doctors wrong. They don't know you. They have no idea how strong you are. And they don't know how much I need you. What will I ever do without you?" The very thought of losing him was tearing her apart. "Remember when I was a kid and you used to watch Muhammad Ali when he fought; how he used to call himself the greatest? Well, you're the greatest to me. And you're the real champ. You're the toughest man alive, Daddy." She squeezed his hand. "Wake up. There's still so much for you to see and do. It's not your time yet. Don't give up, Daddy."

Dominique bowed her head and prayed from the depth of her soul that God would have mercy on her father and spare his life. When she was done, she sat there, still gripping his hand, and talked to him as minutes bled into hours. Finally, Dr. Yang came back over and asked her to step away for a few minutes so that the nurses could clean him up and get some bloodwork. Reluctantly, she stepped out into the waiting area and called her sister. She explained the situation to Whitney and told her what the doctor had said about their father's condition.

"This is terrible," Whitney said. "I'm glad that you were able to drop everything and get there, Dominique. I just can't believe that you are literally watching Dad die."

Dominique frowned. She was stunned by the coldness she heard in her sister's voice. "When will you be here?" she asked.

Whitney sighed. "Well, Dom, I have no money right now. Plus, you know that Chris and I are going through some problems. He's moved out for a while so that we can have some breathing room. You know how it is with the kids, and—"

"Yeah, back to Daddy." Dominique was growing more disgusted by the minute. The last thing she wanted to hear, for the umpteenth time, was how Whitney and her husband were having problems, how money was tight, how everything revolved around Whitney all the time. "He's in serious condition, Whitney. You're saying that you have no money whatsoever to get a flight out here from Florida?"

Whitney could hear the aggravation in her sister's voice, but she felt that Dominique had to understand that not everyone was making the kind of money that she was. Whitney worked for the IRS and made a decent living. But all she ever heard about was Dominique's high-profile, high-paying job as a Def Jam A&R. Their father was constantly telling Whitney how Dominique was flying from one location to the next, meeting all kinds of people and making him proud. Certainly, Dominique could understand that Whitney's life wasn't as glamorous as hers. "I can't drop everything," Whitney said. "I have the kids, remember?"

"I have a kid, too, Whitney."

"Yeah, but you're already in New York. I can't afford it, and I don't think I have enough frequent-flier miles to get me there. And I can't leave the kids behind since Chris is not here with us . . ."

Dominique let out a long, drawn-out sigh. "I will pay for you to come," she said. "If I do that, can you get here?"

Whitney answered quickly. "Yes. I mean, I'll have to find someone to watch the kids, but—"

"Bring the kids, Whitney. I'll pay for them to come, too." Dominique gave her sister her credit card information and hung up before she lost her temper. She was pissed that Whitney was so transparent. It was clear to Dominique that her sister thought she was balling. Despite the fact that Dominique was a single mother and worked hard to achieve the success she enjoyed, Whitney saw only the high-profile nature of her sister's career. While Whitney had a husband and two teenage children and lived in a lovely home, and everyone—including the kids—had their own cars, Dominique was hustling daily to pay single-handedly for the luxury apartment she and Octavia lived in, as well as spending a fortune for the prep school her daughter attended. Still, this was not the time to get into all of that. Dominique feared that her father would lose his battle to survive before both of his daughters were gathered by his side.

Next, she called Toya.

"How is he?" Toya asked.

"Not good." Dominique stood against the wall in the waiting room, looking defeated. "The doctor said that he doesn't expect my dad to make it through the night."

"What the hell happened?"

Dominique recounted what the doctor had told her, including his request that she sign a DNR.

Toya sighed. "Damn. Well, think positive, Dominique. Doctors ain't God, and they don't know everything. He'll pull through."

"What about Octavia? Is she with you?"

"I'm pulling up as we speak," Toya said, making a U-turn in order to pull up in front of the dance school. She saw Octavia standing alone. "What do you want me to tell her?"

Dominique sighed. "Just tell her that her granddad is

sick and in the hospital and I'll pick her up from your place as soon as I know something."

"No problem. Don't worry about Octavia. I got her and she'll be fine. I'll take her back to my house and we'll chill. If you're not back by the morning, I'll take the day off and stay home with her until you get here. Focus on your dad. Don't worry about nothing else."

"Toya, I can't thank you enough for this."

"Please! Stop all that bullshit. We're friends, bitch. Bye!"

Dominique laughed through her tears as she hung up. Only Toya could make her laugh at a time like this. She wiped her eyes, took a deep breath, and headed back inside.

Octavia walked into Toya's big brownstone and looked around. She was impressed by how beautifully decorated it was. She had only met Toya on a number of occasions, but each time she found her to be hilariously funny. Toya had a mouth like a drunken sailor, which Octavia found very entertaining in comparison to her mother. But never in her wildest dreams had Octavia expected that Toya's home would resemble something out of an episode of *MTV Cribs*. She looked at a painting on the wall and recognized immediately that it was a Picasso. She had studied him in her art class and had never expected to see any of his work this up close and personal.

Seeing the young lady standing there looking mesmerized, Toya walked over and smiled at her. "Make yourself at home, darling. Kick off your shoes, relax, and come get something to eat." Toya opened the box of pizza they had picked up on the way home and pulled some plates out of the cabinet.

Still clad in her prep school uniform, Octavia joined her in the dining room and sat down at the table, tapping the wood floors nervously with her stockinged feet.

"So did my mom tell you what exactly happened to Granddad?"

Toya shook her head. "I really don't know much, sweetie. But she said that it's serious. Just say a prayer for him and for your mom, since she's at the hospital with him. This has to be hard on her." Toya glanced at Octavia as she passed her the soda. "Dominique is a good daughter," she said. "She dropped everything and ran to be by her father's side. She's always talking about your grandfather—all the conversations they had and all the funny things he would say. I hope that you're being a good daughter for your mom, because she's giving you a great example to follow."

Octavia nodded, chewing her pizza. She thought about what she'd been doing that afternoon before Toya had called her. She had been at Dashawn's place, moaning and writhing beneath him with her legs in the air as he dug her out. She hated to think that while that was happening, her beloved grandfather was dying. The thought caused her to choke on her pizza. She swallowed a gulp of soda in an effort to wash it down.

Toya noticed the troubled expression on Octavia's face and frowned. "Don't *you* get sick on me now," she said.

Octavia caught her breath and chuckled a little at Toya's attempt at humor. They ate the pizza and talked about what Octavia's favorite subjects in school were and what she hoped to do after graduating from high school. Toya even shared some of her own recollections of her experiences when she was in high school. When they had finished eating, Toya led her downstairs to the basement, where they got comfortable on the leather sofa and turned the TV on.

Toya looked at Octavia. "So," she said. "You got a boyfriend?"

Octavia paused, wondering if she could trust her mother's friend with the truth. Toya seemed so cool and down to earth. And for a moment, Octavia considered asking her opinion about Dashawn. He hadn't told her that he loved her or even referred to her as his girlfriend yet. All that he'd allowed was that she was pretty, sexy, and smart. She was beginning to wonder if their relationship was all about the sex they were continuously having, but she was scared to actually ask him that. Still, she decided not to tell Toya the truth. After all, she was her mother's friend, and that could spell trouble for Octavia if she revealed too much.

"Ummm . . . no. I'm not allowed to have a boyfriend."

Toya wasn't buying it. She had noticed Octavia's hesitation and figured that there was likely some boy in her life. "I didn't ask you what you were allowed to do." She waved her hand as if it didn't matter. "I wasn't born yesterday, honey. There's probably some boy who says he likes you. Most likely he tells you that you're the prettiest girl he's ever seen, that your body is banging, and that he only has eyes for you."

Octavia laughed, wondering how Toya knew that.

"And let me tell you that you are a beautiful girl. No question about it. But don't let guys fill your head with compliments just so that they can get in your pants. Boys will lie like hell in order to get what they want. Trust me! I know it seems foul that your moms is not allowing you to date. But she's got your best interests at heart. Men are nothing but trouble. You can take that shit to the bank!"

Octavia laughed, enjoying Toya's in-your-face personality. The doorbell rang, interrupting them, and Toya went upstairs to answer it. Octavia listened from the bottom of the stairs.

When she reached the front door, Toya was tempted to curse this fool out. But knowing that Octavia was going through a trauma, she didn't want to add to her stress by making a scene.

"Yes, Russell?" she sang as she swung open the door. "What is it now?"

He smiled at her, knowing that she was annoyed. "I just came by to bring you a present." He pulled a bouquet of yellow tulips from behind his back and held them out for her.

Toya took a deep breath and put her hands on her hips. "Flowers, huh?"

Russell nodded. "Beautiful flowers for a beautiful lady."

She resisted the urge to laugh in his face. Reluctantly, she unlatched the screen door and accepted the flowers from the pesky man. "Thank you," she mumbled.

"You're welcome!" Russell shifted his weight from one foot to the other, hoping that she would invite him in.

Toya shot down those hopes. "I have company, so I'll talk to you soon." She noticed Russell's frown fade and wondered why it gave her a thrill to see him so disappointed.

Russell craned his neck to see if there was another man in there with her. Noticing this, Toya blocked his view. "Thanks for the flowers," she said. "Good night."

Before he could protest, she shut the door, locked it, and

tossed the flowers on top of the piano in her living room before going back downstairs to the basement.

Octavia was smiling at her when she came back. "Was that your boyfriend?" she asked.

Toya sucked her teeth. "Hell no! That monster? You should see him! He's the most hideous creature I've ever seen!"

Octavia laughed. "But he brought you flowers!"

Toya shook her head at the young lady, turned the TV off, and said, "See? That's what I'm trying to tell you. Men think they're smarter than us. Every time I see this guy, he's giving me a compliment, asking me to go out with him, and now he's bringing me flowers. All of that is just so that he can distract me from the fact that he's a beast long enough for him to get what he wants. Never that!" She led Octavia upstairs to her guest bedroom. "Don't ever let a guy run game on you. Outsmart them, and they'll respect you more."

Toya handed Octavia a pair of her newly laundered pajamas. Then she led her to the master bathroom and handed her a washcloth and towel. "Go ahead and take a shower. Put these on and get cozy. It's getting late, and Lord knows when your mother will get here from the hospital. If she needs to stay there overnight, we'll both play hooky tomorrow and go up there to meet her. And if she comes in tonight, I'm gonna make her stay here rather than driving all the way back to Manhattan. So you go on and wash up, say a prayer for your grandfather, and get some sleep. I'll see you in the morning."

"Thank you," Octavia said, smiling at Toya. As she shut the bathroom door, Octavia thought about her grandfather and closed her eyes. "God, please don't let Granddad die," she prayed. "And please help me deal with my problems in the best possible way. Amen." She turned the shower on and stepped into the steamy enclave, wishing the water would wash away all of the things that were going wrong in her life, leaving her feeling powerless to stop them.

Love and War

Dominique had been sitting by her father's bedside all night. She looked at her watch and noted that it was close to seven A.M. and Bill was still hanging on. She glanced at the window on the far side of the ER and saw sunlight beginning to peek through the darkness. A slow smile spread across her face.

"Daddy," she said, speaking into her father's ear. "I told you that you were stronger than they thought. They said that you wouldn't survive through the night, but you did. The sun is up and you're still here, fighting. I love you. Don't give up." She stroked his hand. "Whitney is on her way."

Dr. Yang came over and explained that they needed to run a CAT scan on her father. "We want to determine why your father hasn't regained consciousness yet. The scan will tell us if there is brain activity and whether or not that activity is normal. We'll need you to sign a release, giving us permission to perform this test on behalf of your dad."

Dominique nodded, taking the pen he handed to her and signing the paper. "It's a good sign that he's still alive, right? I mean, you said that he wouldn't make it through the night."

Dr. Yang took a deep breath. The last thing he wanted to do was give her false hope. "The fact that he's still alive is a good thing, obviously. We just won't know until we run the necessary tests what, if any, long-term effects there will be."

Dominique thanked Dr. Yang and stood back as they prepped her father in order to transport him for the tests. She said what had to be the hundredth prayer she'd said in the past twenty-four hours. Before they moved her father, she walked over to him and kissed him on the forehead. "I'll be right here when you get back, Daddy."

Once he was taken upstairs, Dominique stepped outdoors for the first time in hours. She looked around at the beautiful, yet blustery, winter day that was unfolding and wondered if her father would live to see another sunrise. As she stood outside, staring aimlessly off into the distance, she heard someone call her name. She looked around and saw Whitney heading in her direction, followed by her teenagers, Janet and Andrew. Dominique breathed a sigh of relief that her sister had finally arrived, and she met them halfway, hugging them all and ushering them inside the hospital. They sat in the waiting room and Dominique brought them up to speed on what was happening with Bill. When she was done, everyone sat in silence, soaking it all up. Everything had happened so fast.

Finally, Whitney spoke. "This is so sudden." She shook her head. "When it rains, it pours, you know?"

Dominique nodded.

"Chris and I are going through problems, too. He has been calling me off the hook because I left town so suddenly that I didn't leave any money behind for him. You know he got laid off from his job, and he's struggling to find a new one. Things have been so tight financially lately, but hopefully that will change soon."

Dominique stared at her sister in silence. Here they were, with their father's life hanging in the balance, and all Whitney could talk about was her husband. "Does Chris realize that your father is in a coma right now? Does he think that you should give a fuck whether or not you left money for him at a time like this?"

Whitney shrugged her shoulders. "That's what I'm saying!" Her cell phone rang and she pulled it out of her purse. Looking at the screen, she pointed and said, "That's him now." She got up and walked over to a secluded section of the waiting room to talk to her husband. Dominique, meanwhile, was growing angrier by the minute. Figuring that she needed to get some much-needed rest, she was relieved when the doctor emerged and told her that Bill had been moved to a private room on the third floor and that his tests had been completed. "It will take a day or two to get the results back," he explained. "In the meantime, we'll just keep hoping that he wakes up soon."

Dominique and Whitney led the kids up to the room where Bill lay still in his bed. Whitney went to her father's side and broke down in tears when she saw his condition. When she composed herself, she asked Dominique what all the machines were for. Dominique, feeling like a pro now that she had asked a ton of questions throughout the night, explained them all to her sister. Finally, fatigue caught up with her and she told Whitney that she was going to take a break from holding vigil at the hospital in order to go and pick up Octavia and get some sleep. Whitney agreed, glad that her sister was going to get a break, and Dominique left the hospital and headed for Toya's place in Brooklyn.

Hours later, Whitney and her two teenagers sat in the hospital waiting room, sleeping with their heads resting on one another's shoulders. Dominique came in with Toya and Octavia in tow and stood there in amazement as she looked at her sister. She turned to Toya in shock.

"This bitch is crazy."

Toya frowned. "Has she even been in to see your father?"

Dominique figured that there was only one way to find out. She walked over and shook Whitney awake. Whitney opened her eyes and stretched, then smiled at her sister. "Hey, sis. Did you get any sleep?"

"I see that you did." Dominique didn't bother to hide her anger. "Have you been in to see Daddy?"

Whitney nodded. "I went in there a couple of hours ago. Nothing has changed."

Toya shook her head. Dominique had told her that her sister was something else, but this was more than she had expected. "So you slept out *here*?" Toya asked. "You could have slept in your father's room instead. If he did wake up, you wouldn't have known. Or worse, if he passed away he would have been all by himself with you out here sleeping."

Whitney was annoyed that this stranger had the nerve to question her. "I'm sorry . . . who are you?"

"Toya Blake, Dominique's friend." There was no softness whatsoever in Toya's tone. In her opinion, this bitch was a sorry excuse for a daughter. When Dominique had come by that morning, she had cried herself to sleep at the thought of losing her father. She had told Toya how she hadn't slept a wink the night before and how she had held vigil at her father's side without so much as a bathroom break. And here Bill's firstborn was, snoozing in the waiting room. Toya had already decided that she didn't like Whitney at all.

Dominique shook her head in disgust. "I'm going in to see Daddy," she said flatly, then turned and went into her father's room. When she stepped inside, she was pleased to see that the nurses had given her father a shave and bathed him. The blood that had been all over his clothes and hands the night before was gone, and he looked so much better. She walked over to him and kissed his face. "It's me, Daddy. Mimi. Told you I would be back soon." She settled into the chair beside his bed as Octavia stepped into the room. Seeing that her grandfather's condition was graver than she had expected, she erupted into sobs, and Dominique rushed over to console her daughter.

Toya watched the scene from the doorway and fought back tears of her own. She thought about her own father and how she didn't give a damn whether he lived or died. She felt her heart break a little at how sad that was, and abruptly left the room, leaving Dominique and her daughter to have some time alone with Mr. Storms. Toya returned to the waiting room and saw that Whitney was on the phone with that husband of hers again, sitting off in the corner while her children watched cartoons on the waiting room TV.

Toya sat down beside Janet and Andrew. "So, guys," she said. "Have you been in to see your grandfather?"

They both shook their heads no. "I'm not good with hospitals," Andrew explained.

Toya frowned slightly. "But this is your grandfather. Don't you think you should make an exception for him?"

Andrew shrugged, and Janet didn't bother to respond at

all. Toya couldn't believe the aloofness coming from Whitney and her kids. While Whitney was over in the corner, seemingly arguing with her husband about something, her father was in the next room fighting for his life. Meanwhile, her kids seemed completely unconcerned about the man who was supposed to be their reason for coming to New York in the first place.

Finally, Whitney hung up the phone. She came over to where Toya sat with the kids and smiled at her. "So you've been friends with my sister for a while now, huh?"

Toya nodded, stared at Whitney, and said nothing.

Whitney nodded as well, searching for a way to fill the awkward silence. "That's good. I'm glad she has friends like you to look out for her since I live so far away."

Toya continued to stare at Whitney for several moments. "Well, you're not so far away now. So here's your chance to be there for your sister."

Whitney frowned. "I don't understand."

"You came all the way here—for free, I might add."

"That's really none of your business. I don't even know you like that." Whitney really didn't like this bitch.

"True, you don't. But you know I'm telling the truth. Your father is in there dying, and you're out here arguing on the phone. Dominique could use your support now. If you keep this up, when all is said and done, she's not gonna want to have shit to do with you. I know I wouldn't." Toya got up and strolled to the ladies' room, leaving Whitney to think about what she'd said. By the time Toya returned, Dominique and Octavia had joined their family in the waiting room.

"Toya, I think it'll be good if we take the kids back to Daddy's house for a little while. They don't need to be up here all day dealing with all this sadness and everything." She held Octavia's hand, since her daughter was falling apart emotionally. "Whitney, you might as well stay there with the kids since you seem to be so sleepy."

Whitney caught the sarcasm in her sister's tone and the sidelong glance Toya shot at her. She nodded and followed Dominique out to the car. They rode back to Bill's apartment in the Mariners Harbor projects in silence, everyone lost in their own thoughts. When they arrived they piled into the elevator for the ride to his apartment on the sixth floor. As soon as the elevator doors shut, Andrew sucked in air in an audible attempt to hold his breath on the project elevator. Toya and Dominique looked over at him as if he had lost his mind.

"Why are you doing that?" Dominique asked her nephew.

"It smells like pee," he explained, his nose scrunched up as if he would pass out if he took a deep breath.

Toya wanted to snatch his bourgeois ass by the neck and toss him off the elevator as they arrived at their designated floor. They all followed Dominique and Octavia as they led the way down the hall to Bill's apartment. Once inside, they began to get comfortable. Dominique turned the TV on and showed Whitney where everything was. Toya found it odd that Whitney didn't know her way around her own father's home, and she questioned it.

"Whitney, when was the last time you've been here to visit your dad?"

Whitney seemed to think about it. "About six years ago, I think. Yeah. It was right around the time he started dialysis."

Toya nodded, really wondering how long it would take before Dominique told her sister off. It sounded to her like Whitney thought she was too good to come home once she'd made it out. Toya saw Octavia kick her shoes off and make herself at home on the sofa, while her cousin Janet sat on the very edge of the couch as if the furniture wasn't even worthy of her ass.

Andrew asked his mother if they could go out and buy some soda or something else to drink. "I'm thirsty," he explained.

Dominique shook her head. "You don't have to go out and buy soda. There's plenty of juice and stuff in Daddy's fridge. Go in there and help yourself."

Andrew frowned and shook his head. "I don't really want to touch anything," he admitted. "It's kinda disgusting in here."

That was the final straw. Dominique lost it. "Let me tell you something, you ungrateful son of a bitch. This is your grandfather's house. He's in that hospital fighting for his life and you're supposed to be here to rally around him in support. Instead, you sit up at the hospital all day without bothering to go inside his room to even see him. Then you're on the elevator holding your breath, and now you're sitting on the edge of the furniture like you're too good to be here." She glared at her niece and nephew. "And you have the fucking nerve to say that it's 'disgusting' in here?" She seemed amazed at their audacity. "Did you know that your mother grew up in the projects? We both did. We were raised in this very apartment. So how dare you act as if this is too far beneath you! If it wasn't for your grandfather, your mother wouldn't even be here. That means that you wouldn't be here, either. So for as long as you're in my presence, you will respect that man and his house. I don't care what your mother lets you get away with, but don't try that shit when I'm around!"

Whitney spoke up. "Your aunt is right," she said, although she herself didn't seem too comfortable in these surroundings.

Toya scowled at Whitney. "*You* should be telling them how to behave, not their aunt!"

Whitney shrugged her shoulders. "I know they're wrong for acting like that, but I'm glad that they feel comfortable enough to express themselves," she said.

Toya had heard enough. "Express, my ass! There's some shit they should be ashamed to express." Seeing that Dominique was on the verge of going completely off, she nudged her friend toward the door. "Let's go back to the hospital," she said. Dominique stormed out, with Toya hot on her heels. They'd both had enough of Whitney and her uppity kids.

Toya was just as vexed as her friend as they headed out to the car. "Do those little stuck-up fuckers know that their mother doesn't have a pot to piss in? Yet they're sitting in there acting like they live in Beverly Hills and they've never been exposed to such filth. I woulda had to kick Whitney's *ass* if I were you!"

Dominique was livid. "They've gotta be fuckin' kidding me! Daddy would be so disappointed in Whitney right now, letting her kids act like that! And what the fuck did she come up here for if she was just gonna sit in the waiting room and sleep?"

Toya shook her head and stared out the window. "Just don't think about her right now. It's all about your father."

They got back to the hospital, and Dominique went straight to her father's room. Toya sat out in the waiting room, astonished by all that she'd witnessed that day. She thought about her own father again. She knew that if her father passed away, she would continue on with her life as if nothing had happened. But that was because of the things she'd endured as a result of living under his tyranny for so long. She wondered what was causing Whitney to behave as if Bill were no more than a stranger to her while Dominique was clearly heartbroken over her father's illness.

Dominique sat beside her father's bed. She held his hand once again and began to cry. She had never felt more alone in her life. She was grateful for Toya, but she still felt as if she had no one to share her pain with. Octavia understood somewhat. After all, she had certainly been closer to her grandfather than any of his other grandchildren. Still, there was no comparison to the hole in Dominique's heart that existed in her father's absence. She leaned in and told her dad that she would give anything to hear his voice again, to see his smile or enjoy his laughter. Dominique laid her head on her father's chest and cried. When she looked up, she was startled to see that his eyes had finally opened.

"Nurse! Somebody!" she yelled. "He's awake!"

Two nurses rushed into the room, followed by Dr. Yang. Dominique watched as they called her father's name and shined a light in his eyes. He was breathing very heavily, and they said that his blood pressure was dropping. His heart rate was extremely high, and they gave him a shot to calm him down. At Dr. Yang's request, Dominique stepped out into the hallway while they attempted to stabilize him. She rushed into the waiting room and told Toya the good news.

"He's awake!" Dominique was overjoyed and Toya was, too. She was praying that Mr. Storms pulled through, because she feared that her friend would never be the same again if he didn't. The two friends jumped up and down together, and Dominique beamed with joy. Then Dr. Yang stepped in and shattered their celebration.

"Miss Storms," he began. "Your father's blood pressure is dropping rapidly. Right now it's at forty over sixty. We've already given him numerous transfusions and we are unable to give him another one due to the fever he's running. I must urge you to sign the DNR—"

"No!" She was angry now. "If it's his time to go, then that's up to God, not me. I'm not giving up on him yet." She pushed past the doctor and headed straight for her father's room. Once inside, she sat by his side and watched as the nurses milled around with defeated expressions on their faces. Toya stood in the doorway and watched as an Indian nurse touched Dominique's back softly.

"He's tired, sweetheart," she said, looking at Mr. Storms. "Sometimes they hold on because we tell them to. Maybe he's just waiting for you to tell him that it's okay to let go."

Dominique was crying softly. "But it's not okay," she said softly. Even as she watched her father struggling to breathe, watched him unable to talk with the tube in his throat, she shook her head in denial. "He's not done living yet."

The nurse patiently soothed her and touched her hand. "Sometimes," she said, "it's not really up to us." She turned and walked out of the room, leaving Dominique to think about what she'd said. Dominique squeezed her father's hand.

"Daddy . . ." Dominique wiped the tears away, determined to be strong despite the fact that she was falling apart inside. "I don't know if they're right. Maybe they are, and I'm the one who's wrong." She sniffled, then swallowed hard. "But I just want to tell you that if you're tired . . . if you're tired, Daddy, and you don't feel like fighting anymore . . . it's okay. You can let go, if you want to. And I'll be okay. I'll make sure that Octavia's okay . . . Whitney and her kids, too. You don't have to fight anymore if you don't want to."

She watched as her father's gaze slowly, ever so slowly, shifted from staring absently at the ceiling to staring in her direction. It was as if he was looking to see if she meant what she said. Dominique smiled at her father. "I love you, Daddy. And I don't want you to go. I don't know what I would ever do without you. You've been there for me when I didn't have anyone else on my side. You've been my best friend for my whole life." Her voice cracked with emotion. "And I will miss you if you go. I will miss you so much." She took a deep breath and looked him in the eye. "But I'll understand if you feel like you can't fight anymore. We'll be okay. I promise you that."

Bill's eyes locked with his daughter's. His gaze was strong and focused on her face. Weakly, he squeezed her hand. And little by little, Dominique could hear the heart monitor slow down. Soon the beeping ceased altogether, Bill's hand went limp in hers, and she knew that her father was gone forever. She broke down in sobs that shook her entire body, as the nurses and doctors came in to officially declare her father deceased. Toya walked in and wrapped her arms around her friend, held her close, and together they cried for Bill's loss.

His funeral was held on a cold November morning with scores of people in attendance to mourn the loss of a class act. Toya, Camille, and Misa came to support her, and Dominique was grateful to have them there with her. She handled all of the arrangements single-handedly, as Whitney was still claiming poverty. But it was an honor for Dominique to give her father the service he deserved. She felt that it was one final act of love through which she could express the gratitude she felt for all the years he had stood solidly by her side, never wavering even for a moment.

At the repast, Whitney pulled her sister to the side. She cleared her throat and looked as if she had worked herself up to this moment for days. She took a deep breath and spoke at last. "Dominique, I just want to tell you that . . . we both lost our father. But you lost more than that. You lost your best friend. I didn't have that relationship with him like you did."

"That wasn't Daddy's fault," Dominique pointed out. "You may not have been as close with him as I was. But that wasn't because he didn't try to be close to you. He did. He used to talk about how I had always been a daddy's girl, while you never were. The minute you finished high school, you ran off and never looked back. I don't blame you for that. We all want to branch out when we become adults. But you never came back, Whitney."

"Yes, I did."

"No, not really. You came back every five or ten years, but that's not really keeping in touch. Look at how your kids act at his house. It's as if they're in the home of a stranger who they feel is beneath them, and that's *your* fault. They should have had a relationship with their family—not just Chris's family, but *your* family as well. And they haven't had that. As angry as I am with them for acting holier than thou, I can't really blame them for it. You're the one who owes it to them to make sure that they know *all* of who they are." Dominique had been praying that God would soften her heart toward her sister. She didn't want to hate Whitney or even dislike her. She knew that their father would want them to be closer than they were. And to honor him, Dominique extended an olive branch to her sister.

"I know that Daddy and I were closer than you were. But let's not have that be the case with our children. They're so close in age that they should have a better relationship than they do now. And so should we."

Whitney nodded, fighting back tears, and hugged her sister. She knew that she had been selfish, condescending, and perhaps even a little callous with regard to family matters. Most of her attention over the past fifteen years had been devoted to keeping her marriage alive, while her own family had received very little of her time. She vowed that from that day forward she would be closer to her sister and to the niece she'd never really gotten to know.

Dominique, meanwhile, was realizing that she had been one of the luckiest women she knew. While she had been seeking unconditional love in the arms of men, she knew now that she had had it all along—from her father. Bill had given her more love, more attention, and more self-confidence than any man could give her. And she was so grateful, so blessed, she now realized, to have been a daddy's girl when so many women had never experienced unconditional love like that. She couldn't completely forgive Whitney for bailing out on their dad the way she had, but with the knowledge that she had been given a gift that Whitney had never seen fit to accept for herself, Dominique put one foot in front of the other and carried on.

Friends with Benefits

December 14, 2007

Misa sat on the chaise inside of Camille's spacious closet, the size of some people's bedrooms. She scanned the dozens of pairs of shoes and wished she could live like this for more than just a few days. But Misa's life was nothing like her sister's. Two months had passed since Baron had been shot at. And during those two months, Misa hadn't been invited over to his house once. She called him, but usually got his voice mail. And she didn't want to show up unannounced at his house, since the last time she'd tried that with a man—Cyrus—it had been a disaster. Misa was miserable, wondering why Baron had bored of her so quickly, and envious of Camille that she was invited to this Nobles family shindig tonight. She had gotten a taste of his lifestyle and was hooked.

"What color are you wearing?" she asked. It was Friday night and Camille was eagerly trying to pick out something sexy.

"Tonight is Doug and Mayra's anniversary party," Camille said, frowning. "That's what makes it so hard to figure out what to wear. Everyone is going to be trying to outdo everyone else."

Misa smiled. "It sounds like a players' ball." She got a far-off look in her eyes as she wished for the thousandth time that she could live the type of lifestyle that Camille was living. She tried hard not to be too envious.

Camille saw the expression on her sister's face and felt sorry for her. "Misa, I know it's hard being alone and having Shane to take care of. But you'll find somebody eventually to share your life with. Somebody just as romantic and caring and perfect for you as Frankie is for me. You'll see." She happily sifted through some dresses, searching for the right look for that evening. She was so anxious that she could hardly keep still.

Misa frowned and looked at her sister as if she had lost her mind. It was times like this that Misa couldn't stand Camille. She was so condescending and thought that everyone wanted to live her life. "What are you talking about, Camille?"

Camille turned to face Misa, seeming confused. "You just look sad and I feel bad being this happy while you're so lonely, sis. That's all."

Misa wanted to curse Camille out. She didn't appreciate being described as "lonely." In fact, Misa was willing to bet that she was happier in her life with little Shane than Camille truly was with Frankie.

"Camille, Frankie's not Prince Charming, you know. You spend so much time bragging about how lucky you are to have him, but I hope you know that the guy's not a saint." Misa thought back to the times she'd seen Frankie with Gillian. Camille had better wake up and realize that her husband wasn't all that she made him out to be.

"I never said he was, Misa. But he treats me like a queen and that's what's important."

"You really believe that? Seriously, Camille, aside from the material things he gives you and the money he hands you, how does he treat you like a queen? He's not even here half the time, so don't fool yourself." Misa stared at her sister in amazement.

Camille shook her head. "Don't be jealous, Misa."

Misa laughed loudly. "Whatever. If you take the blinders off and take a good clear look at your marriage, you'll see that you're not nearly as fortunate as you think you are."

Camille stood in silence and stared at her sister. She didn't even know what to say. Jealousy seemed to have taken Misa over, and Camille was so disappointed in her.

Misa threw up her hands in frustration. "Wear the red dress and have a good time." Misa got up, walked out, and headed home. She had had enough of her sister for one day.

Camille stood dumbfounded for several moments after Misa left, and thought about what she had said. She hadn't meant to talk down to her. And more and more she was being reminded—by Toya and now Misa—that her life with Frankie may not be all that it was cracked up to be. She sat down and looked around the closet at all the shoes, bags, and designer duds and knew that she was lucky.

Camille then thought about the time Frankie spent away from her. She thought about Gillian and her constant presence. Camille reached for the phone and dialed her husband's number, hoping for some reassurance. She wanted him to remind her that she really was lucky. The phone rang twice and went straight to voice mail. Camille hung up and dialed again. Frankie's voice mail picked up again. She thought about something Dominique had mentioned once while

they'd talked over drinks—that men always have predictable
voice mail codes. She chuckled at the thought and, on a whim,
pressed the pound key. The voice mail system prompted her
to enter Frankie's password to check his messages. As a random guess, Camille entered "0310," which was Frankie's
birthday. To her surprise, she had guessed correctly.

"You have three new messages. To hear your messages,
press 'one.'"

Camille hesitated. This was something she had never
done before, and for a brief moment she reconsidered. She
had never snooped on her husband before. She trusted
Frankie. But with her curiosity piqued, she pressed "1" and
listened.

"Yo, Frankie, this is Mikey. Let me know if you want in
on the poker game this Sunday. Get at me."

Camille smirked, happy that Frankie had been telling
the truth about the card games at Mikey's house. She pressed
"9" to save the message and then pressed "1" to hear the
next one.

"Hey, Frankie. It's Gillian." Camille's jaw tensed and
she turned the volume up on her phone as the message
continued. "Remember the night when you kissed me at
B. Smith's? Well, I can't stop thinking about that kiss."
She paused. "I don't know why I'm bringing this up now.
Maybe it's because you brought that dull wife of yours to
Thanksgiving at Daddy's house, and I'm wondering if she
realizes what she has with you. Anyway, I wish everything wasn't so complicated . . . but I guess I just wanted
you to know that I've been thinking about us lately. We'll
talk later."

Camille's heart paused and she held her breath. She
pressed "1" again to repeat the message, praying all the while

that her ears were deceiving her. As she listened to the message again, there was no mistaking it. *"I can't stop thinking about that kiss. . . . I wish everything wasn't so complicated."*

It felt like the whole world stopped spinning. She felt tears roll down her cheek before she even realized that she was crying. She managed to proceed to the next message, though her hands trembled as she did so. She recognized Gillian's voice again.

"Frankie, it's me. Call me back."

Camille sat there with the telephone clenched tightly in her hand. She couldn't move. All she could hear was Gillian's voice confirming her worst fears. Frankie was cheating on her. She wondered how long this had been going on. Frankie had assured her that they were just friends, and she had believed him. Gillian had been in their home, had smiled in her face, and all the while she had been in love with her husband. Camille couldn't believe it.

She hung up the phone and slumped down on the chaise, racked with sobs. Frankie was everything to her. She had invested so many years into their marriage, and had defended him when everyone suggested that his friendship with Gillian was deeper than she thought. Camille felt her heart shatter over and over as she replayed Gillian's voice in her head. She thought back to the night of their barbecue when she had overheard Frankie tell Gillian that he loved her. She had wanted to believe that he meant it in a friendly way. But it was clearer than ever that what he'd said to Gillian that night wasn't as meaningless as she had hoped.

The phone rang, and she fought to stop crying long enough to answer it. She steadied her voice and answered, "Hello."

"Hey, baby. It's me. You almost ready to go? I'll be home

in about an hour." Frankie's sexy baritone resounded in her ears.

Camille couldn't speak. She wanted to tell him that she knew the truth, but part of her was scared to death to do that. What if he really wanted to be with Gillian but just didn't have the heart to tell her? If she told him that she knew about his affair, he might take that as a license to finally leave her. What if he walked away from all they'd built together? Camille wasn't about to let another woman have the man she'd loved for so long.

"Camille? Are you there?"

She steadied her voice and said, "Yeah. I'll be ready."

"Cool. See you in a little while." Frankie hung up, and Camille got to her feet. She walked over to her full-length mirror and looked at her reflection. Her hair was styled perfectly, but she observed that her body was getting a little fat. She shook her head, knowing that all the food and alcohol she'd been consuming over the past few months had caught up to her. Her nails were manicured perfectly. Her makeup was flawless. She worked hard to maintain a perfect appearance so that her husband would never need to stray. But he had done so anyway. Camille wondered what she was missing; what did Gillian have that she didn't? She wiped the few tears that still trickled down her cheek and reached for the red dress that Misa had suggested she wear. She spritzed herself with perfume, put on her jewelry, and got dressed.

Frankie arrived and walked into their bedroom with a bouquet of red roses in his hand. He felt guilty for all the time he had been spending with Gillian, and he was well aware that his relationship with his best friend had taken a more serious tone lately. He felt powerless over his emotions and torn between the wife who had been so faithful to him and the woman to whom his heart truly belonged.

Camille greeted him, looking flawless as usual, and gave him a kiss. She thanked him for the flowers and went to put them in water, thinking about something her mother had always told her: that if a man brought you red roses, you should give them back because he put no thought into that whatsoever. She pondered how ironic that was—that her husband would give her a thoughtless gift on the very night she discovered that he'd been kissing his so-called best friend.

Frankie came up behind her and wrapped his arms around her waist. He sniffed her neck and noticed that she was wearing his favorite perfume. He smiled. "Ready to have fun tonight?"

Camille forced a smile and turned to face her husband. She wondered how he could live a double life so easily. When he looked at her, it was as if she was the only woman in the world. Yet she knew the truth. As she faced Frankie, she thought about Gillian and became more determined than ever to hold on to her husband. She'd rather die than let that bitch have her man. "I love you, Frankie," she said. "Let's go."

Reckoning

Octavia looked down at the home pregnancy test in her hand and cried. It was the third test she'd taken that week and each one gave the same result. Positive. She was pregnant and her mother was going to kill her when she found out.

Octavia had allowed Dashawn to have unprotected sex with her, after he urged her to trust him. He swore that she wouldn't get pregnant, that he would pull out in time to prevent that. But now here she was, at home alone with her heart galloping in her chest.

What am I going to do? she wondered.

Octavia had missed her period that month, and hoped that it was just a fluke. When she confided in her friends at school, they urged her to take a pregnancy test. Seeing the third positive result, she shook her head, wishing this nightmare would end somehow. She hadn't told Dashawn yet. She wasn't sure how he would react, and she was kind of afraid to tell him out of fear of being rejected. Each night as she ate dinner with her mother, she sat in silence as she thought about her situation. Lucky for her, Dominique was preoccupied with mourning the death of her father and keeping in touch with Jamel, so that allowed Octavia's stress to go unnoticed. At night when she crawled into bed, she'd cry herself to sleep and ask God to show her a way out. All she knew for sure was that she was in a world of trouble. Somehow, she had to come up with a plan.

The whole room seemed to sway to "Always and Forever" as the anniversary party wound down at Conga. The lights were low, and everyone was tipsy from the open bar and full from the feast they'd enjoyed all evening long. This was one party that all in attendance would be talking about for a long time. Drinks flowed, flowers peppered the room, and food was everywhere—filet mignon, beef medallions, soul food, and every sweet confection a heart could desire. The deejay had been spinning a mix of old-school and new music, and Nobles and his wife were blissfully happy.

Camille sat nestled in the crook of Frankie's arm as they watched the celebrating couple dance together, gazing lovingly into each other's eyes. Camille tried to recall whether Frankie still looked at her that way, but she came up empty. Looking across the room, she spotted Gillian standing with her brother, who looked like he'd rather be getting a root canal than be at this party tonight.

Camille noticed that Gillian's boyfriend, Sadiq, was standing not very far from Gillian, and Camille stared at her nemesis hatefully. She was still boiling inside about the message she'd heard on Frankie's cell phone, but she was doing her best to push it out of her mind. After all, he was a man, she thought. Men would do whatever their dicks told them to, and Frankie was no different. To Camille, Gillian alone was the problem, and she had to find a way to get her out of their overcrowded marriage for good.

Frankie was looking at Gillian and Sadiq as well. He noticed that Gillian hadn't smiled much all night. Unless someone was snapping a picture of the family, Gillian had been standing around looking like she'd rather be anywhere else in the world but there. She hadn't danced at all, and Frankie couldn't help wondering if Sadiq had done something to piss her off.

"You ready to go?" Camille asked, looking at her husband, who seemed not to be enjoying himself anymore. "Let's get out of here."

Frankie pried his eyes away from Gillian and looked at his wife. "Okay. Let me say good night to everybody." They stood up and bid good night to the others at their table as the song came to an end. Offering congratulations first to Nobles and Mayra, they thanked their hosts for a wonderful evening.

Frankie put his hand on Nobles's shoulder and smiled. "You look good tonight, old man. I'll stop by tomorrow around lunchtime to bring you up to speed on some things."

Nobles smiled and nodded. "No problem, Frankie. Thanks for coming."

Next, Frankie bid Baron farewell, and he and Camille made their way toward the exit. Gillian was standing nearby.

She locked eyes with Frankie as he walked toward her. Camille noticed and gripped her husband's hand tighter. Sadiq stood behind Gillian, talking to a man Camille didn't recognize. As the distance between them diminished, Gillian felt her heartbeat speed up. If they had been alone, Frankie might have told her that his heart did the same.

"We're going home now," he said as he stood in front of

her. He thought she looked sexier than ever with her flowing hair falling in loose curls around her shoulders, and her long eyelashes fluttering over her beautiful brown eyes. "Guess I'll talk to you tomorrow."

Gillian forced a smile. "Have a good night," she managed, looking Frankie in the eye. As she glanced at Camille, her smile was harder to maintain. "You look lovely," she said.

"Thanks," Camille said, smiling on the outside but spitting in the woman's face in her imagination. Camille had squeezed into the dress she was wearing, and was depressed that her overeating had made it hard for her to fit into the size 12 garment. She had to admit that Gillian looked amazing in a sequined one-shoulder gown. Her diamond jewelry was elegant and understated. Camille was growing more insecure in her too-tight dress the longer they stood there, but unfortunately, Frankie seemed not to be in any rush to leave.

He stared at Gillian, wondering what had caused her long face. She had seemed so sad and so distant all night. "Are you all right?" he asked, completely forgetting that Camille was on his arm. All that mattered to him at that moment was whether Gillian was okay.

She looked at Camille, then back at Frankie. She was upset that he hadn't mentioned the message she'd left on his voice mail. Gillian felt like a fool for having called Frankie and expressing what had been on her mind for days, and pissed that he hadn't even acknowledged what she'd said. Just then, Sadiq appeared at her side. He smiled, greeting Frankie and Camille. He had heard Frankie's question, too. "She's mad at me," he said, tilting his head in Gillian's direction. "I got here late tonight, but at least I made it." He smiled as he said this, displaying beautifully capped teeth and adorable dimples. He was handsome and charming, and Camille could instantly understand why Gillian fell for him. She smiled at Sadiq, trying to lighten the mood.

But Gillian wasn't smiling. And neither was Frankie. Camille cleared her throat.

"Okay, baby, let's leave them alone to talk about it. You two have a good night," she said, moving toward the door.

Frankie didn't move. He stood his ground, staring at Gillian and then glancing briefly at Sadiq before looking at Gillian once again. He leaned in close to her and whispered in her ear, "I'm gonna drop Camille off and then I'll be back. Wait for me."

Gillian nodded, eager to explain to Frankie that she wasn't the least bit concerned about Sadiq's lateness. The only thing troubling her was that Frankie kept parading his phony wife around her. She decided that she would lay all her cards on the table once he dropped Camille off. Frankie gave one last menacing glance at Sadiq before he joined his wife at the door.

In the car, Camille couldn't wait to start asking questions. "What was all that about?"

Frankie started the car and looked ahead, avoiding eye contact. "I don't know. She seems upset."

Camille nodded. "Yeah, I saw that. But what was all that about, Frankie?" She was getting more and more pissed by the minute.

"All what?" Frankie wasn't in the mood for this shit right now. "I told you that Gillian is my best friend. Don't you think if one of your friends was upset you would wanna know what's the problem?"

Camille shook her head and looked out the window. "How the hell do you think that makes me feel?" she asked.

Frankie sighed loudly. "What? How what makes you feel? Me asking my friend if she's all right?"

Camille shook her head again. "No. Me hearing my husband refer to another woman as his best friend. *I'm* supposed to be your best friend, Frankie. Not some other woman who hardly even speaks to me when she sees me!"

"Come on!" Frankie said, looking at her like she was crazy. "She speaks to you, she smiles at you, all that. You're making shit up now."

"Really?" Camille asked incredulously. "I imagine a lot of things, I guess. Like you whispering in her ear before you left. Do you know how fucking disrespectful that was, Frankie?" Camille couldn't hold back any longer. Frankie had embarrassed her, leaving her waiting for him to leave with her while he tended to another woman's emotional needs. She was livid. "Do you know how embarrassing that shit was for me, for Sadiq? Do you even care?"

"Fuck Sadiq!"

"Fuck Sadiq, huh? What's really going on, Frankie?" He didn't answer, and it only made her angrier. "Huh? You fucking her? Tell me now!"

Frankie laughed, shook his head in dismay, and ignored his wife.

"You can't even deny it, can you?" Camille was devastated. Tears fell from her eyes, and she didn't bother to wipe them as she imagined Frankie in the arms of someone else. "I heard her on your damn voice mail, Frankie! Talking about kissing my muthafuckin' husband!"

He glanced over at her and grew angrier by the second. "What are you talking about?" He was yelling, and his voice reverberated in the Bentley. He thought Camille had lost her mind. He had gotten no such voice mail from Gillian—at least, not as far as he knew.

"I checked your voice mail, Frankie. And I heard Gillian saying that she can't stop thinking about that kiss at fucking B. Smith's. She said she was jealous when you brought me to Thanksgiving dinner at Nobles's house. Now, I want you to tell me why you betrayed me!"

Frankie gripped the wheel tighter, seething. "You checked my messages, Camille?"

She was crying now and didn't care whether or not he was pissed that she had busted him. "You're damn right I did."

Frankie let her cry and they rode in silence all the way home. He thought about what she said, and figured that Gillian must have left him the message earlier that day while he was putting in an appearance at his barber shop. Obviously, that was why she had seemed so distant all night. He didn't know which emotion was stronger—his happiness that Gillian had been thinking about that night at the restaurant, or his rage that Camille had been spying on him. By the time they got home, Frankie was furious and Camille was distraught.

Frankie pulled the car into the driveway, screeching to a halt and causing Camille to lurch forward slightly in her seat. Before she could protest, Frankie had climbed the stairs leading to their opulent home two at time. She followed closely behind him and watched him charge straight upstairs to their bedroom. He began to pack his things, and, once again, Camille began to cry.

"You leaving me for this bitch now, Frankie?"

He looked at her as if he wanted to jump on her and

wring her neck. "I never fucked Gillian, Camille." He put his hand on the Bible that sat on their nightstand. "I swear. That's my word on everything I love. I never had sex with her."

"But you want to. Don't you? Ain't that why you kissed her—your so-called best fucking friend?"

He looked at her and almost wanted to tell her she was right. He shook his head. "The only reason I refer to her as my best friend is because there's parts of this life that I don't want to expose you to. I don't want to poison you with the shit I deal with. But Gillian is *in* this shit. She's like one of the guys to me, and I talk to her about shit that I would never bring to you." He looked at her sincerely. "I did kiss her once. Weeks ago. And both of us were drunk. That shit just happened, and it only happened that one time. But I never cheated on you with her. I wouldn't disrespect you like that. And I wasn't trying to embarrass you tonight, Camille. I was just concerned about my friend. But this whole situation showed me how you don't trust me."

He kept packing, and Camille rushed over to try and stop him. She grabbed him by the arm and turned him toward her. "Don't walk out on me. I've been trying so hard to make you happy, Frankie."

He laughed. "Yeah? Is that what you've been doing? All I ever see you do is sit around here eating all fuckin' day and getting fat, drinking every night, letting your sister use you, checking my muthafuckin' voice mail, and listening to your little miserable friends filling your head with shit. I'm not dealing with that no more. I got enough shit to deal with every day."

"Don't leave, Frankie," Camille said, trying not to sob, but feeling wounded by her husband's words. He had never acknowledged that he'd noticed her weight gain or her drinking until now, and she was ashamed. She was also so sorry that she had accused him wrongly. "I'm sorry."

"Yeah, me too," he said, as he breezed past her and walked down the stairs and out the front door.

Frankie got into his car and was on his way back to the party when his cell phone began to ring. He answered it as he fastened his seat belt.

"*Frankie!*" Gillian was crying hard, and he froze as he heard her anguished voice.

"What's wrong, Gigi?"

"They shot them, Frankie. Please!" she cried. "Come back. Hurry up, and come back!"

"Who got shot?" Frankie was breathless now.

"*Daddy!*" Her voice was racked with sobs, and Frankie's heart sank instantly.

"*What?*" He was shaken, and hoped he had heard her wrong.

"They shot him. And Baron, too. It was Jojo and them, Frankie . . ."

Frankie instinctively started the car and peeled off in the direction of the Verrazano Bridge. Gillian could hardly talk. She spoke in a hoarse whisper, and her words dripped with grief and pain. "They were outside. They ambushed Daddy and they shot him . . . they killed him!"

Frankie felt hot tears falling as he thought of his mentor suffering at the hands of Jojo. All because of something Baron had done. "And Baron?"

"They shot him so many times, Frankie." She sobbed some more. "Please hurry up." She hung up the phone and

Frankie drove the rest of the way to the restaurant in a daze. He thought about Nobles. The man had saved his life in more ways than one. And now he was gone. His thoughts drifted to Baron, and Frankie was filled with rage. It was Baron's beef that had cost Nobles his life, and Frankie hoped that Baron survived so that he could be plagued with guilt for the rest of his days. When he thought of Gillian, Frankie pushed way past the speed limit to get to her side. She needed him now, more than ever before.

Casualties

Frankie finally pulled up in front of Conga and left his car double-parked at the curb behind the droves of emergency vehicles at the scene. He jumped out and jogged toward the entrance.

"Are you okay?" Frankie asked Mrs. Nobles as he walked into the restaurant. She nodded, though she appeared to be dazed, possibly even sedated. She was surrounded by police officers as well as family members. After explaining that he was a member of the family to the officers who were asking a thousand questions, Frankie started asking questions of his own. They told him that Nobles had been killed by two shots to the head, and he had died instantly. Baron had suffered numerous gunshot wounds and had been rushed to the hospital with his life hanging in the balance. His mother had been notified and was flying to New York immediately. One valet assistant had also been shot, but the wound was superficial and he was expected to be treated and released.

"Where's Gillian?"

Mrs. Nobles's sister pointed toward the corner, where he saw Gillian sitting alone staring at the wall. Frankie strode over and sat down across from her. He took both of her hands in his and looked in her eyes. He was fighting the urge to cry because he knew that Gillian needed his strength at this moment.

"You all right?" He knew it was a stupid question, but he didn't know what else to say. Gillian looked so fragile, like she was teetering somewhere between sanity and snapping. He felt so much grief in his heart at that moment, so he couldn't imagine how she must feel. Since she had positioned herself so far away from her grieving family, he didn't know what state of mind she was in.

She simply stared at him blankly. Tears slid down her cheeks slowly. She shook her head no, and he pulled her into his arms and held her tightly to his chest. She cried and he felt her body quake from the force of her sobs. Frankie cried, too. He stroked her back, and whispered to her that it was all right, that he was there for her. Gillian cried until her tears wouldn't come anymore. She finally sat back and caught her breath.

Gently, he asked her, "What happened when I left?"

She shook her head and looked up toward the sky. "It happened so fast, Frankie. Everybody was leaving for the night. My mom was wheeling Daddy out, and a whole bunch of people were outside. Valets and people going to their cars, that kind of activity. Then, all of a sudden, somebody just started firing. I heard shots and so did Baron. He told me to stay put and he ran out there. By then Daddy was already dead." She paused, shook her head as if still in disbelief, and took a deep breath before continuing. "When Baron went outside, the shots started all over again. I don't know if Baron got any shots off or if there was more than just one person shooting at them. But I could tell that there was more than one gun being fired. People were screaming and running, but Baron couldn't run. They shot him and he was defenseless." She paused to blow her nose with a tissue Frankie handed to her. "They just kept firing. Jojo was there. Mikey and Tremaine said they saw his face when they ran outside. They saw him shooting at Baron and they shot back, but nobody hit him. Then he got back in the car and they sped off."

Frankie sat soaking up all that she'd told him. He tried to picture it all happening, and he realized how lucky he was that he had left before all hell broke loose. He knew that if he had been there, Jojo would have had to kill him, too. Nobles was probably the one man that Frankie would gladly lay down his life for. He looked at Gillian and his heart broke. He had never seen her look so defeated.

"He killed my father. My brother might not make it. I want Jojo dead." Gillian's voice was deliberate and flat. Her eyes and nose were puffy and red from crying so hard. Frankie looked around, noticing that her lame boyfriend was nowhere in sight.

"Where's Sincere?"

"Sadiq, Frankie."

"Where's he at?"

"He left not long after you did. I told him to go home and that I'd call him tomorrow." Gillian shook her head, wiped the tears that fell from her eyes. She knew that Sadiq had been with a woman, because he'd arrived smelling like Chanel No. 5. And when she'd suggested that he go home and leave her to retire with her family for the night, he'd gone along with it all too eagerly. She was done with his punk ass. Her thoughts went back to her father, and she dissolved into tears again. The pain was so palpable that she felt an ache in her chest. She couldn't believe that he was gone.

Frankie was feeling so much all at once. Nobles was dead and he couldn't believe it. He hadn't even had a chance to say good-bye. He never thought when he bid the old man good night that it would be the last time they'd ever get to talk to one another. He sat there, lost in thought, while Gillian was interviewed by the officers at the scene. When they were finished, Gillian was eager to get to the hospital to check on her brother's condition. Frankie told her that he would bring her there, and they rose to leave. One of the crew members came over and explained to Frankie that Mayra was going home with her sister and would be watched around the clock by the crew to ensure her safety. No one expected Jojo and his goons to push things any further that night, but they would take extra precautions just in case.

Frankie and Gillian rode to the hospital in silence, both lost in thought over everything that had happened. Gillian stared out the window into the night, feeling lost and so alone now that the father she loved so deeply was gone. She thought about his face, the sound of his voice, all the things he taught her. She cried so hard that Frankie almost pulled over. Instead, he reached for her hand and held it tightly, assuring her softly that it was gonna be all right. But they both knew that without Nobles, things would never be the same.

When they got to the hospital, they rushed through the corridors still dressed in their formal attire. Frankie's suit jacket swung open as he walked, and his tie was loosened. Gillian trotted to keep up in her three-inch heels. When they got to the emergency room, they asked about Baron's condition. Several members of the Nobles crew were already there. The doctor spoke with them only briefly, informing them that Baron had been hit numerous times and had lost a lot of blood. They had him in surgery that was expected to last for several hours. When the doctor returned to the operating room, Frankie looked at Gillian. She looked so hopeless and heartbroken. He walked over and assured the crew that he would look after Gillian while they held vigil at the hospital with Baron. "Call me as soon as his mother gets here. And let me know when he comes out of surgery." The crew agreed, and Frankie took Gillian by the hand and led her out of the hospital. When they got inside the car, she looked at him.

"I'm scared," she said, her voice barely above a whisper.

Frankie looked back at her and brushed his hand across her cheek. "Don't be," he said. "I got you. Nobody's gonna hurt you." He started the car and left the hospital parking lot. But instead of driving her home, Frankie drove to the Plaza Hotel in Midtown Manhattan.

Gillian was confused. She turned to Frankie and asked, "What's Camille gonna say when she hears—"

"I walked out on her tonight, Gigi. So she can't say shit." He looked at Gillian seriously. "You can't go home right now. So I'm gonna stay with you until it's safe enough for you to go back." He checked them into a suite, then led the way with Gillian right behind him.

"What happened with your wife?" she asked as they walked down the long carpeted hallway.

"Shit got heated," he said. "You seemed upset tonight, and when I was asking you what's wrong, Camille got mad. We had a fight and I bounced."

Gillian was speechless. She wanted so badly to spend the

next few days and nights safely at the Plaza with Frankie. But was it right? Then she thought about her father sitting slumped over in his wheelchair, pictured Baron sprawled out across the sidewalk bleeding from all the gunshot wounds he had sustained. She heard her mother's voice mixing with her own as they screamed in the midst of the melee. And she looked at Frankie, tall and strong and ready to remain by her side for as long as she needed him. Gillian pushed the fact that he was married out of her mind and walked into the room with him.

Frankie tossed his bags on the floor beside the sofa. There were steps leading to a huge, beautiful claw-foot tub in the center of the room, a flat-screen TV and surround-sound system, a big California king–size bed near the wall. Frankie took off his tie and unbuttoned his shirt to reveal a crisp wifebeater beneath his tuxedo. He put the radio on *The Quiet Storm* and helped himself to the champagne chilling on the table. Gillian kicked off her shoes and lay across the bed, propping herself up on one elbow amid a huge mountain of pillows. Frankie walked over to her and handed her a glass of champagne, which she happily accepted. He lay beside her at a safe distance, watching her in silence.

The two of them lay there for a few minutes before Frankie spoke up. He took a deep breath and exhaled. "I met your father at the perfect time," he said. "I was probably twelve or thirteen, and I was lost."

Gillian was all ears because she could never recall when exactly Frankie became a part of the family. For as long as she could remember, he had been there. But she had been too young to recall the specifics of how it all happened.

Frankie drained his glass and refilled it before he continued.

"My father was crazy, you know what I'm saying? He used to bug the fuck out at the drop of a dime." He paused. "I never told nobody this."

Gillian felt honored. "Keep going."

He cleared his throat. He wasn't sure why he felt like telling Gillian his story tonight. But he was so eager to get it off his chest. He realized that he trusted her, because he had never shared with anyone—even his wife—what he was about to share with Gillian.

"He was crazy. I guess maybe nowadays they would call it bipolar or some shit. Back then I just knew the mutha-fucka was crazy. He would be different people at any given time."

"Like schizophrenic? He had different names and personalities and all that?" she asked.

He shook his head. "No. Not like that. Like . . . he would be cool one minute. He'd sit down to eat dinner and tell my moms that it was delicious. We were always quiet, me and my brother, 'cuz if we ever said the wrong thing at the wrong time, it would set him off. So he would compliment my moms on the food, everybody's quiet, and then *bam*! Why the fuck was she looking at him like that? What, did she poison his food? How come she wasn't eating the food she had just served him? And he would bug the fuck out."

Gillian listened carefully, picturing young Frankie in her mind, scared and confused. "Did he hit y'all?"

He nodded. "Hell yeah. He used to knock my mother around a little. Nothing major. But he bullied her. He would corner her and punch the wall behind her, scream in her face and make her cry. She was scared of him. So were me and my brother. Then, when I got to be like eleven or twelve years old, I had a growth spurt and I got taller than him almost overnight. He didn't like that shit. So he started taking his anger out on me, challenging me to kick his ass so he could kill me and be justified. I used to take the beatings at first. I felt like I was the biggest one and I'd rather him beat me than beat my little brother or my moms. But as I got older it got harder to keep taking ass whippings and not hitting back—father or no father."

"Damn," Gillian said, her brow furrowed with genuine compassion for what Frankie had endured. She thought of her own father and all the love he had lavished upon her over the years, and she was intensely grateful. It made her realize how blessed she had been to have the loving, doting father she had been given. She missed him so much already.

"We were all scared of him," Frankie admitted again. "I felt that if I challenged him that he really would kill me. I really felt he would do that shit. So I ran away instead. I slept at my friend Mikey's house when his moms was out smoking crack. Sometimes she would come home and try to sober up. When she was clean, she stopped letting me be there all the time and started asking questions about why I never went home. So I would find someplace else to sleep for a few nights. Then she would start using again and I could come back. Then Mikey told me that if I wanted to get money with him, he could put me on with your pops. I didn't believe him. We were shorties, and your father was a big fucking deal in the hood. I didn't think he had ever even spoken to Nobles, let alone that he had the hookup for me to get on, too. But he was telling the truth and he introduced me to your father. I was like . . . I froze when I met him for the first time. He talked all smooth and he was just such a G. I wanted to impress him, so I worked around the clock to get his attention.

I stopped going to school, stopped doing anything but hustling."

"You were still staying with Mikey?"

"Yeah. I figured out that if I gave his moms crack every now and then, she didn't beef as much. It became like home to me. We had our whole operation running out of there pretty much. That's the closest thing to home I had at that time." He paused, thinking back on those days. "But then his moms got arrested and he got put in foster care. I didn't know where the fuck I was going. I just knew I wasn't going back home."

Gillian nodded. "What about your mother and your brother? Did they know where you were?"

"Yeah. I saw my brother, Steven, all the time. I felt bad because by then he was older and I figured my father was probably fucking him up, too." He paused again, thinking that this was why he allowed Steven to take advantage of him. "He was smaller than me, you know what I'm saying. Shorter and skinny as hell. I worried about him a lot. I would sneak and see him and give him money to bring to Mommy, and he told me that my father wasn't hitting my mother no more since I left." Frankie paused, thinking about that. "I don't know if Steven was telling me the truth. Maybe he just said that so I wouldn't feel bad about leaving. He knew I didn't want to go back, but I would if I needed to protect them. Now that I was making a little money, I felt like I was invincible." He paused again briefly. "I didn't get to see my mother much, though. . . ." His voice trailed off at the end. He seemed pained by the truth of that. He felt guilty that he'd been the only one to escape the abuse. "She was so beat down after being with my father for so long that she used to just sit and be quiet. She would hum a song every now and then or answer you if you asked her a question. But other than that, she never talked too much. And even now, she's like that. It's hard for me to see her." He looked at Gillian. "I'm embarrassed to admit that my mother is still alive and I don't go see her because it's too hard."

Gillian reached and took his hand in hers. "I can understand that," she said softly. "Is your father still alive?"

Frankie chuckled. "Nope. He put a .45 in his mouth and blew his brains out on a random Tuesday night while everyone in the house was asleep. It was the middle of the night, and my family woke up when they heard the shot. My mother found him in the bathroom. She hasn't been the same since."

Gillian was so saddened by Frankie's story that she momentarily forgot her own pain. "How did you feel when he killed himself?"

He thought about that and admitted to himself that he had felt no grief. He shrugged his shoulders. "I was just glad that he chose to kill himself and not my moms or my little brother."

They sat quietly, lost in thought for a while.

Frankie broke out of his reverie. "That's when your pops took me under his wing. He asked me one day why I never had to go home at night and why I never went to school. I told him I *was* going to school, every day out there in them streets. And he laughed. He liked that. I was a young dude with a gift of gab and a lot of heart. And I respected the fact that he didn't pry. He only asked me once, and he accepted the answer I gave him. I was glad, too. 'Cuz I was too embarrassed to admit that my crazy father was terrorizing my family all along and now he was dead and I had to hold it down." He shrugged. "He must've known something about me in order to trust me like he did. He noticed that after I did my business with him, I would talk to Baron and we hit it off. So he encouraged us to chill together. Then, as we got to know each other, I started staying over. He never told me to go home or asked about my family or education again. He just let me in."

Gillian smiled through the tears in her eyes. "He loved you, Frankie," she whispered.

He nodded, wiped the tear that fell from her beautiful eyes. "I loved Pops more than I loved my own father," he said. "Now that he's gone, whether Baron makes it or not, I'm gonna take care of you. You're not alone, Gigi. I got you."

She looked at him, and he stared right back. They both took in the features of each other's faces with new eyes. Frankie noticed a few faint freckles scattered across her nose, and she noticed a lone gray hair in his goatee. She also looked at his lush lips and intoxicating eyes and felt herself being drawn in.

"How come you never told your wife what you just told me? About your family."

Frankie licked his lips. He wanted so badly to kiss her. "Because our relationship isn't like that," he answered honestly. "She met me when I was already in the game and never asked me how I became who I am. We were young and having fun and she just took me at face value, and I was cool with that. My family history is uncomfortable for me, so I never talk about it. She knows Steven and she's met my mother, but I never told her why things are the way they are in my family. You're the first person I feel like I can trust to know everything."

She smiled. "I'm glad that you know you can trust me."

He nodded and looked at her intently. "You can trust me, too."

Luther crooned in the background, and both of them felt swept up in the moment. Gillian figured it was a mixture of grief, sadness, shock, and the undeniable chemistry between them. Not to mention the champagne. But to Frankie it was something altogether different. He looked at her and thought she was the most beautiful woman he had ever seen. She was so vulnerable and so fragile that he just wanted to wrap his arms around her and never let go.

"Camille listened to my voice mail and she heard the message you left me." He looked at her seriously. "I didn't know you even left me a message until we were on our way home from the party and she told me."

Gillian was relieved to hear that. She hadn't wanted to believe that Frankie would ignore her feelings. "So she knows about the kiss."

Frankie nodded. Gillian didn't know how to feel. Part of her felt slightly guilty for hurting Camille. But the other part of her was glad that the truth was finally out.

"Come here," he coaxed, at a loss for words to fill the silence.

Gillian moved close to him until their bodies were merely inches apart. He moved a stray hair out of her face and stroked her cheek. Then he pulled her closer so that she was wrapped tightly in his embrace, their faces so close that she could smell the champagne on his breath. He could hear her heartbeat and her breath quickening despite the sound of the music playing in the background. Searching her eyes, Frankie gazed at her, hoping that she wouldn't tell him no. He kissed her. She held on to him and kissed him back. He pulled her tightly to him until she was nearly on top of him. He tasted the sweetness of her tongue and it made him want to kiss her deeper. Finally, he pulled away and stared at her once more.

She touched his face now. Touched that gray hair she'd noticed earlier and wondered how many gray hairs he'd grown over the years with all the burdens he had shouldered in his lifetime. She felt her heart swell with affection for him.

Frankie was undressing her and she silently let him. He zipped her out of her dress until she lay before him clad in only a pair of La Perla panties and a matching bra. He could not take his eyes off her. Every inch of her was beautiful. He caught her eyes again.

Frankie stripped out of his shirt and slacks, and realized that he was actually shy at that moment. He knew he was working with a well-endowed package. But he was still a little shy to be with Gillian in this way. She'd been his friend for so long and now here she was, nearly naked before him. He could sense her own hesitation as he lay on top of her still wearing his boxer shorts.

He kissed her. His hands ran the length of her body, stopping at her hips. She also reached for him, stroking his face, his chest, his back, and finally his rock-hard dick. She could feel how hard it was, how long and thick, and she creamed in anticipation. He pulled her panties down to her ankles and licked her from her toes all the way up her long, thick legs. He parted her thighs, feeling them quivering in anticipation. He looked at her beautiful pussy, thinking he had never seen a more exquisite work of art. He touched it, licked it, sucked it, and devoured it until she was screaming his name. Gillian was overcome by the feeling of Frankie—the man she'd loved for years in silence—between her legs, taking her to heights she'd never reached. Frankie didn't stop until she begged him to. He loved the way his name sounded as it rolled off her lips while she came.

Gillian was spent and Frankie was rock hard. Eagerly sliding on a condom, he watched her feeling the aftereffects of multiple orgasms. He climbed on top of her, slipping her bra off and sucking her nipples till they stood rock hard against his chest as he entered her. He slid within her wetness and took his time, stroking her, kissing her, whispering in her ear that she felt so good.

Gillian grabbed Frankie's back and grinded back at him, loving the way he felt inside of her. She had never felt anything like this and didn't want it to ever end. He held her tightly to him as he stroked her, held her so close that their sweat mixed together and their breathless kisses made her emotions overflow. Gillian began to cry and Frankie kissed her tears, slowed his pace, and looked in her eyes.

"You want me to stop?"

She shook her head and grabbed him tighter, wrapping her legs around him as if to pull him in deeper. "No," she whispered. "No, don't stop."

For the rest of the night they expressed the love they'd felt for each other for so long. As the sun came up, Frankie watched her sleep and knew that her sleeping face was the first thing he wanted to see every morning for the rest of his life.

Steal Away

Toya could not believe her ears. Camille was bugging the fuck out about Frankie on the phone. "Slow down!" she demanded. "I can hardly understand what you're saying!"

"Frankie might be hurt!" Camille yelled, holding the phone closer to her mouth as she shouted, as if Toya were deaf. "Nobles got killed last night, and Frankie hasn't called and he never came home."

Toya sat down at her desk at her real estate office and held her head in anguish. Once again, one of her dearest friends was in crisis. "Oh God!" she lamented. "Tell me what happened, from the beginning. The last time I spoke to you, you were going to the old man's anniversary party."

Camille poured herself a glass of cognac and sat down. "We went to the party. Everything was nice and we had a good time. But everybody was acting tense, and Frankie took me home so I would be out of harm's way just in case something popped off." Even as she said it, she knew it was a lie. She was conveniently leaving out her argument with Frankie and the fact that he had moved his things out.

"How did he know that something was gonna happen? He just sensed it?" Toya was frowning.

"I don't know. He just said something didn't feel right and he wanted to take me home." As she lied, Camille wished that was all there was to it.

"Okay, so he takes you home and goes back there. Then what?"

"That's what I'm trying to tell you. I haven't heard from him since. Now he's not answering his phone and I only heard about Nobles when I looked at the newspaper this morning. The story about his murder is on the front page." She looked at the headline of the *New York Daily News*, which blared, NOTORIOUS NOBLES DEAD IN AMBUSH. "It's not like Frankie not to answer his phone when I call, Toya. I'm scared."

"Did you call that bitch Gillian?" Toya felt that she had to ask.

Camille hated to admit that she had. In fact, she had been repeatedly dialing Gillian's home number since about an hour after Frankie stormed out. "I got her number off the caller ID and I've been calling her and she's not answering, either. But her father is dead and her brother is not going to make it, according to the newspaper. She could be anywhere."

Toya searched to find the right words to say. She put her inner bitch on the shelf in order to show compassion to her friend. "Camille, just relax. I'm sure he's fine. Did you call the hospital?"

Camille fought back tears. "I called St. Vincent's, where they took Baron, but Frankie wasn't admitted there. What if he's dead, Toya?"

"Stop thinking like that! Here's what we'll do. Meet me at St. Vincent's Hospital. I'll leave now. If Baron is there, somebody has to know where Frankie is. We'll ask questions. Stop panicking and meet me there now."

Toya hung up before Camille could protest.

By the time Gillian woke up, Frankie had a full report on Baron's condition. She rose out of bed, naked as a newborn child, and walked into the bathroom, where Frankie was shaving. She felt like last night had been both a terrible nightmare and a dream come true. She had ended the night in the arms of the man she loved. But her beloved father was gone and her brother's life hung in the balance. "Good morning." She looked at him expectantly.

Frankie looked back at her and felt guilty for wanting her all over again. Her body made him bite his lip with longing. "Good morning, gorgeous," he greeted her. Then he kissed her, morning breath and all.

"Did anybody call about Baron yet?"

He nodded. "His mother is here. She's at the hospital with him, and he made it out of surgery. They just don't know how long it will take him to wake up. He's not sedated anymore, but so far, he's still unresponsive."

Gillian stood there, digesting that. Her brother was in a coma. Her father was dead. What she had hoped was just a nightmare was actually very real.

Frankie pulled her close to him and tilted her chin to face him. "Everything is gonna be okay. I promise."

She wanted to believe him but couldn't see how things could ever be okay again. "What do I do now, Frankie?"

"First we'll get you some clothes and go to the hospital and check in on Baron and see if Celia needs anything. Then we'll go get your mother and take her to make arrangements for Pops." Frankie felt himself getting choked up as he said it. "Then we're gonna come back here and lay low for the time being."

"We can't lay low forever." Gillian felt like everything had fallen apart. "Eventually, we have to handle the business. What then?"

"By then, Jojo won't be a problem anymore." Frankie said it so firmly that Gillian knew he had a plan.

She stepped back and looked at Frankie, caught off guard. "I don't want you to get hurt or go to jail, Frankie. I can't take that on top of everything else. My brother is dying and Daddy is already gone. I can't deal with losing you, too."

"Don't worry about me. Just let me do what needs to be done," he said. "And Baron is gonna be okay, Gigi. Trust me." Frankie hated even uttering Baron's name. He was still furious that Baron's beef with Jojo had cost Nobles his life.

She nodded, feeling reassured. It was amazing how this man could make her feel like no matter what happened, she could handle it with him by her side. She went to the sink and brushed her teeth with the brand-new toothbrush lying in the package on the counter. She looked at Frankie's reflection in the mirror. He looked so good standing there, all chocolate and brown. She thought back to last night and how they'd lain together, their lovemaking bringing her to tears. He'd held her so close to him that their heartbeats seemed to synchronize. Gillian wanted to feel that again. She finished and set her toothbrush down, then turned the water off and faced Frankie.

"Take a shower with me."

Frankie didn't need to be asked twice. He stripped out of his wifebeater and boxers and turned the shower on full steam. Stepping into the hot streaming water, he held Gillian's hand as she stepped in after him. They slid the glass door shut, and Gillian reached for the soap. She lathered Frankie's sexy brown body from head to toe, and when she was done, he reciprocated. He ran his fingers through her long, thick hair and kissed and sucked on her every hot spot. She moaned his name as he fingered her, and she felt her juices flowing like a river between her thighs. She pulled away and bent on her knees and slowly took all ten inches of Frankie into her mouth. He had to fight the urge to moan like a female. It felt so good! Not able to hold back any longer, he pulled her to her feet and scooped her up in his arms with her ass resting firmly in his big hands. Frankie pressed his back against the wall and, using his bulging arms, lifted her easily onto his rock-hard dick. Bouncing her up and down on his manhood, he watched her face twist into ecstasy and could feel her throbbing on his dick as she reached her climax. She wrapped her arms tightly around his neck and began to writhe on him, grinding her pussy onto him until finally he exploded.

They rinsed off and emerged from the shower, both of them light-headed from the sex. He followed her into the bedroom and pulled her down to lay beside him on the king-size mattress. Frankie looked into her eyes and realized that he was definitely in love with Gillian.

"You don't love Sadiq," he said.

"How do you know?" Gillian asked, smiling and noticing that Frankie had gotten her boyfriend's name right for the first time ever.

" 'Cuz I know you." Frankie touched her nose, tracing the freckles that were now his favorite part of her face.

She didn't deny it. "You're right. I don't love Sadiq."

"So why do you stay with him?"

She hesitated. "Because he keeps my mind off of you."

Frankie had suspected that. But hearing her say it was music to his ears.

"You don't love Camille like you used to." Gillian was turning the tables on him.

He sat in silence for a long time. He thought about their fight last night—how he'd been waiting for an excuse to leave Camille. She had finally given him a way out. "You're right. I don't."

Gillian exhaled, pulled him toward her, and kissed him softly.

"So why do you stay with her?" she asked, meeting his gaze.

Frankie sighed. "Part of me feels obligated to her. Like I told you, in the early days, I didn't have shit. I was making money, but I was spending just as much as I made. I needed to make more, but I didn't have the cash to do it. Your pops helped me out a lot, but I was too proud to ask for more at that time. Camille was doing her modeling shit back then." When Frankie had begun dating Camille, she had the face and figure of a top model. Long legs, slim waist, and big boobs, plus a chiseled face with beautiful warm brown skin. She was stunning. And Frankie had been smitten with her. "She handed me eight grand one time, which was all the money she made doing a shoot. She told me she could tell that I was struggling and she wanted to help me get on. We weren't even married at the time."

Gillian nodded. "That's real."

"It is." Frankie cleared his throat. "And I did love her at first." He remembered that their love was unparalleled in those days. It seemed so long ago. "Because she rode it out with me in the beginning, I stayed with her even though the love wasn't the same. The thing is, it's getting harder for me to pretend like I'm happy. And now . . . I think it's safe to say it's over. I don't really enjoy being around her anymore. She's so uptight all the time, always concerned about what people will think about her or about us. I want her to let loose sometimes and rock a Yankee fitted."

Gillian laughed.

"It's like everything she does gets on my nerves. And on top of that, she gained weight. And I don't want to be an asshole about it, but I don't like her looking like that. She used to take care of herself better than she does now." He shook his head. "I do love Camille. There's a lot of history between us. So I got love for her. But it's not how it used to be. With you . . . it's different."

Gillian felt her heart two-step again. "What's different?"

Frankie stared into her dancing eyes and grinned slightly. "The way I love you is different."

Gillian wasn't smiling. "You don't really mean that, Frankie." Her expression turned sad. "And I don't need to be lied to right now."

He kissed her hand and stared at her for a few moments before he responded. "Have I ever lied to you before?"

She shook her head no, felt herself getting choked up.

"I'm not gonna start lying now." He kissed her lips. "I love you, Gigi. I'm dead serious about that."

She smiled and touched his face gently. "I love you, too."

Frankie kissed her deeply, and they both knew that things would never be the same again.

Misled

"Here he comes." Toya nudged Camille and nodded toward her approaching husband.

Camille's heart sank. She sat and watched Frankie and Gillian walking down the hospital corridor in her direction. She had been calling her husband all night and day, and he never picked up his phone. She had called every hospital in Manhattan in search of him. She had even called the medical examiner's office, worrying and praying the whole time that he was safe. Now here he was, looking perfectly healthy, headed in her direction with the bitch she now despised for being the reason their marriage was imploding.

Thoughts raced through her head at lightning speed. She was heated that, by the looks of it, her husband had spent the night with Gillian. But what enraged her even more was the fact that Toya was present to witness Frankie's brazen infidelity. Camille prayed silently that Frankie wouldn't play her by ignoring her or disrespecting her in front of her friend.

"Hmmm!" Toya mumbled, seeing Frankie and Gillian striding down the long hallway. It was a cold December morning, and Gillian looked adorable in her curve-hugging Seven jeans, a fitted black and gray striped sweater, and black leather booties. A cropped black motorcycle jacket completed the look, and her long hair blew slightly from the swiftness of her stride. Frankie walked beside her wearing jeans and a black button up. To Toya, they looked like a sexy Hollywood supercouple with their coordinated outfits. She wondered if Camille was finally realizing that her husband was sleeping with his best friend.

Meanwhile, Frankie had spotted Camille sitting beside Toya almost immediately. "Shit," he said under his breath. Gillian looked at him and slowed her pace.

"She's been waiting here for you all night?" she asked.

Frankie shook his head. "She must've come after I called this morning, because if she had been here all night Tremaine would've told me."

Gillian didn't need a confrontation with Frankie's wife after having just lost her father. With her only sibling's life hanging in the balance, she was in no mood for Camille's melodrama. As they got closer, she felt her adrenaline rushing. If Camille made a scene, Gillian would not hesitate to beat her prissy ass senseless.

They got to where Camille was now standing, and Gillian wasted no time making a hasty exit. "Hi, Camille," she said, and greeted Toya politely as well. Toya responded, but couldn't help noticing that her friend did not. Gillian didn't seem to care. Instead, she moved past the ladies and walked over to Baron's mother, who was seated nearby. Hugging her, Celia burst into tears, and Gillian consoled her. Celia was distraught. Not only was her only child comatose with a grim prognosis, but her ex-husband—whom she had never stopped loving—was gone. Gillian cried tears of her own as the two women headed to Baron's room to hold vigil at his bedside.

Frankie was now standing with Camille and Toya, awkwardly silent.

"Hi, stranger," Toya greeted Frankie. "I'm glad to see that you're all right. Your wife has been extremely worried about you."

Frankie looked at Toya and nodded, his hands in his pockets. She noticed that he still hadn't even greeted his wife. No hug, no kiss, not even a hello. Such a contrast from the man she'd seen at Camille's birthday party rubbing her back and professing his love for her. She wondered what was really going on with the Binghams.

The awkward silence returned, and Toya figured that she was the odd one out. She turned to Camille. "I'm gonna go now," she said. "Call me if you need me."

Camille nodded, terribly embarrassed by how distant Frankie was acting toward her. "Thanks, Toya. I appreciate you coming down here to meet me." She hugged her friend and watched as Toya sauntered off toward the elevators.

When her friend was out of earshot, Camille scowled at Frankie, fighting to keep her voice down. "First you walk out on me. Then you spend the night with Gillian. All night and all morning long your phone has been going straight to voice mail, and I've been thinking the worst. I have to pick up the newspaper to find out what's going on in my own husband's life, and now you stroll in here and you can't even acknowledge me, Frankie? What the fuck is wrong with you?"

He looked at his wife, and suddenly felt guilty. He had no regrets about what happened between him and Gillian the night before. But he did feel bad that Camille—who clearly loved him deeply—would inevitably be hurt because his heart just wasn't in their marriage any longer.

"Listen," he said, taking a deep breath. "You played yourself last night. Going through my voice mail, accusing me of fucking around on you . . . Camille . . ." Frankie's voice trailed off as he struggled to find the words to say. "I'm tired of it. Tired of you always being jealous of my friendship with Gillian." He looked at her seriously. "Nobles is dead." Each time he said it, the reality of it hit him like a freight train. "And you know he was like a father to me."

Camille nodded. As soon as she'd seen the *Daily News* headline that day and a picture of the bloody carnage that the anniversary party had erupted into, Camille had known that Frankie would be devastated by the loss of his mentor. "I don't even know what happened. All I know is what I read in the paper, because you haven't picked up your phone."

Ignoring her subtle dig, he shook his head. "I got back to the party and it was chaos. Pops was dead, Baron was in emergency surgery, and the decision was made that Mayra and Gillian should be kept safe in case they were targets."

"I see," Camille said, folding her arms across her chest. "So you volunteered to protect Gillian, am I right?"

Frankie stared at her blankly, not bothering to answer her.

She was getting more and more angry. "Right, Frankie? You spent the whole night protecting Gillian instead of making sure that I was okay? It was so important for you to keep a good eye on her that you couldn't answer a single one of my phone calls?" Hearing herself speak, Camille realized that she was fighting a losing battle. Frankie hadn't called or come home to her because he didn't want to be with her anymore. She shook her head and started to cry.

Frankie rolled his eyes. This shit was so unwelcome right now! "Camille, stop crying."

"I've been trying so hard," she said between gasps. "Trying to look good enough for you, and keep the house clean and cook like I'm the fucking black Rachael Ray! All this time I've been the perfect wife. I tried everything I could to keep you happy. And the first chance you get . . . the first mistake I make, you go running off with that bitch and you can't even be bothered to call me. To check in and let me know that even though the guys you do business with were shot the fuck up, that you were okay. I sat up all night calling you, Frankie! Then you walk in here, you see me sitting here with my friend, waiting for someone to tell me where you are, if you're okay. And your fake-ass friends won't tell me anything because the whole time they knew that you were laying up with that bitch! And you can't even say hello to me? Not even a hug or a fucking handshake? Why do you hate me all of a sudden, Frankie? What did I do wrong?"

Camille's sobbing caught the attention of several passing hospital staff members. Frankie was embarrassed, both of Camille's public outburst and of his own selfish behavior.

"It's not even like that," he lied.

Camille looked at him in disbelief. "You spent the night with her, Frankie!"

Frankie couldn't take this. "Camille, the woman just lost her father. Her brother is in there fighting for his life, and your selfish ass is standing here acting like it's all about you. Poor you! *You* sat up all night calling me. *You* called all over town looking for me. *You* tried so hard to be the perfect wife. How do you sound?" Frankie was so disgusted by his wife, who sat before him with tears in her eyes and snot in her nose. "Your friend came and sat with you all morning here at the hospital. She dropped everything for you, didn't she? So my best friend just watched her father and brother get gunned down and I'm wrong for dropping everything for her?"

Camille didn't have an immediate comeback.

"This is the type of shit I can't take anymore, Camille. Gillian's not the fucking problem. You are. And the only reason you keep talking shit about her is because you're jealous of her. She's more interesting than you. She's more independent than you. And you feel like less of a woman because I enjoy being around her." Camille looked wounded by his words, so he stopped. Maybe he was being mean because he was going through some serious emotional turmoil after the events of the last twenty-four hours. He tried to tone it down. "You keep talking about how hard you tried in this relationship. I've been trying, too, Camille. I try to ignore your nephew being at our house more than he's ever at his own and I try to ignore you nagging me about a baby every few minutes. Your sister takes advantage, you spend money on her like she's one of our dependents, and I keep my mouth shut about it. You're not the only one trying."

Camille looked in her husband's eyes and wondered if they were at a point of no return. "So what now, Frankie? You seriously want to leave me now? Just like that? All these years and it's over just like that?" She was trying not to cry again.

Frankie looked toward Baron's room, thought about Gillian in there. He thought about the night he spent with her and the way he felt waking up beside her that morning. Then he looked at his wife and could see that she was falling apart right before his eyes. He loved her, but not the way he used to. Still, he couldn't shake the sense of obligation he felt toward her. She had been a good and faithful wife to him over the years. Even in the early days, when he was far from rich, she'd been in his corner. Was it her fault that he was bored with her? He shook his head, frustrated by the fork in the road he was facing.

"I got a lot of shit going on right now. Now that Pops is gone and Baron's out of commission, I have to help hold everything together." He was tap-dancing around the truth. He wanted out of his marriage, but seeing his wife crying a river was making it hard for him to say that. "I'm gonna need some space, Camille. Seriously. We both need that."

Camille didn't respond. She stared at Frankie, wishing she could wave a magic wand and make everything all right. But she knew that it wouldn't be that easy. Relieved that he hadn't flat-out said that their marriage was over, she took a deep breath. "So now I'm supposed to turn around and go home alone?"

He nodded. "Yeah. I have to help make Pops's funeral arrangements when I leave here."

"And after that?"

He looked at her, wondering why she was pressing him to tell her what she didn't want to hear.

Realizing that Frankie wasn't going to deny that he would be with Gillian that night, Camille nodded slowly. She looked at the floor, then turned and picked up her clutch bag from the chair behind her. She turned back to her husband and said, "I'll be waiting for you to come home, Frankie."

He didn't respond. Finally, Camille walked away, fighting back a flood of tears and nursing her wounded pride.

Love Is a Losing Game

As soon as Misa found out what had happened to Baron, she rushed to the hospital and held vigil at his side. Celia was there each day, too, wondering why her son had never told her about the young lady who showed up each day when visiting hours began and stayed until they ended each night. Misa explained that she and Baron had only recently begun seeing each other, and that she had fallen in love with her son. Celia was, quite honestly, grateful for the company as she waited and prayed for her son to regain consciousness.

Meanwhile, Camille held out hope that her marriage wasn't really over. Frankie hadn't been home since the night of the shooting. She hadn't spoken to him, either, since he wouldn't answer her phone calls. Still, she wouldn't give up. As the day of Nobles's funeral neared, she continued to play the role of Mrs. Bingham, getting food ready to take over to Mayra's house and purchasing a beautiful black Tahari suit to wear to the funeral service. She was in denial about the state of her marriage. She didn't think about the fact that Frankie was avoiding her. Instead, she attributed his absence to the fact that he was stepping up in order to honor

his mentor one last time. She understood Frankie's love for
Doug Nobles, and that love, she believed, was the only reason her husband was away from her for so long. What did
bother her was the thought of Frankie being intimate with
Gillian. Even after witnessing the two of them together at the
hospital the day after the shooting, Camille refused to accept that there was anything serious going on between them.

That all changed on the day of Doug Nobles's grand funeral at the Frank E. Campbell funeral chapel on Madison
Avenue in Manhattan. Cars lined the surrounding blocks as
droves of mourners showed up to pay their respects to
Nobles. Fur coats and diamonds of all sizes and colors
adorned them as they poured in through the large doors
leading into the chapel. The smell of flowers filled the air,
and arrangements of all kinds—sprays, large bouquets, and
plants—dotted the room. Beside the heavy mahogany casket where Nobles lay in repose, a large canvas portrait sat
atop an easel. Camille recognized the image of Nobles as
one she'd seen on a number of occasions. In it, he was
dressed in his favorite blue velvet bathrobe as he sat in his
favorite chair, which resembled a throne. His face bore a
slight grin and his right hand held one of his fine Cuban ci-
gars. The canvas was elegantly framed with an engraved
brass nameplate affixed at the bottom. A pianist played
softly in the corner, and Camille noticed a videographer
capturing the service on film. Camille took a seat in the row
closest to where the family would be seated. After all, she
was married to the deceased's surrogate son.

The family began their processional into the chapel, led
by Mayra, who was escorted by Tremaine. Celia followed,
escorted by Mikey. Next came Gillian, who walked in
hand in hand with Frankie.

As they neared her row, Frankie locked eyes with his wife. Camille's jaw tightened. Frankie turned away and continued as if he barely noticed her presence. While the rest of the family, including Doug's sister and her children, filed in, Camille's gaze was fixed on her husband. Even as the officiator began the service, all Camille could do was stare ahead at Frankie, who was seated in the row ahead of her. She saw Gillian bow her head and cry and watched as Frankie wiped her tears with his handkerchief. As tears fell from her own eyes—mourning the demise of her marriage more than the fall of Doug Nobles—Camille couldn't help but ponder the fact that her husband was not there to wipe them away. He was too busy with Gillian instead. Their hands still clasped, the two of them spoke softly to one another throughout the service. Camille could make out some of what they were saying to each other. At one point Frankie leaned in to Gillian and tenderly swept a lock of hair out of her face. "It's all right, baby," he whispered. "It's okay."

Camille could hardly stand it, and she felt terribly embarrassed. She was relieved that her sister and her friends were not there to witness the spectacle her husband was making with another woman. Still, there were dozens of people there who knew that she and Frankie were married, and she could certainly imagine what they must be saying or thinking as Frankie wrapped his arms around Gillian, who was now sobbing hard. Finally, as the service came to an end, the minister invited the attendees to come up for the final viewing, beginning from the last row of the chapel. Camille sat still in her seat, her eyes shielded by Gucci sunglasses, which did a wonderful job of masking the hurt and palpable sadness she felt as she watched her husband.

When the time came for her row to move forward, Camille fell in line with the mourners ahead of her as they
inched toward the casket. Passing Frankie's row, she stared
at him and was dismayed that he didn't even seem to notice
her at all. He certainly made no attempt to acknowledge
her, his attention focused solely on Gillian, who seemed to
be coming undone. She was crying harder than ever now,
no doubt dreading saying her final good-bye to her beloved father. Camille lingered at the casket and touched
Nobles's cold hand as she said a silent prayer for him. Then
she moved along and watched from the back of the chapel as
Frankie tenderly led Gillian toward her father's casket.

The sound of Gillian's sobs reverberated throughout the
room as she all but passed out at the sight of her father lying
still in his coffin. She appeared to go weak in the knees, and
Frankie held her up with his arms, supporting her around
her small waist. She cried into his chest, and he stroked her
hair softly while his own tears fell. As she watched the two
of them, so united in their grief and in their love for the man
who had been taken from them so suddenly, Camille's heart
broke into a thousand pieces. She began to understand what
drew them together so strongly, and she did her best to fight
the feeling of defeat that crept up within her.

"Oh, Daddy . . ." Gillian's voice was so filled with sorrow
and misery that Camille almost felt sorry for her. But that
soon changed when Frankie gripped Gillian tightly and led
her out of the chapel, and right past Camille as if she were
invisible.

"Frankie," Camille called out to her husband. But he ignored her and walked Gillian out and ushered her into the
limousine that awaited them.

Camille stood alone at the back of the chapel and

watched as Mayra and Celia cried out in anguish as they bid farewell to the man both women had loved a great deal. Camille, too, cried—finally accepting that she was mourning the loss of her husband as well.

When all of the mourners had exited the chapel, pallbearers loaded Nobles's casket into a waiting horse-drawn hearse. Once the funeral sprays were laid on top of it, the coachman set off toward the cemetery with a long processional of cars trailing behind it. Camille followed in her SL600, crying bitter tears of shame, anger, and pure pain.

At the cemetery, a large crowd gathered around as the minister prayed. All heads were bowed, except for Camille's. She was staring directly at Frankie, watching as he linked arms with Gillian. When the prayers were done, Mayra set a flower on the casket and broke down. Gillian went to her mother's side and wrapped her arms around her, and the two of them embraced warmly as they headed back to their car. Frankie stood at the casket, and tears slid slowly from his eyes. He missed Nobles so much and felt a loss he hadn't felt when his own father had passed away.

"I love you, Pops," Frankie said softly. He set his flower down on the solid casket and turned to walk away, and came face-to-face with Camille.

"Hello, Frankie," she said. "Can I talk to you for a minute?"

Frankie looked at her with a slight snarl and then glanced over her shoulder at Gillian, who was watching from the limo. "What's up?"

Camille's long hair blew in the cold winter breeze and she pulled her mink tighter against her body. She looked up at Frankie and took a deep breath.

"Frankie, what's going on with us?" she asked. "Since the

shooting, you haven't even called me or answered any of my messages. I've been waiting to talk to you so we can figure out what went wrong and try to fix it." She reached and took his hand in hers. "I love you, Frankie. And I miss you so much. When are you coming back home?"

Frankie shook his head and looked at the ground. He hated to break her heart, but he had to be honest about what he was feeling. Still holding his wife's hand, he led her a few feet away from the other mourners, and sighed.

"Camille . . . I wish you wouldn't have come here."

She felt like she'd been punched in the face. "Don't I belong here? Am I not your wife?"

He nodded. "Yes, you are." He looked her in her eyes in order to convey his sincerity. "But I think it's safe to say that me and you have gone in different directions, Camille. I'm not happy with you. I haven't been for a long time."

"Don't say that, Frankie." Camille's voice cracked with emotion. "Don't give up on us like this."

He shook his head. "I'm not gonna keep telling you what you want to hear. Or avoiding you because I'm not eager to hurt your feelings. I never wanted to hurt you, sweetheart. You're a good woman. Just not good for me anymore."

Camille's tears ceased, and she felt a venomous rage build up within her. "You are not leaving me for that bitch!"

"I'm not gonna do this with you right now, Camille. This ain't the time or the place—"

"*What is the right time, Frankie?*" Camille lost all decorum.

He turned and began to walk away from her.

"*Frankie! Frankie, don't you dare walk away from me!*" Camille couldn't believe that he was ignoring her and acting as if she were a stranger to him.

Celia came over and hugged Camille. She had watched the whole scene unfold and could see that Camille was unraveling. Celia consoled her as she dissolved into tears, and stroked her back in an attempt to comfort the heartbroken woman. Everyone had seen Frankie cozying up to Gillian all day while ignoring his wife. Celia, for one, was appalled by his behavior. "Keep your dignity, Camille," she said. "Don't let anybody take you outside of your character." She smoothed Camille's hair. "Wait here."

Celia walked off after Frankie. She called out his name, and he stopped walking and turned around to face her. She caught up to where he was and shook her head.

"Don't do this."

He frowned. "Do what?"

"Years ago, Doug did to me exactly what you're doing to your wife right now. When he decided that he was in love with Mayra and that he was no longer happy with me, he didn't have the guts to tell me that. Instead, he just began to spend more and more of his time away from home and in essence abandoned me. He left me no choice but to end my marriage, and he never really told me why. Maybe he just got bored with me, or maybe he ran out of love. Who knows? But you make vows to stay with someone till death do you part. You owe Camille more respect than you're showing her right now. You keep ignoring her and, yeah, eventually she will go away. But you owe her better than that. Talk to your wife, Frankie. If Gillian loves you, she'll be patient and give you the space that you need to do that.

"Doug loved you very, very much," Celia said. "He was so proud of you. Now I need you to handle this the right way so that you can be proud of yourself."

Frankie breathed deeply and exhaled. He had always

respected Celia, and he had to admit that she had a point right now. He didn't want to have this difficult conversation with Camille. But Celia made him realize that even though it would be difficult, it was necessary. He nodded and kissed Celia on the cheek. "You're right," he said. "Thank you."

Celia gave him a sympathetic smile. "I'll tell Gillian to give you a few minutes alone." Celia walked away, and Frankie slowly walked back toward his wife. Camille had dried her tears and was standing bravely against the cold.

"I owe you an explanation," Frankie said, trying hard to man up and level with Camille. "I'm in love with Gillian."

Camille shook her head and fought back tears. "No, you're not."

"I am. And I love you, too, Camille. But it's not the way it used to be. It hasn't been that way for a while between us. Whenever you bring up the subject of us having a baby, it makes me so mad because having a kid would be like putting a Band-Aid on a gunshot wound. It's not gonna fix the problem. I'm in love with somebody else. And I'm so sorry that I hurt you. I didn't handle this the way that I should have. But I really didn't mean to break your heart, Camille. You deserve better than that."

She stared at her husband, so angry that she refused to cry anymore. She laughed at the irony that they were standing in a cemetery as their marriage died. "So that's just it?" she asked. "All these years, and after everything we've been through . . . that's it?"

He shrugged his shoulders and shook his head, feeling truly sorry that he was letting her down. But losing Nobles had shown him just how fragile life could be. He wanted to spend his with the woman who made him happy. And that woman was Gillian.

"I know that we still have a lot to figure out. Marriages don't get dissolved overnight. But I need to ask you to give me some space for a while so that I can sort everything out. Let me deal with everything that's happening with Baron . . . and then I'll come by the house and we'll talk. Is that fair?"

"None of this shit is fair. You're quitting on us." She shook her head and threw up her hands in frustration. "Go," she said. "Just go, Frankie."

He stood there for a few awkward moments, and then he turned around and walked away, leaving Camille to cry alone.

One Way or Another

It was Christmas Day and Celia was on her way to the hospital to see about her son. She was still mourning the loss of Nobles, who still held the keys to her heart even after so many years apart. Now her son was fighting for his life, and she prayed each day that God would spare her only child so that he could have a second chance to get it right.

Her cell phone rang as she drove into the hospital parking lot, and she answered it. She had to pull it away from her ear when she heard Misa screaming into the phone. Celia's heart paused and immediately she thought the worst. But Misa was screaming for a good reason.

"He's awake, Miss Celia! Baron woke up! Where are you? He's asking for you."

"*Thank you, Jesus!*" Celia jumped out of her car and began running toward the entrance. "I'm right downstairs. I'm on my way up. Tell him that Mama's on her way!" Celia did a happy dance as she jogged toward the elevator. This was the best Christmas present she could have ever received!

She entered Baron's room and found him lying with his

eyes barely open and Misa holding an ice pack on his forehead. When she saw Celia, a huge smile spread across her face.

"He has a fever, Miss Celia. But they said he's gonna be okay."

Celia inched toward the bed crying happy tears. "Baby, I love you so much. I've been praying so hard and Misa has, too. She's been here every day. I'm so happy to see you back with us, baby." She watched as Baron managed a weak smile. He was happy to be alive and even happier to see his mother. The night of the shooting was still a blur to him. But he remembered seeing his father slumped over in his wheelchair. He winced a little, both from the memory and from the pain that seared through his chest whenever he tried to move.

"How's Pops?" he asked. "Where is he?"

Celia glanced at Misa and they both looked saddened by the news they had to give him. Celia sat on the edge of her son's bed and held his hand in hers. "Baron . . . your father didn't make it."

He started to cry, sobbing so hard that both women melted into tears of their own. "No, Ma . . . no . . . please tell me that he's okay. Please!"

Misa felt so sorry for him. She couldn't imagine how he must feel. Celia, too, was devastated for her son. She wished there were some way she could take on all of his pain and suffering. She would have gladly felt it for him so that he wouldn't need to suffer the way he clearly was now.

What neither woman knew was that Baron was distraught not just over the loss of his father, but because he knew that it was his fault. It was his problems with Jojo, particularly the

fact that he had killed his brother, that caused Jojo to shoot
up the anniversary party. And now his father was dead. He
blamed himself.

"His funeral was a few days ago, Baron. It was very beautiful. And he's not suffering anymore, son. That's what matters right now."

He continued to cry, and Misa decided that she should
excuse herself. She figured this was a private family moment
and that she should allow them time to talk alone.

"Baron, Miss Celia, I'm gonna step out for a while. Go
check on my son and get something to eat. I'll come back up
later on tonight."

Celia nodded and smiled at Misa. "Thank you, sweetheart. Go on and spend Christmas with your boy. You've
been up here so much that I know he misses you. I'll be here
for the entire day, so Baron will be fine."

Misa smiled and nodded. Then she blew Baron a kiss
and left the two of them to mourn Doug Nobles in private.

She went to her sister's house, anxious to see her son on
Christmas morning. He had been staying at Camille's place
ever since Baron was wounded. Shane was on break from
school until after the new year, which made it easier for her
to spend the time that she needed to at Baron's bedside. She
felt that nursing him back to health was her chance to solidify her position in Baron's life, and she didn't want to let
it slip away no matter what. She was grateful that Camille
had been caring for Shane during that time, and that she
hadn't complained about it. Since she hadn't spoken to Camille in at least two days, she had no idea that Camille and
Frankie's marriage had ended.

Misa rang her sister's doorbell and was dismayed when
Steven answered the door instead of Camille.

"Well, well, well, stranger," he said, smiling. "Welcome back."

"Hi, Steven," Misa said, breezing past him into the foyer. "Where's my sister?" Looking around, she noticed some of Shane's toys on the couch, though he was nowhere to be found.

Steven followed behind her and shrugged his shoulders. "Camille went out. I don't know where she went. She didn't tell me. You know her and Frankie broke up, right?"

Misa's head snapped around, and she looked at Steven in shock. "They did?"

He nodded. "Ever since then, Camille's been out and about a lot more than usual. Since I don't be going nowhere I've been keeping an eye on Shane."

She frowned. She felt like a bad sister for not knowing what was going on with Camille and Frankie. "Okay, then. Where is Shane?"

Steven shrugged and looked around. "I don't know where lil homie went. He was sitting in the living room with me watching TV a little while ago, but then he broke out."

Misa walked into the living room and glanced at the TV, which was tuned to Cartoon Network, and she frowned. She wondered where Shane had disappeared to and why he hadn't come running when he heard her voice. She felt a surge of guilt, wondering if her son was unhappy that she had returned. Seeing the dejected look on Misa's face, Steven tried to ease her mind a bit.

"He's probably playing hide-and-go-seek again. He likes to do that, especially since Camille's been so busy running in and out. She's usually too tired to play it with him, and I'm always willing. He does it like every day." Steven laughed. Misa, however, was searching for her baby. She opened closet doors and searched the kitchen, calling Shane's name all the while.

Finally, she wandered into the bathroom down the hall and found Shane crouched into a ball in the bathtub. He was crying, and her heart seized in her chest.

"Baby, what's wrong?" she asked, pulling him close to her. "You're not happy to see Mommy?"

Shane pushed her away. "No!"

Misa's eyes watered, and her mother's words echoed in her ears. "*You better get back to parenting your son before he forgets that you're his mother.*"

"Shane, stop it," she said, as he pushed her harder. "I'm sorry it took so long for me to come back and get you. But Santa brought you so much stuff. Come home with me so you can see what he got for you." Misa stood up and held her hand out for him. He didn't reach back.

Shane's arms were still folded tightly across his chest, and Misa had never seen him look so sad and angry at the same time. She heard Steven's voice behind her and jumped, startled.

"Shane, go with your mommy. She missed you."

To Misa's surprise, her son peeked up and looked sheepishly at Steven. Steven nodded slightly and, just like that, Shane stepped out of the tub and reluctantly took his mother's hand. Steven seemed to have Shane in check, and Misa felt like she had lost control of her own child.

She turned to Steven, angered by the fact that it took his encouragement to get her son to listen to her. But she checked herself. After all, it wasn't his fault that Shane wasn't thrilled by her return. Misa's guilt brought tears to her eyes as she looked at Steven. "Thank you," she said. "I appreciate you looking out for him while I was gone."

Steven nodded. "My pleasure."

Misa led Shane upstairs to get his belongings, feeling slighted but hoping that his mood would change once she got him home again. She tried to make idle conversation with him, asking if he missed her and inquiring about the things he did with his aunt while she was away. Shane gave her the silent treatment no matter how hard she tried to coax him to talk to her.

Misa was crushed. But she stopped pressing Shane, and gave him time to come around. They gathered his things in silence and left Camille's house with Steven standing in the doorway to see them off. He patted Shane on the head softly.

"See you soon, little homie."

Shane ran quickly to the car, happy to be going home at last.

Hours later, Misa sat on the couch watching a ridiculous VH1 reality show. She couldn't recall a worse Christmas than this one. Shane was still mad at her, and he was holed up in his room playing with the toys he had unwrapped only hours earlier. She had decided to leave him alone, hoping that with time he'd come around and be his old self again. Her cell phone rang, and she happily answered it upon seeing Celia's cell phone number flash across the screen.

"Hey, Miss Celia," she said. "How is he?"

"He's sleeping now," Celia answered. "His friend Angelle came by to visit him and she's going to stay here for a while. I'm about to step out and grab some dinner, so Angelle is going to sit with Baron while I'm gone. I've decided to spend the night here, so there's no need for you to come back tonight if you don't want to. We've got him covered. Enjoy your Christmas with your son," she said.

Misa frowned. She knew all about Angelle. Baron had

interrupted their time together on a number of occasions in order to talk to that bitch about business. But she could tell by the way he had spoken to her that there was more to their relationship than just business. She didn't like the thought of her being there unsupervised with Baron. And she also didn't like the idea that the bitch might come back again the next day or the day after that. Misa was more determined than ever to solidify her position as Baron's wifey. Angelle was not part of that plan. The only problem was that Camille was too busy running around trying to save her marriage, which meant that Misa had to take full responsibility for Shane, and he was too young to be allowed in Baron's hospital room. She thought long and hard to come up with a solution.

The last thing Misa wanted was to wind up like her sister. Camille's marriage had self-destructed, and Misa felt sorry for her. She pondered how the tables had been turned not so long ago, when Camille had been saying that she felt sorry for her sister instead of the other way around. No one would have guessed that Camille's picture-perfect marriage to Frankie would have dissolved so horribly and that Misa would be the one to find a chance at true happiness with Baron. She thought about Shane then, and how blessed she was to have him. Camille's own hope for a child had been dashed, and Misa realized that she had taken motherhood for granted. Shane's behavior today had shown her how much she was neglecting him. She decided to go talk to her son.

Walking into Shane's room, she saw him sitting on the floor surrounded by his toy cars. Misa smiled.

"Hey, papa."

Shane ignored her and continued pushing his favorite car across the carpeted floor.

"I came to play with you, Shane."

Silence still.

Misa was getting annoyed. "Shane, I'm talking to you."

He kept playing. "No talk to me," he said softly.

Misa was trying to remain patient with the three-year-old. "Why not, papa? I thought you would be happy to see me."

He shook his head.

Misa sat on the edge of his bed. "You're not happy to see me?"

"No." Shane pushed the cars around on the floor.

"You want to go back to Aunt Camille's house?"

He stopped playing and stared at the floor.

Misa took that as a yes. "Fine," she said, assuming that her son had gotten accustomed to the posh surroundings of his aunt's house. She guessed that her modest home wasn't good enough for him anymore after spending so much time at Camille's bigger, more opulent abode. "You can go back there tomorrow since you like it so much. Uncle Steven can watch you while I go out."

Suddenly, Shane stood up and tossed the car he was holding at Misa's head. He started crying and yelled at the top of his lungs, "*I hate you!*"

Misa stood dumbfounded, her mouth agape in pure shock.

"No! I wanna go with my *daddy*!"

Misa was furious. The toy car had missed her by mere inches, and, once the shock wore off, she was enraged. Shane was longing for the father who had abandoned them without a second thought. Before she knew it, she was on her feet charging at her son. To her dismay, he threw himself on the floor and curled himself into a ball, hiding his face with his hands. Misa stopped in her tracks and took a deep breath. The last thing she wanted was for her son to be afraid of her.

"You know what?" she said. "I'm gonna call your father and tell him to come and get you. That's what you want, right?"

Her heart broke a little when he nodded, his face still covered with his hands. "I want Daddy," he said, his voice barely above a whisper.

Misa stormed off angrily and dialed her ex-husband's number. With every punch of the keypad, she felt more and more betrayed. When Louis answered the phone, she wasted no time getting to the point. "Your son is crying for you, Louis. Come and get him tonight or stay out of his life for good. This is ridiculous!"

"Hello to you, too, Misa," Louis said.

"Are you coming or not?"

Louis had been thinking about Shane more than ever lately. It had been weeks since he'd last seen his son. And even though his girlfriend, Nahla, wasn't a big fan of children, he was eager to reestablish a relationship with his only child before it was too late. "Yeah," he said. "I'll be there in about an hour."

Misa hung up the phone and went to pour herself a drink. She was hurt that her son was being mean to her, but relieved that Louis was willing to finally spend time with Shane. They could rebuild their father/son relationship, and she could work on establishing a permanent spot in Baron's life. As she downed the coconut rum she'd had in her cabinet for months, she told herself that things couldn't have worked out better.

Just Call My Name

"Oh God, Frankie!" Gillian purred. She dug her nails into his back and clung to him tightly. He was fucking her better than she'd ever imagined possible. Her thick brown legs were twisted around him like a pretzel as she tried to draw him in even deeper.

He wrapped her hair around his hand and gently pulled her head back, licking her neck, kissing it, sucking on it. Gillian could no longer hold back. She erupted in orgasmic spasms, and Frankie felt every pulsing motion. It didn't take long before he was gushing, too.

They lay sweaty together afterward, and Gillian reached over and flicked on the lamp on the night table. She looked at the beautiful man lying beside her. He stroked her thigh softly and she smiled. She loved the tender way he treated her. Frankie made her feel so good. And he was feeling things for her that he had never expected to feel. She was a beautiful girl with eyes that danced and lips that seemed to invite him to kiss them. He was so in love with her that nothing else mattered.

In the days since Frankie had left her, Camille had been coming apart at the seams. She couldn't understand how he could end their marriage so easily. Since she no longer had to look after Shane while Misa was up at the hospital playing Florence Nightingale to Baron, Camille had more time on her hands than ever. She felt frustrated and helpless, and so she did the unthinkable.

Camille had started following Frankie. She had followed them after they left the funeral repast and watched them go up to their room at the Plaza Hotel. She had watched the next morning as they checked out of the hotel and went back to Gillian's place. She had watched the day after that as the pizza deliveryman climbed the steps of the Upper East Side town house and brought the couple a large pie; watched as Frankie came to the door shirtless and smiling. Camille had followed them days later when they walked hand in hand to the Italian restaurant two blocks away. She was watching the house now, wondering why she hadn't stopped crying since Frankie walked away from her; wondering why she was letting this happen instead of doing something about it. She had a bombshell to drop on her husband and his mistress. And there was no time like the present.

She got out of her car, headed toward the ritzy town house, and climbed the stairs. When she reached the door, she took a deep breath and rang the doorbell. It was showtime.

Toya came home from the mall exhausted. She noticed that her screen door was unlocked and cursed herself for being careless and not locking it when she left for work that morning. When she realized that her front door was also unlocked, she knew immediately that something was wrong. She pulled her gun out of her purse and slowly opened the door, stepping quietly into her house.

She looked around for her dog. Ginger usually met her at the door, eager for a walk after being locked up all day. But Ginger was nowhere to be found. She noticed the kitchen light on, and knew that someone was in there. She slowly inched toward the kitchen, ready to fire at the slightest movement. Entering the room, she cocked her gun and stood stunned by what she saw.

Her father, Nate, stood against the kitchen counter holding her dog in his arms. He had picked her locks and waited for her to get home. Toya would have shot him on sight, but he had the upper hand. Ginger was her weakness, and there was no way she would ever put her in danger. Nate knew this, and he used it to his advantage.

"I just want to talk to you, Latoya. Now, I've tried to call you, tried to come by here, and you keep refusing. I didn't want to go this route, but you forced me."

She wanted to spit in his face. "Talk, bitch! And it better be good, or I swear 'fo God, I'll kill your ass tonight."

Dominique didn't get home until close to eight o'clock in the evening. Since her father's death, she and Octavia were on their own on late nights such as this. She hated worrying about what Octavia would eat for dinner each time she had to work late. But so far it had gone well. Dominique would pick up food from one of the restaurants near her office, and she and Octavia would sit and eat together and catch up on each other's days. Tonight, it was Italian food, and she couldn't wait to see her daughter's face when she found out that she had gotten her favorite pasta dish.

The apartment was quieter than usual. Dominique set the food down on the counter and began sifting through the mail. She called her daughter's name as she strolled down the hallway toward her bedroom, but got no answer. She knocked on Octavia's bedroom door and still got no response. Pushing the door open, she was mortified to find that Octavia wasn't in there.

Dominique began to panic. Where the hell could her daughter be at such a late hour? She went into her own bedroom to get the house phone and noticed that the answering machine light was blinking. Pressing the playback button, she listened, hopeful that the message was from her daughter.

"Miss Storms, this is Vickie Murphy from the Bardwell Dance School. I'm calling again about Octavia's attendance. It's been more than four weeks since we have seen her in class. I've left a number of messages for you, but we haven't heard back. Her tuition is all paid up, and she is a pleasure to teach. We really miss her in class, so if you could give me a call just to confirm that she's okay, I'd appreciate it. We hope to see her return to class on Monday. Have a great weekend."

Dominique was completely confused. To her knowledge, Octavia had never missed a dance class. And she was more worried than ever about her daughter's whereabouts. She went into Octavia's room and turned the light on to

look for clues as to where she may have gone. She didn't
have to look very far.

An envelope sat atop the pillows on Octavia's bed. On it,
she had written MOMMY in her fancy cursive handwriting.
Dominique tore the envelope open and read the contents.

> Ma,
> I got myself in some trouble. I'm not really who
> you think I am and I don't want to let you down
> anymore. It's time for me to grow up sooner
> than I thought I would and to take responsibil-
> ity. I love you and I'll be in touch soon. Don't
> worry about me. I'm okay. You just have to ac-
> cept that I'm not your baby girl anymore. In
> time you'll understand.
>
> Octavia

Dominique was confused. She felt like she was reading
some kind of puzzle that she was supposed to decipher. She
ran back to the kitchen, grabbed her purse off the counter,
and headed back out the door in search of her child.

Misa arrived home on the evening of January fourth and couldn't
wait to see Shane. It had been days since Louis had picked
him up, and she missed her son. She kicked off her BCBG
heels and plopped down on the couch to call Louis. As the
phone rang, she toyed with the diamond ring Baron had
given her, hoping to replace it soon with an actual engagement ring. She figured that if she played her cards right, it
would only be a matter of time before she was Mrs. Baron
Nobles.

Finally Louis answered the phone.

"Well, well, well, stranger," Louis said when he answered. "How nice of you to finally call."

"Hi, Louis," Misa said, detecting the anger in her ex-husband's voice. She wasn't in the mood for bullshit today. "Where's my baby?" she asked. "I miss him."

"You irresponsible bitch! You don't have a son anymore!" Louis bellowed into the phone.

Misa was taken aback, and was completely speechless for several seconds. "Who the fuck are you talking to like that?"

"I'm talking to you, you filthy bitch! You haven't been home in days and you never even bothered to call to check up on this little boy!"

"That little boy is my son, you idiot. And he's been with you—his fucking part-time father—for the past week. Why would I call to check up on him when he's with you? I trusted that you'd take care of him like a real father would." Misa did feel badly that she hadn't been the best mother to Shane. But she believed that Louis was the last person who should dare to lecture her about parenting skills. "Now put my son on the phone."

"I told you that you don't have a son anymore. He is *my* son. And you'll never see him again by the time I'm finished with you."

"Louis, I don't know what your problem is, but—"

"You're so busy running around chasing after some dick that you never thought about protecting Shane. What kind of fucking mother does that make you? He doesn't even ask for you. You know who he asks for? Camille!"

Misa felt hot tears spill from her eyes. "Louis, all right," she said. "That's enough. I'm sorry it took so long for me to call and talk to Shane. But I've been up at the hospital—"

"*You let somebody molest my son!*" Louis bellowed. He sounded out of breath after he said it. His chest heaved with rage and he knew that if Misa had been there, he would have strangled her.

Misa's heart seized in her chest. "What?" She wondered what had made him come up with this ridiculous theory. She figured that this was Louis's latest attempt at battling her—making up lies in order to seek custody of their son. "Ain't nobody molesting Shane, Louis! What the fuck are you talking about?"

"I swear to God, if you were here right now I would kill you with my bare hands and happily do the time. You selfish bitch."

"Wait a minute, Louis. Please tell me what the fuck you're talking about. And stop calling me out my name."

"Somebody has been raping my fucking son and all you can say is that you been at the fucking hospital?" Louis was livid.

"Raping Shane?" Misa's head was suddenly pounding. "You're bugging out."

"That's right. *I'm* bugging out." Louis chuckled at Misa's audaciousness. "You know what happened last night? Shane was acting up, being real disrespectful, and that's not like him. So I started to spank him." Louis paused, and Misa could tell that he was crying now. She felt like her world stopped spinning as she listened. "And he started to cry and begged me not to hurt him back there. He told me, Misa. He told me that some nigga has been touching him, *raping my muthafuckin' son!* And that's *your* fault!"

She felt at that moment as if something inside of her shifted. She went numb, and her own voice seemed to echo

in her ears. "Louis, what are you talking about? Who would do that to Shane?" Misa was crying now.

"He won't tell me," Louis said, his voice barely above a whisper. "He won't even tell me because whoever it is, they scared him to death so he won't say nothing. All he keeps saying is that he don't want to go home. That he don't want to play those games no more and that he's gonna be good; he keeps swearing that he's gonna be good. And as long as I have breath in my body, he will never come back to you again."

"Louis, can I talk to him?" She sniffled as tears cascaded down her cheeks. "Please, let me speak to him so I can find out what's wrong."

"Fuck you," Louis said, wiping his own tears, which he had shed ever since learning of his son's victimization. "I'm calling the cops and I'm getting a lawyer so that I can get sole custody. You and your family stay the fuck away from my son until you figure out who did this to him. Until then, don't call here again, Misa. If you do, I'll kill you myself." He hung up on her and she sat there in silence, still holding her phone in her hand.

Misa wasn't thinking straight. This whole thing was like a horrible nightmare. She sat there and racked her brain for who might have been lecherous enough to harm poor, innocent Shane. She thought of his teachers at school. None of them seemed predatory, at least not to her. Louis had mentioned that Shane didn't want to play "those games" anymore. She thought about who her child played with most often, wondering who could be responsible. Outside of the teachers at his school, the only other people who had ever had prolonged access to Shane were his family members. Camille, the aunt who adored him, and Frankie—who rarely even interacted with his nephew. When Misa's thoughts turned to Frankie's brother, Steven, her heart all but stopped.

She thought back on times when Shane would tell her how much Uncle Steven loved to play with him. She thought about the way she had found her son weeks earlier—curled up in the fetal position in Camille's bathtub. She recalled telling her that Shane played hide-and-go-seek all the time this way. That it was "his pleasure" to babysit Shane.

Steven certainly fit the profile. He was always playing with Shane, always willing to look after him, always hanging around little kids. Misa's stomach flip-flopped as she realized that the only person capable of such a depraved act was her brother-in-law. She cried for her son, overcome with intense guilt. When her tears finally dried, she pulled herself up off the couch, vowing that no one was ever going to hurt him again.

In Cold Blood

It was slightly after midnight when Misa walked into the house. She was in a daze, feeling like her feet were carrying her forward all on their own. Her mind was reeling, and all she could think about was confronting the man who had molested her innocent son. Misa had driven to Camille's house in a fog. Having a spare set of keys to her sister's place, Misa let herself into the sprawling home and saw that no one was there.

She walked into the dining room and sat down at the table. Seeing a candle sitting in the center, she picked up a nearby match and lit it. She sat there in the flickering darkness and waited. The diamond ring and bracelets she wore sparkled in the candlelight. She knew it wouldn't be long before that bastard returned. And when he did, she'd be waiting.

It was close to one in the morning when Steven came in from the guest house and went to the kitchen. He took a beer out of the refrigerator, although he was already drunk, and guzzled it. He thought about Shane. Guilt tugged at him for what he had done repeatedly to the little boy who had been left in his care. He flashed back to the abuse he had suffered at the hands of his tyrannical father. Frankie had been beaten by him, but their father had saved the worst of the abuse for Steven.

With these thoughts on his mind, Steven turned to leave and came face-to-face with Misa. She saw him standing there, startled, with a beer in his hand. Her heart roared in her chest.

Steven laughed after being caught off guard, and smiled at her. "Damn, girl. You scared me."

Misa looked at Steven and her jaw clenched. Her hands balled up involuntarily into fists, and she shook slightly.

"What did you do to my son?"

Steven was still smiling, but she could see the surprise in his eyes upon hearing her question.

"What are you talking about?" he asked, frowning.

Misa inched closer to him. "He said that you touched him." Her voice shook, and she kept advancing on him. "He said that you hurt him, you fucking freak!" Misa was crying now, and her lips quivered as she spoke. "You molested my son!"

The smirk on his face remained, but Steven shook his head. "He's lying."

Misa reached in her coat pocket and pulled out the .38 special that Louis had given her for protection years ago. She pointed it at Steven, though her hands shook as she did so. The smile immediately drained from his face.

"Put that away," he urged her. "The little muthafucka is lying."

Pop! Misa pulled the trigger, hitting Steven in his chest.

He fell back against the counter and looked at her in shock. He staggered toward her and she fired again and again, hitting him twice in the head and then riddling his body with even more shots. Even after he fell to the floor in a dead heap, she kept on shooting, letting off all the rounds that remained. Soon the trigger just clicked as the chamber was now empty. She continued firing, as if entranced, staring down at Steven's lifeless body crumpled on her sister's kitchen floor.

Finally, Misa lowered the gun and dropped it at her feet. She cried from the pit of her soul for her son and for the torture he had suffered at the hands of the monster she had just slain. She only wished that she had saved a bullet for herself. This was all her fault, she thought. Everything that had happened to her son was her fault. She should have never left him alone with this sick muthafucka who lay sprawled across the kitchen floor.

She stumbled, sobbing, out of the kitchen and into the dining room, where she leaned against the wall and cried. Some of Steven's blood had splattered onto her clothes and she tried to wipe it off with her hands. Absentmindedly, she wiped her bloody hands on the wall. Thoughts of poor, sweet Shane being victimized by a grown man flooded her mind, and she squeezed her eyes closed in anguish. She slumped down into a chair, still trembling. As Misa sat there staring at the wall, reality set in. She had just committed murder, and her life as she knew it before this day was over.

The phone rang and snapped her out of her trance. She wondered who was calling, but didn't dare answer it. The house was empty except for her and the body lying on the kitchen floor. The phone seemed to ring forever, each ring sounding louder than the last. Soon all she could hear was the shrill volume of the ringing in her ears. She knew she couldn't hide forever, but she wasn't ready to face what she had done. Not until she made sense of it herself. All she could think about was what she had done. And the only thing she felt was numbness.

The ringing finally stopped. It was over, she reassured herself. She sat there in the stillness of the house and closed her eyes, realizing that nothing would ever be the same. She heard someone come in through the front door and held her breath. She waited to see who it was, but didn't move from where she sat transfixed.

Camille walked into the house and immediately sensed that something was awry. First of all, Misa's car was parked outside, which was odd since Shane had been with Louis for several days. Second, the house was dark and quiet, even though most nights Steven came into the house and drank up the beer in the fridge while watching TV in the living room until the wee hours of the morning. Instead, tonight the house was empty and silent.

She walked into the kitchen and screamed. Steven's cold, dead body was lying in the middle of the floor, and blood was splattered all across the walls and all over the floor. A gun lay on the floor near the body. Steven's eyes were wide open, and a broken beer bottle lay near his right hand.

She saw a dim light coming from the dining room and walked toward it. She took a knife from the block on the counter and followed the glimmering light. As she stepped into the room, she was amazed to see who was sitting at the dining room table, and slowly inched toward her.

"Jesus . . . oh my God, girl, what have you done?"